OTHER TITLES BY SUZANNE BROCKMANN

Heartthrob
Bodyguard
The Unsung Hero
The Defiant Hero
Over the Edge
Out of Control
Into the Night
Gone Too Far
Flashpoint
Hot Target
Breaking Point

INTO THE STORM

SUZANNE BROCKMANN

INTO THE STORM

A NOVEL

BALLANTINE BOOKS • NEW YORK

Copyright © 2006 by Suzanne Brockmann

Published in the United States by Ballantine Books, an imprint of The Random House Publishing Group, a division of Random House, Inc., New York.

BALLANTINE and colophon are registered trademarks of Random House, Inc.

ISBN: 0-345-48014-7

Printed in the United States of America on acid-free paper

www.ballantinebooks.com

9 8 7 6 5 4 3 2 1

First Edition

For Ed, Eric, and Bill. Thank you for letting me be a witness to your solid, special, funny, sometimes rude, and always loyal friendship. Jenk, Izzy, Lopez, and Gillman's banter might sound familiar at times. Thanks for that, too.

ACKNOWLEDGMENTS

Thank you, first and foremost, to everyone at Ballantine Books for allowing me to push back my deadline and take some desperately needed time off. Extra-special thanks to Gina Centrello, Linda Marrow, Dan Mallory, and my wonderful editor Shauna Summers, for going the extra mile to get *Into the Storm* into readers' hands as quickly as possible.

Eternal thanks to home team: Ed Gaffney and my monkey-dog, Sugar, the world's greatest schnauzer. Thanks, also, to my daughter Melanie, an aspiring author in her own right, and to my son Jason, who is Broadway bound. I'm so proud of both of you.

Thanks, as always, to Steve Axelrod and Eric Ruben—for way too many things to count—and to my parents, Fred and Lee Brockmann.

Thank you to real-life hero Tom Rancich for cold weather survival information, as well as your friendly presence on the BB. You continue to be an inspiration. Finish writing your book already, will you? I can't wait to read it.

Super snaps to everyone who helped with my July 2006 reader event in Atlanta: Maya Stosskopf of EMA, Gilly Hailparn and the publicity team at Ballantine Books, and my wonderful guests Alesia Holliday, Virginia Kantra, Catherine Mann, and Tom Rancich. Thank you, too, to my hardworking, brainstorming volunteers: Elizabeth and Lee Benjamin, Suzie Bernhardt, Stephanie Hyacinth, Beki & Jim Keene, Laura Luke, Jeanne Mangano, Heather McHugh, Peggy Mitchell, Dorbert Ogle, Gail Reddin, Erike Schutte (Hah! I spelled it right this time!), and Sue Smallwood. Thank you, too, to everyone who attended the event! You know I'd list you all if I could—I so enjoyed hanging out with each and every one of you!

Check my website at www.SuzanneBrockmann.com/appearances.htm for information about my next readers weekend. You'll also find the schedule for my August/September 2006 *Into the Storm* book tour.

Thank you to Stephen Syta for lending me his name. (My apologies to Stephen's mom!)

Last but never least, thank you to my readers for giving me this crazy, exciting, wonderful career that I adore. I hope you enjoy reading Mark and Lindsey's story as much as I enjoyed writing it.

As always, any mistakes I've made or liberties I've taken are completely my own.

INTO THE STORM

PROLOGUE

Mark Jenkins was having a meltdown.

It was not a particularly good emotional state to be in right now. It was not helping him hide in the cool autumn night just a few shadows away from the valley where the enemy was setting up camp.

He double-checked his MP4.

It was locked and loaded.

His hands, however, were still shaking.

Jenk used sheer will and several dozen steadying breaths to try to bring himself back.

Some guys in the SEAL teams, like Izzy Zanella who was eyeing him now from several yards away, operated in a perpetual state of pissed. Izzy set his anger on simmer and used it as fuel. Jenk had always thought that was dangerous—until tonight.

Because simmer was a million times better than the rolling boil of rage that had hit him at the sight of those familiar black running shoes hanging limply, lifelessly above his head.

God damn it.

He forced himself to breathe. In. And out.

Smooth, not ragged.

Focus.

He smelled the smoke before he saw the flicker of flames in the distance.

Someone had lit a campfire—proof that the enemy believed they owned this godforsaken patch of dusty land, that they thought they were alone out here in the night.

That was good.

It was also good that the new guy, John Orlikowski, was RTO for this SEAL patrol, a job Jenk himself usually handled.

Being radioman would've required Jenk to glue himself to Lieutenant Jacquette's mountainous side.

Which would've made it hard for them both to pretend Jenk's hands weren't shaking.

Not that the lieutenant hadn't already noticed.

On the other side of Izzy, Jenk could see Jacquette and Orlikowski fading back, away from the enemy's camp. The lieutenant motioned to Izzy, who followed.

Jacquette then glanced at Jenk, signaling for him to hold his position.

Yeah, perfect. You, over there, with the emotional diarrhea: Stay put, don't move, don't mess this up by tripping over your no doubt equally shaking feet.

It was weird not to be in the thick of things, not to know what the lieutenant was planning.

Although, if Jenk knew Jacquette—and he most certainly did—the lieutenant was going to send someone to check out the encampment.

Which was why he'd pulled Izzy over. Irving Zanella may not have been anyone's first choice for taking tea with the queen, but he was fast and silent and, despite his tall, lean build, he was invisible, especially after the sun went down.

Jacquette's goal would be to find out how many of the enemy were out there. Were any of the leaders identifiable as being on the current list of top al Qaeda terrorists, wanted by the world in the GWOT?

Could the SEAL team get away with killing them all? Just gunning them down—ending their miserable lives a whole lot less painfully than the motherfuckers had done to those civilians when they'd tortured and hanged them—

No, wait. That last bit was Jenk's own personal goal.

Which was why he was sitting over here in the virtual corner, taking a time-out, trying to turn his grief and rage into something useful.

Not that it mattered. With an eight-man platoon—larger than usual— Jacquette could simply ignore him until it was time to exfiltrate.

As it was, Jenk's job was to carry the backup radio, in case Johnny O. fell prey to Superman Syndrome. As a newbie, John still felt compelled not to pancake when bad shit started to fly. Like he had to prove to his teammates that his *cojones* were extra *grande*. Fucking new guys took a while to learn that getting their balls shot off didn't make 'em bigger. It made 'em gone.

If it weren't for the fact that Jenk had been determined to be part of this op, he wouldn't be here right now. He was only along for this ride because two was one and one was none. Because being suddenly ball-less tended to make a newbie's voice go up about seven octaves. Dogs everywhere would come running, but talking on the radio would become a challenge, and someone else would have to do it.

Of course, the flip side of Superman Syndrome was the possibility that young John would become ball-less sans altercation—unlikely, but not impossible. Jenk had seen it happen. A guy who aced the intense BUD/S training could become immobilized when out in the real world for the very first time.

Their voices wobbled and their hands shook.

Shit.

It was flipping unfair that anger and fear were manifested in such similar ways.

Izzy elbow-crawled over to him. "Y'okay?"

Jenk nodded.

Iz was looking at him with the strangest expression in his usually mocking eyes. Coming from anyone else, Jenk would have called it concern. Sympathy. Maybe even compassion.

"Sorry about Suhayla," Izzy said nearly silently. "That *was* her, right?"

Jenk nodded again, a curt affirmative.

It had indeed been Suhayla's body hanging, with three other civilians, from the bridge that had been rebuilt after American troops had come in last year and liberated this remote mountain town.

For the third time.

Jenk had been there. He'd seen the Marines set up camp and believed what Suhayla and her friends had believed—that real assistance was finally here to stay.

Suhayla Naaz—a medical doctor educated in London—had been brave enough to step forward and help organize the local government after the first invasion, at the very start of Operation Enduring Freedom. She'd been forced to go into hiding the first two times the Americans had pulled back to Kabul, barely escaping with her life.

She hadn't been as lucky this time around.

"That's rough," Izzy said. "Seeing her all dead like that."

Jenk managed another terse nod. Yeah.

"Don't go and get yourself killed, Marky-Mark. I don't want to have to lug your body all the way back to Jalalabad."

Typical Izzy. He couldn't just say, "Dude, I'm worried about you."

Jenk changed the subject. "You going out for a look?" Normally he would've used a hand signal to ask the simple question. Instead, he kept his fists tightly clenched.

Izzy nodded. "In a sec." He paused. "Fishboy said you've known Suhayla a coupla years now. That you got e-mail from her just last week."

And Jenk knew why Izzy had crawled over here. He was on a fact-finding expedition.

"Were you really banging her all that time?" Iz asked. And yes, that probably *was* admiration in his voice.

Izzy's world was a simple one. He believed that a man and a woman couldn't possibly have a relationship that didn't include — in Izzy-speak — bumping uglies.

Jenk stared into the night.

"I'll take that as a no. But you wanted to, right?" In Izzyland, there were only two types of women. Those you wanted to have sex with and those you didn't.

Suhayla Naaz was, before being cruelly murdered, a beautiful, articulate, intelligent woman. She was also forty-seven years old and married to an English doctor who lived with their three children in Liverpool. In the course of the fourteen days Jenk had spent in her remote hometown last year while ridding the surrounding countryside of various bad guys, she had noted that he was very good at getting things done.

He'd managed to help her gain possession of a truckload of medical supplies and generators. Food. Blankets. Clothing and shoes for children who'd lost everything.

They'd recognized that they were kindred spirits and had become friends.

"That's why we're here," Izzy continued. "Isn't it? You pulled your usual voodoo and set it up for us to get this assignment."

Jenk shook his head. "You're an idiot."

"Seriously," Izzy said. "I don't know how you do it, Eminem. But Gillman said he saw the e-mail — your ladyfriend said there was some serious problem, but no one would listen to her. So, you, I don't know, mind-control some admiral so that we all come running, and you get to save the day. She's so grateful, next thing you know you're boldly going. Only bad luck. We get here too late. No wonder you're freaking."

Yeah. *That* was why he was freaking. Because now that Suhayla Naaz had been brutally tortured and killed, her body hung from a bridge to warn others against working with the Americans, Jenk was never going to get a chance to boldly go.

And just like that, the game was over. Izzy had pushed him too far.

"You are *such* an asshole. You have no clue," Jenk whispered through clenched teeth. "Dr. Naaz was amazing. She was smart, she was brave, and she was dedicated to democracy. She was everything all the fucking politicos say we need to find over here, and they left her to swing while they sit in safety and agree that war is hell. You can tell the lieutenant I'm okay," Jenk told Izzy. "I'm not going postal. But I'm *furious* at the ineptitude. Why build a bridge if we're just going to let the sector fall back into the insurgents' hands?"

"Good question. I'm sure some desk jockey somewhere back in the States has what they think is an answer."

"The thought that these bastards"—Jenk pointed into the night toward that campfire—"are the ones who killed her . . . But we helped. God *damn* it." He let out a stream of profanity that would've made even his father's eyebrows curl.

Izzy, however, was unperturbed. "Maybe after we neutralize these scumbags who murdered your friend, I'll go to DC, find the policy makers and ask some pointed questions."

Yeah right. Jenk made a disparaging noise.

"You don't think I've got the balls?" Iz shrugged. "Hey, I'm not the chickenshit whose hands are shaking." He held out his own to demonstrate.

"Fuck you." Jenk accompanied his words with a flip of the bird—with a hand that was finally steady.

Izzy nodded, clearly pleased that Jenk was solidly back in control. Which, more than obviously now, had been the real reason he'd slithered over here. He patted Jenk's shoulder. "Venting, even just a little, keeps the apeshits away."

Words of wisdom from Irving Zanella, psychotherapist.

It was a new one for the Iz—three additional syllables added to his usual descriptive postname suffix.

"So come on," Izzy said. "You and me, Marky. Lieutenant Jacquette wants us to take a little midnight stroll. He thought the brisk night air would cure your girlish vapors."

And Jenk knew that even though his shaking hands were gone, they wouldn't ever be forgotten. *Girlish vapors.* No doubt about it, he would be reminded of this night right up until the day he left the Navy.

Of course, he wouldn't need any reminders from his teammates. He was never going to forget Dr. Suhayla Naaz, who should never have died.

"Although, word of advice, Mark?" Izzy stopped him.

Jenk couldn't quite see his eyes in the darkness of the night—but he knew that the taller man was deadly serious.

"It won't help," Iz said quietly, definitely. "Even if we find out this is a terrorist cell with direct ties to Osama bin Laden? Even if we have proof these are the mothers who strung Suhayla up and left her hanging . . . Even if we make sure none of 'em ever hurts another human being again . . ." He shook his head. "It won't really help." He smiled then, morphing back into his usual irreverence, as if suddenly aware he'd given too much of himself away. "Of course, Auntie M, it sure as hell won't hurt."

There were too many of them.

It was unreal. Insurgents usually knew better than to occupy the same small piece of real estate, for fear of airstrike. Yet here so many of them were, like some kind of Taliban reunion.

Izzy had gone farther north, leaving Jenk to count heads and scan faces and . . . Wait a sec, wasn't that . . . ?

Jenk tightened the focus of his night-vision glasses.

Yes, it was definitely Yusaf Ghulam-Khan. The interpreter who'd worked for both the SEALs and the Marines, back when Jenk was here last. He'd been on the Americans' payroll.

What was it Suhayla had said about him? "I wouldn't trust him any farther than I could pitch him."

She'd been a baseball fan.

Back when Jenk had known him, Yusaf had been privy to all sorts of information. He'd sworn an oath of loyalty—not that that meant anything.

Currently, he wasn't a prisoner. He was walking around, clearly a popular guy, being offered what looked like congratulations . . . ?

And just like that Jenk knew.

This massive gathering was the trouble that Suhayla had written about. She'd sent her brother into Kabul, where there was Internet access, to send an e-mail to one of the few people she still trusted.

Jenk.

Knowing that Suhayla would try to warn the Americans, and not knowing that he was already too late, Yusaf had helped to silence her. At the very least, he'd identified her. It was entirely possible, though, that he'd tied the rope around her neck.

Jenk's hands were shaking again.

What was it Iz had said? Vent.

"Motherfucker, motherfucker, motherfucker," he muttered.

Izzy reappeared, materializing from the night as if summoned. He silently signaled Jenk. He'd counted 112 men. Jenk flashed his number— 147. Combined, that was nearly 260 enemy combatants.

What the hell was going on?

The insurgents weren't amassing in preparation for a coming battle. There was nothing out here in the freaking middle of nowhere to attack.

At least not since the Americans had pulled out. Again.

Jenk faded back, far enough away from the encampment to speak, and Iz followed him.

"It's a supply drop," Izzy confirmed. "Ammo, weapons, explosives— they've got an arsenal in that cave."

And there was the answer. A resupply. The big question about why the insurgents weren't running out of ammunition and explosives hadn't been a mystery for a while. It came in over the border with remarkable ease.

But this ballsy gathering was troubling. It was a show of power—a clear message to the people of this region. It was a clear shout out that the insurgents no longer considered the Americans to be a threat.

Izzy kept moving, heading back toward Jacquette. It was obvious, to him, what needed to be done. They had to report to the lieutenant, who would call in an airstrike while the supplies were still at these coordinates.

If they let it disperse into the mountainous countryside, it would come back at the Americans one bullet and mortar at a time.

But calling in an airstrike was a major problem, and not *just* because lately air support had to be reserved days in advance. Jenk stopped Izzy.

"How're you feeling about the eight against two-sixty odds?" he asked the taller man. The equipment he'd seen in the enemy camp wasn't limited to weapons and ammo. "They've got DF equipment—state of the art."

Jenk had used similar radio detection-finding equipment in a training op, and the bad news was that it worked. Extremely well. Technology tended to play leapfrog. It wouldn't be long before the whiz kids in the lab came up with a radio that wouldn't be detectable by this latest round of equipment, but they hadn't done it yet.

Bottom line, if Jacquette broke radio silence, it would be like announcing their presence—and location—to the enemy over a loudspeaker.

Combined with that artillery Jenk had glimpsed in the flickering firelight . . . No, that was not a good idea.

"So we clear out," Izzy said. "Get out of mortar range, and then call in the airstrike."

"They're blocking our route down the mountain," Jenk pointed out.

"So we go over the mountains and through the fucking woods if we have to. There's more than one way to get to Grandmother's house."

Unlike Izzy, Jenk knew this area well. "That'll take us over the border." At Izzy's expression of exasperation, he added, "Look, *I* don't have a problem with it. The weapons came from over the border. Fucking Osama's probably over there, too, being treated like royalty. But I can tell you right now, that as soon as we give him this information, the lieutenant is going to start muttering about not wanting to cause an . . ."

". . . international incident," Lieutenant Jacquette said grimly, just as Mark Jenkins had predicted. It was hardwired into all officers in the U.S. military. But unlike many of the top brass, Jacquette had studied under the best commanding officer of all time, Lieutenant Commander—now retired, which was a real shame—Tom Paoletti. "Other options?"

Like Tommy Paoletti, Jazz Jacquette believed in brainstorming with his men, in a give-and-take of ideas. He actually thought it was a good idea to make full use of all the thousands of hours of training his enlisted SEALs had had in thinking outside of the box.

Izzy scratched his nose as he tried now to do just that. They had to blow up those weapons and explosives, and not die doing it. This was a real Apollo 13 scenario. The SEALs were restricted extensively by the impassable mountain terrain, and the equipment, weaponry, and supplies they carried were limited.

"We could just walk right through their camp," Izzy suggested. "Collect a few head scarves, cover our faces, and boot-scoot down the trail. Call in the airstrike when we're out of range."

"Like no one would notice us," Silverman scoffed.

"Maybe they wouldn't," Izzy said. But if they did, the SEALs were all dead.

"They'd still pick up our radio signal," Jenkins pointed out. "They'll know we're calling in an airstrike and be out of here in minutes."

They had to figure out a way to keep the insurgents here until the bombs started falling. *And* not die in the process. Sheesh. It was easy to do one or the other. It was doing both that was going to be a challenge.

"I've got enough C4 to blow that cave shut," Gillman said.

"Yeah, with you in it," Silverman pointed out. Mr. Doom and Gloom.

"Not necessarily," Izzy said.

"Are *you* volunteering?" Silverman came back at him, his normally half-closed eyes opening wide. "Because that's a strong sign that a plan is totally fucked." He looked to Jacquette for confirmation. "If Psycho here actually wants to—"

"I didn't say that," Izzy spoke over him. "I say we call in the airstrike, then run like hell to safety, which just happens to be across the border. With an immediate extraction, who's going to know?"

Jenkie glanced at his watch, on top of every detail, as usual. "Helo's not available for extraction for another six hours," he reported.

"What the fuck?" Izzy said, speaking for all of them, looking to Jacquette for confirmation. Six *hours*? "Sir?"

The lieutenant nodded. "Secretary of Defense is visiting Kabul today."

Holy Jesus. Was that really a mission with priority over this one?

So in other words, they didn't just have to run, they also had to hide. For six freaking hours. And yes, there were caves aplenty out there in the mountains, but the enemy had the advantage. They knew this terrain inside and out. Plus, *they* didn't give a flying fuck about any alleged borders.

"We can take photos, get faces for intel to identify," Silverman suggested.

"But if we don't stop them . . ." The new guy, Orlikowski, started to protest as if it were an actual possibility that all they'd do was take snapshots.

Doing that—the equivalent of nothing—wouldn't sit well with any of them. Izzy knew that each time some boots-on-the-ground grunt was killed by a sniper or an IED, they'd all get a bad taste in their mouths and a twisting in their gut, thinking about all those weapons and ammo that got away.

"We're not walking away from this," the lieutenant intoned in his best voice-of-God imitation.

Jenk spoke up. "I got an idea," he said, in that barely-old-enough-to-vote, gee-whiz-sounding voice that made Izzy think his next words were going to be *We can hold the pep rally in my dad's barn!* "Permission to liberate one of the insurgents, sir."

Lieutenant Jacquette was African American. He had a broad face, with dark skin and a nose similar to the one Jacko had traded in, back when he was handsome. Jacquette was a very good-looking man—Izzy knew because he'd dated plenty of women who'd made a point to tell him so. But the lieutenant's default expression was of having just stepped in shit. It could have won him a fortune playing Texas Hold 'Em, because it never changed.

Never.

Well, okay, maybe it changed a little, depending on whether the shit he'd stepped in came from a dog or a bull. But you had to know him really well to be able to tell that difference.

The man was also about twice the size of Jenkins. But Jacquette clearly knew Jenk well enough not to be fooled by his about-to-turn-nineteen, grade-A student, baby-faced Boy Scout appearance.

"Anyone in particular?" he asked Jenk dryly. "Or just any old insurgent?"

"His name's Yusaf Ghulam-Khan," Jenk said, because no matter where they went and what they were doing, he automatically knew everything and everyone. And the best way to manipulate them. Izzy knew right then that the SEALs were not going to leave this mountainside dissatisfied. Or in body bags.

Jenk continued. "Let me tell you, sir, exactly how he can help us. . . ."

"Yusaf! Thank God!" Jenk dug deep, using all of his experience and talent as the team's best liar to give the man a sincere-sounding greeting. It took everything he had in him to look into the bastard's eyes without fear of betraying his true desire, which involved use of his KA-BAR knife.

The man was terrified. Who wouldn't be after getting grabbed by Izzy and Danny Gillman and dragged into the night? He was also more than a little confused that he was still alive. He was making random not-my-fault, please-don't-kill-me noises from beneath Danny's hand, which was securely covering his mouth.

"Relax, dude," Jenk said, playing the role of the stupid American soldier. "We were out on a sneak and peek—just a standard op, you know, a small squad? Then we ran into this mess." He gestured toward the insurgents' camp. "I saw that you were with them, working undercover"—yeah, right, but Yusaf stopped weeping—"and realized that, together, we can bring these fuckers down."

Yusaf was nodding now—loyal to whoever held the gun to his head. At least for as long as the weapon was locked and loaded.

Jenk nodded at Danny, who took his hand from Yusaf's mouth.

"Thank God you are here," Yusaf threw his arms around Jenk. "I didn't know what to do. They killed Mrs. Naaz—"

Jenk may have been good at lying his ass off, but there was no way he was going to stand here and discuss Suhayla with this scumbag.

He pushed free from the embrace. "We don't have much time before someone notices you're missing. Here's what we need you to do."

Jenk went into detail, outlining a seriously flawed plan to "fool" the insurgents into thinking they were surrounded by coalition forces. The SEALs in his squad would move into place around the perimeter of the camp, to send up flares that would mark the "position" of each of two "battalions."

Jenk, meanwhile, would man the radio—ready to contact the insurgent leader, to "negotiate" their surrender.

Of course, Yusaf would return to the insurgents' camp and tell the leader exactly how many—or in this case how few—SEALs were out there in the night.

They'd send up those flares, and the insurgents would charge up into the mountains, leaving the downward-heading trail clear for the SEALs to make their escape. After calling in that airstrike, of course.

And this was where Jenk's plan got a little sketchy. With that dog and pony show going on in Kabul, an immediate airstrike might not be possible.

So Jenk embellished, filling his story with the usual diplocrapic debris: They were virtually certain that they'd identified one of the men in the cave as a high-ranking official of an allegedly neutral country, which would help provide proof that that country had terrorist ties.

"Which is why we can't just call in an airstrike and blow them to shit," Jenk lied. "We need the weapons and ammo as proof of this man's criminal activity, do you follow?"

Yusaf nodded.

Jenk dropped his final disinformation bomb. "We just need to stall them," he told the man. "For a solid twenty-four hours, until the real coalition forces arrive." He paused, giving his words added weight. "Will you help? Will you go in there and tell them that these mountains are filled with American soldiers? Will you tell them we'll be contacting them via radio to negotiate their surrender?"

Yusaf just kept on nodding. "Of course," he said.

Of course.

Jenk clasped the older man's hand and poured on the sincerity. "We're counting on you."

"I understand," Yusaf said.

Jenk nodded at Izzy and Danny, who'd volunteered to set up those flares. "Move into position. Let's do this."

*   *   *

Lieutenant Jacquette was brilliant—letting Marky-Mark have free rein with this sitch.

The lieutenant and the rest of the team in place, ready to boogie down the mountain, no border crossing necessary, as they destroyed the insurgents' ammunition and didn't die in the process.

Izzy positioned his flare, rigging it with extra det cord. After he lit this puppy, he didn't want to be anywhere in the neighborhood, and having a superlong fuse would allow him to get out of Dodge.

Mark Jenkins had known just how to put a similar slow-burning fuse on Yusaf and his insurgent cronies.

He'd even given them a reason to stick around—SEALs in them thar hills. If these insurgents could not just kill but capture a team of SEALs, they could parade them on al-Jazeera television and be real heroes.

Little did they realize, thanks to the simple wonder of a slow-burning fuse, that the SEALs would be nowhere near the flares. The bad guys would charge the mountain and find nothing. No one.

Well, except for Marky-Mark Jenkins. But he was small and fast and good at hiding.

The coolest part of Jenk's little subterfuge was that he had told Yusaf that he would be sending a radio message to the insurgents—an attempt to negotiate, aka stall for time, before the additional fictional American troops arrived.

Hence, it was a given that the insurgents would pick up the SEALs' radio signal on their DF equipment.

Izzy knew that Jenk was banking on the fact that the insurgents wouldn't know how to use that equipment as skillfully as he himself apparently did. An important but as of yet still unknown part of the plan depended on the insurgents failing to recognize that, while sending his "Prepare to surrender" message, Jenk would also be simultaneously calling for the aforementioned airstrike.

Which brought them to goatfuck factor one. Jenk had to convince the numbnuts at command to send an airstrike now, rather than three days from now. That was important.

Once Jenk made radio contact, much depended on his ability to connect with someone back at HQ who would forgo the red tape and paperwork and actually send the help they needed.

Nah, on second thought, the goatfuck factor was handled. Jenk knew everyone. And he knew how to charm, trick or mind-control them into getting exactly what he wanted. No human on earth was immune to Jenk's talent.

From his vantage point overlooking the enemy camp, Izzy scanned the area, searching for Yusaf. He was still back in the cave, no doubt deep in conference with the insurgent leaders, like a good little turncoat, helping to work out the details of their counterplan.

But the level of activity around the radio, the DF equipment, and an entire array of rocket launchers had increased. And, yes, slowly but surely the insurgents were moving—away from the trail down the mountain and into attack position.

Excellent.

Izzy looked at his watch.

Showtime.

Jenk sent the coordinates for the airstrike on the backup radio, then fired off his flare.

The other two flares lit the sky as he ran like hell.

Luck and the small-world factor were on their side. Jenk had gotten through to HQ, to an Air Farce colonel he'd actually met once at an airport bar. Dude was smart for an officer—he was a regular guy. He'd gotten the picture immediately.

He was getting them the air support they needed. And, instead of days or even hours, it was going to arrive in minutes.

Which meant they all had to haul ass out of this area.

Which also meant breaking radio silence.

"Seven minutes," he informed Jacquette and the rest of the SEALs over the headsets they all wore, as he scrambled down the mountainside.

"Get out of there," the lieutenant thundered.

"Working on it," Jenk replied.

Jenk's position was the most vulnerable. In working within the parameters of the worst-case scenario—the one where they'd had to be put on a waiting list for that airstrike—they'd had to make sure that Jenk was close to the radio that was sending the surrender demand—recorded and on a loop—to the insurgents. The theory was, if the baddies picked up the two different signals, maybe they'd think the second was some kind of shadow or reflection.

At least that was the theory as Jenk had described it when proposing his plan to the lieutenant.

At the time, though, he'd left out the *maybe*.

The possibility that the insurgents had a radioman who was as well trained as a Navy SEAL was still floating around out there, about number fifteen on the list with the heading "Ways that Mark Jenkins Could Die Tonight."

Possible but unlikely.

Of course, now "friendly fire" had been moved to the very top of that list.

As opposed to "Hudson River sailing accident," which was still down at about thirty thousand.

As Jenk slipped and slid in the dust and rocks, making his way toward the surer footing of the trail, he could hear distant shouting from the campground. Although languages weren't his particular strength, he could tell from the inflection and tone that the words he was hearing were military commands.

Yeah, that was definitely a "Ready, aim, fire!"

It was followed by the thump and hiss of rockets launching.

Thump. Thump, thump-thump, thump. Thump thump. Thump.

Shit, lots of them.

He'd misjudged the insurgents' bloodlust. He'd thought they'd have a hard-on for capturing a team of SEALs. Apparently, they preferred to blow the Americans off the face of the earth. Which made the next few minutes of Jenk's life both easier and harder.

He couldn't tell where the rockets were heading—there was never any way to know. Although if you heard the whine of one falling toward you, it was probably too late to duck.

Damnit, he hated artillery attacks most in the launch phase.

But then he changed his mind. He *really* hated them most as the bombs started to fall, exploding with a roar of noise and sprays of fire and dirt, shaking the earth.

The urge to hit the deck and crawl for cover was overcome by the need to move as quickly as possible, so he stayed on his feet.

Thump. Thump, thump. Thump-thump. Thump.

At least the trail was clear. It opened up ahead to a fork, and Jenk didn't hesitate. He went toward the river.

Bad choice.

He heard the rocket screaming and he knew he was dead. But survival instincts were hard to overcome, and he dove headfirst beneath an outcropping of rocks, even while thinking, *too late, too late.*

The pain was immediate as he scraped and bounced across the grit and dirt. It was like sandpapering the palms of his hands, his chin, his cheek.

And still he tried to go farther, to fit in a narrow little crack between the ground and a rock. He'd never been a quitter, not ever in his life, why should he start now during his impending death?

The noise of the explosion was deafening, and the force of the shock waves lifted him, pushing him even farther back.

Dirt and dust and smoke filled his lungs and stung his eyes and he found himself thinking about his mother, his sister Ginny, his dad. He saw their faces clearly, like a slide show. It was not his life as he'd lived it that flashed through his mind, but rather the people he'd loved. Ex-girlfriends. Amanda. Christy. Heather. Even Shelly the perfectionist, who had annoyed the hell out of him whenever they weren't having sex.

Little Charlie Paoletti, with his big, drooly-chinned grin . . .

Jenk coughed, ears ringing, choking on both dust and regret. There was so much more he'd wanted to do, so much of life yet to live.

But then he realized the fact that he was choking meant that he still had lungs—that his head was still attached to his chest.

He moved his right leg. His right arm. His—

Pain shot through him—proof along with the choking thing that he was still very much alive.

His entire left side was pinned. He shifted, trying to pull himself free, or at least to see how badly he was injured, and he heard himself howl.

He checked to make sure his microphone was turned off, and realized that his entire headset was broken. He couldn't hear his teammates, and they couldn't hear him.

His watch, however, was still ticking—and still counting down. There were two minutes and seventeen seconds before the enemy artillery—which was still coming—would be the least of his worries. Two minutes and seventeen—sixteen—seconds before the U.S. airstrike wiped 260 insurgents off the face of the planet.

And Jenk with them.

He was too close. And he had no idea how badly he was injured. There was no way he could crawl to safety in two minutes, even if he got himself out from underneath this rubble.

There was also no way that one of his teammates would find him in time since he was heading away from, not toward, the planned extraction point.

But his litany of *no way*'s wasn't going to get him out of here. It hurt like hell, but he started to dig, twisting in a way that would have made his middle school gymnastics coach proud.

Another rocket fell, but this time Jenk was able to cover his mouth and nose, burying his face into the crook of his elbow.

And as the roar of the explosion turned to ringing in his ears, as he got back to work, he heard . . .

"Jenkins!"

Izzy?

"Over here!" Jenk shouted, and then, thank you Jesus, Izzy was there, helping to dig him out, tossing aside the smaller chunks of rock, rolling away larger pieces, pulling him free.

The pain was incredible as Izzy helped haul him to his feet—feet that were still attached to his legs, feet upon which he could miraculously still stand.

His left shoulder was a different story.

Of course, he didn't need his shoulder to run.

Or did he? Jesus, every step he took sent pain knifing through him.

Izzy seemed to know, and he looped Jenk's good arm over his shoulder. He was talking to the lieutenant over his radio headset, even as he pushed Jenk to move faster. "Got the radio. Oh, yeah, and bitsy little Jenkins, too. I almost couldn't find him. He's so tiny, he'd crawled beneath a rock. Don't tell the other guys, but I think he might've shit his pants."

"Fuck you, dickhead," Jenk gasped, laughing despite the pain, through the pain.

"It's going to be close," Izzy reported to Jacquette, "but we'll make it."

They were going to make it. It was a miracle—the most painful miracle of Jenk's life, but a miracle just the same.

And Izzy Zanella was his angel sent from heaven.

Somehow Iz had known where to find him. He'd known just where Jenk would be.

"I cut her down for you," Izzy said, talking now to Jenk, who realized they'd made it over to the bridge.

Sure enough, the bodies—Suhayla and the others—were lined up along the road, faces respectfully covered.

"I figured you'd be heading over here," Izzy told him. "When you didn't show, I did the job before heading back to fetch you. I hope you don't mind."

"No," Jenk managed. "Thanks, man."

"FYI, they shot her, Mark. In the head. It was quick. Before they, you know, strung her up. I know it doesn't make it better. Dead is dead. I just thought . . . you'd prolly want to know."

Izzy had known Jenk was headed here, to the bridge, to make sure that Suhalya's body was cut down. It didn't make it any less of a miracle—the idea of Izzy being that sensitive and perceptive was almost as absurd as the idea of Izzy-the-Omnipotent-Angel.

"We'll make sure she gets buried," Izzy promised him now, his voice quiet in his certainty.

There was no time to stop to pay his respects.

They were barely out of range when the first of the American bombs began to fall. Through the haze of pain, Jenk heard Izzy singing. "And the rockets' red glare! The bombs bursting in air . . ."

He sounded practically gleeful—more like the Izzy Jenk had thought he'd known and kept his careful distance from after hours. The Izzy that no one really called friend, but everyone wanted by their side when out on an op.

They paused on the mountain trail as the insurgents' ammo dump took a direct hit. The explosion was massive—all those weapons and ammunition and dynamite going up in smoke.

Weapons that would not be used to kill Americans—or innocent people like Suhayla, who had only wanted to live and work in her own country, free from oppression, free from fear.

As they started back up the trail, heading for the team's extraction point, Jenk knew that Izzy had been right.

It didn't help. As far as Suhalya was concerned, it was too little, too late.

But it sure as hell didn't hurt.

CHAPTER ONE

Lindsey Fontaine knocked on her boss's door. It was ajar, so she pushed it open, peeking in. "You wanted to see me, sir," she started, but then realized there was someone in a Navy uniform sitting across from his desk. "Oh, I'm sorry."

"No, come on in, Linds." Her boss, Tom Paoletti, waved her into the room. "You've met Mark Jenkins, haven't you?"

"Not officially," Lindsey told him. She'd seen Jenkins earlier this morning. Hanging out at the new receptionist's desk.

Reading rank wasn't one of her strengths, but Tom was a former Navy SEAL. His company, Troubleshooters Incorporated, did a great deal of business with the government, including the military. Which meant lots of uniforms walked through their door.

The very young man—Jeez, were they really taking them this fresh out of diapers these days?—pushing himself to his feet while favoring his left side was a petty officer, first class.

And oh, yes, he was definitely first-class—in more ways than one. Extra cute, with muscles.

But wait. His rank meant he'd been in the Navy for a number of years, because petty officers started at third class and worked their way up to first. And *that* meant he couldn't be as young as he looked.

Shame on her for making assumptions. She should've known better—as someone who still got carded. At the movies. When she went to see an R-rated film.

Lindsey knew firsthand what a pain in the butt it was to look far younger than her years.

"Nice to meet you, Lindsey," Jenkins said as he shook her hand.

Good grip. Solid eye contact. Pretty, *pretty* hazel eyes. Great smile. Cute freckles. And not too tall, either. She liked him already.

Except for the fact that he was clearly infatuated with Tracy Shapiro, Troubleshooters Incorporated's remarkably inept new receptionist. Of course, most men seemed to turn into idiots around women who looked like Tracy, the brainless hairdo.

Not that Lindsey had exchanged more than a casual greeting with Tracy, who'd started working there just a few days ago. But there was no doubt about it, Tracy had set Lindsey's Brainless Hair-Do-o-meter clacking right away. It might've had something to do with Tracy bumming five bucks for lunch off of Alyssa—after flat-out flirting with Alyssa's husband, Sam.

But okay, to be fair, it wasn't the flirting-with-Sam part that was a problem. Alyssa had to be good and used to that.

The Real Hair-Do Action came from Tracy lamenting her lack of money for lunch, accepting a fiver from Alyssa with only the vaguest of promises to pay it back, and then, without taking a breath, launching into an explanation of how she'd seen the shoes she was wearing on sale, and she just had to buy them, and could they believe she'd actually gotten them for only three hundred dollars?

When Lindsey came to work, she wore sneakers or clunky-heeled boots, bought on sale for $29.95, so . . . No. She could not believe that any pair of shoes, even those made by mermaids off the coast of Sicily, could be worth three hundred dollars.

"Jenk found Tracy for us," Tom Paoletti told Lindsey now. "They were friends back in high school."

"Ah," she said. *They were friends back in high school* was guy code for *Jenk had always wanted to jump her bones.* Apparently, he hadn't given up trying. He no doubt thought helping her get a job might work. "That explains it."

Oops, she probably shouldn't have said that aloud.

"I mean, I'm sure she's just feeling her way, first days and all," Lindsey added, putting on what she hoped would be perceived as an optimistic expression. "I mean, we've all had 'em, right? First days. Kind of scary. Kind of overwhelming . . ."

"Absolutely," Jenk said, flashing her a grateful smile.

And first days of work had to be doubly hard for Tracy, who'd apparently been intercepted midway through her quest to see the Wizard and finally get a brain.

Cleverly, Lindsey didn't say *that* aloud.

"Have a seat," Tom ordered in that easygoing way he had of making a demand sound like an invitation.

She sat. Jenkins sat, too.

Tom Paoletti was the best boss Lindsey had ever had. Not only was he good-looking in that Captain-Picard-make-it-so, bald-men-can-be-sexy way, but he was also smart and unbelievably kind.

Maybe too kind. Lindsey made a mental note to offer to volunteer to fire Tracy for him. After the past few years she'd had, firing someone would be a cakewalk. She wouldn't even blink.

She'd mention that to Tom later, when Mark Jenkins wasn't around.

"We're going to be playing the part of Red Cell—the terrorists—in a training op with SEAL Team Sixteen," Tom told her now. "Jenk is going to be liaison as we work out the logistics."

"Really." Lindsey looked at the SEAL. "How . . ." *Convenient*, she was about to say, since his being liaison would give him even more access to Tracy. Except, Tracy was not a multi-tasker, and his distracting presence would be far less convenient for everyone else in the office. She, for one, was extremely tired of answering the phones because Tracy had managed to screw up the voice mail system again. "Interesting," she said instead, because they were both waiting for her to finish her sentence.

Day-am, the freckles across Jenk's nose were positively adorable, especially when he frowned. Combined with those hazel eyes, rimmed by thick, dark lashes . . .

He was beyond cute, but it was probably in a way that he himself hated. Baby-faced cute. His mouth tightened slightly, because he misunderstood her comment. *Interesting.* . . . "I'm twenty-eight years old."

"Oh," she said. "No, I wasn't—"

"You were wondering," Jenk said. "I could see that you were wondering, so . . . Now you know. I'm old enough to vote."

"Actually, I wasn't wondering." Lindsey glanced at Tom, who smiled, apparently in no hurry to talk about that training op. Red Cell. That was going to be some kind of fun. "I mean, I was earlier, but then I did the math, figuring that you probably went to college and then . . . I had you at more like thirty, if you want to know the truth."

She'd surprised him. "You really thought . . . ?"

She shrugged. "Hey. Without makeup, I look about twelve."

He looked at her—really looked.

"Being flat-chested helps with the illusion," she said. "I'm five feet and three-eighths of an inch tall—you better believe I count every eighth. I'm also the same age as my bra size—30A. The A is for my four-oh average at UCLA, which I attended before my seven years with the LAPD." She smiled at him. "I'm one of Tom's best bodyguards, by the way. I specialize in the protection of people who might not want their friends, business associates, and/or enemies to know they're being protected. Because I could tell that *you* were wondering." She'd stunned him, so she turned to Tom who was now flat-out grinning. "Red Cell, huh? So you called me in here, boss, because you want me to play the part of Dr. Evil, the terrorist mastermind, right?"

Lindsey liked Tom for a lot of reasons, but particularly because she made him laugh. Some people didn't get her sense of humor, although Cutie-pie Jenkins seemed to be on the same page after he'd shaken off his shock.

"Sorry, I'm the terrorist mastermind of this one," Tom told her. "It was a direct request from Admiral Tucker."

Ah. "Which makes me . . ." She let her voice trail off. "Mini Me?"

Tom laughed again. "Tempting, but no. Not quite."

Uh-oh. "Please don't say that I'm—"

He spoke in unison with her. "The hostage."

Lindsey stared at him.

"Someone's got to be the hostage," Tom pointed out, undaunted by her scathing disbelief.

"Yeah, but come on. How realistic is it for the hostage to weigh only ninety-two pounds?" She leaned forward to argue. "Don't you want to give the SEALs a challenge?" Lindsey turned to Jenk. "Tell him you want a challenge. Tell him you want, I don't know, Sam Starrett to play the hostage. What is he? Six and a half feet tall? Two ten? Now if only he had a heart condition, too, he'd be a perfect hostage."

"This time it's going to be you," Tom told her.

She knew when to stop pushing, so instead she sighed heavily. "All right."

"We'll talk more later," Tom said, four little words made even more intriguing by the gleam in his eyes. Was it possible she was going to be more than the hostage? Suddenly this was back to maybe being fun.

Maybe.

"I just wanted you to meet Jenk," Tom continued. "If he needs help with the scheduling—or really anything," he added addressing Jenkins directly, "he's going to come to you, Linds."

Oh, good. She was going to get to be the secretary, as well as the hostage, helping out with scheduling. Whoo-freakin'-hoo. She would have complained that she never saw Tom assigning Sam Starrett to help out with the scheduling—except for the fact that Sam was bitching about Tom giving him a similar task just last week.

"I was thinking it might be a good idea to have the two teams meet, sometime in the next week," Jenk suggested. "Maybe over at the Ladybug Lounge?"

"Really?" Lindsey was skeptical. "That doesn't seem very realistic. Meeting in advance, at a bar?"

Hello, Osama, can the boys in your San Diego sleeper cell make it to a party on Tuesday night?

"This is a silver bullet assignment," Jenk informed her, then translated. "Just short of R&R. Or it was supposed to be. Before Admiral Tucker got it into his head that it would be a kick to pit Tommy here against the new CO of Team Sixteen."

Yikes. Lindsey looked at her boss. "Your old team versus your new?" she asked. "That's gotta suck. For your old team." She turned back to Jenk. "We are *so* going to kick your butts."

"Yeah, I don't think so. We're SEALs. And—no offense, Tommy—Commander Koehl's a good CO, so—"

"The poor guy," Lindsey said. "Because, like, isn't Team Sixteen still referred to as 'Tom's Team'? I mean, that's gotta sting. Koehl's been there, what? At least a year already. That must be frustrating. And now if he loses—*when* he loses—"

Tom interrupted. "Training ops arc not about winning and losing. They're about learning. About improving."

Lindsey looked at Jenk, who was looking back at Lindsey with an expression equally disbelieving. Not about winning? Who did Tom think he was kidding?

"And yes," Tom continued. "This *was* supposed to be fun. So let's see if we can't find the time for that social event. Don't forget to invite Lew Koehl. Let's try to downplay the winning and losing thing. Starting right here and now."

Lindsey looked over at Jenk again. "I'm down with learning," she said, even as she gazed pointedly at the spot where his rear was planted in that chair, making a tiny kicking motion with her foot.

"Totally into improving," he agreed, shooting her back a discreet L for loser, shaped with his thumb and forefinger, out of Tom's line of sight.

Lindsey couldn't help it. She laughed, covering it quickly with a cough.

Tom, of course, wasn't fooled. He rubbed his forehead. "I'm serious, people. This is going to be . . . at best, difficult. Both for Commander

Koehl and for me. I want you working together. Let's turn this into a win for everyone." He smiled tightly. "Except maybe Admiral Tucker."

"We should look at a calendar," Jenk told Lindsey. "And exchange cell phone numbers."

Those words coming from those lips should have made her heart beat harder. Mark Jenkins wanted her phone number. He was cute and funny and smart—and tremendously flawed. He had, after all, the hots for the Hair-Do. And his wanting Lindsey's number was purely work-related.

No doubt about it, he was Lindsey's type. Perfectly, cleanly out of reach, unless, of course he got a little drunk and ended up going home with Lindsey as his solid second choice.

Oh, yeah, if she played her cards right, she could get totally skewered by this one.

Although it had been quite some time since she'd been skewered—or preskewered, which was far more enjoyable.

Still, a little distance would probably be prudent.

"Wouldn't Tracy be a better person to assist Jenkins with this?" she suggested, even as she took one of the Troubleshooters Incorporated business cards off of the little holder on Tom's desk. She wrote her number on the back. "I mean, I'm happy to do it, of course. I was just thinking, since they're, you know, old friends"—wink, wink—"Jenk might appreciate spending time with her."

Jenkins liked that idea. "Thanks," he said, pocketing the business card, still rummaging for one of his own. Yeah, she had been right about him favoring one side. He definitely didn't have full range of motion in his left arm.

Her own shoulder—her right one—twinged in sympathy.

If she hadn't just decided to keep her distance, she could've given him some rehab and recovery tips.

Tom, meanwhile, wasn't as thrilled as Jenk was about her Tracy idea. "You're the official TS Inc liaison," he told Lindsey. "If I need answers, I'm going to come to you. But you can absolutely let Tracy help. That's what she's been hired to do. In fact, you can use this opportunity to get to know her, help bring her up to speed."

Oh, whee.

Tom was an excellent leader. He was capable of reading his subordinates even when, like Lindsey was doing right now, they were wearing their best poker faces.

"We'll talk about that later, as well," he said. "I've got a few more things to discuss with Jenk."

"First days are always tough," Jenk reminded them, as Lindsey got to her feet. He rose, too, terminally polite, as he handed her his card.

"I'll see if I can't find the office calendar," Lindsey said.

"Are you going to be around for a while?" Jenk asked.

"All afternoon."

He nodded. "Great. Then I'll catch you after lunch." No doubt he was going out with Tracy. What a waste. Still, his smile was infectious, and Lindsey smiled back—but distantly, she hoped—as she closed the door behind her.

Out in the reception area, Tracy was making copies as she tried to keep up with answering the phones. Slender, but with curves in all the right places, with long brown hair, startlingly blue eyes, and an exotically beautiful face, she could have made a fortune as a fashion model if only she were five inches taller.

She teetered precariously on the too-high heels of those ridiculous three-hundred-dollar shoes, as she ran back and forth between the copier and the phones.

"Oh, hi, Sam," she said, as she answered the phone, putting on a sugary voice reserved for anyone who had dangling genitalia. "No, Decker hasn't called in. Can I help?" The other lines were all lighting up, and the copy machine had stopped, but Tracy ignored it all because Sam Starrett was on the phone.

Lindsey sighed, and went to the other desk, picking up the ringing lines. "Troubleshooters Incorporated. Hold please. Troubleshooters Incorporated, sorry, can you hold?"

Tracy Shapiro was beautiful, there was no question about that. She had a body that all women wished for but few ever achieved. She seemed friendly enough—a little too friendly where Sam Starrett was concerned, though. And, yes, okay, maybe Lindsey was wrong about the no-brains thing. Maybe she was a rocket scientist. Some of the rocket scientists Lindsey had met at UCLA couldn't answer more than one phone at a time, either.

There was a lot Lindsey didn't know about Tracy, but there was one thing she would've bet big money on if she'd found a taker.

And that was that the Tracy Shapiros of the world didn't hook up with the Mark Jenkinses.

The man didn't have a Smurf's chance in a wolf fight.

Which seriously increased Lindsey's odds of getting skewered.

She pushed the last lit button as Tracy dragged out her phone call with Sam by asking him about the traffic on the Five. Jesus. If Lindsey were Sam's wife Alyssa, she'd sit down right here in the lobby, at this desk across from Tracy's. And she'd clean her entire collection of handguns. Hint, hint, beeyotch. "Troubleshooters Incorporated, how may I direct your call?"

LOCATION: UNCERTAIN
DATE: UNKNOWN

She was cold. Always cold.

Hungry, too.

He kept the damp basement freezing, kept her carefully underfed.

And almost always in the dark. There were no windows. No way to tell the difference between night and day.

Sometimes he turned on the lights just to disorient her. There was never any rhyme to it, never any reason.

She tried to keep track of time, but it was impossible to do, especially during days like these, when she hadn't heard his footsteps in the kitchen overhead for what felt like weeks on end.

She couldn't remember the last time he'd brought her food. All she knew was that the supply she'd been hoarding was gone. She started to believe that she would starve to death, locked down here, cold and alone.

She tried to tell herself that that would be okay. It would be better than what he'd done to Number Four.

But then she heard it. Footsteps overhead.

His footsteps. She'd know them anywhere.

He was sliding something across the kitchen floor.

Someone.

She knew that he hadn't been shopping while he was gone all that time. She knew it wasn't a hundred-pound bag of potatoes that he'd dragged in from his car.

There was little she could be certain of in her life—in this nightmare that her life had become. But that he hadn't come home alone was definite.

And sure enough, he opened the door and came partly down the stairs. The glow from the kitchen spilled into the basement, lighting him from behind, making it hard for her to see his face.

"I'm back, Number Five. Did you miss me?"

She couldn't remember what he looked like. And she'd never really seen his eyes. Not without the sunglasses he'd worn when she'd gotten into his car. Time was a blur, but she knew it had been months since he'd first locked her down here. Maybe even years.

She'd had a name once—Beth. But now she was a number. Five.

He called her that, called her his champion, too, in his flat Yankee accent, when he opened the door to bring her food. Sometimes he brought fresh water, so she wouldn't have to drink the brackish liquid that seeped up in a pool, in the corner of this prison.

Lord, how she hated him, how she feared him—yet how she looked forward to those dazzling moments of light.

This time, he threw something at her. She ducked, and it hit the wall before she realized what it was. A loaf of bread. A jar of peanut butter. She tore it open and ate it, as quickly as she could. Because she'd learned that everything he gave her, he could easily take away.

She would have liked to save it, because she never knew if the food and water he'd brought was all she'd get for God knows how long. If he'd gone right back up the stairs, she would have rationed it, both dreading and praying for his swift return.

Sometimes he left food well out of range of her chains, with no way for her to reach it. She'd sit in the darkness, starving, smelling it, even over the constant stench of death.

Sometimes he took and emptied the bucket he'd given her for her waste. Sometimes he wouldn't bring it back downstairs again for days on end. Sometimes he did. Sometimes he threw it at her, covering her with her own filth if she didn't move quickly enough out of the way.

All the while calling her Number Five. "You've been a good girl, Number Five."

"You've been a bad girl, Number Five."

It didn't matter what she did. God knows she tried being good, doing what she thought he wanted, but it soon became clear that the very thing she was praised for on one day would invoke his wrath on the next.

It was an awful way to live.

Only one thing was certain.

After he'd been gone for so long, he'd tell her it was time to get cleaned up. He'd get out his hose and spray her with water that stung and bruised her, that left her soaked and colder than ever. He'd toss her the key that would unlock the chain around her ankle.

But before that, he'd say the words she dreaded hearing, words she could count on hearing, words he spoke to her now.

"I've brought you a new friend."

SAN DIEGO, CALIFORNIA
FRIDAY, DECEMBER 2, 2005

Dave brought two mugs of coffee into her office.

"Did you make that?" Sophia asked.

He nodded as he slumped down into the chair across from her desk.
He had terrible posture. Maybe his brain was just too heavy, and he didn't
have the strength to hold his head up for great lengths of time. "Yeah. I
arranged for an accident with the previous pot."

"So," Sophia said as she took a sip. "She can't make coffee, she can't
work the voice mail system, the copies of my report went out missing page
five . . ."

"She's only been here a few days," Dave said mildly. "Give her a
chance."

"The Phoenix client was on hold for twenty minutes," Sophia said.
"And I'm sorry, but it was a six-page document. How hard could it be to
make sure page five was there?"

"I've taken a nonscientific poll. Lindsey hates her as much as you do."
Dave leaned even farther back in his chair, stretching his legs out in front
of him. "Alyssa grits her teeth and Tess rolls her eyes whenever her name
is mentioned. The *men*, on the other hand, all agree that the job just might
be harder than it looks."

"So what are you saying?" Sophia asked. "That we're insecure and
jealous? Or that you're all just blinded by the wonder of Tracy's sweater?"

"It is a lovely sweater," he agreed. Out of all the people she'd met since
coming to work for Troubleshooters Incorporated, David Malkoff was the
most unassuming. He dressed like tech support, in stoner T-shirts and
baggy shorts, with long hair waving around what was very definitely not a
long-haired face. "It matches the color of her eyes."

Sophia laughed. "Yes, I'm sure the color was what everyone noticed."

"I did," he told her. He looked, in fact, like an accountant dressed up
as Jerry Garcia for Halloween.

"Right."

Dave sat up slightly, blinking at her in mild offense. "I *did*."

He looked, well . . . silly, to be honest. Ignorable. The gelding in a stable of stallions.

He was, in fact, a former CIA operative—brilliant and extremely capable.

"You know, you've got a shirt that you sometimes wear," he continued earnestly. "It's kind of like a T-shirt only fancier. It's the same color blue as *your* eyes. It's striking. And of course the fabric manages to . . . hang isn't the right word, but you know what I mean. It clings. To you. As does the shirt you're wearing right now, which is . . ." He was actually starting to blush. "Also very nice. But it's the color. Blue. Of the T-shirt. It's the same color as your eyes, that . . . I noticed. First."

It was quite possible that Sophia was blushing now, too. Considering her checkered past, she made a point never to dress provocatively. The blouse she was wearing today was nothing special. It covered her—even with the top button comfortably undone. Yet it wasn't a cardboard box. The fabric did drape around her body.

A body that Dave—among plenty of others—had seen, completely unclad. It wasn't something they'd ever discussed, but there were times—such as this one—where Sophia could see the memory of her nakedness in his eyes.

"You can't not know that your . . . figure is . . . what it is," Dave slogged on, hip deep in dangerous territory, but honing in on his point. "And yet you wear that blue shirt. Or the shirt you have on. Instead of a Kevlar vest, which would completely conceal . . . you know. You. Tracy is a beautiful woman, too. It's not her fault that she—same as you—looks good in the clothes she wears to work."

"Maybe I *should* get a Kevlar vest," Sophia said. She slipped her arms into her jacket, needing to feel more covered. Dave, the least threatening man on the planet, was aware of her body.

"I'm sorry," he said, visibly distressed. "I didn't mean to make you uncomfortable." Like a true gentleman, he changed the subject. "Have you decided yet if you're going to Boston?"

Leave it to Dave to leap upon the one subject that made her equally uncomfortable. Going to Boston—or not—was not something she wanted to *think* about, let alone discuss. Not even with him.

"Have you talked to Tom about that team leader position he wants you to take?" she countered.

He grimaced, clearly recognizing her subtext. His answer was as giant a *no* as hers. Still, he hesitated. "You know, if you decide you want to talk about it . . ."

"Ditto with the job thing," Sophia told him.

Their boss, Tom Paoletti, was convinced Dave would make a top-notch team leader. Sophia agreed. Dave was fair, he was honest—yes, sometimes brutally so—and he was highly respected. It was time for him to start giving orders, not taking them.

But the words that Dave had used when they'd last discussed it included "not a chance in hell" and "over my dead body." There was no need for it, he insisted. Not so long as he worked for a company where there were already plenty of people with team leader written all over them.

Alyssa Locke, Tom Paoletti's second-in-command at TS Inc, was former FBI, as well as a former naval officer. Her husband, Sam Starrett was, like Tom, former SEAL. Lindsey Fontaine was former LAPD. Tess Bailey and Jimmy Nash had both worked at a mysterious no-name agency. PJ Prescott had been an Air Force Pararescue Jumper.

"Deck's coming in this afternoon," Dave reported now.

And then there was Lawrence Decker.

Former chief in the Navy SEALs, former Agency operative, champion of freedom, protector of the downtrodden, dedicated to truth and justice, Decker was quietly, relentlessly a true American hero.

He'd made only one mistake in his entire life—and it was when he'd first met Sophia Ghaffari.

He'd yet to forgive himself for it.

He'd yet to forgive her, as well.

Sophia nodded, shuffling the files on her desk, unable to meet the now-steady kindness of Dave's gaze. "Thanks for the heads-up."

This was the real reason he'd stopped in. The coffee was just a cover, the talk about the new receptionist just a distraction. Even the mention of Boston was a warm-up to an even more difficult topic.

Dave was a good friend—always looking out for her. He was always taking care of her, even while making it clear that he knew she was completely capable of taking care of herself.

"I overheard Tom talking to Lindsey," Dave told her. "We're doing some kind of war-gaming thing with SEAL Team Sixteen."

Sophia nodded, her heart sinking. She already knew. About the impending op, not about Decker.

Lindsey had stopped in to see if Sophia wanted to help out. The way she'd described it had sounded fun. A training mission—low-key and casual. A chance to get to know the SEALs in Team Sixteen.

It was, at the very least, an opportunity to get dressed up in cammie gear and war paint, and run around in the woods. Sophia didn't have that kind of training—the work she did for Troubleshooters Incorporated was mostly client interface. Presentations, meetings, business matters.

She'd actually been excited at the idea of trying something new.

But now . . .

"Deck's coming in to be part of that," Dave confirmed her suspicions.

"We're all supposed to participate. Everyone who's not currently on assignment. Which includes you, by the way."

She looked up at him at that. She'd just finished that report for Cleveland and hadn't yet scheduled her impending trip to Phoenix. But . . . "Deck won't work with me."

Dave shrugged. "I don't think he has a choice this time."

She put her hand on her telephone, ready to call Phoenix. That's all it would take—one phone call—to change her status instantly to *on assignment*. But Dave knew what she was thinking, and he leaned forward, covering her hand with his own, so she couldn't lift the handset.

"Deck comes in, you go out for lunch. Or to Cleveland," he continued.

"I make him uncomfortable," Sophia said. "The least I can do is—"

"Why do you always do what Decker wants?" Dave asked her.

It was a good question.

But the answer was easy. "I owe him," she whispered, "so much. You know that."

She still had nightmares. Her dreams were a twisting of her memories, of fleeing for her life on the streets of the lawless city of Kazabek, hunted by a man who wouldn't have hesitated to separate her head from her shoulders. Sometimes, in her dreams, he caught her. Sometimes, though, it was Decker who found her first.

Either way, she woke up with her heart pounding.

Dave moved her hand off the phone, squeezing it before he let her go. "It's been almost two years," he told her. "I think you probably paid him back. It's time to start thinking about what you owe yourself." He stood up. "If you want to go out to lunch, my schedule's clear—I'll go with you. But maybe, today, we should eat in."

After he got back from grabbing a quick sandwich, Jenk found Lindsey Fontaine in Troubleshooter XO Alyssa Locke's office.

She was showing Alyssa how to input information onto the office calendar, leaning over her shoulder to gaze at the computer monitor.

"That's right," Lindsey said. "Now, see, it comes up in blue on the screen because it's a personal appointment. And you don't need to be specific, because it's no one's business *why* you're taking lost time, but at the same time, it lets the rest of us know that you're unavailable on Tuesday between two and five."

Jenk knocked on the door, and both women looked up at him—one

African American, one Asian American. With white boy Jenk in the room, it was like being part of the "Small World" ride at Disney.

Or in a video game.

More than Lindsey's name was androgynous. With her black hair cut short, almost like a bathing cap on her head, she reminded him of a character in a Japanese anime adventure. Of course, much of that had to do with the way she dressed. In that Hawaiian shirt and cargo pants, sandals on her feet, she could have passed for a Japanese boy.

A very, very pretty Japanese boy, with huge brown eyes, a heart-shaped face, delicate gracefully shaped lips, and an almost-elfishly pointed chin.

"Excuse me, ma'am," he addressed Alyssa. "Lindsey, when you're done here, would you mind . . . ?"

Alyssa glanced at the smaller woman. "We're done. I get how the program works."

"Yeah, well, see, there's more to it than *getting* it," Lindsey told her. It was impressive—she was talking to Alyssa as if Alyssa didn't totally intimidate her. Jenk had known the Troubleshooters' executive officer for years, and he still ma'amed her to death whenever he spoke to her. Maybe it was out of fear that if he didn't, she would smite him with her evil eye.

Of course, since she and Jenk's old teammate Sam Starrett had gotten married, her use of her evil eye had dramatically decreased. Probably because—in the past—it had been Sam himself that she'd used it on most often.

Lindsey actually leaned on Alyssa's desk. And spoke to her sternly. "The calendar program doesn't work unless we all *use* it. Which means that after I leave here, you will actually have to take the ten minutes and input all of your upcoming appointments. And I'm talking now, not later. Not an hour from now or tomorrow. Not even *in a minute*. Now. Do we have an understanding here?"

"Now," Alyssa repeated obediently.

"If you're lying to me," Lindsey warned her, as she came out from behind Alyssa's desk, toward Jenk, "I'm going to come back here, and it's going to get ugly."

"I'm doing it," Alyssa said. "Right now. See? Doing it . . ."

Lindsey sent her one more dark look as she followed Jenk into the hall. "I'm leaving the door open so I can hear you," she called back to Alyssa, who was obediently clacking away on her computer keyboard. She turned to Jenk. "You're welcome—because I know that you're thinking *thank you*. You know, for doing your girlfriend's job?"

Of course. Tracy should have been in charge of maintaining the office calendar. "She's not my girlfriend," Jenk pointed out, leading the way into Tommy's conference room.

"You mean *yet*, right?"

"We're friends."

Lindsey wasn't convinced. "Yeah, and you've only been crushing on her for how long? Since, what? Ninth grade?"

He had to laugh—she'd pegged it so exactly. He closed the door behind her. "Seventh."

"Oh, you poor thing." She sat on the table, putting them more at eye level, which was a shame. He liked the fact that she had to tilt her head to look up at him. That didn't happen very often. Even women who were shorter than average, like Tracy, tended to wear heels. In fact, the shoes she was wearing today, combined with her hairstyle, made her seem to tower over him.

The beach. He had to invite Tracy out to the beach. Get her barefoot . . .

"You're even further gone than I thought." Lindsey was talking to him, and he forced himself to focus. "May I be honest with you?" she asked.

"More than you've already been?" Jenk was bemused.

"In my opinion, Tracy was not born with a receptionist's gene," she said. "You may want to take her out to dinner tonight, ply her with wine, and prepare her for the fact that a gold watch upon retirement after thirty years of employment is probably not in her future. Maybe you can convince her to bear your children. You know, it's actually been proven that space-shots—both male and female, I'm not being sexist here—they become more efficient and organized after having kids. I think it's part of that whole Darwinian survival of the fittest thing."

Jenk wasn't sure what to say, especially since Lindsey kept going.

"It's a full moon tonight, too. People act impulsively during a full moon. More knife fights, but also more sex. I'm betting that Tracy might not be so good at knife fights."

Was she honestly suggesting that he . . . ? It was hard to tell when she was serious and when she was kidding.

"I'm, um, babysitting tonight," Jenk told Lindsey. It was nice to surprise her, for a change. "For Tommy and Kelly. They've got some kind of rehearsal dinner thing."

Tommy's niece was getting married tomorrow.

"Wow," Lindsey said. "Okay, I'm totally impressed. An alpha male who isn't terrified by the idea of spending an evening with a seven-month-old?"

This time she wasn't kidding. At least he didn't think so. Her smile was sincere, her eyes warm, her admiration more than evident. She was definitely attracted to him. He hadn't just imagined that back in Tommy's office. Wasn't that . . . interesting? At any other time, he would've taken advantage, because the attraction was definitely mutual.

But the woman of his dreams was finally available. She'd moved to San Diego, she'd broken up with her longtime scumbag boyfriend, she was looking for a change. These days Jenk was setting his sights higher than a mere mutual attraction. So he took a step back, tried to make his smile more friend-ish.

"It's going to be fun," he said. "I mean, kids, you know? Kids are great."

Lindsey's smile was definitely sincere. And his suspicions were confirmed. Women really did have a soft spot for men who liked children. Running out of cash during last month's poker game over at Tommy's house had been a gift in disguise. He just hadn't realized it at the time.

Jenk had been holding a beautiful, beautiful boat. Aces and kings. But Tommy had refused to fold, betting everything he'd had to try to force Jenk out of the game. He'd written up an IOU for five nights of babysitting, just to call Tommy's bluff.

Of course, Tommy hadn't been bluffing. He'd had a straight flush, beating Jenk's full house. The man had incredible luck.

Not just at poker, but in life and in love.

Tom Paoletti had actually gone and married his high school crush. He was Jenk's inspiration. If Tommy could win his wife Kelly's heart, then Jenk could win Tracy's.

He'd yet to tell her he was babysitting tonight—telling Lindsey had been a practice run. But now he couldn't wait to see that same softness in Tracy's eyes.

As for the babysitting, Charlie Paoletti was pretty cute. How hard could it be?

"Have you ever babysat before?" Lindsey asked him. The softness had been replaced by concern. And quite possibly amusement. It was hard to tell, because the amusement was usually always present in Lindsey's dark brown eyes.

Jenk shook his head no. "A friend is coming along, to help." It still felt weird, calling Izzy his friend. "He has something like nine brothers and sisters. He's the youngest—all his older brothers and sisters were having kids when he was, like, ten."

Tom had been uncertain about leaving Charlie alone with Jenk—until Izzy had volunteered to assist. Apparently the Iz-Meister had sat for Charlie before.

Strange, but true.

"That's good," Lindsey said. "That you'll have help. It'll also be better for, you know, your shoulder."

"Did Tommy tell you . . . ?" He realized that he'd unconsciously reached up to rub it.

She shook her head. "You've been favoring it. Only slightly, though. I only noticed because I can relate. I was in an accident about five years ago. Really messed mine up." She rotated her right arm. "I'm now prone to dislocating it, which is barrels of fun."

"I'm still rehabbing," Jenk admitted.

She nodded. "Pain in the butt, huh?"

And there they were, just smiling at each other again. Friendly smiles, he reminded himself. Tracy, Tracy, Tracy. "Tommy thinks very highly of you," Jenk told her.

She waved the compliment away. "I'm serious about Tracy," she said. "I know she's your . . . friend, but this just isn't the right job for her."

"Working the front desk is not that hard."

"That's right," she said. "It's not. And yet . . ."

Tracy wasn't getting it done. Damn it. "I'll talk to her," Jenk said.

"What this office really needs is a Mrs. Landingham. You know, the President's old secretary from . . . ? I guess you don't watch *West Wing*."

"I don't watch much TV."

"Not even *Lost?*" she asked.

Jenk shook his head.

"Or *Boston Legal?* I'm thinking of starting a new religion, with William Shatner as my god."

"When do I have time to watch TV? All the stories are connected, I turn it on, and it's like watching the Spanish station. What the eff is a hatch doing in the freaking jungle, anyway? So I flip to ESPN. You can come into the middle of a football game and know exactly what's up. Some of these shows—you have to plan your life around watching them."

"Yeah, I don't have a life," Lindsey admitted. "I go to work, I come home. My most intimate relationship is with my TiVo. I'd get a cat, but I'm allergic. And by the way, it's okay if you drop the f-bomb on me. After seven years with the LAPD, I've heard it before. At least, oh, six, seven times."

Jenk laughed. "That many, huh?"

"Back to Tracy," Lindsey reminded him. "How well do you know her?"

"Not very well," he admitted. "I mean, it's been a long time since high school. I'm sure she's changed. I have, too."

"It's just that she's so easily distracted. She seems so much more suited for retail sales. Working at the mall with all the twinkly, shiny things to sell?"

"We can help her get up to speed," Jenk said.

"We," Lindsey repeated.

She was sitting there, enormously skeptical. But not uninterested. That was good. She had a solid sense of humor, which was important when dealing with Tracy, who sometimes spiraled into one of her "I'm not good enough" moods.

Lately that attitude had been front and center. Jenk's sister, Ginny, had told him Tracy'd been fired from her job of appointment scheduler at a dentist's office in the same week that she'd walked in on her cheating lawyer boyfriend and his latest affair. Her move out here, to California, was part of an attempt to start fresh.

But playing the pity card wasn't likely to work with Lindsey. No, Jenk knew just how to get her on board this particular train.

"If you help me with Tracy," he told Lindsey, "I'll talk Tommy out of using you as hostage during the op."

Her eyes widened. "Wow. You could do that?"

"Yes, I could." Considering he was the one who'd orchestrated this entire training op. But he didn't want to cop to that, not after Admiral Fucker stirred some of his ugly into the pot by making it a showdown between Tommy and Commander Koehl.

"Wow," she said again.

"Do we have a deal?"

"Thanks, but no thanks. I talked to Tom while you were at lunch. I'm good with the hostage thing now."

She was serious. He found himself searching her eyes. They were totally unreadable—except for the amusement dancing there. And as for that small smile playing about the edges of her delicate lips . . . If he weren't a SEAL, it might've scared him.

Particularly when she continued. "We both know that, no matter what Tom says, this training op is going to be a competition. You against us. So here's the deal. I'll help you try to help Tracy over the next few days, until the op. If your SEAL team wins, I'll give her another full month. But if you lose, then you'll have to get her to hand in her resignation within that month, so Tom doesn't have to fire her."

Jesus. What had Tom told her? Something that had made her convinced the TS Inc team was going to win this thing.

Of course, Tommy didn't really know Commander Lew Koehl all that well.

Lindsey reached out with her foot, kicking him lightly on the leg. "Unless you don't think your SEALs can win. I mean, that's understandable. You probably know Tommy better than I do. He's formidable. And Sam Starrett, Alyssa Locke, Larry Decker . . . We've got quite the team. I personally wouldn't agree to this deal. I mean, if I were you."

She was totally manipulating him, working and molding him like a piece of clay. He oughta know, he'd used similar tactics himself, plenty of times before.

Still, Jenk found himself holding out his hand. "We've got a deal," he said, as they shook.

She had small hands with slender fingers that were cool to the touch.

Her smile, though, had one hell of a spark. "You," she told him happily, "are totally toast."

CHAPTER
TWO

I t happened in the office lobby. In the reception area, right under the
curious eyes of TS Inc's new receptionist.

Sophia and Decker.

Face-to-face for the first time in what had to be months.

Dave Malkoff stood awkwardly off to the side, certain that the last
thing they needed was an audience for this, but unwilling to desert Sophia.

"How are you?" Decker had to clear his throat before the words came
out.

"Fine." She managed a smile. "You look . . . like you're doing well."

Decker, in fact, looked like shit. He looked like *tired* shit. Of course,
to Dave, he always looked both like shit and bone tired, which probably
translated to *doing well*. For him, anyway.

"Yeah," Deck said to Sophia. "Thanks. You, too. You look . . . fit."

Fit? *Fit?* Sophia was, without a doubt, one of the most beautiful
women ever to walk the planet. With her long blond hair and porcelain
complexion, she was ethereal in her beauty, like some half-fairy, half-
human sprite, created when a moonbeam mixed with lightning and magically came to life.

Okay, so maybe Dave had watched *LOTR* one too many times, but
really, the best Decker could come up with was *fit?*

Unbelievable.

It was Sophia's turn to clear her throat. Dave's heart ached for her.
Why did Decker have to make this so hard? "You're here because you're
helping Tom with the, um . . ."

"Training op for Team Sixteen," Deck finished for her. "Yeah, that's, uh, it's a good opportunity for all of us, you know, the operatives here, to do some training, too. We don't want to get soft."

Amazing words to be spoken by this particular man. If there was one word that no one would ever use to describe Decker, it was *soft*. He was, in fact, relentlessly hard beneath that unassuming appearance. And his ferocious intensity, as he threw himself into his work as one of the top civilian counterterrorist team leaders in the country, made him seem not just hard, but razor-sharp, too. If someone got too close to him, they would risk getting cut.

Yet, here was Sophia, with her heart plainly on her sleeve, wanting nothing more than to be close to Decker.

The insensitive prick.

"Or softer than some of us already are," Decker amended.

His words were probably supposed to be a joke. At least Dave thought they were intended that way. But he didn't feel the urge to join Sophia in forcing a laugh as Decker glanced around the room, his gaze landing on Dave, as if he were a living example of the downhill slide they were all experiencing. "Hey, Dave. Nice to see you."

There was nothing to do but shake Decker's hand. "Deck."

"Have you heard anything from Murphy?" Decker asked.

Dave shook his head. "No." Murph had nearly been killed by a sniper, on a bodyguard assignment in Hollywood nearly a year ago. His wife had died in the same incident. Like everyone else in the TS Inc office, Decker was haunted by it. "He's dropped off the map."

Decker nodded grimly, as if he'd expected as much. He turned back to Sophia. "When are you leaving for Phoenix?" he asked her, his meaning clear. *Since I'm going to be in town for the next few weeks, it's your turn to disappear.*

Sophia didn't say it. Dave could see from her expression that she wasn't going to say it. So he said it for her. "She's not going to Phoenix. She's helping out with the training op."

Sophia put her hand on his arm. Her fingers were cold, despite the day's heat. "Dave," she murmured, ready, as usual to back down.

And Dave lost his temper. "What?" he said to her. "You're just gonna go to Phoenix?"

"It's not that big a deal," she told him.

"Yeah?" he said, as mad at her as he was at Decker, the selfish coward. "That's not what it sounded like when I heard you talking to Lindsey about it. It actually sounded as if you thought this op might be fun. Tell me this, Sophia, when was the last time you had fun?"

She didn't answer him. Instead, she was looking at Decker and apologizing. Again.

"*You* want to make a guess at when she last had fun?" Dave interrupted, stepping between them, getting into Decker's face. "No? I will, then. I'll guess it's been at least a coupla years, probably not since her husband was murdered in front of her—is that about right, Soph?"

Tracy, the new receptionist tried to intervene. "Would anyone like some coffee?"

"Go back to your desk," Dave snarled at her, and she backed off, wide-eyed.

Sophia was tugging on his arm again. "What are you doing?"

"I'm getting angry for you," Dave told her. "Since you can't seem to get angry for yourself."

"But I'm not angry." She was, however, mortified. "If this is your idea of help, stop, because I really don't need it!"

But he couldn't stop. "Yes, you do. Because you *should* be angry. You wanted to be part of this op. I heard you talking about it—You said you were going to play the part of a crazy commando-wannabe chick, dressed in high-fashion camouflage. I heard you laughing." He turned back to Decker. "I heard her *laughing*." Sophia never laughed—not really. Sure, she made this laughterlike noise and moved her face into a smile. She was really good at it. It sounded realistic, but Dave knew better. It wasn't genuine laughter. Except this time it had been. "And then you appeared, and whammo, she's going to Phoenix. Because you're not man enough to deal with your mistakes!"

Okay, that last part came out a little too loud. Heads were being poked out of doors.

But Dave still wasn't done. "Maybe you think I'm *soft*, because I was never a Navy SEAL. Maybe I *am* soft. But maybe I don't give a damn what you think. Not anymore."

Tom Paoletti came all the way into the lobby. Probably because Tracy had finally done something right and called him on his intercom. "How about we finish this in my office?" he said.

"Thank you, sir, but no. I'm done." Dave couldn't look at Sophia because the expression on her face would have broken his heart. "Go to Phoenix," he told her. "Have a nice trip."

Tracy was still watching them, her eyes wide. "I'll take that coffee now," he said, as he went into his office and slammed the door.

*   *   *

Izzy loved dropping by the Troubleshooters Incorporated office. There was always some crazy shit going on.

"May I help you?" The hot babe with the coffeepot and the mile-long legs had finally spotted him lurking here by the front door, as Tommy Paoletti ushered a former frog named Decker and the incredibly sexy Sophia Ghaffari into his office.

Tommy was saying something about clearing this up, but really, what was to clear up? The situation was obvious to anyone with eyes. Decker—the lucky bastard—had, at some point in the past, thrown Sophia a bang. She, the way most women did, had wanted a Re-Lay-Tion-Ship. Deckaroonie had activated his super-Y chromosome, exfiltrated pronto, and now, whenever they did an eyeball to eyeball, awkwardness ensued.

Meanwhile, crazy Dave Malkoff, who spent a lot of time pretending to be fair Sophia's friend when what he *really* wanted was to get in her panties, was jealous. Hence the meltdown Izzy had just witnessed.

Case closed.

Izzy turned his attention to a far more fascinating mystery. Could Miss Legs here help him?

She was like something out of a music video. Collagen lips—just slightly done to be enticingly pouty, a body that could hypnotize when in motion. She had gorgeous hair, long and shiny and kind of reddish brown, and eyes that were almost as big and blue as the Little Mermaid's.

Please, Heavenly Father, let her be able to help him.

She was checking out his BDUs, checking *him* out beneath his BDUs. The smile she gave him was beautiful. It was laced with a palpable amount of *hello, and who might you be?* Which, in Izzy's vast experience with hot babes, whether wielding coffeepots or not, usually led to another kind of smile—the kind that accompanied the sound of his zipper being pulled south.

Not immediately, of course. After a certain number of days. Or, if he was really lucky, hours. Depending on the proximity of copious amounts of alcohol.

"Are you one of Tom's SEALs?" she asked.

"Good guess," he said. "Yeah. I'm Izzy."

"Izzy," she repeated, like she liked the way his name felt, rolling around in her mouth. "Tom's in a meeting. Would you like something? Coffee? While you wait?"

"I'm good, thanks, and actually, I'm not here to see Tommy."

She set the coffeepot down, settled herself into the chair behind her reception desk, and smiled up at him. "Do you just drop in, randomly? Not that I mind. It's raining Navy SEALs—alleluia."

Sweet Jesus, she was practically waving semaphore flags at him. He could probably close this deal with two beers, maybe three. Tops. Except for one potential problem. Praying he was wrong, he asked, "Are you Tracy Shapiro?"

Dimples appeared. Damn, he loved dimples. "I am."

And just like that, all of his hopes and dreams crashed and burned around him. "I'm a friend of Jenk's," he told her. "I'm meeting him here. I'm a few minutes early."

She shook her head. "I'm sorry. A friend of . . . ?"

"Jenkins?" Izzy said, but she still looked at him blankly.

Alrighty then. This did not bode well for Mark's so-called impending romantic relationship with this woman. The way Eminem had described it, he and Tracy were practically engaged. Talk about wishful thinking.

Still, Jenk had invoked the girlfriend rule. It was not something that could be broken. At least not without bloodshed and loss of friendship.

"Mark?" Izzy tried.

"Oh, *Mark*," she said, laughing at herself. She had a terrific laugh, low and musical. "Right. Jenk. Jenkins. Duh. Ginny—his sister, she's Ginny Genaro now—we were best friends in high school."

"No kidding." If he were attempting to move this to the next level, Izzy would have perched on the edge of her desk. But screw it, just because he now knew there would be no next level didn't mean he couldn't be comfortable. He perched. "So, you've known Mark since he was a kid, huh?"

Her body language was an anthropology exercise. One moment she was sitting back in her chair, completely open. If she'd wanted to be any more inviting, she'd have been on her back, knees apart. But then she shifted, crossing her arms, closing. Another shift, and she was open again. Then closed. Then open. If Izzy was reading her right, she was a good girl who burned to be bad.

Why, oh why did God hate him so?

"We used to call him Weeble," Tracy told him. "You know, like, weebles wobble, but they don't fall down?"

Of course, maybe it was Jenk that God hated.

"Yeah," Izzy said. "I remember weebles, and . . . You know what, Tracy? That old nickname is probably something that Mark wouldn't appreciate your spreading around. I mean, it's perfect blackmail material, so if I were you, I'd save it for the exact right moment."

She laughed again, catching her lower lip between her teeth as she gazed up at him. "Do you want me to find Mark for you?" Damn, she was gorgeous.

Izzy made himself stand. Move back. "Nah, I'm okay to wait. I'll just let you get back to work." The phone had started ringing.

"Are you sure I can't . . . get you anything?" Chin in her hand, she watched him as he crossed the room, toward the leather sofas in the waiting area.

"I'm good," he said again.

"I bet you are," she said, but then actually looked embarrassed or even shy. She may have blushed.

Mother of God.

There was no woman on earth who could make him regret saving a teammate's life. But at this moment, this one came pretty damn close.

Sophia was going to kill Dave.

She would have done it already, but he'd so completely surprised her. She hadn't thought he was capable of losing his temper. She'd never imagined he'd say the things he'd said right up in Decker's face like that. Like he was ready to bring it out into the street.

It would have been funny, if it weren't so horribly unfunny.

As she sat down in Tom's office, Decker sat beside her, looking virtually identical to the last time Sophia had seen him. It was possible he was even wearing the exact same T-shirt. Gray with maroon ribbing at the very edges of the sleeves and around the neck.

He was not a big man—he was probably a perfect size medium. He was not particularly good-looking, either, with his average brown hair and unremarkably brown eyes. His face was pleasant enough, with a chin he kept always carefully shaved and comfortable crow's-feet around his eyes. Nothing wrong with the way he looked, that was for sure. He was just . . . Decker. Steady. Reliable. Quiet.

Until life got dangerous. And then there was nothing average or even remotely medium about him.

He sat silently now as their boss chose his words carefully.

"I'm sure you're aware I have no rules for my employees regarding personal relationships," Tom told them. "But this tension between the two of you is starting to get old."

Decker shifted slightly, clearing his throat to speak, but Tom cut him off.

"Everyone in this office is aware of the game you two have been playing—that you're never in the same location at the same time—at least not for long. Everyone is also aware of the toll that's taking on the both of you—and it *is* taking a toll. I've seen you expend an enormous amount of energy avoiding one another. As for how much of the company's money you've wasted"—Tom put up his hand to silence Deck's protests—"on unnecessary business trips, I don't know. It may not be much, but I *am* sure that it's not zero. Bottom line is this. I'm tired of it. Everyone else in this office—except maybe Tracy, who's new—is tired of it, too, and it's going to stop. Right now."

Tom continued, "You're going to iron out your differences, and you're going to work together on this assignment with Team Sixteen."

Sophia didn't dare look at Decker, but she could feel him glance at her.

"And if, after this assignment is over, you decide, for whatever reason, that you can't do that"—Tom's voice was not unkind, just absolute—"I will expect letters of resignation on my desk."

"There's no need to wait." Decker got to his feet. "I'll get that for you now, sir."

Sophia stood, too. He'd misunderstood. "No, Deck—"

He turned to her, and his intensity made her take a step back, bumping into her chair. She couldn't remember the last time he'd looked at her, *really* looked at her like that.

"I'm not going to let you be the one to leave," he told her.

"He said *letters*. Plural."

Decker turned to look at Tom, who was still sitting behind his desk.

"You both stay or you both go," their boss confirmed. "No one gets to play the martyr here. I won't facilitate that game." He let that sink in. "The choice is yours. I suggest you use this training op as a trial, to see if your differences really are irreconcilable."

"Sir," Decker started, but Tom didn't let him speak.

"You're dismissed."

Silently, Decker led the way to the door. He opened it, stood back to let Sophia exit first.

Always the gentleman.

Well, almost always.

"I'm so sorry," he told Sophia, as he closed Tom's door behind them.

She spoke before he could get to the *but*. *But I just can't work with you. But I can't handle seeing you every day.* "I really like this job," she said.

His mouth tightened, but she pressed on. "Why don't we try to make this work?" she asked him. "You know, I actually thought—back in Kazbekistan—that we'd managed to become friends."

Talking about this, even half in code the way they were doing, was hard for him. "And seeing me doesn't remind you of . . ."

"Of the fact that you saved my life?" she asked him. "Definitely. It also reminds me that you helped me get back on my feet again. You lent me money, you helped me get this job. Yes, I'm very much reminded of that when I see you."

"I've tried," he said, his voice low. "But I just can't forget that I took advantage of you."

"I happen to disagree," Sophia told him, her voice shaking slightly despite her best effort. "You didn't take advantage. But whether you did or not, isn't it time you stopped punishing me for it?"

He didn't have a comeback for that one, so she left him there, heading down the hall to her office, half-hoping he would follow.

Fully knowing that he wouldn't.

Jenk sat in silence as Izzy drove them over to Tom Paoletti's house.

That hadn't gone the way he'd hoped it would.

In his fantasy version, he'd walk into the Troubleshooters Incorporated reception area to find that Tracy was finally getting the hang of manipulating the voice mail system. She'd smile at him, holding up one perfectly manicured finger, asking him to wait just a sec as she flawlessly connected the caller who'd requested operator assistance. Then she'd smile at him again, thanking him for helping her find this wonderful job.

He'd remind her that he'd promised to take her to the furniture store with his truck, to pick up the dinette set she'd gotten on sale. He'd also promised he'd help bring it up to her second-floor apartment, help her put it together.

She'd suggest they go that evening, right after work. At which point he'd tell her he was babysitting for little Charlie Paoletti, and her eyes would widen the way Lindsey's had.

Izzy glanced at him now. "Dude, I hate to break it to you, but your girlfriend wants to jump me."

What?

Izzy nodded. "It's true."

"Why do people say *I hate to break it to you* when they're obviously gleeful about the news they're going to share?" Jenk asked.

"I'm not gleeful," Izzy said.

"Yeah, *dude*, you are."

"I'm actually depressed, because I really think I could have scored with her tonight."

God. "Yeah, I don't think so."

Instead of his fantasy with its meaningful eye contact and warm smiles, Tracy had been on the phone with Lyle. Her scum-sucking ex-boyfriend. Jenk had walked into the reception area to find every other phone line ringing as Tracy took a personal call—forgetting to switch on the voice mail system.

Lindsey was right behind him, and the two of them got the phones back under control. Of course, by then Tracy was focusing all of her energy on trying to hide the fact that talking to Lyle had made her cry.

The news that Jenk was babysitting for Tom tonight got absolutely zero reaction.

Nothing at all. Not even a blink in his direction.

"Tracy's got this ex who just won't leave her alone," Jenk told Izzy now. "He's trying to get them back together, and . . . She's pretty hung up on him. I have to figure out a way to—"

"Jenkins. Read my lips, okay? You're seriously deluded about this girl. And even if she was interested in you, I'd be advising you to hit-and-run. Did you check out her shoes? And her handbag? She's a shopper. Shag her, for sure, but then move on—before you're stuck paying her credit card bills for the rest of your life."

Shag her and move on. Jenk had done *shag her and move on*. His almost dying in Afghanistan had woken him up to a new reality. He didn't want *shag her and move on* anymore. He wanted the kind of closeness that Tom and his wife Kelly shared. He wanted the magic that the senior chief shared with his wife.

He wanted someone waiting for him when he came home at night.

Even crazy-assed Chief Karmody had found his soulmate. If *he* could do it, Jenk could, too.

And why shouldn't it be Tracy Shapiro?

When his sister Ginny had called, telling Jenk that Tracy was finally moving out of New York, that she wanted to come to San Diego to make a fresh start, it had seemed like a sign from God.

He'd helped her get this job—coaching her via e-mail to say all the right things during her interview with Tommy.

Sure, she was flawed. No one was perfect. But as far as vices went, shopping was a pretty minor one. Her relentless attraction to Lyle, a man who had hurt her—repeatedly—in the past, was more troubling, though, but not insurmountable.

She was funny, and sweet, and beautiful, and kind, and yes, she was even smart.

Even though Lindsey didn't think so.

And Jenk had been crazy about her, for forever.

So why not Tracy Shapiro?

Sure, okay, she still didn't know he existed. She still saw him as Ginny's annoying little brother. That was a perception he was going to have to change.

Was it going to be easy? No.

Was the fact that it wasn't going to be easy going to stop him? No.

He was a Navy SEAL. He'd done difficult things in the past.

He *would* get Tracy to notice him, to fall in love with him, and yes, even to marry him, if that's what he decided he wanted.

It might take a while, but there was one thing he'd learned about himself over the past few years—he was a patient man.

"That Lindsey's pretty hot," Izzy said, as they took the turn onto Tommy's street. "I think she liked me, too."

"Lindsey?" Jenk couldn't keep the disbelief from his voice.

"You don't think she's hot?" Izzy misunderstood. "Asian women, man . . . They're unbelievably beautiful. And smart."

Oh, God. "Lookit, do me a favor," Jenk said. "Just stay away from Lindsey, okay? She's—"

"Whoa," Izzy said. "Time out, Marky-Mark. You can't call dibs on everyone. One at a time, right? Fair's fair. So which is it, Tracy or Lindsey?"

Shit. "Tracy," Jenk said. "But seriously, Zanella, Lindsey's . . . different."

"Is she, you know, a friend of Ellen?" Izzy parked in front of the Paoletti's house. "That would be so cool. Do you think she's got a girlfriend, because I've always wanted to get with some lesbians." He laughed at the expression on Jenk's face. "Look at you. I'm kidding. That's the joke, right? Some asshole's all like, *Lesbians are so hot, do you think they'll do me?* Only he's too stupid to know that they're lesbians because they're not into men and . . . never mind."

"No, I get it," Jenk said. "But Jesus, Izzy, sometimes you frighten me."

"So what do you think? *Is* she a dyke?"

Jenk exhaled his exasperation as he got out of Izzy's truck. "I don't

know—it wasn't on the questionnaire I gave her about her sexual prefer-
ences. And frankly, I don't care. I like her, all right? As a friend. I don't
want you to mess with her."

"You can call dibs on her if you want, but then you've gotta toss Tracy
back. Otherwise, you've got no right. Unless, you know, you discover Lindsey's your long-lost sister. Then you can invoke the sister rule. But looking
at the two of you, I don't think that's gonna fly."

Jenk followed Izzy up the path to the front door. "I don't know what
I'm worried about. Lindsey's gonna break your balls."

"Perfect," Izzy said. "I'm into pain. Weeble."

Jenk stared at him. Had he just said . . .

"Tracy told me she used to call you that—right after she implied that
she wanted to do me."

It was probably all true. Tracy had dreadful taste in men. Izzy was almost as big of an asshole as Lyle, so why shouldn't she be attracted to him?

This was going to be more difficult than he'd imagined.

Izzy grinned. "I'm guessing you were rounder when you were a kid,
Wobble-Man."

"Fuck you."

"Fuck *you*," Izzy said cheerfully, as if it were some sort of blessing Jenk
had bestowed on him, and that he was bestowing on Jenk in return.

From inside of the house, they could hear a baby crying. Ferociously.
Izzy rang the doorbell. "Two Navy SEALs versus one angry seven-month-
old," he mused. "The odds could go either way."

LOCATION: UNCERTAIN
DATE: UNKNOWN

Number Twenty was a fighter.

The lights were up in the basement, which was also a treat. Although
Five knew from experience that he could turn them off at any moment.
Just to increase the challenge, to ramp up the level of fear.

He fed on the fear, and tonight he was getting a feast.

Twenty was sobbing as Five rushed her. She was terrified—as well she
should be.

But she'd had some kind of rudimentary self-defense training. She
knew not to let Five get close enough to her head to land a blow, close
enough to her throat to get a grip.

So Five kicked her in the back, and she slammed against the wall.

She made herself hate Twenty—for her relatively clean jeans, her untangled hair, the traces of makeup on her butt-ugly face—as she kicked her again.

Fear could make the prettiest girl on the planet look like a freak show.

She also hated Twenty for what her being here meant that Five would have to do.

But it was always easier with a fighter. Number Nineteen had done little more than curl up into a ball and cry.

He was on the stairs, watching, lapping up the fear, laughing as Five drove Twenty back into the corner. "Use it," he called. "Come on Twenty, use it now!"

Use what?

And then Twenty turned, a tumble of golden curls, a flash of something else as she lashed out at Five with her fist.

She blocked the blow easily with her arm, but there was a sharp burst of pain.

She retreated. She'd been cut—her arm was . . . bleeding?

Twenty still sobbed, light flashing again on the blade she held awkwardly in front of her, as if to defend herself.

That son of a bitch had given Twenty a knife.

Chapter
Three

Lindsey's post-workout pizza had just been delivered, in all its extra cheese glory, when her cell phone rang.

She glanced at it, ready to ignore it unless it was her father or work, and saw that the caller was none other than Mark Jenkins.

So she answered it. " 'Lo?"

"Lindsey. It's Izzy Zanella. You know, Jenk's alarmingly handsome friend?"

Jenk's alarmingly handsome friend. Lindsey had thought that the tall, dangerous-looking SEAL was a little too convinced he was all that, but now he was mocking himself. At least she hoped he was mocking himself.

"You got a sec?" he asked.

"Is this more important than a portobello mushroom pizza?"

"In my opinion, no," he said. "But Jenk asked me to call you, so I'm calling you. You know anything about kids?"

"If you're calling me with your babysitting woes, simply because I'm female—"

"Actually, Jenk thought to call you because you used to be a cop. He thought maybe you'd run into a sick kid a time or two."

Lindsey sat up. "Is Charlie sick?"

"Nah," Izzy said. "Well, *I* don't think so. Marky-Mark, however, is not convinced. But everyone we know who has kids is out. It must be American Annual Date Night or something. Seriously, no one's home. And most of the babysitters we've talked to sound like they're thirteen, so . . . We're now up to calling everyone who may have *seen* a kid at one point in their lives."

"What's the problem?" Lindsey asked.

"It's diaper-related," Izzy said.

"As in, you want me to come over there and change Charlie's diaper?"

"Oh, please," Izzy said in disgust. "Give us more credit than that. We're trained in recon. I once didn't leave my position for fifty hours. I'm talking *didn't move*. I crapped in my pants three times."

"Wow," Lindsey said. "That's more information about you than I ever wanted to know."

He laughed. "So, you're, uh, finding me irresistible, huh?"

"Um," Lindsey said.

He *did* have a nice laugh. "My point here being that a baby diaper doesn't scare me."

"So what's the problem?" she asked.

"Well, in two words . . ."

Lindsey just knew they were going to be two very good words.

"Green poop."

"Green poop," she repeated.

"Like, seriously green," Izzy reported. "Hey, you live just a few blocks away, don't you? Is there any chance—"

"Hold up. And you would know where I live because . . ." She let her voice trail off dangerously.

"Choice A, I'm a serial killer and I've already built a shrine to you in the glove compartment of my truck. Choice B, Tommy's got you on a list of emergency contacts on his fridge," Izzy told her.

"He does?" Wow, this was turning into some kind of great day. First, in their private meeting, Tom had referred to her as his "secret weapon," and now, to find out that her contact info was on his refrigerator . . .

"Yeah." Izzy wasn't as impressed by the fact. "So can you come over and do a visual? And as long as you're coming, you know, bring your pizza?"

"I don't think so." Lindsey could hear Jenk shouting something in the background. There was a dog barking back there, too. Since when had Tom and Kelly gotten a dog? "Does Charlie seem sick? Is he crying or—"

"Crying's like his specialitee. Hang on," Izzy said, and she heard the murmur of another voice. "Oh, really?" He spoke into the phone again. "Jenk says you're prolly too busy watching *American Idol* to come help us out with our green poop situation, which is pathetic. You really like Ryan Seacrest better than me and Jenk?"

Lindsey wondered what he'd say if she told him the truth. *No, actually, I'm already well on my way to developing a full-blown crush on Mark*

Jenkins, so I thought I'd limit my face time with him to work hours only. In a futile attempt to keep a train wreck from happening.

Instead, she said, "*American Idol* doesn't start until February. But if it were on tonight? I can guarantee that Ryan wouldn't want to eat my pizza."

"Ryan's also not a Navy SEAL," Izzy pointed out, after transmitting her words to Jenkins. "He won't come and save your life if you ever need saving."

"Hmmm," Lindsey said, pretending to think about it. "Nope. Won't ever need saving—completely capable of doing that myself. I'd still stick with Ryan. If you want my opinion, for whatever it's worth, I think the green poop means that Charlie ate something green for lunch. But if you have any doubts, you should call Tom and Kelly. You know, Kelly's a pediatrician."

"Yeah, but Jenk doesn't want to bother them. Oops, I'm getting a beep. Someone's calling me back. Ooh, it's Tracy Shapiro. She's definitely not a lesbian."

"A what?" Lindsey said, totally confused.

"I bet I can talk *her* into coming over," Izzy said. "She digs me. Later, babe."

"Izzy, wait," Lindsey said. Didn't he know that Jenk had a serious thing for Tracy? God, wouldn't *that* be a mess. But he'd already cut the connection.

She returned to her pizza, only now it didn't taste very good.

Lindsey went to her spice cabinet, rummaging for her red pepper, disgusted with herself for worrying about the guy that she maybe could have liked, had the timing and situation been different. Yeah, worrying that Tracy was going to break Jenk's heart was healthy—in an alternate universe.

She shook the pepper onto her slice of pizza, and when she took a bite, her mouth practically exploded. Much better.

And yet, she kept eyeing her phone. Like she should maybe call Izzy back, make sure he didn't inadvertently hurt his friend.

Maybe she should just go ahead and skewer herself now.

California was working.

Lyle, the rat-bastard, was coming to San Diego next weekend.

He was flying into LA for business, but then he was going to hire a car and make the short drive down the coast to see her.

Tracy parked on the street in front of a trim little house, its yard all but bursting with neatly kept flowering plants. She double-checked the address she'd written on the back of an envelope—this was definitely it. Her boss's house.

Little was the key word despite the gorgeous gardens and pretty solar lamps lighting the front path. She'd been expecting something . . . more.

A whole lot more. In quantity and quality.

Something a little less relentlessly middle-class.

Tom Paoletti was the owner and CEO of Troubleshooters Incorporated. He had to be making money hand over fist. And his wife was not just a doctor, but a doctor with a trust fund. And yet, they lived here.

Go figure. Of course, it *was* a nice little neighborhood, reminiscent of the kid-friendly cul-de-sac where she'd grown up. And not everyone was like social-climbing, law-firm-partner-wannabe Lyle.

Tracy pulled down the sun visor, checking her makeup in the mirror.

People were strange and stupid. Of course, she'd have to include herself in that generalization.

She grabbed the bottle of chardonnay that she'd picked up on her way over, got out of the car, headed down the path to the house, her heels tapping on the pink bricks.

She'd come to California to get Lyle's attention. But really, what did it say about their relationship—the fact that in order to communicate effectively, she had to move out of their condo? And not just to Brooklyn. No, she'd had to travel thousands of miles to make her point.

Straighten up and fly right.

And oh, by the way, that left hand of Tracy's that was without a ring? A return trip to NYC would require both a diamond and a wedding band.

Mark Jenkins opened the door before she even rang the bell. "Hey, Trace. Thanks for coming." He pushed open the screen, giving her a dazzling smile.

He had a terrific smile. She'd always thought Mark was cute in a little brother kind of way, but it wasn't his smile that immobilized her now, making her stand and gawk at him, feet glued to the bricks like an idiot.

He wasn't wearing a shirt. Dressed in only blue-patterned jams and sandals, with that golden tan and all those muscles—holy moly, little Weeble was *all* muscle—he looked like one of the surfers she'd seen out on the beach.

No, actually, he looked like their king.

Sure, he was on the shorter side of short, but that six-pack more than made up for it. And the way those jams hung low on his trim hips. . . .

"Sorry, about the . . ." He motioned to his bare chest as if it might be a problem for her. "Apparently babies hurl as part of their regular routine. My T-shirt's in the wash."

Her heels made her taller than him, but he smiled up at her quite sunnily, as if he didn't care. Why should he, with that body? He closed the door behind her and led the way into the house.

Tracy realized that she hadn't seen him out of uniform since she'd arrived in California, since he'd gotten back from overseas. He'd helped her find her apartment and her job via e-mail, from a hospital in Germany.

His shorts went down all the way below his knees, but they fit him extremely well. Unbelievably well. Dear God, she was standing here, ogling Weeble's fantastically tight little butt.

And she'd thought his friend, what's-his-name, Izzy, was the hottie.

Mark turned back to look at her, amusement in his pretty green eyes. Ginny had always hated the fact that, out of the two of them, he'd gotten the long eyelashes. "You coming?"

"Yeah. Sorry." Tracy kicked off her shoes, leaving them by the door, and, still carrying the wine, followed him into her boss's remarkably average-looking little house.

Tracy Shapiro knew dick about babies.

Izzy had just gotten Charlie quieted down, when she came in and woke him up. The sound of a female voice laughing loudly caught the Chazster's attention.

It probably wasn't intentional. Still, it wouldn't have taken a whole lot of figuring for Tracy, arriving on the scene of a babysitting emergency—so to speak—to notice that said baby was finally quiet and to keep her voice low.

The good news was that she was on Izzy and Lindsey's side in the green poop debate. It was now three to one that it was nothing to worry about, and Jenk finally seemed down with that.

Anyone want some wine? She'd brought a bottle with her, of course.

Izzy slipped out onto the back patio while Charlie was still in the snuffling, maybe-going-to-cry phase, hoping the cool night air would distract the kid.

Also, he'd noticed that Charlie stopped crying when Izzy sang to him. Of course the kid wasn't interested in Bruce Springsteen or Dire Straits or anything else that could be sung aloud in public. No, it had to be either Elton John or The Carpenters. Or Celine Dion, but damn. Izzy had to draw the line somewhere.

"Don't you remember you told me you love me, baby," Izzy sang, as he watched Tracy do her weird hot/cold thing to Marky-Mark. The big glass sliders gave him a clear view of both the kitchen and the living room.

He couldn't hear what they were saying, but their body language told the whole story as Charlie clutched Izzy's little finger with his teeny little fist, enthralled by his rendition of the song.

In the living room, Tracy's hands fluttered, fixing her already perfect hair after she sat on one end of the sofa. "Your naked, manly chest has sent my estrogen levels soaring."

Jenk came out of the kitchen, carrying a glass of wine and a plate of cheese and crackers. "Here, let me provide for you, for I am a strong alpha male despite being height-challenged."

"Jesus, Chaz," Izzy sang to the same melody, which was okay with Charlie. Getting the lyrics right wasn't that big a deal for the under-two set. "Can you believe this crap?"

Inside the house, Tracy smiled up at Jenk. Accepted the glass and a microscopic piece of something from the plate. Took a nibble, turning so that her body was open to him as he crossed to the other end of the couch. "Ooh, this nourishment you have brought to me is delicious," Izzy imagined her saying. "You are indeed a most worthy candidate for a mate. I will sit like this, so you can more easily imagine me naked."

Jenk sat, too, but not on the sofa. Instead he perched on the arm. It both gave him height and added definition to his abs. He braced himself with one arm against the back cushion, sly devil, which put even more muscles into play. "I see that you have noticed that I am too sexy for my shirt." He laughed, but it was one of those awkward, mixed-company laughs—definitely not a funny-joke laugh.

Tracy laughed, too, and adjusted her sweater, pulling it down by the bottom. "I see that you, too, have noticed my generous, womanly bosom. You must earn the right to look directly at it, although I will never let you forget that it is there."

On and on and *on* it went, with Izzy hanging out on the deck long after Charlie's eyes had rolled back in his head.

He could totally relate to the little dude.

Jenk was working it like a pro, loading on the charm, letting Tracy talk, nodding to show he was listening, always giving her plenty of sincere eye contact. It was only occasionally that he let his massive confusion show on his face, but he always covered it by smiling or even laughing. "You are as odd as all of the others of your fair sex, but I will pretend that I understand whatever the fuck you say to me in my single-minded quest to nail you to the wall."

Tracy stood up, pointing toward the kitchen. "I will walk over here, mate-candidate, so you can check out my ass. Because that is what I want you to do, even though if I caught you doing it, I would pretend to be most upset."

She put her glass down on the kitchen counter and vanished down the hall.

On the arm of the sofa, Jenk took the opportunity to adjust his balls. Good man. It may have been hard work, but he had the right to be comfortable while doing it. Give 'em a scratch, too. There you go.

He then rotated his bum shoulder. It was clearly bothering him, especially in the cool air with no shirt on. He flexed his neck muscles, too, as if he were running a marathon or preparing for round two of a boxing match.

It was crazy. What did Jenk think? That the hard work he was doing here tonight would ever end? The little dude wanted Tracy to be his girl-friend, or—even worse—his wife. But a woman like Tracy wouldn't be content to do the laundry, cook dinner every now and then, perform gymnastic sex acts on command, and then cheerfully wave good-bye when duty called. "Have fun with your SEAL pals, honey! See you in a few weeks! I'll be fine here on my own, doing jigsaw puzzles and watching Jane Austen movies until you come home."

No, with Tracy, there would be tears. Demands. Endless hours of confusing conversations on the couch. The gymnastics would be all Jenk's—as he leaped through hoops in a futile attempt to placate her.

Still, Izzy couldn't help feeling jealous. Apparently, when Tracy had done her weird half-flirting thing with *him* back at the TS Inc office, it hadn't meant dick. Although he guessed it was possible she flirted like that with every and anyone—like it was her default mode.

From the other end of the deck, another door slid open. It was the door to the guest room and . . . "Oz!" Izzy shouted. "No! Sit! Stay! *Shit!*"

The dog streaked past him, ignoring him completely, going hell for leather across Tommy's perfect lawn. He disappeared into the darkness of the privacy shrubs on the property line.

Charlie woke up, because of course Izzy'd shouted into his ear. He started to cry as Tracy stepped uncertainly out onto the porch. "He was at the door," she said, pointing out to where the dog had last been, "as if he needed to go out."

Jenk must've heard the commotion, because he came to the other slider.

"Tracy let the dog out," Izzy informed him. "Arf. Arf, arf, arf."

"*What?*" Jenk came outside. "Oz!" he called into the night, snapping his fingers and whistling. "Here, boy!"

"Yeah, you know, the way he was going, I think he's in Laguna Beach by now." Izzy sang as softly as he could into Charlie's ear, jiggling him slightly. "Get back, honky cat. This living in the city just ain't where it's at . . ."

"I'm so sorry," Tracy said, her Little Mermaid eyes opened wide. "I thought the yard was fenced."

"It's not," Izzy and Jenk said in unison.

"Oz—the dog—is a wedding present for Tommy's niece Mallory," Jenk said.

And that was an understatement. Oz was *the* wedding present—from the groom to the bride. Mal had been doing a photography job at an animal shelter and had fallen in love with the little dog, whose owner had just died. The apartment she and her intended, David Sullivan, were living in didn't accept pets. But Sully managed to make some kind of deal with the landlord and, voilà.

"It was a surprise," Jenk continued. "Tommy was hiding Oz here, as a favor to Sully, the groom.

"I think we better call him, tell him to hit the mall. Slippers make a lovely gift," Izzy suggested. "Get back, honky cat—whoo!"

Charlie actually laughed—the only one of them enjoying himself.

"Oh, my God," Tracy said, lowering herself down onto one of the deck chairs, her head in her hands. "I am *so* fired."

The evening had gone completely into the crapper.

Jenk had been on the phone for the past twenty minutes, rounding up a search party, calling in all the favors from his teammates in Team Sixteen that he'd ever been owed.

He hated wasting all those favors on a lost dog.

Yeah, the night had definitely tanked.

And that was *after* having to listen to Tracy go on and on and *on* about her ex-boyfriend, Lyle, the superlawyer. It was obvious that she was still completely hung up on him, although, okay. Small victories. The no-shirt trick had worked like a charm.

Tracy no longer saw him as Ginny Jenkins's Cheez-Doodle-eating, chubby little brother. That mission was accomplished.

But the campaign was far from over and looking to be a lengthy one.

And not particularly pleasant, because it was clear Jenk hadn't heard the last of Lyle, who apparently billed upwards of—holy shit—six hundred dollars an hour. The son of a bitch was coming to visit next week. That oughta be tons of fun, before, during, and after.

But right now, his goal was to find a schnauzer in a haystack.

Lindsey had come right over, God bless her. She, in turn, had made some phone calls, too. As a result, a large portion of the crew from TS Inc were either here or on their way to help. Right now, Sophia Ghaffari, Tess Bailey, and Jim Nash had teamed up with Petty Officers Danny Gillman and Jay Lopez. They were working their way north, armed with a leash and chunks of microwave-defrosted hamburger that Lindsey had grabbed from her own freezer after getting Jenk's call.

The woman was not only efficient, she was also a quick thinker and good at taking charge of a chaotic situation.

Chief WildCard Karmody was helping out from his own house. He'd called up a map of the area on his computer, and Lindsey had quickly put him in touch with all of the searchers via cell phone, so he could direct them and coordinate their movements.

Two other chiefs from Team Sixteen—Stan and Cosmo—had brought their wives along to help. They were both using their own cars, looking to spot the missing dog as they drove slowly through the neighborhood—also Lindsey's idea.

Izzy was keeping Charlie occupied by singing to him in a surprisingly pleasant voice.

Tracy—God help them all—was in Tommy's kitchen, making coffee.

Jenk's phone rang. It was Lindsey. "Sam and Alyssa called me back. They're on their way over." She was talking really quietly. It was hard to hear her, and he put his finger in his other ear. "I told them to call Chief Karmody—to work out of their car, trying to spot Oz, is that okay with you?"

Not only did she take charge, but she made sure everything she did had his approval.

"Yeah," he said. "Thank you."

"S'all right," she said. "Happy to help."

"Which group are you out with?" he asked.

"I'm solo," she said. "I'm just a few houses away. I'm trying to think like a frightened schnauzer. Remind me again what a schnauzer looks like?"

"Small," he told her. "This one's about fifteen pounds. Kind of like a terrier, but with softer hair. Salt and pepper—black hair with white eyebrows that make him look like he's perpetually surprised. He's pretty cute. Floppy ears, stubby tail."

"Does he bite?" she asked.

Good question. "I don't think so, but be careful. Any animal that's cornered could bite."

"Speaking of cornered animals," Lindsey said. "Both Dave Malkoff and Larry Decker are on their way over. You might want to organize that so they go in two different directions."

"Yeah," Jenk said. "Wow. Thanks for the heads-up. That could be . . ." He had to laugh. "Exactly what this evening doesn't need."

"Or you could just leave Tracy and Izzy to handle it," Lindsey suggested. "And you could come help me, because I think . . . I'm face-to-face . . . with . . . Hello, baby. Hello, aren't you a cutie? Look at your big brown eyes. . . . a very nervous schnauzer named Oz."

Well, this was just perfect.

Dave got out of his car just as Decker got out of his truck.

And of course, he came right over to Dave. Apparently Sophia was the only person Deck hid from.

"I came to your office, but you'd already left for the day," Decker said, no greeting, just boom, right into it. Just like the man Dave had always admired would have done.

Dave nodded. "Yeah, I was, um, avoiding the possibility of violence." Even after he'd vented, he'd retained an overwhelming urge to slam his fist into Decker's face.

Which probably would've ended with Dave in the hospital, with a broken hand. So he'd gone home early.

"I know you don't think so, but everything I've done has been to make things easier for Sophia," Decker started to explain, but Dave wouldn't have it.

"Bullshit! You've been making it easier for yourself." Dave was thoroughly disgusted. And that potential cast on his hand still hovered out there in the extremely likely future. Never before had he wanted to hit someone so badly. "You know, I used to like you. No, not just like. Respect. Admire. Adore even. Yes, I adored you. That was before I realized what a selfish prick you really were. Or maybe you weren't at the time. Maybe you've just turned into one."

Decker was silent, denying nothing, and Dave couldn't stop himself.

"Come on, Deck," he said. "Run your pattern. What is it you usually say? *Dave, you have no idea what Sophia went through.* Except, guess what? I do. I have an idea. Why? Because I've spent the past year and a half talking to her. Ready to listen if and when she was ever ready to talk. Which she was and she did. A little. Not much. She probably would have said more about what she went through if I'd've been you. For some reason she trusts you. Cares about you. Yeah, funny, isn't it? She still thinks of you as a friend. Maybe even as her hero."

Decker turned.

"Perfect," Dave got louder. "Walk away. What is it you tell yourself, huh? That the best way to be Sophia's friend is to stay away from her? Stop lying." His voice shook. "You're better than that. And she needs you to be her friend. Still. Even after all this time, she needs you."

"To be her friend," Decker repeated. He'd stopped walking, but now he turned back to look at Dave. In the dim streetlight, his eyes were shadowed but not impossible to read. He was unsure of himself, even though his stance was pure alpha certainty.

And Dave knew exactly what he was thinking. "Her friend," he repeated, too. His stomach hurt, but he said the words. "Or even . . . more."

And there it was. Sitting between them. The truth about Sophia.

"She'd want that?" Decker asked quietly.

It was hard to believe he hadn't known—that this wasn't what he'd been hiding from all these months.

But Dave answered him anyway, because apparently some things needed to be said aloud. "Eventually," he told Deck. "I believe so. Yes."

"I don't . . ." Decker started. "I've made a point never to fraternize with people I work with."

Fraternize? "So don't work with her," Dave told him. "Talk to Tom. After this training op, make it clear that you want separate assignments. It won't be hard to do."

Decker just stood there, looking at him. "These past few months," he finally said, "when I've requested you be on my team . . . Your unavailability wasn't an accident, was it?"

Dave gave him the truth about that, too, as he started toward the house. "No, sir."

Deck nodded again, following him. "I wish you'd been up front with me about that."

"I wish," Dave said, as he rang the doorbell, "that I still gave a damn what you wish."

Izzy assigned Dave and Decker to two different search parties on two different ends of the neighborhood, got a finally-sleeping Charlie settled in his crib, then went in search of Tracy.

He found her in the kitchen, no longer trying to pretend that she wasn't crying.

"Hey," he said.

"Go away," she told him. "Just leave me alone in my misery."

It was high drama. He half expected her to turn triumphantly toward him, her arm in the air, proclaiming, "Acting!"

He'd say, "Genius!" She'd say, "Thank you!"

Although she was probably too young to remember Jon Lovitz on *Saturday Night Live*. Unless she'd caught it on reruns. But no, she was *Sex and the City* all the way. No doubt she'd studied that program to know how to dress, how to think, what to do, how to feel.

Right now, for example, it was the proper time for stormy tears. God damn, but he was tired of crying babies.

"It's a little bit funny," he sang. "This feeling inside . . ."

She turned to stare at him. "What?"

What do you know? It worked with Tracy, too.

"Why are you singing that song from *Moulin Rouge?*" she asked.

"It's not from *Moulin Rouge*," he educated her. "It was *in Moulin Rouge*, but it's an Elton John song." If she didn't know who Elton John was, he'd put her out of her pain. He'd just snap her neck right here and now.

She wiped her nose on the back of her hand. "I know it's an Elton John song," she sounded vaguely insulted. "Why are you singing it to me?"

"Because I'm tragically in love with you," he said, then realized that she actually believed him. "I'm kidding," he quickly backpedaled, but he could tell from the look in her eyes that it was too late.

So he tried to prove he was only kidding by slamming her with reality. "You know, the chances of finding Oz before Tommy gets home are slim to none. The chances of finding him at all are . . ." He shrugged. "Highly unlikely."

It was a shame he'd had to do that, because she'd stopped crying. Of course now her eyes filled up again.

"I know," she said bravely. "I'm so stupid. This is all my fault."

She was looking at him as if she wanted to be comforted. No doubt about it, she wanted strong arms around her, with a little, *Aw, honey, no it's not. It was a mistake anyone could've made. Cheer up, we'll find the dog . . .*

"Damn straight it's all your fault," Izzy told her instead, opening the fridge and helping himself to a can of soda. "You totally blew it. Didn't it occur to you to ask before you opened that door? That *was* stupid. What were you thinking?"

To her credit, she didn't immediately dissolve into tears. She defended herself. "I heard the dog whining and tapping on the sliding glass door when I went past on my way to the bathroom. On the way back, I didn't hear anything, so I opened the door and peeked in, and he was in that squat that dogs do? And all I could think was, outside—do it outside! I was trying to help." The tears finally came. "I always screw everything up."

Again, she wanted him to tell her she was wrong.

Again, he didn't give it to her. But wow, it wasn't easy. She so wanted to cry on his shoulder, even though she'd been doing that mating ritual fox-trot with Jenk just a short time ago.

Crying on his shoulder would involve her pressing her entire amazing body against his, which would've been a nice reward for having to sing *Rainy Days and Mondays* to Master Chaz. Seven times in a row.

Walking around, some kind of lonely clown . . .

He'd been right about Tracy, though. She flirted with anyone with a dick. Poor Weeble. All that hard work he'd done tonight was for naught.

"I suck at my job, in case you didn't notice," Tracy told Izzy, starting to get angry with him for just standing there like an idiot, watching her cry.

He took his time answering, taking a long drink of his soda. "I *have* heard rumors that it's not going well," he finally said, which, again, was way not what she wanted to hear. "But I thought you did okay this afternoon. Calling Tommy to tell him that the circus had come to town? That was good. I mean, basic common sense, sure, but still the right choice."

"Great," she said. "I did one *basic* thing right. In four days. And now there are rumors . . . ? Everyone hates me, don't they?"

Ach, Christ. "Come on, Shapiro, that's overkill, even for you. Jenk doesn't hate you," Izzy pointed out. "He's out there, right now, scrambling to save your ass. You know, that's what you should be doing instead of having this pity party. You should be figuring out the best way to pay him back."

Oh, yeah. Now she was frosty. Her tears instantly freeze-dried. "Are you telling me that Mark is doing all this because he wants to be *paid back*?"

The way she said it was pretty funny, like she was some kind of virgin high priestess being told she should sacrifice herself on the altar as a tip for the pizza deliveryman.

Izzy made *no way* noises. "Marky-Mark? He's too nice. And he's had a thing for you for ages. He wouldn't expect it. He wouldn't even think it. But he's bent over backwards for you—getting you this job, and now cleaning up after your mistakes? So I'm just saying. You might want to return the favor."

Now there was uncertainty in her eyes. "Mark has a thing for me?"

"Hello," Izzy said. "Didn't you just spend the past hour flirting with him. Are you blind? He's extremely into you."

"Well, yeah," she said. "I could tell, but . . ." She shook her head, a furrow between her brows. There were definitely some deep thoughts going on inside that head. Her mouth quirked into a rueful smile. "Who knew he'd grow up to look like . . . that."

"He's pretty hot, our Marky," Izzy agreed. "Although he's a little short for me. I like my men taller."

She looked at him.

"Kidding," Izzy said. "Don't you ever read body language? I've been sending out an *I would sell my sainted grandmother's soul to the devil just to do you once* message ever since I first laid eyes on you."

"Really?" she whispered.

And okay. All that eye contact was making the kitchen just a little too warm. She should have been offended. And yet . . .

She definitely wasn't.

She was thinking again. Looking at him, and thinking.

Izzy backed out of the room. "I better go check on Charlie."

The dog bolted.

It must've heard Jenk coming, and it just took off.

"Don't," Lindsey said, but Jenk was already in motion, diving for the dog, about to scare the poor thing out of his wits—and maybe get bitten for his trouble.

So she did the only thing she could.

She blocked him.

Which meant that instead of grabbing Oz, Jenk hit her like a wrecking ball. She was strong but a lightweight, and she would've gone flying into a chain-link fence if he hadn't grabbed on to her and brought her to the ground with him.

It was the old "six of one, half dozen of another" adage in play, because although Lindsey didn't wind up with permanent chain-link marks on her forehead, she did find herself between the very hard ground and a very solid man.

"Jesus, I'm sorry," Jenk said, trying to untangle himself from her and race off after Oz. "What are you doing? I coulda had him."

Lindsey clutched at him and, ew. His T-shirt was cold and wet. Still, she hung on. "Let him go," she wheezed, sounding like a dying mob boss.

The wind had been completely knocked out of her, and she struggled to breathe. "Get help," she managed to gasp.

Her death rattle imitation was evidently even scarier for Jenk than it was for her, because he immediately got onto his phone. He tucked it between his ear and his shoulder. "Lopez! Where are you? I need a medic! Now!"

He was fumbling with her buttons, and he dropped his phone, to give her shirt his full attention. He was trying to loosen it, which was ridiculous, because it was already comfortably loose. But then Lindsey realized he was checking to see if he'd hit her windpipe, or damaged some other vital part of her breathing apparatus.

And as long as she couldn't speak to correct him, it was fun to pretend that he was unbuttoning her shirt with such urgency for another reason entirely. She might've let him keep going if he weren't so upset.

It took all the energy she should have been using to get air back into her lungs, but she managed a weak, "I'm okay."

Jenk didn't believe her. Or maybe he did, but he was just one of those people who had to see things for themselves. He touched her—her throat, her neck, her collarbone—as if he'd had some medical training. Which he surely had, being a SEAL. His hands were warm as he ran them across her, as if he would be able to tell just from touching that she was uninjured. And yet he hesitated, just slightly—which made it very different from a doctor or paramedic's ultraconfident, impersonal touch.

It felt far more like that of a first-time lover.

Which was not at all helpful in the getting-her-breath-back department. Especially when he touched her neck and throat for the second time.

"God," he breathed, more of an exhale than an actual word. For a half a second, time froze.

And Lindsey knew that she was doomed. If he kissed her, she was going to kiss him back. Try as she might, she would not be able to resist that temptation.

But reality crashed through.

"You have, like, the skinniest neck," he told her, wonder in his voice. "How does it hold your head up?"

And people claimed that the days of romance were gone.

Jenk's hands moved up to surround her head, checking to see if she'd hit it when she'd fallen—or so she thought until he laughed. "Your head's tiny, too. That's how it works."

Lindsey tried to push his hands away. "I happen to be perfectly proportioned for a woman of my height, thank you," she wheezed.

"Are you really okay?" he asked, catching her hands in his, peering down at her. Relief was a funny emotion. Even in the dimness of the night, Lindsey could read Jenk's clearly in his eyes.

"Yeah." Although she was still unable to do more than whisper. "I just lost my air. The help we need is to corner Oz. The way he went, he's trapped. It's fenced in back there." She shifted against him. "Do you mind . . . ?"

And then there was something else in his eyes entirely, as he realized that he was on top of her. Lindsey could see that he really hadn't been aware of it before, but he was straddling her, his thighs warm against hers, his hands still holding hers.

For several long seconds he sat there, just looking down at her in the moonlight, as if maybe her having a pencil-neck wasn't such a bad thing.

His phone rang, breaking the spell, thank God. He climbed off of her, answering it even as he helped her to sit up.

"Yeah, Card, sorry—belay that last order," he said into the phone, obviously talking to WildCard Karmody, their makeshift dispatcher. "We don't need a medic. Lindsey's fine. Will you let everyone know where we are? We're . . . Okay, good, that's exactly where we are. The dog's cornered, we'll need to create a net. Tell 'em to move in quietly, though. He's pretty spooked."

He hung up, then reached to pull the two open sides of her shirt together. "Sorry," he said. "I, uh . . ."

She'd been sitting there—lying there, too—with her Hawaiian shirt completely unbuttoned, revealing . . .

Oh, goody. She was wearing *that* bra. The transparent one. She had bras that covered more of her than her bathing suit did, but was she wearing one of those today? Of course not.

It really shouldn't have been that big a deal. She had, after all, already told him her bra size.

And so what if he'd seen her nipples? She could see his in the moonlight, too, clearly outlined beneath his snug-fitting, disgustingly cold and soggy T-shirt.

Of course his "skinny neck, tiny head" comment was still ringing in her ears. Thankfully, he kept any similar critiques of her breasts to himself.

He did clear his throat about three times. "I'm confused about your strategy," he finally said. "I could've had him."

"I didn't want him to bite you." Lindsey could hear the others coming and tried to button her shirt more quickly. It was hard to see in the darkness.

"There are worse things," Jenk told her.

"Such as Tom getting home to find the dog missing?"

She heard more than saw him smile. "That's definitely on the list."

"I scouted out this area," she said. Shit, her buttons were askew, the whole front of her shirt off-kilter. "I knew there were two fences creating a corner. If he headed the way he headed, I knew he'd be trapped."

He saw what was happening and helped, reaching out and matching up the first button with the correct buttonhole.

"There are also plenty of dense shrubs, perfect for hiding." She pretended that having their fingers bump as he kept going and she tried to take over didn't affect her. "I got it, thanks," she said, and he turned his attention to removing the pieces of grass and leaves in her hair.

Okay, so that felt a little too good, too.

Lindsey cleared her throat. "My plan is to go in there, with more hamburger—he already ate everything I had with me," she continued. "You have more, don't you?"

He reached into his pocket. "Oh, crap."

She knew before he told her, and tried not to laugh. "Green crap or regular?"

"Very funny. The baggie broke, and I now have raw hamburger in my pocket, and . . . Oh, *crap.*"

Lindsey gave up trying not to laugh. Instead, she tried to laugh quietly, so as not to frighten poor Oz.

"These pockets are mesh and it's, like, all down my leg. Oh, man." He lay back in the grass. "Congratulations to me. I have uncooked picnic food where the sun doesn't shine. My evening is now truly complete."

"Not quite," Lindsey said. "We've still got a dog to catch, and you're the bait. I think you've got a few more new experiences still in store."

He rolled his head to look at her. "One new experience I'd particularly like to avoid has to do with getting too close to Oz."

"Oh, come on, Jenkins," she said, holding out her hands to help him to his feet. "Where's your sense of adventure? You haven't lived until you've risked getting your balls licked by a hungry lapdog."

Jenk cracked up.

"I'd like to point out that said risk, although present, will be extremely low," she continued. "Because I'll be with you. I'll protect you."

He took her hands and let her haul him up.

But as he followed her into the deeper darkness of the yard, she couldn't keep herself from adding, "Yes, indeed. Me and my pencil-neck and pin-head will keep you safe from the tiny little doggy."

"Hey." He stopped her with a hand on her arm. "Hang on. I didn't say that. And I certainly didn't mean it like . . ." He took his hand away as if touching her felt too intimate as they stood there in the light from the moon. "It's, well, I don't often get a chance to feel, you know . . . Large. And please don't make a dick joke, because that's not what I mean, and you know it."

"I wasn't going to make a dick joke," Lindsey said, "and actually, I prefer to call them johnson jokes. It's more dignified. Classier."

He smiled, shaking his head. "Aren't you ever serious?"

She nodded. "Yeah. When I have to be."

"Can you be serious for a sec, right now?"

She knew it wasn't a good idea. Serious meant being honest, and honestly, she wasn't up for that. Not with this guy, in the moonlight. But he was looking at her so imploringly, she caved. "All right."

"I used the wrong word," Jenk told her, and as she looked into his eyes, she realized that she'd been wrong about him. Intensity, determination, assertiveness, fortitude. He had it all, along with an inability to understand the word *quit*. "I shouldn't have said *skinny*. I should have said *willowy*, or I don't know . . . *graceful*. *Delicate* maybe. Bottom line, I happen to think you're extremely beautiful. And, yes, very nicely proportioned."

Oh, God. Lindsey had to look away, afraid that he'd see her crush on him blooming into a redwood-sized monster, right there in her eyes.

And okay, that was all the seriousness she could take, without fainting. "Thanks," she said. "I think you're full of it, but thanks. Good effort. Good attempt at a save."

"I'm serious," he insisted, God help her. "If I were single, I'd be all over you."

Oh, great. He'd figured out that she was enormously attracted to him. It probably had something to do with the way she drooled whenever he touched her.

"You *are* single," she pointed out, determined to keep this light. "And you *were* all over me. Although I'm pretty sure it was better for you than it was for me."

"You know that's not what I meant," he said. "And as for being single . . . I think, after tonight anyway, I'm kind of seeing Tracy."

"Really?" Lindsey couldn't disguise her disbelief.

Jenk's smile twisted. "Yeah, well, maybe that's too optimistic a statement. She's still pretty entangled with her former boyfriend. She talks about him endlessly. But I managed to, you know, catch her attention at least. It's a step in the right direction. Anyway, I didn't want to give you the wrong idea."

Boom, it was over. Lindsey now officially had it bad for him. She was a sucker when it came to men who were honorable.

Make that: unattainable men who were honorable.

She mustered up a smile. Tracy, apparently, was smarter than Lindsey had thought if she'd allowed her attention to be caught. "Impressive. Especially considering this was way before the hamburger in the pants thing, which always works for me, when I'm trying to catch someone's attention."

He laughed.

"So, how'd you do it?" Lindsey asked. "Recite Shakespeare, cook a twelve-course meal, or—"

"I took off my shirt," Jenk told her.

She snickered. "No, really." Oops. He wasn't kidding. "Wow," she said. "Okay. Sure. That could do it." Provided the attention get-ee was incredibly shallow and utterly unworthy. "For the record, you didn't have to take off your shirt to get *my* attention."

There was uncertainty in his eyes now, as if he wasn't sure if that was a joke, a half a joke, or no joke at all.

"But I'm glad it worked," Lindsey continued, "because I know how much you like her."

"Thanks," he said, but he still looked wary.

Probably because his super-SEAL senses were tingling.

"Don't move," Lindsey told him as quietly as she could. "Hungry dog at eight o'clock . . ."

CHAPTER
FOUR

LOCATION: UNCERTAIN
DATE: UNKNOWN

He'd given Number Twenty a knife.

The really sick thing was that beneath the pain-laced fear that Number Five was feeling, with the blood from her arm running through her fingers as she tried to apply pressure to the wound, she was jealous.

Did he like Twenty, with her pretty blond hair, more than he liked Five? Was he tired of Five? Was he bored with her? Did he really want Twenty to win?

Or was he merely tired of Five's methods? Did he want to see blood? Did he need more drama, or higher stakes?

Twenty awkwardly swiped at her, and Five had to jump back.

Twenty did it again. The same move, leaving herself open in the same way. This time Five was ready, and she hit Twenty, square in the temple.

The blonde lost her balance, slamming into the basement wall, dropping the knife. It skittered across the floor.

Number Five didn't need a knife. She hit Twenty again. In the head. Again. And again.

Twenty dropped to her hands and knees, and Five kicked her, right on the chin. She rag-dolled, hitting the floor with a thud, the whites of her eyes showing.

Five turned to the stairs, but where he was standing, she still couldn't see his face. He was busy with himself, or so she thought before he spoke.

"Use the knife."

She crossed to it. Picked it up. Closed it. She didn't like blood, he knew that. Twenty was wearing a belt. She crouched beside the woman, unfastening the buckle.

He spoke again. "Use the knife or leave her for me."

Fuck you. She wouldn't say it aloud. She didn't dare. But he couldn't stop her from thinking it. She yanked the belt out of Twenty's jeans.

She should have known he'd planned this. He had, after all, given Twenty that knife.

She should have known he'd be ready for her, too.

Instead she was surprised by the water from the pressure hose. It hit her like a two-by-four to the shoulder, spinning her back, away from Twenty, knocking the belt out of her hands, pushing her to the basement floor.

Just as suddenly as it had started, the force of the water stopped, leaving her dripping and battered, her head ringing from hitting it on the concrete.

"You have seven seconds," he told her, "before I take her upstairs. Six . . ."

It wasn't long enough to do it with the belt.

"Five . . ."

As always, he'd won, forcing her to choose between two unthinkable evils.

"Four . . ."

She had no choice. She opened the knife.

Twenty was rousing—he'd hit her with the water, too. Of course. He'd have planned for that. She saw Five coming, saw the knife blade gleaming, reflecting the light. And the noise she made, so full of fear and desperation, was one that he would feed on for many nights to come.

"Three . . ." He was laughing. "Two . . ."

"I'm so sorry," Five whispered, and cut Number Twenty's throat.

San Diego, California
Friday night, December 2, 2005

The party that started in Tom Paoletti's living room was moved, rather effortlessly, over to the Ladybug Lounge.

Sophia slipped into the booth across from Dave, who was already drinking his second beer of the evening. Either that, or he was trying to live up to his grunge-biker image and had ordered a bottle for each hand.

He slid one in front of her.

Or . . . he'd ordered for her.

"Am I that predictable?" she asked. "What if I'd wanted wine tonight?"

"You didn't." Dave smiled as he tucked his hair behind his ear. It was getting really long, and he was wearing it down instead of back in his usual ponytail. His smile faded. "Look, I'm sorry about this afternoon. It might seem like otherwise, but I didn't purposely set out to humiliate you."

"I know."

Decker was over by the bar, talking to his friend Nash and the soon-to-be Mrs. Nash, Tess Bailey. Sophia tried not to glance in his direction.

She made herself look around instead.

She hadn't lived in the United States for very long—her parents had taken her abroad when she was quite young. Aside from occasional visits to her grandparents in New England, she'd spent most of her life overseas. Living in America was full of discoveries and surprises, but apparently, as was the case anywhere in the world, a bar was a bar was a bar.

Dimly lit, with neon signs and mirrors to allow even the toughest customers to watch their own backs, the Ladybug Lounge could have been situated in any city in just about any country in the world. Music pulsed, at lower decibels than a dance club, but loud enough to create a party atmosphere. Conversations had to be held loudly, too, and there were frequent bursts of laughter.

A cell phone shrilled, and everyone in the place checked their pockets.

The winner was Tracy. As Sophia watched, the receptionist hurried out of the noisy bar and into the relative quiet of the parking lot.

The SEAL named Izzy moved from where he was sitting, over to a table by the window. No doubt keeping an eye on her. This wasn't the best part of town.

Dave, too, saw Tracy go outside. He also automatically shifted so he could watch out the window. He noticed that Sophia noticed, and he smiled. "She doesn't have all that much common sense, does she?"

Sophia shook her head no. "She surprised me tonight."

"Me, too," he said.

Tom and Kelly Paoletti had come home from their dinner to find nine operatives from TS Inc and eight SEALs in their living room.

Mark Jenkins had been ready to take the blame for the evening's impromptu search and rescue op. He started in on a long explanation—beginning with something about changing little Charlie's diaper.

Tracy easily could have stayed quietly in the background. But she stepped forward, cutting Jenk's story short. "I was the one who let the dog out," she confessed. "It was all my fault."

Apparently, she wasn't a total loser after all.

Across the bar, Decker glanced over, and Sophia quickly pulled her gaze away. She hadn't even realized she was staring at him again, but apparently she was. Talk about losers . . .

Dave was peeling the label off his bottle of beer. "So," he said. "On a scale from one to ten, just how badly does this suck—this decree that you and Decker have to work together on this op or both resign? For me, it's around an eight point five. I'm solidly miserable. I know I've been on your back, trying to get you to confront Deck, but to *force* it . . . ? I don't think Tom Paoletti has the right to . . . I mean, just watching you two tonight was . . ." He shook his head. "Painful."

"I'm sorry," she said. "I didn't expect to see him, and then I didn't know what to say."

He leaned forward slightly. "Have you told Tom anything about—"

"No." Sophia knew what he was going to ask—whether she'd told their boss what had transpired between her and Decker all those months ago. "And I'm not going to."

"If you did," Dave pointed out, "you might be able to file some kind of official complaint against Decker—"

Official . . . ? "No," she said. "No."

"—that would allow you to stay—"

"I'm not going to file a complaint," Sophia was adamant. "Any wrongdoing was as much mine as it was his. More, actually. It was *more* mine. He said no, and I . . ." She took another sip of her beer.

"It would allow you to stay employed at TS Inc, and for Decker to leave," Dave finished. "It might be a technical way around this particular rock and hard place. That's all I'm saying. If Tom knew the reason . . ."

"No," she said again.

"Just think about it."

"No. The wrongdoing was mine." She put her bottle down on the table forcefully. "What did Decker tell you about it? Did he go into detail?"

"Of course not," he said.

"What did he tell you?" Sophia pushed.

Dave had been part of a Troubleshooters Incorporated team sent to Kazbekistan, a Middle Eastern country that had suffered a terrible earthquake. A terrorist leader had been killed in the quake, and the team had been assigned to find that terrorist's missing laptop computer, believed to hold information on impending attacks.

Decker had been team leader.

He'd been searching for a man that he believed could help them—a businessman who'd lived in that country for years—a man who happened to be Sophia's husband, Dimitri Ghaffari. But Dimitri was dead, killed by a warlord named Padsha Bashir, who had then taken possession of his business, his bank accounts, his house.

His wife.

After months as a prisoner in Bashir's palace, Sophia had escaped. But the warlord put a reward on her head. If he found her, he would have killed her, of that there was no doubt.

When Decker and Sophia had first met, neither of them had trusted the other. Sophia was convinced he was a bounty hunter who would sell her out to Bashir. She was certain, unless she escaped from Decker, that she was going to die. Horribly.

And so she'd done what she'd had to, to ensure her survival.

Here in the Ladybug Lounge, thousands of miles and many months away from that awful encounter, Dave wasn't quite able to meet her gaze.

"What did Decker tell you?" Sophia asked again.

Dave cleared his throat. "That he—and you—had a power struggle that, um, got out of hand. Resulting in a, uh, encounter of, um, a sexual nature."

Good grief. That was an even more antiseptic version than she'd imagined possible. Still, Sophia nodded. "Did he mention that I tried to kill him? I had a gun, and I shot him. At him. I missed."

"Good thing," Dave said, finally meeting her eyes. "And yes. He mentioned that."

"Are those your words?" Sophia asked. "Or his? *Encounter of a sexual nature . . . ?*"

"His," Dave reported. "Although, I'm pretty sure he was more concise. A sexual encounter. That's what he called it."

"What do you think he meant by that?" she persisted.

Dave shook his head. "It doesn't really matter."

"Doesn't it?" Sophia asked. "If I'm going to file a complaint? Things like who touched who first, who said no?"

Dave shrugged. "I know that Deck said no, for what it's worth. I know he hasn't forgiven himself for what happened despite the fact that he said no. And I can certainly guess—" He stopped himself, took a deep breath. Started again. "It doesn't matter. The details are moot. You were the victim, Sophia." She opened her mouth to argue, but he cut her off. "You were Bashir's victim. And Decker was, too."

"So you're not even a little curious?"

"No," he said mildly. "I'm curious about a lot of things where you're concerned. Are you going to go to Mass General Hospital to visit your father? I'd like to know what you're going to do about that—time's running out. I'd like to know more about Dimitri, too. I know you loved him. From what little you've told me, well, I wish I'd known him, too. I'm also curious about those months you spent as Bashir's prisoner—but not about what happened. I can guess that. What I'm dying to find out is when you're going to take my advice and get professional help in dealing with everything you've been through. I'm curious as to when you're truly going to rejoin the human race and allow yourself another chance at happiness. I'm curious about the important things." He shrugged again. "Who went down on whom as an attempted distraction, an entire lifetime ago . . . ? It just doesn't rate."

"What doesn't rate?"

Sophia looked up to see three of the SEALs from Team Sixteen standing next to the booth. She'd been on a search team with two of them tonight.

"May we join you, ma'am? Dr. Malkoff?" Jay Lopez politely asked.

Sophia looked at Dave. "Doctor?" she asked.

"Ph.D.," he told her, waving it off as if it were nothing. "Didn't you say you had to leave early?"

He was giving her an out if she didn't want the added company.

But SEALs would be SEALs, and they were already sitting down. At least Danny Gillman was, sliding in next to her. Tall and tan, and, yes, young and lovely, he'd lightened the mood earlier by telling the entire search team about winning a turkey-calling contest back when he was eleven. Schnauzers apparently had their own unique way of barking. He'd demonstrated that, too.

"We come bearing gifts," he said, pushing another beer in front of her.

Lopez put a second bottle down, waiting until Dave slid over to join them. The third SEAL pulled a chair over and sat at the end of the table.

It was Izzy Zanella and . . . Sophia looked, and sure enough, Tracy Shapiro was back inside. She was at the bar with Mark Jenkins and about fifteen drooling Marines.

"Rumor has it, ma'am, that you'll be helping out with the training op," Izzy said.

It was funny, his ma'am had a different ring to it than Lopez's.

They were all waiting for her answer, all eyes on her—all that testosterone aimed in her direction.

"For once a rumor is right," she said.

"That's really great," Gillman enthused. Lopez smiled at her, too.

Izzy was back to checking out Tracy Shapiro, who was leaving with Mark Jenkins.

They weren't the only ones who were going home.

As Gillman launched into a story about one of the SEALs' previous training ops, Sophia could see Decker, still over by the bar, saying good-bye to his friends. He picked up his beer, and, with resolution in the set of his shoulders, he turned.

His intention was to join her and Dave. She knew this because she saw him hesitate—just slightly—as he saw that their table was now full.

He didn't stop short, though. He didn't even meet her eyes. He just went on past, pretending that his intended destination had been the juke-box.

He was good at pretending.

Of course, Sophia was, too.

Tracy unlocked her car door, then turned back to look at Jenk. "I'm going to risk embarrassing myself here," she said with a nervous laugh, "but there's something I have to tell you."

The moon was gleaming, making her hair shine, casting shadows on her already exotically beautiful face. Her eyes were colorless and dark and filled with uncertainty.

It was freaking amazing. Maybe it was because Jenk had dreamed about this moment countless times that he felt oddly detached. Distanced.

Even when she moistened her lips with the tip of her tongue.

"I'm listening," he said, because she seemed to need some encourage-ment.

But she didn't speak. She just looked at him.

So Jenk did the only thing he could do, given the moonlit circum-stances.

He kissed her.

He caught her off guard, and he tasted her surprise, along with a little salt from her recent trip to Margaritaville. Her mouth was soft and warm and sweet, and his heart should have been pounding because, for the love of God, he was finally kissing Tracy Shapiro and instead of pushing him away, she was kissing him back.

Her arms were around him, pulling him even closer, her hands on his back, in his hair.

Her incredible body was pressed against him.

His heart should have been hammering, his knees turned to Jell-O, his brain seizing.

Instead, he was thinking an entire array of stupid things.

His cell phone was in the front pocket of the shorts he'd borrowed from Gillman, who'd had his seabag in the trunk of his car. Would Tracy feel that as he kissed her, and think he had a hard-on? If she did, would she also think, because his phone was tiny, that he wasn't very well endowed? Or would she know it was his phone, and therefore notice that he *wasn't* revved up? And would she realize that he wasn't revved up because he'd self-gratified in the shower he'd had back at Tom Paoletti's house after the hamburger in his pants incident? Would she then think he was a perv, jacking off in his former CO's shower, too turned on by picnic food simply to let his overly enthusiastic body subside on its own?

Truth was, it wasn't the hamburger that had turned him on.

And where *had* Lindsey gone, leaving so abruptly like that, while he was getting cleaned up? She hadn't even said good-bye.

His cell phone rang its standard ring, bumping and vibrating, and he pulled back.

Tracy turned away, breathless and gorgeous and quite possibly trembling, as Jenk took his phone from his pocket.

"Sorry," he said.

"No," Tracy said. "It's probably a good thing."

He glanced at the incoming number and . . .

It was Lindsey. Why was she calling?

The devil in him wanted to answer it, but that same devil had provided some truly genius ideas in the past. Snowboarding off the roof when he was ten, with a bedsheet for a combination parachute and sail. That had worked out well.

As had the drinking contest he'd had with Alec MacInnough, the officer known in the teams as Big Mac because he was enormous. Or that time that he and Silverman had borrowed Chief O'Leary's motorcycle without asking. Sending flowers to blowhard Admiral Tucker's wife with a card that said, "Thank you, darling, for your very special personal contribution to my campaign," and signing the President's name. That impromptu trip to Hawaii, to stand up at Knox's equally impromptu wedding—his first one—that would have made Jenk UA if the senior chief hadn't saved his ass . . .

Jenk silenced both that devil and the ringer, putting his phone back into his pocket, where it continued to shake.

Tracy, meanwhile, had opened her car door and tossed her handbag onto the passenger's seat. "That was a mistake," she said, with her back still to him, talking about that kiss.

"It didn't feel like one to me," Jenk countered.

"Izzy told me you like me." She turned to face him as if that news created some kind of problem for her.

"I do," he admitted.

"I don't want to hurt you," Tracy told him. She was really upset, but of course she'd always been into high drama. "But that's what I'm going to do."

"I appreciate your concern, and consider myself warned."

"I'm serious," she said.

Maybe her problem was that she was always too serious. Everything was life or death with Tracy. She couldn't just relax and let life happen. But, man, she was pretty.

His phone beeped again. Lindsey had left voice mail. She'd probably been unable to resist making one last hamburger-in-his-pants joke. He smiled, which pissed off Tracy.

"I am," she insisted. "I'm going to end up going back to Lyle," she told him. "I always do. That's what I was going to tell you. I mean, I want to punish him, but . . ."

She wanted to *punish* Lyle. Okay.

"Look, maybe you'll go back to him, maybe you won't," Jenk countered. "I think it's worth a gamble."

Her eyes filled with tears. "Yeah, well, it's not," she said. "I'm not worth it." She got into her car, started the engine with a roar. She put her car into drive, and then, as if on second thought, she lowered her window. "Don't follow me," she added.

I wasn't planning to, definitely wasn't the right thing to say. And yet she seemed to want some kind of response. *I think you need to find your melodrama button and dial it down about seventeen notches.* Also not a good choice.

God, he was exhausted. Talking to Tracy was a workout and a half. Far harder than looking at her, that was for sure.

"I don't really know you," Jenk finally said. "And I'm pretty sure you don't know me. I think we've both changed a lot since high school. So maybe what we should do is go out sometime. Just the two of us, though. No Lyle. No talking about him, no thinking about him even."

She was already shaking her head. "That's impossible."

Jenk laughed. "Yeah, see, you really don't know me, because if you did, you'd know not to say that. I don't accept impossible. I never have, never will." He knocked on the roof of her car before stepping back. "Drive carefully."

And then, thank you Jesus, she was gone, the taillights of her car fading into the night.

Jenk took out his phone and dialed Lindsey's number as he walked home. His apartment was just a few blocks away. It wasn't worth bothering Izzy for a ride.

"Hey." Lindsey answered the phone. "I didn't expect you to call me back."

"You called me," he pointed out.

"I left a message," she said.

"I didn't listen to it," Jenk admitted. "It was easier just to call back."

"Are you always so lazy," Lindsey asked, "or did your ground beef body wrap tire you out?"

He laughed. "I knew you had to make just one more hamburger joke before you could go to sleep."

"Just one?" she said.

"FYI, I've got fifteen messages. I'd have to wade through all of them before I got to yours. So are you going to tell me what's up, or are you going to make me work for it?"

"I solved the mystery of . . ." Lindsey paused dramatically. "The green poop. In the spirit of Sherlock Holmes, with a kindred quest for knowledge, a restless thirst for answers . . ." She switched back to her regular voice. "While you were in the shower, I asked Kelly Paoletti what Charlie had had for lunch, perhaps . . . spinach? Why, indeed, he did. I questioned her further, and discovered yes, that would give him, ta-da, green poop."

"Hey, why'd you leave so soon—running home to catch the end of *American Idol?*" Jenk asked.

"Ha, you're almost as funny as your friend Izzy. No, actually, my dad called me on my cell," Lindsey said. "We hardly ever get to talk—we play a lot of phone tag—so I left to take his call."

"Ah," Jenk said. "Tommy told me your dad's some big deal professor at Stanford." As the words left his mouth, he kicked himself. That was not a hey-we're-just-friends thing to say. Letting her know that he'd been asking Tommy about her?

She didn't seem to notice. Or if she did, she hid it well. "Yup. Economics. Kill me now. I'm one of those people who can't even balance her checkbook, and he's always trying to talk me into investing. We couldn't be less alike if I were adopted. Anyway, by the time I got off the phone with him, it was too late to head over to the Ladybug. Was it fun? Did you and Izzy get up and pole dance? I would like to have seen that."

"It's not that kind of bar. No poles, no dancers."

"Too bad." He could hear laughter in her voice. "Anyway. I just called because I didn't want you up all night fretting over the diaper thing."

"Thanks."

"We still on for Monday, Hamburger Buns?" Lindsey asked. "Get this op scheduled and ready for go-time?"

"Yes, but did you really just call me . . . ?"

"Yeah, that was a good one, wasn't it? And by the way, after tonight, the bad jokes are done. Finito. This won't go on and on, ad nauseam. I promise."

"I'm going to hold you to that," Jenk said. "Thanks again for helping me tonight."

"Anytime." Lindsey's voice was warm in his ear. "See you Monday."

She cut the connection before Jenk could ask her about tomorrow— if she was going to the wedding. But it was probably just as good that he didn't ask. Besides, if she *were* going, he'd see her there.

He pocketed his phone. *Hamburger Buns.* He walked the rest of the way home, smiling, through the quiet of the night.

Izzy was getting another beer from the bar when the door opened, and Tracy Shapiro came back in.

She stood for a moment, looking around. Scanning the place as if she were looking for someone.

As her head slowly turned toward him, Izzy shifted, turning, too, so that he wasn't looking directly at her, but rather monitoring her in his peripheral vision.

As he watched without quite watching, she found the person she was looking for and began moving toward him.

Toward *him.*

Yes, there truly was no God. She'd been looking for Izzy.

He had two choices. Ignore her and hope he was wrong, or turn and watch her approach. She was a good-looking woman in repose, but when she was moving . . .

Ouch.

There was a third option. Run like hell.

"These colors don't run," he said to her in his best John Wayne when she got within earshot.

She stopped short. "You know, half the time, I don't have the slightest clue *what* you're talking about."

"I gotta be me," he told her. "Where's Mark?"

"He went home," Tracy said. "I was halfway to my apartment when I realized I left my jacket here. So . . . I came back for it."

Her body language was damn near making his head explode. She was contradicting herself all over the place again—open, closed, inviting him closer, warning him to stay back. And then there was the subtext behind her words. She left her *jacket* here. Of course, Izzy was willing to answer to just about any name she wanted.

Or he would've been willing, he reminded himself. If Tracy weren't the future Mrs. Jenkins. God, wouldn't *that* suck—if Marky really did marry this crazy chick . . .

"Did you find it?" he asked, even though he'd been watching her since she came back in, and she'd picked nothing up.

"Yeah," she said. She was a terrible liar, and to top it off, she was carrying nothing in her hands.

"So what'd you do, lose it again already?"

"No," she said. "When I got here, I realized that it was in my car—on the floor in the back—all that time."

So she'd come back inside to . . . ? Izzy didn't put his question into words. He just raised his eyebrows and waited.

She chewed on her lower lip, and wrapped her arms around herself and lied her ass off. "When I tried to start my car again . . . it won't, it doesn't . . . I don't know what's wrong with it. I was hoping you could maybe . . . help me?"

Waka-chicka, waka-chicka.

Word for word, it was the kind of dialogue that would show up in a low-budget porno flick. Spoken breathily by some buxom brunette nympho who had more than car repair on her mind.

"Why sure, lil' lady," Izzy drawled. John Wayne as porno star. "I'll he'p you out."

The look she gave him was lacking a certain *come do me* quality. In fact, it was almost a hundred percent *what the fuck was this asshole doing, talking like an idiot?* Still, she led him out into the parking lot, where the moon was hanging like a swollen blister in the hazy night sky.

Tracy stopped short, and he nearly bumped into her.

"Whoa," she breathed, entranced. "We don't have moons like that back East."

Maybe Izzy had been a SEAL for too long, but he just couldn't look at the moon and ooh and ah over how pretty it was. For him, first and foremost, the moon was a pain in the ass, lighting up the protective dark cover of the night.

Although he had to admit that Tracy looked particularly lovely bathed in its light. And yes, probably if she danced for him, naked, on a moonlit beach, he'd regain at least part of his lost appreciation for the damned thing.

"I always wanted to be an astronaut," she told him dreamily. "When I was little, I was sure that someday I'd walk on the moon."

Okay, so that wasn't part of a typical porno flick's dialogue. Unless walking on the moon was a euphemism for, say, sex on a trampoline or maybe in a zero-G chamber.

But, hello. There her car sat, at the edge of the lot, with its hood up. As if she were really having trouble starting it.

Maybe she was telling the truth.

She was still gazing at the moon, lost in a time long past in which she still allowed herself to dream that which she now deemed impossible. When had it happened? When had she changed from the little girl who was convinced she had the right stuff, to this desperately insecure woman who was so wrapped up in the mundane, daily problems of life that she couldn't hold a simple receptionist position without messing it up?

Tracy turned back to him, back to business. "When I turned the key, nothing happened. The engine didn't even whatchamacallit. Turn over." She laughed. "God, I'm a ditz when it comes to cars."

Like being a ditz was something she was proud of . . . ?

"Sounds like it might be the alternator." Izzy took a brief look at the engine—everything seemed fine in terms of hoses and connections—and then opened the driver's side door for her. "Let me take a listen."

She sat behind the wheel and her skirt, already short, rode even farther up her smooth, tanned thighs. She didn't push it back down, didn't close the door. "It won't do any—" She turned the key and it started. With a roar. "Oh, my God, thank you so much!"

"You're welcome, but I didn't do anything," he told her.

Her eyes were brimming with wonder and gratitude—and disbelief. "This is another one of your weird jokes, right?"

"No. I didn't touch the engine." Izzy shrugged, and backed away from that open car door and that moonlit view of Tracy's world-class legs. "It sounds like everything's fine now."

The wonder turned to worry. "But if it is the alternator . . . I once had a car where the alternator died. I was on the Saw Mill Parkway, at night. The lights—even the hazards—didn't work. It was really scary."

She was looking for him to comment, and "Okay, Buh-bye!" probably wasn't going to fly. "It must've been," he said.

"Could you . . . Would you . . . Would it be very much of an imposition—God, I know it is—if I asked you to . . ." Her voice was down to a whisper. "Follow me home?"

Waka-chicka, waka-chicka. They were suddenly back in porno-flick dialogue land.

"I'm picking up a weird vibe here," Izzy told her. "Is sending out a weird vibe really your intention, because—"

"Never mind." She slammed the car door, locking in those legs. "Forget it. I just thought . . ." She shook her head and used both hands to push her hair off her face. "I must be some kind of complete and utter moron."

She put her car into gear and, tires squealing, pulled away.

"What just happened here?" Izzy asked the moon.

It didn't answer, but it may have smiled.

CHAPTER
FIVE

L t. Commander Lewis Koehl, CO of SEAL Team Sixteen, was a good-looking man. Dark, wavy hair, a square jaw, and quite the ability to fill out a military uniform worked well in combination.

And then there were his eyes. A matinee idol shade of dark brown, he was using them to check Lindsey out.

In fact, every time she looked up, Lew Koehl was watching her.

And, yes, he was also frowning, so he probably wasn't checking her out in any kind of exciting, romantic-dinner-in-her-future way. He was probably wondering whose teenage daughter had been allowed out here, onto the potentially dangerous site of the SEAL Team Sixteen/Troubleshooters Incorporated training exercise.

Tom Paoletti had told Lindsey to dress like a pop-star wannabe for today's op, so she'd complied. Her jeans were low on her hips, leaving way too many exposed inches of bare skin—skin that was getting decidedly chilly. How did girls today manage to hang out at the subzero, over-air-conditioned malls without freezing to death?

Her top was more accessory than actual shirt, and she longed for a sweater. But that would ruin a look that was straight out of the lingerie department, enhanced by a padded push-up bra that created the illusion of cleavage.

At least her feet were warm in her clunky boots. For footwear when undercover, Lindsey would always choose the Sheryl Crow crunchy granola look over the four-inch *there better be a valet because I'm not walking in these things all the way from the parking lot* stilettos of Christina Aguilera.

She'd clipped her short hair over in the front, in a style she'd seen on the high school girl who worked behind the counter at the video store. It was definitely young-ifying, and she'd chosen pinker shades of makeup to enhance the effect.

Although she obviously didn't look *too* young, because Mark Jenkins had nearly dropped the box of equipment he was helping to carry in when he'd first spotted her.

He seemed to have wrenched his injured shoulder as he'd overcompensated, because after he put the box down he stood there rubbing it. He continued to watch her as she listened to Tom tell her—hopefully for the final time—just how important it was that she keep herself as safe as humanly possible during the course of this exercise.

Talking about personal safety was something that the CO of TS Inc did in advance of every mission, training or other, to every member of the company. It wasn't that they didn't all know that there were risks in their business. She, for one, was well aware that people died while on the job.

Even in training ops.

But probably not in this one.

Still, Tom had to give what amounted to his "be careful" reminder. To let it slide, undone, was tantamount to laughing in the face of fate. It was the equivalent of giving a double-devil-dog dare to bad luck.

And Lindsey had been in the law enforcement business long enough to recognize that luck played a definite role in deciding who lived and who died.

So even though she herself didn't have any rituals or superstitions, she was not about to get in the way of anyone else's. And Tom was not the only one. Dave Malkoff always carried a small polished chunk of beach glass that no doubt meant something special to him. Tess Bailey and Jimmy Nash had some kind of eye contact thing that they always did anytime anyone made a toast. Alyssa Locke had what Lindsey had come to recognize as her pre-kicking-ass CD. If strains of Aretha Franklin could be heard coming from her office, everyone but her husband, Sam Starrett, had learned to run.

And Sam himself had some doozies in the superstitions department. They'd all learned the hard way never to sit in his special chair when he was stressed. And God forbid anyone mess up his desk. Although Lindsey suspected that Sam's insistence that he needed to spend at least six solid hours in isolation with his wife following an overseas assignment, or he'd have bad luck the next op, was at least partially contrived.

Still, the deal was this: If all the rituals had been executed, and all the superstitions followed to the letter, and bad luck still managed to rear its ugly head, then at least, in the aftermath of tragedy, there would be that much less what-if-ing.

Lindsey couldn't imagine how truly dreadful it must be for a leader—or even a CO up the chain of command—to lose a member of his or her team.

It hadn't been that long since Tom and Decker had lost Vinh Murphy—or technically, Murphy's wife. Her shooting death had been beyond terrible, a tragedy happening during an assignment that, like this one, was supposed to be easy. And they *had* lost Murph. He was just as irrevocably gone as if he'd been buried alongside his Angelina. Lindsey's heart still ached for him. God, she missed them both so much.

So it really wasn't any wonder that Tom was still spooked and that Decker was still walking around with a permanent case of grim.

It was possible, from the way Deck clenched his jaw these days, that he'd soon have to go on a soft food diet. His teeth were probably on the verge of being ground down to his gums. And then, of course, there was his thing with Sophia—whatever that was about. It was more than a romance gone bad. Lindsey knew that much. Not that anyone would talk about it.

Which was fine with Lindsey. She had her own list of topics she would not discuss. Her mother's death. Her father's remoteness and withdrawal from life that started when he discovered the identity of his biological father. Her seven years of ugliness and suffering witnessed as a matter of course while on the job, culminating in the ultimate destruction and despair. Yeah, her partner Dale and the shooting. Bring *that* up and watch her run.

But they all had their luggage, their hot buttons, their pain. Letting Tom talk about safety was not a hardship, and it obviously helped him, so . . .

He finally finished his speech, leaving Lindsey free to wander over in Jenk's direction.

She skipped the niceties of a greeting. "You suck," she told him point-blank. But she could tell from his eyes that this was something he already knew.

"I'm sorry. It's been a crazy week." Jenk was still working on his shoulder. It must've really been hurting him—not that he'd ever complain. He looked exhausted, and she felt herself melting. Forgiving him.

"Lindsey, holy sha-moly." Izzy was already wearing full camouflage, and with the brown and green streaks on his face, he looked fierce and primitive. But then he smiled, which made him look even odder. A happy, friendly monster. "What happened to you?"

"If you think this is bad, you should see my pross clothes from when I worked Vice," Lindsey told them. "I have to lock my closet when my father comes to visit. God forbid he wander in there and think I actually wear red spandex."

"Hold on just a minute there," Izzy said. "No one thinks there's anything even remotely bad about this amazing, new improved Lindsey. You are smokin', baby." He nudged Jenk. "Isn't she smokin'? Who knew she was packing this kind of heat?"

Jenkins sighed. "Zanella." He grimaced as he met Lindsey's eyes. "Sorry."

"What? Like Lindsey doesn't know she's a walking hard—"

"Please don't say—"

". . . attack. *Heart* attack." Izzy grinned at Lindsey. It was clear that it wasn't what he'd intended to say.

"I'm a grown-up," Lindsey reminded Jenk. "I worked for years with a predominantly male police force. Believe me, I've heard every stupid comment and lame joke possible. It comes with the territory. Why do you think I'm so good at johnson jokes?"

"Whoa," Izzy said. "Wait. You two've been telling dick jokes without me?"

"We prefer to call them johnson jokes," Jenk said, with a completely straight face. "It's classier."

It wasn't until she laughed that he cracked a smile, and then they stood there, just grinning at each other as Izzy echoed, "Classier?"

"Much," Jenk said, holding Lindsey's gaze.

It was a crying shame that Tracy existed.

She forced away her foolish smile. "As far as your apology goes, Jenkins, I'm going to need some serious groveling to make up for your amazing quadruple Houdini. *My* week was pretty crazy, too. Considering I was doing both my job and Tracy's."

"I really am sorry about that," he said as if he actually meant it. "I would have helped you if I could."

"So what happened?" she asked.

"It's not so much what happened as what didn't happen," Izzy interjected.

"It started early Saturday morning," Jenk said. "We got a call saying we're going wheels up, destination unknown, except we all know it's Afghanistan, and everyone's pissed because we're going to have to miss Mallory Paoletti's wedding and—you know, I thought you'd be there."

"At the wedding?" Lindsey asked, surprised. Had he actually looked for her? "No. I mean, sure, Tom invited me, but I'd only met Mallory once, and I knew she wanted a small wedding, so . . . I figured sending my regrets would be the best gift."

"You should have come," Jenk said. "It was a good party. Great band."

"There was a serious shortage of women," Izzy added. "Particularly gorgeous ones whose waists I can probably span with . . ." He moved as if to demonstrate, and Lindsey took a step back.

"You are *so* not touching me with those hands," she informed him.

He looked down and actually seemed surprised that his fingers bore the green and brown residue of his cammie paint.

"So, you, uh, didn't bring a date?" Lindsey asked Jenk. She was pretty sure he hadn't taken Tracy. If he had, she would have heard about it, endlessly, over the past four days. Or maybe not. Maybe the only person Tracy talked about endlessly was Lyle.

"Nah. I RSVP'ed months ago, telling them I was coming solo." Jenk perched on the edge of a stack of boxes. He was trying to look casual, but she could tell he was still trying to stretch out his shoulder.

She wanted to offer to rub it, but she knew he'd think she was hitting on him.

The bitch of it was, he'd be right.

Damnit. Lindsey hadn't seen the man for close to a week. She'd spent large amounts of time with Tracy, the woman of his dreams. Which should have been a total turnoff, since Tracy was an idiot.

Okay, that was mean. Tracy wasn't an idiot. She just had the habit of making some truly idiotic life choices. She really was quite funny, and she did have a good heart, and she wanted so desperately to succeed—it was hard not to like her at least a little. But the woman could not do two things at the same time—to the point that Lindsey was starting to wonder if she wasn't maybe learning disabled.

Still, it was so beyond obvious that Tracy hadn't truly left Lyle. Sure, she'd moved out of his apartment and across the country, but the man was under her skin.

If Mark Jenkins couldn't see that, then he was a major idiot, too.

Lindsey had gone a long way toward convincing herself of that. Until he'd walked in, nearly dropped his box, and smiled at her.

"You know," Izzy said, still holding out his green-and-brown-streaked hands. "This reminds me of a really good johnson joke. Actually, it's more of a johnson story. Right, Marky-Mark?"

Jenk suddenly looked as if he'd been struck by lightning. Surprised and stunned and totally horrified.

"No," he said. "Nuh-uh. Don't even *think* about—"

"Oh, come on," Izzy said. "You were young. Just a tadpole. It *is* a great story."

"No, it is not. Zanella, I swear to God, if you start this story circulating again . . ." Jenk said, but he probably knew there was no stopping Izzy. He turned to Lindsey. "It's not even true. This story. It's, like, like . . . an urban legend that someone just went and put my name into." He turned back to Izzy. "Find me one person who was there. Just one. You can't, can you?"

"Yeah, that's because you've transferred them all to the East Coast."

"*I've* transferred them," Jenk repeated. He looked at Lindsey again. "I'm not an officer. Am I an officer?" He didn't wait for her to answer. "No. I'm not even close. So how exactly did I *transfer* an entire platoon of SEALs?"

Izzy shrugged. "I don't know. The same way you do everything. The same way you set up this little training op."

"I didn't . . ." Jenk made an exasperated noise. "I *may* have planted the seeds for the idea . . ."

"Now he's just being modest," Izzy told Lindsey. "You need something done—a war started, significant troop movements, lunch at the White House . . . Just ask Jenk. He'll get it done."

"How about a dinner date with Lew Koehl?" Lindsey asked. Oh, God, had she really just said that? What was she, crazy? This was total middle school tactics. Pretending she liked Lewis so Mark would be jealous.

Both Jenk and Izzy were staring at her.

"Are you insane?" Izzy asked. "Because the CO is . . ." He glanced at Jenk. "Damn. What's the word I'm looking for?"

"Straightlaced?" Jenk supplied.

"That's the polite one. Stuffy applies. I'd also say stiff, but since we were just referencing johnson jokes that might be misinterpreted as a plus," Izzy said. "Bottom line, the man is seriously comedically challenged."

"Yeah, you don't know that," Jenk said. "I think somewhere back there he's got a sense of humor. He's got to have one. Look what he deals with on a daily basis. He's just a very formal person. Very old-fashioned. Conservative. To be honest, I don't think he's Lindsey's type."

"He's definitely never laughed at a johnson joke in his life," Izzy agreed.

"Old-fashioned actually might be kind of nice," Lindsey said, because obviously she had the mental age of a twelve-year-old. "And, you know, I don't *have* to tell jokes about any part of the human anatomy."

"Oh, I do," Izzy said, and Jenk sighed loudly in exasperation. "Just relax, all right?" Iz addressed his friend. "It's not like I'm telling Tracy. You won't tell Tracy, will you, Linds?"

Jenkins surely knew he was fighting a losing battle, but giving up didn't come naturally. "Zanella."

"Is it funny?" Lindsey inquired, "or just crude?"

"Oh, it's funny." Izzy clearly loved Jenk's discomfort. "*And* crude. Considering the subject matter. You know what? Here's what I'll do. I'll tell it without using any names."

"Oh, right," Jenk said. "That really works after you already freaking told her it was *me*." He turned to Lindsey. "Which it wasn't." He took a deep breath. "Will you please just tell Zanella that you don't want to hear his totally fictional story that never happened?"

Lindsey made a face. "Well, I guess I could, but . . . I'd be lying."

"Great. Thanks, Iz. You know how you saved my life? Well, now we're even." He gestured to Izzy. "Go ahead. Tell the story. Ruin our friendship."

"Ruin our friendship," Izzy scoffed. "You'll get over it. You always do." He turned to Lindsey. "This story circulates every few years or so. It hasn't killed Jenkie yet. Okay, here we go. Ready?"

She nodded. This was going to be good.

"So we got this new guy on the team, right? He's a good guy, but he's really young. Extremely green. And about to get even greener." Izzy started to giggle.

Jenk stood up. "You know what? I changed my mind. I've heard this story too many times to be able to sit through it again. Lindsey, it really wasn't me, and I'll see you later—"

"Okay, wait." Lindsey stopped him. "First I have to hear about the wedding. I assume something happened that allowed you to go . . . ?"

"Yeah, we got a twelve-hour delay, so we brought our equipment to the church. Just in case."

"But then we got a twenty-four-hour delay on top of that," Izzy added. "And finally on Sunday, we got a call telling us to stand down, we're not needed. Only, a few hours later, what was it, oh-three-hundred, Monday morning?" he asked Jenk.

"Do you hear some kind of noise?" Jenk asked Lindsey, "that sounds like oxygen being wasted?"

"It was definitely early Monday," Izzy said. "Way predawn. Prolly around three."

"On Monday we got a second call," Jenk continued to ignore Izzy.

"This time, we're told it's real. We're definitely going. When you and I spoke on the phone on Tuesday . . ."

He'd called Lindsey's cell, but he'd only had about thirty seconds to talk, and he'd spent most of it apologizing for having to leave town.

". . . I was in Virginia," Jenk reported, "getting ready to head for parts unknown."

"Again," Izzy said. "Hoo-yah, take two."

"We were in Europe, in Germany, before we got *that* stand down order."

"One thing's sure—something's up in the sandbox," Izzy said.

"It's only a matter of time before we do go," Jenk told her. "Which is why we're rushing to do this exercise now."

Lindsey nodded. "TS Inc has gotten an increase in phone calls from the alphabet agencies." She shot Jenk a look. "And the reason I know this is because I've spent the past four days helping Tracy try to learn how to use the phone system."

The task that Jenk had promised to come into the office to assist with.

"How's she doing?" he asked.

"What has *she* told *you*?" Lindsey countered. Did he know that Lyle had come into town several days early, that he and Tracy were having dinner together tonight? God, she was not going to be the one to break that news to Jenk. Or the fact that Tracy had been talking, nonstop, about whether or not Lyle would attempt a reconciliation.

Jenk shook his head. "I haven't spoken to her all week. I haven't even text messaged her. After the word came down that today was our window of opportunity to do this exercise, well, you're lucky I had time for a shower."

Someone had to tell him. God forbid he come into the TS Inc office tomorrow and see Tracy packing up her desk, a big ol' diamond ring on her finger. There'd been a lot of speculation over the past few days that Lyle would play the "Marry me" card to get Tracy back. Lindsey had kept her own thoughts to herself, but she suspected that that had been Tracy's game plan all along.

"It's funny," Jenk was saying. "I thought most of the work would be done over at Tommy's office. I got that wrong."

"See?" Izzy was triumphant. "You *did* set up this training op, didn't you?"

"Yes," Jenk said. "Okay? Yes. Just tell your story and—No. You know what? *I'm* going to tell Lindsey the story. Let's just get this over with, and move on, okay? How does it start?"

Lindsey made up her mind. She'd tell Jenk about Tracy and Lyle immediately after the op.

"There's this new guy on the team named Mark Jenkins," Izzy supplied.

"Bite me," Jenk said. "I'm telling it with your name in the fill-in-the-blank slot, see how *you* like it, dickweed." He took a deep breath. "There's a new guy on the team named Irving Zanella, and he's going out on a real-world op for the first time, and he's scared, but he's ready. It's a simple sneak and peak—get in, get some basic info on the enemy's camp, how many guards are posted, what kind of weapons are in view, get back out."

"He can pretend that it was me," Izzy interjected, "but it was really him. How else would he know so much about the assignment?"

Jenk grimly ignored him as Lindsey tried not to laugh. "They're in the middle of the jungle," he continued with the story, "just collecting information, blending with the scenery. Turns out they need to stay longer than they'd anticipated, so they settle in, tear open some MREs, have a little chow. About an hour later, the new guy, *Izzy*, goes, 'Damn, I didn't bring my Magic Markers. I don't even have any extra cammie paint.' "

It wasn't me, Izzy mouthed to Lindsey, from behind Jenk, who elbowed him without missing a beat. "Ow!"

"And the chief looks at him and, you know, tries to reassure him," Jenk said. " 'Zanella, you're fine.' His paint's a little muddy from sweat, but that's no big deal. The chief doesn't know what this kid means by his Magic Markers, though. What, is he going to make a sign or maybe write a letter home? You never know with the new guys. But this is not the time or place for lengthy conversations.

"But Izzy goes, 'No, chief, really, I gotta take a crap, but I didn't camouflage my ass. I didn't think we'd be gone this long, so . . .' And the chief is like, 'What?' "

Lindsey, knowing full well what was coming, started to laugh.

"Yeah," Jenk said. "You guessed it. Turns out, back at the base when they were gearing up for this op, some cruel bastards tell Izzy that he's got to use paint on every part of him that's going to peek out from beneath his uniform—including his . . . johnson. Especially his johnson, because he definitely doesn't want *that* to get shot off, right? And they tell him, as far as that piece of his anatomy is concerned, it's easier just to use permanent markers. That way he doesn't have to keep drawing on himself every time he's going out into the world. So there he is, with a jungle cammie print— apparently he did a very good job of it—on his unit, for like, two months."

"Gillman! Zanella! Lopez!" On the other side of the Quonset hut, the senior chief was handing out gear.

"I thought it was more like four months," Izzy said. "But, hey, you should know."

Jenk gritted his teeth. "Rumor has it, if you look really close, you can still see a trace of it. Even after all these years."

"If that's the case," Izzy said, his hands on his belt, "I can prove right here that it wasn't me."

"No, thank you," Lindsey said quickly.

"It's an urban legend," Jenk said. "Go to Fort Bragg, and you'll hear a version where the new guy is an army grunt. Go to Eglin Air Force Base and the story takes place during pilot SERE training. It didn't happen. It's fiction."

"Zanella!"

"Later, babe." Izzy was gone.

Jenk looked imploringly at Lindsey. "You believe me, right?"

She didn't get a chance to respond before the senior chief bellowed for him. "Jenkins!"

Jenk didn't move as quickly as Izzy had, walking backwards so that he could still talk to her. "I probably won't see you until the rescue."

"In that case," Lindsey told him, "you won't see me until the exercise is over. Team Sixteen's not going to win this thing, remember?"

He laughed, supremely confident. "Prepare to be disappointed."

"Back at you," she said. "You know, I couldn't help but notice that you didn't volunteer to prove that that story's not about you."

Something may have sparked in his eyes. Or maybe it was just a combination of the setting sun and wishful thinking on her part.

"I don't feel the need to prove anything," he said. "Besides, I'm too old-fashioned."

Now, okay, *that* was flirting. Wasn't it?

"Lindsey," Tom Paoletti called. "It's time."

The intentionally motley-looking collection of TS Inc operatives had their equipment. They were ready to vanish with their hostage—her—into the desert.

When Lindsey glanced back, Jenk was still watching her walk away, and her heart actually skipped a beat.

LOCATION: UNKNOWN
DATE: UNCERTAIN

She used to have a name.

Beth Foster.

She sometimes said it aloud in the darkness, just to hear something besides the sound of her own breathing, the endless drip of the water, the occasional squeaking of his feet on the kitchen floor overhead.

Sometimes she said all of their names. Connie Smith was the latest. It was the scent of Connie Smith's blood, metallic and sharp, pooled on the concrete floor, that hung in the dark basement air, making her stomach churn and her head ache.

Alive. Alive. Her heart still beat. Her own blood was safe in her veins. Most of it, anyway. Alive. Alive. Alive.

And Connie Smith, Lord Jesus save her soul, had gone to a far better place.

"Connie Smith," she whispered.

He always made a point of telling her their names, but never while they were still alive. Only after their suffering was over. After she'd finished them.

"Connie Smith, Jennifer Denfield, Yvette Wallace, Paula Kettering, Wendy Marino, Julia Telman, Debra Perez, Liana Bergeron, Cathy Quinn, Maris Olietto, Nancy Stein, Michelle Kulhagen, Brianna Martin, Jennifer Denfield . . . No wait. Jennifer Denfield was Jennifer Two. Jennifer McBride was Jennifer One. Jennifer McBride and . . . Number Four."

Number Four had been Beth's first.

She didn't know her name.

Possibly, according to some twisted set of rules that he followed, she hadn't earned the right to know it.

But more likely, he hadn't yet discovered that telling her their names was another way to torment her.

It turned them from nameless lumps of frightened flesh into people. People who had had lives and families who loved them, who would mourn them—the same as she did.

Once upon a time, she'd had a mother. Strict and overbearing. Full of rules and disapproval. *How will you get a real job without an education? Why don't you reenlist? How will you ever stop drinking if you keep on working in a bar? If you dress like a slut, you'll be treated like a slut. He was married? And you're actually surprised? What goes around, comes around . . .*

Once upon a time, Beth had thought she'd had problems, troubles, pain.

She'd had no idea.

East of San Diego, California
Thursday night, December 8, 2005

The training op's SNAFU started when Dave called for a break about an hour after they'd entered phase two of Tom Paoletti's plan.

Phase two—for Dave's little team and their hostage—was all about keeping moving, always moving. They allowed themselves only the briefest of respites in the clear desert night.

Lindsey, however, was purposely dragging, slowing them down as a real hostage would. Someone had given her a blanket because the night air had a crisp chill, but she tripped over it more often than not.

Still, it was Sophia who had really needed the chance to stop and catch her breath.

So Dave concocted some reason to go and consult with Decker, leaving Lindsey sitting on a rock, guarded by Tom and Sophia.

Sophia had, indeed, dressed like a commando-wannabe in cammie-print pants and T-shirt, no doubt purchased off the rack from some fashionable department store. The pants fit very nicely, and both they and the shirt had shiny designer labels that glittered, kind of defeating their purpose.

It also didn't help that the print was intended for camouflage in the jungle rather than the desert.

But it was Sophia's bandana, worn biker-style on her head, that truly completed her look. And it was quite a look, especially since she'd arranged her long hair into dozens of skinny braids that hung down her back.

She looked Hollywood ferocious—particularly since the way she wielded her weapon broadcast her lack of skill in using it.

The really funny part of Sophia's appearance was that, while out in the field, Dave had seen enemy combatants dressed just as carefully and holding their weapons just as awkwardly. It was as if they believed that looking like a soldier was more important than, oh, say, training . . . ?

And Sophia had more than the appearance down pat. She'd made them all laugh back in the Quonset hut, before the op got into gear. Clutching that weapon that was almost as big as she was, her eyes had actually sparkled as she'd haughtily informed Tom that she would only answer to her new nickname, Señorita Diablo, which according to her meant, with poetic license, "Devil Woman."

She was totally in character. She'd completely cracked Dave up, but his heart had gone into his throat, too. If he'd had any last doubts, they were now gone. Sophia Ghaffari had definitely decided to return to the world of the living.

Apparently with or without Decker's help.

As for Deck, he'd been intent on keeping his distance, but of course Tom, who was calling all the shots, had divided the Troubleshooter operatives into three cells. He had assigned both Deck and Sophia to the hostage-handling patrol. His final insult had been to name Dave as their team leader.

A command position was the one job Dave vehemently didn't want, not ever. And particularly not now with this particular grouping of operatives.

But Dave had no choice in the matter. Tom had gently pointed out that training ops such as this one were for experimentation. How, he'd asked in his blandly reasonable voice, did Dave know for sure that he didn't want to be a team leader if he never tried being a team leader? And what better time to try than here and now?

So here Dave was with his very first command, in charge of a five-person unit that included that oil and water of Troubleshooters Incorporated, Sophia and Decker.

Dave's first command decision had been to make Decker their point person. Deck would lead their way through the growing darkness, all by himself, way out in front. As far as possible from Sophia.

Dave then assigned Tess the radio—letting her maintain communications with the other two "terrorist" cells led by Sam and Alyssa—although their hardware was ancient and didn't work more often than not.

He, himself, and Sophia, ahem, *Señorita Diablo*, were in charge of handling the prisoner, leaving Nash at the rear, guarding their six and covering up their trail.

Phase one of Tom's master plan to keep Lindsey out of the SEALs' hands had worked like a dream. Of course it helped that the TS Inc team—with the exception of Lindsey—had spent the past few days exploring this area, both during the day and at night. The SEAL officers leading the opposing team, however, had only a few hours spent studying maps and charts. They were out here for the very first time tonight, as would be the case in most rescue scenarios.

Phase one, part A, involved little more than letting the SEAL scouts find Dave's team—and the hostage. Their SEAL opponents were highly skilled—it didn't take long at all before Tess got a crackly message from Alyssa's team that they'd spotted at least one SEAL who was now following the hostage.

Phase one, part B, was more complicated. It involved a stealthy trek through the hills, filled with backtracking and following their own footsteps, as if they were trying their best—which they were—to cover their trail.

They ended up at an abandoned mine that Decker and Nash had found several days earlier. This area was littered with the ramshackle structures. But this one was special. It had a back door, so to speak. There was more than one way in and out.

Dave's mirthless band had brought the hostage into the mine, meeting up with Alyssa's cell. They'd traded Nash and Tess—who stayed outside, as if guarding the hostage—for who else but Tom Paoletti.

Like *that* wasn't at all intimidating—having his boss suddenly on his team during his first-ever command. Still, there was no time to bitch and moan. Like a trip to the dentist, this, too, would eventually end. And it would hurt less if they just kept moving.

So Dave's new, smaller, more compact cell took the hostage and boogied out the back door. As did the rest of Alyssa's. Sam's group was already in place, ready to ambush the SEALs who approached the mine to rescue the hostage.

It was going to be a bloodbath. Or at least a virtual one. The weapons both sides were using didn't fire bullets, although they made the same attention-drawing racket of real machine guns. They were, however, just a higher-tech version of laser tag. There were sensors in the uniform jackets they all wore. A hit would render the wearer KIA, and turn a stripe on the sleeves a telling deathly shade of black. His or her weapon would cease to fire, and, according to the rules, that person would sit out the rest of the op, neither moving—unless carried out on teammate's backs—nor speaking.

"What's the word from Alyssa?" Dave now asked Decker, who had taken over Tess's radio duties.

"She says we weren't followed," Deck reported.

The words were barely out of his mouth when a woman's voice shouted. "Tom!" Then a scream that sounded much too real. Was that Sophia or Lindsey? The sound of gunshots exploded, all from just down the trail.

It was hard to say who moved faster. Decker may have gotten there first, but his lead over Dave could have been measured in mere inches. They rounded the corner, neck and neck and . . .

Sophia was sprawled on the ground. Tom Paoletti was, too. His jacket had a black stripe on the sleeve.

"Shit!" Dave wildly looked around for Lindsey, who was gone. He should have known better than to take a break. His team had been slaughtered, and the hostage had been grabbed.

Like Dave, Decker had his weapon up and ready, but whoever had taken Lindsey wasn't hanging around. "Find the hostage," Dave ordered Deck, who responded by dropping both his weapon and the radio and crouching in the dust next to Sophia?

She hadn't been killed—her sleeves were unchanged. She was on the ground because she was . . . hurt? Dave went onto his knees beside her, too. "Are you all right?"

"I think I killed Tom." She pushed herself up, reaching for the weapon she'd dropped.

"*You* killed Tom?" Dave couldn't keep the incredulity from his voice as Decker dragged her weapon closer to her.

Sophia nodded, embarrassed. "Thanks," she told Deck, wincing as she discovered that she'd skinned her knee. It was bleeding through a tear in her pants.

"What happened?" Dave asked.

"Someone pushed her, knocking her off her feet while they snatched the hostage, that's what happened," Decker said. "And when I find them, they're going to die."

"I was sort of asking Sophia," Dave told Deck mildly. "Although I'm sure she appreciates the macho warrior rhetoric. You want to beat your chest for us, too?"

It was possible that Tom, although dead, laughed.

"No one pushed me," Sophia said. "And if you two are going to fight, I'm out of here."

"Find Lindsey," Dave ordered Decker again, as if he were a mentally challenged dog. He took the radio. He had to let Alyssa and Sam know that they'd lost the hostage. They had to start working on a plan to get her back. But, of course, the radio was completely dead. He couldn't keep his frustration from his voice. "What's wrong with this thing?"

"You'll have to go to a higher elevation to get a signal." Decker gathered up his weapon, smoothly pulling himself up in that athletic way he had that made everything he did look graceful. Dave was going to grunt at least twice, elbows and knees awkwardly akimbo, as he hauled himself to his feet.

"Which way did they take her?" Deck asked Sophia.

She shrugged apologetically. "I don't know. That way, I think, from process of elimination." She pointed north. "She was sitting on that rock. I was over here." She pointed nearby. "I heard a noise and I stood up to check it out, and when I turned back, Lindsey was gone." She turned back to Dave. "I didn't hear anyone. It was like . . . she just vanished."

"And no one pushed you," Deck repeated, as if he didn't quite believe it.

"No one was anywhere near me," she admitted. "I was so surprised that Lindsey was gone. I shouted for Tom—I don't know where he went, either—and I think I took a step backward and tripped. I must've grabbed my gun the wrong way—the only training I've had is with small arms. It started firing and . . . That's when I must've killed Tom." She looked over at him. "Sorry, sir."

Dave again gave the order to Decker. Maybe third time would be the charm. "Go, now, and track the team that took Lindsey. Sophia and I will get a message to Alyssa, try to recoup the damage that's been done." He got to his feet with only one grunt, holding out his hand to help Sophia up. "We better move, because those gunshots surely drew some attention."

Yet Deck still lingered. "You're sure you're all right?" he asked Sophia, who nodded.

It was only then that he left.

"Come on," Dave said, leading Sophia in the other direction.

It was her turn to hesitate. "Are we really just supposed to leave Tom?"

"We're terrorist scum," Dave pointed out. "We're supposed to remove his gold teeth, strip him of his boots and clothing, and leave him for the bobcats to eat for a midnight snack."

"I'm so sorry," Sophia told Tom again, as Dave pulled her with him down the trail.

"I'm not," Dave grumbled. "It's his fault entirely for making me a team leader."

Shots had been fired.

Jenk had been sent to investigate, along with Izzy, Lopez, Orlikowski, and Gillman.

Izzy found the enemy first. "Tommy's dead," he reported gleefully.

"No way." Danny Gillman couldn't believe it.

"Go see for yourself, Fishboy," Izzy countered. "He's lying by the side of the trail. Black stripe."

"No," Jenk said. There was no time for Gillman to do his doubting Thomas routine. "Iz, did you see Lindsey?"

"No sign of her, M. Which could confirm they left her in that mine."

"What this could confirm is that the mine has a second entrance," Jenk said. It was true that Lindsey hadn't been seen leaving the mine, but what about Sophia, Dave, or Decker? They hadn't been seen leaving it, either.

"I didn't get close enough to hear what they were saying," Izzy continued, "but it looks like they're splitting up. Decker's going one way, Malkoff and Sophia are going another."

"I'll follow Sophia," Danny and Lopez unisoned. What a surprise.

"You think you can keep up with Decker?" Jenk asked Izzy.

"Depends," Izzy said. "Am I going to be dragging your sorry ass with me?"

"Fuck you," Jenk said.

"I'll take that as a yes."

Jenk turned to Johnny O. "Run this info back to Commander Koehl." Their radios were down, which sucked, but was probably intentional. Technology was a gift, a pleasant bonus during those times that all the equipment worked as it should. But they always had to be ready to go without, which was why they could navigate using the stars and start a fire with a pair of sticks. Among other things, like resorting to message runners to communicate.

Orlikowski vanished.

"Follow Dave and Sophia," Jenk told Gillman and Lopez. "Can you do that without tripping over your dicks?"

Izzy answered for them, even though they left just as quickly as Orlikowski had. "Lopez, yes. Gillman, no. But stupidity is contagious, so you just upped our side's body count by two."

"Maybe they'll learn something," Jenk said.

"Maybe." Izzy paused. "When the fuck did we become the wise old-timers?"

"I don't know," Jenk said. But he was lying. He'd started growing up the first time one of his teammates died on an op. His recent trip to A-stan that nearly resulted in his own death was just the frosting. This particular cake had already been baking for some time.

"You ever think about crossing over?" Izzy asked. "You know, going to OCS before you get too old?"

Izzy was actually talking about becoming an officer, going to Officer Candidate School. And Jesus, he was serious.

Or was he? It was hard to tell with Zanella.

Especially when he segued directly into a different topic. "So Sophia Ghaffari," he said. "She has the kids drooling. Doesn't do it for *you*, though, huh?"

"She's beautiful," Jenk said. "But . . . I don't know."

"Remote," Izzy agreed. "But I'd do her if she asked. I mean, who'd say no to that? Now Lindsey Fontaine. Totally bangable, right?"

Jenk sighed.

"Yeah, yeah," Izzy said. "You pretend she's just your friend, but I've seen you looking at her like you got a rocket in your pocket. On the Mark Jenkins Wham-Bang scoreboard, with a high-scoring ten being who? Julie Andrews?"

"Fuck you." Jenk laughed. They had to get moving.

But Izzy had more to say. "There's a solid affirmative. And dude, really, no need to be ashamed. Mary Poppins is hot. So Julie's a ten, which means Lindsey's, what? Off the charts with a never-before-seen fifteen? Ow."

"We should probably shut up now," Jenk said. They wanted to find Decker, not have Decker find them.

"And, again, I'll take that as a yes." Izzy was satisfied.

Which was fine with Jenk. Let him have the last word. Let him think he was right. Even though he wasn't.

On Jenk's nonexistent scoreboard, if he'd had such a thing, Lindsey Fontaine would have come in much higher than fifteen.

CHAPTER
SIX

Sophia couldn't believe that she had, in one magnificent screwup, lost their hostage and killed her boss.

Although maybe it was worth it—just for that one moment when Decker was crouching there next to her, concern in his eyes. *Are you sure you're all right?*

Her knee was badly bruised, and it stung where she'd scraped it. And the heels of her hands were pretty raw, too. She'd managed to conceal that from both Decker and Dave. Well, Decker, anyway. It was clear that Dave knew her hands were sore as he took her by the wrist and swiftly pulled her with him into a cave that was barely more than a crevice among the rocks.

"What—"

He shook his head, pressing a finger to his lips, then touching his ear. He'd heard something. Someone was following them.

How many? She mouthed the words.

Dave shook his head. He didn't know. He touched his ear again. He was listening.

There were only a few men on the planet with whom Sophia felt safe enough to occupy the same few square inches of space without discomfort, and Dave Malkoff was one of them.

He'd put on quite a bit of weight since the last time they'd been squeezed in together in a tight spot. It was funny that she hadn't noticed, although come to think of it, he *had* mentioned recently that he'd joined a gym. And he did tend to wear loose T-shirts and baggy shorts.

His arms around her felt warming rather than threatening. She could hear him trying to slow his breathing, feel his heart. It was pounding. They were, no doubt, in even worse trouble than she'd thought.

It was entirely possible that they were surrounded by the SEALs who took Lindsey. Although why, if they wanted to kill them, had they waited until now to do it? It didn't make sense.

Dave loosened his hold on her as he quietly attempted to work the radio.

Sophia tapped his arm.

Why are they following us? she silently asked when he blinked down at her, their faces mere inches apart.

He leaned close enough to speak to her.

"I think they realized we don't have radio contact with the other cells," he said almost noiselessly, his breath warm against her ear.

Okay, now, this was awkward. Or it would have been if it were anyone but her good buddy Dave. She was pressed against him from shoulders to thighs, her left hand pinned between his chest and her breasts. Straightening her arm would mean her hand would dangle near a place she didn't want her hand dangling.

"They know that as soon as we spread the word that Lindsey's gone," he explained, "our team's priority is going to be to get her back. They probably realize that neutralizing us puts them at a serious advantage."

Sophia's wrist was on the verge of breaking, so she shifted her shoulder, moving her arm back around him. Which resulted in her upper body plastered against his, and his mouth not just close to her ear, but pressed against it as he continued, "I'm pretty sure they're—Sorry. I'm . . ."

He pulled back, which was even more awkward because now he was looking directly into her eyes. His lips moved silently. *Sorry.*

For several long seconds something hung in the air between them. Something palpable and aware and warmly sexual—and she wanted to cry, because this was Dave, for heaven's sake.

He was her friend.

Or maybe he wasn't. Maybe he was just another man who wanted to possess her. Maybe he was trying to worm his way into her bed indirectly. Maybe he was even worse than the others who were, at least, up front about what they really wanted.

And now Sophia had the choice of putting her left hand along his shoulder or his waist. Both were equally suggestive and she wanted to do neither.

"Shit," he said. "*Shit.* How could you be afraid of me?"

How did he know? Was she really that transparent? Apparently, yes.

"Look," he said, taking her face between his hands, obviously no longer trying to be silent, no longer caring who overheard them. "You're a very attractive woman. I find you attractive—I'd have to be dead for, like, two years not to, and . . . I guess it's sometimes hard for me to hide it. But please, *please* don't think that I would ever act in any way that would jeopardize our friendship. Think about it, Sophia. I'm one of the few people who can actually guess the kind of abuse you survived in Kazbekistan. I would never take advantage of you. *Never.* I would rather die first."

The look in his eyes was so completely Dave—sincere and honest and desperately true, and Sophia suddenly had the perfect place for her left arm. She wrapped it around him, as she held him tightly. "I'm sorry. I'm so stupid." Stupid and twisted and broken. Would she ever completely trust anyone ever again?

"No, this was my fault," Dave told her, kissing the top of her head. "This is just a . . . a silly game, and I let the idea of winning it matter more than . . ." He shifted, as if to pull her out of the narrow cover that the rocks provided. "Let's surrender. We can just walk out there, hands up. End this right now."

She pulled back to look up at him, shocked that he would even suggest such a thing. And grateful to him, too, at the same time.

"I bet they'll give us chocolate," he said enticingly.

"You'd betray the cause for chocolate?" she asked, straightening her bandana and giving him her haughtiest glare. "Señorita Diablo spits on your shoe." She pretended to do just that, and he laughed.

But his smile quickly faded. "You know, the fact that you're out here at all is . . . I'm so proud of you."

Dave was standing slightly bent over, shoulders hunched, so as to give her as much room as possible. How could she have ever thought he was a threat of any kind? He was *proud* of her. She wanted to cry.

"So okay," he said. "We've lost Lindsey and killed Tom. You don't want chocolate, so what's next on the agenda?"

But now she had to laugh. "That was a very generous use of *we.*"

Dave shrugged. "I'm team leader. You might do it, but I own it. With that in mind, what are *we* doing next?"

"We need to get that message to Alyssa," Sophia told him. "Try the radio again."

He did, holding the headphones to one ear. "Still nothing."

"Okay," Sophia said. "Here's what I think we should do."

Jenkins rematerialized next to Izzy, sending a silent message with a shake of his head.

No one was following them.

This was surreal.

Izzy and Jenk were following Decker, who had gone in circles for quite some time, searching for something that he didn't appear to find.

Deck had backtracked then, heading in the direction that Lopez and Gilligan had traveled as they'd followed Sophia and Dave Malkoff.

It wasn't long before Decker—a former SEAL—had picked up Lopez and Gillman's trail. He was now following them as they followed Sophia and Dave—and as Iz and Jenk followed him.

The Jenkster had clearly been thinking the same thing Izzy was, because he'd used hand signals to communicate that he was going to circle around behind them, make sure *they* weren't being followed.

He'd ninja-ed into human mist and drifted away.

For all of Izzy's disparaging comments, Jenkins was one of the better operators on Team Sixteen. Sure, he was no Irving Zanella, but he was tolerably close.

Jenk, now back, hand-signaled a well-deserved *What the fuck?*

There was no way Izzy was going to be able to explain nonverbally why they'd all stopped moving, so he leaned over and spoke into Jenk's ear.

"Sophia and Malkoff got spooked and ducked into a cave." He quickly sketched out the location of the various other players in this game of Follow the Terrorist Leader. Jenk used his night-vision glasses to locate first Decker and then Lopez and Gillman, and finally the entrance to the cave.

No one had moved, for going on ten minutes now.

"What are they doing in there?" Jenk muttered, his glasses trained on that cave.

"Maybe that's where they've got Lindsey," Izzy suggested. "Or maybe they're having a quickie."

As if on cue, Sophia spoke, her voice ringing in the stillness. "Dave?"

Everyone froze. Izzy used his own NVGs to scan the areas where Decker and the SEALs were hiding. They'd all been nearly invisible before, but now they had completely become one with the rocks and desert scrub around them.

Sophia's voice got louder. "Dave? Oh, my God, *Dave!* Help me, somebody, oh my God!"

It was the oldest trick in the book. Call for help, draw the enemy out into the open, and turn them into hamburger.

But Sophia didn't stay concealed in the rocks. She ran out into the open herself. "Please, I know someone's out there. We need a radio. We need a medic—please, Dave's . . . I think he's having a heart attack."

Izzy looked at Jenk, who looked at Izzy.

"She's shitting us, right?" Izzy asked.

"This is real!" Sophia sobbed. Her weapon dropped with a clatter on the ground and she held her hands up. "I'm unarmed, and I need help! Shoot me if you have to, but damn it, *help* us!"

Jenk shook his head, serious doubt in his eyes. Damn, if *they* were wondering if maybe Dave really was having a medical emergency, then Dumb and Dumber up there closer to the action were probably . . .

Izzy trained his NVGs on Gillman and Lopez. Fucking A, they were coming out of cover. Lopez, usually the smarter one, was leading the way. But Lopez was a hospital corpsman. He was physically unable not to risk his own life when the call went out for a medic. That, plus the promise of gratitude brimming in Sophia's tear-filled eyes had significantly lowered his IQ.

As for Gilligan following him—he had no excuse.

"Yup, she's shitting us," Jenkins announced.

Izzy swung the NVGs over to the cave where, sure enough, Dave Malkoff was very much not in the throes of death. From the other SEALs' and even Decker's position he would be completely hidden, but Izzy and Jenk had a clear, unobstructed view of Dave tippy-toeing through the tulips, making a run for freedom.

Sophia, meanwhile, had collapsed, sobbing, onto her dusty stage.

And here was Lopez, trusting that just because her weapon was five feet away from her, she wasn't going to up and shoot him.

Izzy looked up from his green-tinted view of the world as Jenk rapidly moved forward. What the fuck . . . ?

But then he saw that Decker was moving, too. Moving just to the edge of the clearing, still hidden by the scrub brush, his weapon ready to blow Lopez and Gillman away. Jenk was trying to get close enough to eliminate Decker, but he never had a chance.

Because as Lopez and Gillman, the freaking idiots, approached Sophia, she pulled another weapon—Dave's presumably—smaller and concealable, from beneath her jacket.

And she whaled on the trigger, sweeping the barrel, emptying the magazine.

Jenkie pancaked, good man.

Decker wasn't as fortunate. He was as dead as Lopez and Gillman. Izzy could see the stripes on his sleeves reading bright green in his NVGs—which translated to black as seen by the naked eye. The dude rolled onto his back in exasperation. Sophia had killed him, and the big irony was that she didn't even know it.

"Oh, man," Gilligan said as he sat down next to Lopez. Their role in the game was over, and they both knew that the debrief was going to suck. They were going to have some 'splainin' to do. Lopez would play the medic card and as a result would receive at least a sliver of a pardon. But Gilligan was going to be hammered. Because what could the fishboy use as an excuse for following Lopez? *I'm sorry, sir, but I was afraid if Lopez went out there by himself and saved the day, he'd end up getting a gratitude screw, and I just wanted to make sure I was eligible for the honors, too.*

"Sorry, boys," Sophia said, as she shouldered both weapons.

"Come on, we better move." Good ol' Dave had hung back, waiting for her, instead of running like hell when he'd had the chance.

Sophia scolded him. "You should be long gone."

"Yeah, well, you should be dead." He held out his hand, first to re-claim his weapon and then to help her over the rocky terrain. "Good job, by the way."

"Thank you. I can't say the same to you—what if they'd killed me? They would have caught you right away."

"But they didn't," Dave said evenly. "Shhh. We need to be quiet now."

Izzy followed them. Jenk was behind him again, too.

"Yeah," Sophia scoffed. "Shhh. You don't want to talk about this, be-cause you know I'm right. You should have started running as soon as I started distracting them. I'm telling Tom on you."

"Kind of hard to do," Dave commented, "considering you killed him."

"But now I have more than just losing Lindsey and killing Tom on my résumé," Sophia said. "I've got two SEAL notches on my belt. Well, I would if I were wearing a belt . . ."

Jenk was tugging on his sleeve, so Izzy turned. *Losing Lindsey,* Jenk mouthed. "Is she saying . . . ?"

Izzy put his finger to his lips, not because they might be overheard— no chance of that with the way these two chattered. But Sophia was speak-ing again.

"We should split up," she said. "We need to get that message to Alyssa. Why don't you give me the radio, and I'll go to a higher elevation and—"

"I'm not leaving you alone out here," Dave said.

"Don't be ridiculous," she said.

Dave was climbing, his intention obvious—to try that radio he was clutching like it was his favorite teddy bear.

Sophia scrambled after him.

"Okay," Dave said, "wait, wait . . ." He moved even higher, slipping the headphones over both his ears. "Yes!"

"Finally!" Sophia said.

"Yes," Dave said into the microphone. "Malkoff here, with an important message for Alyssa Locke, over."

"Just broadcast it," Sophia said. "Because if the radio goes out again . . ."

Dave held up his hand in an attempt to quiet her. "Yes," he said. "We'll need to change the plan drastically. The enemy's taken the hostage. Repeat, the SEALs have Lindsey, over."

"Tell 'em it was my fault," Sophia said.

Dave said something to her that Izzy missed, because Jenk was not just tugging on his sleeve, but flat-out hauling him backwards.

"We don't have Lindsey," he told Izzy.

"What? How do you know?"

"Our radio's working now, too," Jenk informed him grimly. "I just spoke to the senior chief. We do *not* have Lindsey."

LOCATION: UNKNOWN
DATE: UNCERTAIN

The putrid smell of blood was making her sick.

Five had vomited, all night long, until her stomach was empty, until there was nothing left to purge, and still she'd heaved and coughed.

The darkness surrounded her, sometimes heavy and hot, sometimes brittle and cold, as she alternately shivered and sweated.

Number Four came, as she often did when he left her alone and the night went on and on and endlessly on, but this time she still had all of her face. This time, she sobbed and begged, "Finish me, please, finish me," as her blood seeped through her fingers, onto the concrete basement floor. "Don't let him take me upstairs!"

"I didn't know," Five tried to tell her, tried to explain.

But then she was gone, and the light was up even brighter, glistening off of Connie Smith's golden hair, flashing off that knife blade as it slashed Five's arm.

And then she was on the floor, *her* blood oozing through her fingers, as Connie Smith advanced.

But Connie's eyes filled with fear before she could move any closer. They filled with sheer terror and shock and hurt—*how could you?* And then they glazed as her life sprayed, warm and wet across Five's face and arms.

Her mouth moved, small and tight above that giant gaping grin. *How could you?*

"I couldn't," Five gasped as her body spasmed with the endless wrenching pain, "let him take you upstairs."

EAST OF SAN DIEGO, CALIFORNIA
THURSDAY NIGHT, DECEMBER 8, 2005

Jenk went Rambo.

Izzy had seen it happen among the SEALs of Team Sixteen only a few times before, and of course one of the times he himself had been the guilty party, but he'd never in his wildest dreams imagined that Marky-Mark would ever do it.

But he did.

He just took off in the same direction that Sophia and Dave had gone, as if Izzy didn't exist. He didn't mention a plan, he didn't even say good-bye. He didn't try to be quiet, he didn't try to conceal himself. He just elephanted up the trail.

Of course, Starsky and Hutch were too busy yakking about their deep innermost feelings to notice an elephant attack, so it probably didn't matter. Except for the fact that there was going to be an unavoidable point of contact.

And what then, Marky-Mark, huh?

Izzy loped after him, staying far enough back to be able to dive for cover, but close enough to watch the action unfold.

Not that there was more than about two seconds of action.

Dave heard Jenk coming just as Jenk shouted, "Hey!" breaking war-gaming rule number three: Never engage the enemy with a shout calling yourself to their attention.

Sophia and Dave both turned, but Sophia managed to mess Dave up. She was too close to him, making it impossible for him to sweep his weapon into firing position.

And Jenk—WTF, M?—just blasted them. Rat-a-tat-tat-tat-tat.

Sophia and Dave looked at each other, looked at the now-black stripes on their sleeves, looked back at Jenk, who was still running toward them, still talking to them.

"Where did you lose Lindsey?"

They looked at each other again, like, who did Jenk think he was, Haley Joel Osment? "We're dead," Dave said.

"Fuck that. Excuse me, ma'am. I heard your radio transmission," Jenk said, "I know your team doesn't have Lindsey. We don't have her, either."

"You don't?" Sophia said.

Dave was sitting down, and he tugged on the bottom edge of Sophia's jacket, trying to get her to sit, too. "The rules state—"

"Fuck the rules," Jenk said. "Excuse me, ma'am. Look, I've come to know Lindsey a little bit over the past week, and this would be something she'd definitely do. Try to escape on her own. But the desert is very different from the streets of LA. There are dangers she may not even know about. Bobcats, coyotes, wild dogs—"

Izzy came closer. "Dude, she has a better chance of being abducted by aliens than attacked by wild dogs or coyotes. They just don't go after people—"

"Yeah, the attacks I've heard about have all been children," Jenk said. "But Lindsey's tiny—"

"She's also a competent, trained police officer—"

"Who is currently unarmed." Whoa. Jenk was seriously, ferociously worried.

"I'm sure she's all right," Dave tried to reassure him. "You know, I shouldn't be telling you anything, but Decker is tracking her. I'm sure he's found her by now."

"Decker's dead," Izzy told them. "Sophia killed him when she iced Lopez and Gillman."

"What?" She was indignant. "I did not."

"Yeah, you did," Jenk confirmed.

She turned her intensity onto Dave. "Did you know . . . ?"

"No." He was shaking his head. "I didn't. Honest."

"We were following him. He didn't find Lindsey," Izzy said.

"Yeah," Jenk said, "but maybe he knows where she is."

"He's dead," Izzy reminded him—like that was going to stop Jenk-bo.

He was already striding back to where they'd seen Decker die. Sophia was following.

"We're dead," Dave reminded her.

"Fuck dead," Sophia said, in a damn good imitation of Jenkins. "I'm helping Mark find Lindsey."

"I tried to pick up her trail," Decker said. "But there was nothing there."

"She's still out there somewhere." Lieutenant MacInnough was convinced of this. The big burly SEAL officer had been in charge of setting up a perimeter and containing the "terrorists" to one area. "She didn't get past my men."

Tom and Commander Koehl had called a halt to the exercise, using the radios they all wore to send a "game over" message, asking everyone to gather down by the parking lot near the Quonset hut—both the living and the dead.

Although, Dave noticed, a rather large percentage of participants on both sides of the exercise had black stripes on their sleeves. Usually, in an exercise like this, it was easy to identify the winners from the losers. Here, however, they were all losers, since the main goal was possession of the hostage.

And no one knew where that hostage was.

Jenkins was a pit bull. He wanted to bring searchlights back to the place where Lindsey had last been seen, to check the area more carefully. He wanted to call in a helicopter and do an infrared search from the air. He wanted to bring in loudspeakers, so they could make an announcement telling Lindsey to come in. He wanted his own head, on a platter, for sending Lindsey out without a radio of her own.

He wanted to do anything besides stand around and talk. Especially not in this faintly party atmosphere, where both mistakes and triumphs were being discussed and—quite often—laughed about.

Sophia was surrounded by her fan club—including the two SEALs she'd killed. Dave knew that, as usual, she was keenly aware of Decker. She kept glancing in his direction. But despite that, Dave could hear her laughing, which still felt like a miracle. He was never going to forget the look on her face when he'd had her penned in, in that cave. He was still kicking himself for putting her in that situation, for forgetting just how terribly vulnerable she was.

She was vulnerable, and fragile, and courageous as hell, simply for getting out of bed each morning. Forget about participating in an exercise like this one.

Dave wandered back over to Jenk, who looked ready to grab one of the weapons and kill them, all over again.

Alyssa Locke beat him over there. She was trying—like everyone else—to reassure Jenk. "I know it's hard for you, coming from the boys-only atmosphere of the SEALs, but Lindsey *can* take care of herself. Tom had her dress like a bar bunny for a reason—so that you and your team-mates would underestimate her."

"I'm not underestimating her," Jenk insisted.

"She's nothing like Tracy," Alyssa pointed out. "If it were Tracy out here, *then* I'd be worried."

"Yeah." Jenk was seriously distracted. The moon had risen, and he was looking out at the variety of cars and trucks in the parking lot. "Excuse me, ma'am, I'm sorry, do you know—did Lindsey drive here?"

"I'm not sure," Alyssa said.

"Yeah, she did," Dave volunteered. "When we first got here, she told me about stopping for dinner, and how this cop asked to see her driver's license because he thought she'd stolen her mother's car and . . ."

Jenk was gone.

He was running down the rows of cars. Dave followed, curious. Izzy was right behind him.

"What's he up to now?" Izzy asked.

"I think he's checking to see if Lindsey's car is still here," Dave told him.

"Yo, she drives a white hybrid," Izzy shouted.

"I know," Jenk shouted back. "It's not here. Throw me your keys."

Izzy fished in his pocket, tossed a key ring over to him.

"What's he doing?" It was Dave's turn to ask as he watched Jenk open-ing the passenger-side door of a truck.

"I don't know," Izzy admitted. "But that's my ride. We drove down here together. Maybe he's getting something from his bag."

As they got closer, they could see that Jenk had indeed gotten something—his cell phone. He held it to his ear, pointing to a parking space in the next row over, empty in the midst of all those vehicles.

"You don't know she was parked there," Izzy said.

"Were you parked almost directly across from Zanella?" Jenk said into his phone.

Was he talking to . . . ?

"She was parked there," Jenk announced.

"Looks like he found her," Izzy said. "Did you find her?" he asked Jenk who nodded. Yes. "Jenk found her," he shouted—words to draw a crowd.

Jenk was laughing at whatever Lindsey was telling him, his relief making him lean against the truck. He wiped the sweat from his face with his free hand. "Jesus, you scared the crap out of me. Yeah . . . Yeah, okay. I will. I'm . . . glad you're safe." He hung up his phone. "Lindsey's at the Ladybug Lounge," he told them. "She wants to know what's taking us so long."

"She got past us?" Some of the SEALs still couldn't believe it. "No way."

Both Commander Koehl and Tom Paoletti had come over.

"About time someone checked the parking lot," Tom said to the commander.

"It was one of mine," Koehl pointed out. "Good job, Jenkins."

"Yeah, you guys lost, and you know it," Tom scoffed.

"Your team lost, too."

"Yup." Tom smiled happily. "Losing provides such good life lessons, don't you think, Lew?"

"Absolutely, Tom."

Jenk was staring at them both, his mouth open. He finally found his voice. "You set this up? You knew where Lindsey was this whole time?"

"I didn't know she was at the Bug. Did you?" Tom asked Koehl, who shook his head, no. "That's pretty impressive. She's definitely the winner here." He shot a pointed look at Koehl. "*She's* one of *mine.*"

Jenk interrupted, raising his voice so everyone could hear him. "Lindsey says if we can get over to the Bug in the next forty minutes, the first round's on Tommy and Commander Koehl."

"Oh, really?" Tom said.

Jenkins shrugged expansively. "Sorry, sirs. I'm just reporting what she said to me."

Tom exchanged a glance with the commander. Apparently words weren't needed between the two COs of SEAL Team Sixteen, one past, one present. Koehl nodded, and Tom said, "Well then, what's everyone still standing around here for?"

CHAPTER SEVEN

Mark Jenkins must've been on his cell phone for the entire drive over to the Ladybug Lounge.

Lindsey knew this because the Troubleshooters and the SEALs from Team Sixteen came into the bar in one huge, massively organized group that could only be Jenk's doing. They all dropped to their knees on the grungy wood floor, kowtowing before her.

Sam Starrett and Alyssa Locke. Decker, Nash, and Tess. The SEALs' scary-looking senior chief. The team's even scarier XO, Jazz Jacquette. Enlisted and officers alike—Nilsson, Muldoon, MacInnough, and many more whose names she couldn't remember. They were all grinning at her.

Tom Paoletti and Commander Koehl didn't get down on the floor, but they did come over to shake her hand.

"Excellent job," Tom said. "I have to admit, you exceeded my expectations by about a thousand percent."

Lindsey narrowed her eyes at him. "So what are you saying, boss? You didn't believe me? You thought I was maybe exaggerating?"

"Yeah," he admitted. "It's one thing to have E&E experience. It's another thing entirely to evade personnel who have the kind of training and skill our people have. Larry Decker tried to track you, Linds—he found no trail. None. At all."

"I should hope not," Lindsey said. She lifted her glass. "To Grandpa Henry, who taught me everything I know. Well, almost everything."

There was much laughter at that, but then everyone in the room lifted their glasses—at least those who'd managed to get their drink orders filled. "To Grandpa Henry!"

Jenkins was standing to Tom's left smiling his ass off at her, with Izzy behind him. This was what it must've felt like to be Tracy Shapiro. Always surrounded by attractive, attentive men, at least one of whom found her . . . What was that quaint expression? *Bangable.*

"I want you to do a debrief with my men," Commander Koehl told her. It was amazing how different his delivery was from Tom's. Tom made orders sound like requests. Koehl made requests sound like orders.

Straightlaced, Jenk had called him. Stuffy. Formal. Old-fashioned. But *day*-am, Skippy. His jawline was a work of art.

"I'm sure we can arrange that, sir," Lindsey told Koehl.

"With all due respect, sir, I can't believe you were in on this," Jenk accused the commander.

"It was Paoletti's idea," Koehl admitted with a far-too-fleeting smile. "Create a lose/lose scenario. Make it a total Charlie Foxtrot. Get Admiral Tucker's grudge match out of the way, so we can get down to some real training."

Apparently, this was a night of surprises for Jenk. "We're doing additional training with Tommy's Troubleshooters?" he asked his commanding officer.

"Isn't it obvious we need it?" Koehl's cell phone was ringing, and he glanced at it. "Excuse me. Ma'am." He nodded at Lindsey as he escaped to find a quiet corner to take his call.

"We haven't discussed a timetable yet," Tom said, "but as much as we'd like for it to happen ASAP, it's probably not going to happen until early next year." He, too, backed away. "I'm proud you're on my team," he told Lindsey.

"Thank you, sir," she said.

Tom grabbed Izzy by the arm, pulling the SEAL with him. "Got a minute, Zanella?"

Her boss was as subtle as a two-by-four to the face. It was embarrassingly obvious that he knew that Lindsey wanted some one-on-one time with Jenk—not easy in a crowded bar where she'd been crowned Queen for a Day.

Still, Jenk didn't seem to notice. Or if he did, it didn't frighten him. He put his bottle of beer down and slipped onto the barstool next to her. "So, wow."

"Yeah," Lindsey said. "Tom's pretty smart, isn't he? This was all his idea."

"The hostage vanishes, and no one wins." Jenkins laughed. It was funny, he looked far less tired now that the exercise was over, despite the hours spent running and hiding. She knew from experience that hiding took up an enormous amount of energy. She, herself, was going to sleep very well tonight. "It's brilliant."

"When Tom spoke to me about it," Lindsey admitted, "he was very concerned for your morale—you know, of Team Sixteen's. I think he was afraid if you won, some of you would have a mixed reaction to having beaten him, since he's your former commander. He's very aware that many of the guys in Sixteen are still extremely loyal to him. And he's equally aware that the jury's still out on Koehl."

"Yeah." Jenk took a sip of his beer, and the movement of his arm made his T-shirt tighten across his chest. He had a streak of dirt on his sleeve and his arm. In fact, he looked as if a cloud of dust would shake free from his clothes if he stood in front of a fan. "Koehl's not . . . He's respected. He's a solid leader, no one disputes that. It's just . . ."

"He's not Tom," Lindsey finished for him, and he smiled as he met her eyes.

Lindsey's heart flipped. God help her.

"Yeah, he's very much not Tommy," he admitted, gazing down at his beer, angling the bottle slightly so he could see the label. Was he as freaked out by the spark from that brief eye contact as she was? Probably not, because he looked back at her almost right away. "He's a different kind of leader. He's old-school. More regular Navy. All *yes sir* and *aye, aye sir* all the time. Tommy, on the other hand, was a cookout CO. You know, always inviting the team—officers and enlisted—over to his house for burgers and beer."

Lindsey had to laugh as she polished off the last of her wine. "He does love a good party." She risked another glance back at Jenk. He was watching her, so she pretended to be fascinated by the dregs in the bottom of her glass.

"I miss him." Jenk sighed. "We all do. Still, it could be worse."

He began making patterns on the bar with the condensation from his bottle, which meant that Lindsey could look at him without risk of meltdown.

"Think about how hard it must be for Lew Koehl," she pointed out. "Trying to fill Tom's shoes? And can you imagine how awful it would have been for Lew if he lost this exercise—if Tom's new team had beaten him? Nightmare."

Jenk rolled his eyes. "And way to trigger discord among the men. Team Sixteen doesn't need that—it's been a hard enough year."

"So Tom sets it up so that everyone loses in glorious unison. SEAL

Team Sixteen and TS Inc are in the exact same boat—no one's officially better than anyone else."

"Except for you," Jenk pointed out, as the bartender set a fresh glass of wine in front of her.

"That," Lindsey said, "is a given. I won our bet, by the way."

"No, you didn't," he said. "TS Inc didn't win."

She could handle eye contact when self-righteousness was involved. "No, but the bet wasn't about whether we won, it was about whether Team Sixteen lost."

"Oh, shit," he said, as realization dawned. But then he added, "But we're going to be doing more training together."

"Yeah, I heard Tom say that. Maybe in January." Lindsey rested her chin in her hand, elbow on the bar. "What are you suggesting? Double or nothing? If I win again, you quit the Navy and become our new reception-ist?"

Jenk laughed. "Yeah, I don't think so."

"Still, if I have to wait until January for the next exercise . . ."

"What do I get?" he asked. "If I win?"

And okay. The eye contact was no longer self-righteous. It was defi-nitely getting warm in there.

"Tracy gets to stay forever," Lindsey said, before she realized that using the T-word was probably a mood-killer. And indeed. The sizzle, whether real or imagined, was instantly DOA. But as long as she'd brought up the topic . . . "Although there's a good chance she won't want to." She braced herself for his disappointment. "Her ex is in town tonight. He came in early."

"Yeah, I heard." Jenk laughed his disbelief. "So you knew about this, too, huh? What, was I the last to know?"

"I spent the past week with her," Lindsey pointed out.

"You could have told me before the exercise," he countered.

"Yeah," she said. "I could've. But I didn't. Shoot me. Talking to you about Tracy is not on my list of fun things to do."

Well, that shut him up.

Desperate to change the subject, Lindsey caught the bartender's eye in the mirror. "Aren't you supposed to see if I have enough money in my wallet before you give me more wine?" She turned back to Jenk. "I've also been here for a while. If I'm going to drive home . . ."

"I'll drive you home," he said.

And there it was again. That glint of something extra in Jenk's eyes. This time it definitely wasn't a reflection of the setting sun.

It probably meant that Lindsey was Jenk's Plan B. She tried to get indignant or even upset about that, but she just couldn't.

"Thank you," she said instead. "I might take you up on that." Like she would actually turn him down.

"The wine's from the commander," the bartender told her on his way past, with a toss of his head toward the SEAL CO, who was at the end of the bar.

Well, goodness gracious. "Lew Koehl bought me a drink," Lindsey mused.

"He's buying a round for everyone."

"Thanks a million for completely killing that little fantasy. You know, he might be old-school and old-fashioned, but he's so . . . what's the word I'm looking for here . . . ? Hmm . . . Oh, I know. Totally *bangable*."

Jenk knew he was in trouble. Lindsey could see his confusion as he tried to make sense of what she was saying. As she watched, he recognized first that bangable was an Izzy-word. He tried to access memories of a conversation with both Lindsey and Izzy—and failed.

Lindsey took a sip of her wine. Ooh, lovely. It was far more expensive than her first few glasses. "You know, *Marky-Mark*, on the Lindsey Fontaine Wham-Bang Scoreboard, Lew Koehl rates a solid eleven."

"Oh, fuck," Jenkins said, then quickly apologized. "God, I'm sorry."

"For your language?" she asked. "Or for your hideous taste in friends?"

"Both?" he asked. The expression on his face quickly morphed into wonder. "You were actually out there, close enough to overhear us?"

"Baby-cakes, I was close enough to brush the dust from your clothes," Lindsey told him as she did just that. It was one thing to admire his muscles from afar, another entirely to touch him. His skin was warm, his arm solid. And yes, there were worse things in life than being the Plan B for someone like Mark Jenkins.

There'd be no rude surprises. Just a week, maybe two, of laughter and sex as he rebounded from his disappointment with Tracy. After a while, he'd lose interest. And he'd either just drift away or . . . No, Jenk wouldn't drift. He'd sit down with her. He'd hold her hand and gently explain that the timing just wasn't right, that he had to focus on his career or his car or his microbrewery or his new girlfriend, although he probably wouldn't mention that last one.

But it would be okay because she knew it was coming. Even now, before it started.

"That's . . . really amazing," he said.

"You weren't looking for me," Lindsey said, taking her hand back, even though she knew he wanted her to keep it there. He did, after all, find her bangable, and Tracy had left the playing field. "No one was looking for me, out there all by myself. That was the biggest failure of the op, in my opinion. Both sides assumed that I'd be part of a group—either a prisoner of the terrorists, or being rescued by the SEALs. One person, particularly one my size, is a whole lot harder to find and track."

"I did finally figure it out," he told her, and oh, there was double meaning in that, since he moved his boot over to the footrest on her stool, which made his knee touch her leg. Just lightly. Just enough.

"Yeah, but by then I was long gone." As far as hidden messages went, that was a complete lie, since she was sitting right here. Still, it was probably good to let him wonder.

"Hey, gorgeous." Izzy slid onto the stool next to Jenk, leaning around him to smile at Lindsey.

"I am sorry," Jenk said to Lindsey. "About . . . you know."

"Your degrading objectification of the women that you work with?" Lindsey shrugged. "It could be worse. I could've rated lower than Julie Andrews."

"Uh-oh," Izzy said.

"Maybe," Lindsey said to Jenk, amazed at her daring even as the words were coming out of her mouth, as she reached out once again, this time to brush some dirt from the front of his shirt, "if I give it some thought, I'll come up with a way you can make it up to me."

Izzy knew it was probably best to remain absolutely silent as Lindsey slid down off her barstool.

He was intending to wait until she was nearly all the way across the room, way out of earshot and over by the door to the women's head, before he turned to Jenkins and said, *Dude, you are so getting laid tonight.*

And Jenkins wouldn't disagree. He wouldn't deny it. He wouldn't even try to pretend that he wasn't thinking the exact same thought. How could he possibly? Lindsey couldn't have been any more clear if she'd taken a bullhorn and shouted directly into Mark's ear.

After they high-fived, then Izzy would say, *Does this mean I can have Tracy?*

Okay, wait. That was probably not the best way to put it. And yeah, sure, the going consensus was that Tracy was going to be packing her desk and heading back East, which was a bummer for Marky-Mark since he'd wanted a fifty-year relationship. Izzy, however, only wanted forty minutes in a broom closet, and he hadn't yet given up hope of a tryst with Miss Born-to-be-Bad.

But Jenk turned to Izzy first. "I think she's had too much to drink."

Oh no. No, no. "M., she's fine."

"Yeah, I don't think so."

"What, Lindsey has to be shit-faced to hit on you?" Izzy couldn't believe this. "Jenkins, read my lips. She's a sure thing. Celebrate this. Don't turn it into a problem."

"She's definitely feeling the alcohol."

"Yeah," Izzy said. "That's why people drink. To feel the alcohol. To facilitate getting laid."

Jenkins was shaking his head. But he was also sneaking looks over to where Lindsey had stopped to talk to a table filled with SEAL officers, past and present. "What about Tracy?"

"What about Tracy?" Izzy countered.

Jenk glanced at him. "Eventually she's going to figure out that Lyle is a lying piece of shit."

"Eventually the polar ice caps will melt. You gonna be celibate until *that* happens, too?"

"Don't be stupid," Jenk scoffed.

"Said the man who's getting ready to be crowned the stupid king," Izzy pointed out.

"If I'm so in love with her," Jenk mused, the *her* in question being Tracy, "why am I even thinking about going home with another woman?"

"Because you're not a fool," Izzy said. "Yeah, maybe pining away for her is romantic, but it's also fucking stupid. What do you think *she's* doing tonight?"

Jenk shook his head.

"She's seeing her ex tonight, right?" Izzy pressed him. "Right?"

"Right," Jenk said. "But—"

"Fuck but," Izzy said. "She's definitely seeing this guy—and I mean that in the how could she miss seeing him when he's right on top of her, going, *oh baby, yes baby, come now baby, I'm right behind you, I missed you sooo much . . .*"

"Thank you for that image," Jenk said.

"You know," Izzy mused, "I had a girlfriend where the sex after we broke up was a hundred times better than it was when we were officially seeing each other. Renee. She was into some na-a-a-sty shit." She still called him every now and then, although he'd learned—the hard way—to just say no. But oh, Renee, Renee . . .

Except this tangent, lovely as it was, wasn't helping Jenk who, although he wouldn't admit it, was looking for a good excuse or a solid rationalization so he could go home tonight with Lindsey.

"Look," Izzy said. "Maybe Tracy's the one. And in a couple months when she's finally done having breakup sex with what's-his-name—"

"Lyle."

"Right. Maybe after she's dumped Lyle for good, you guys'll hook up, and it'll be great. And birds will sing and flowers will bloom and you'll marry her, tra la, tra la, and live happily ever after—which, I should point out, includes never, ever having another encounter with a gorgeous, smart, funny, sexy-as-shit woman who wants to rock your world for a night or two, no strings." And that one clearly hit home, so Izzy added another "Never, ever again," for good measure. Unless, of course, Jenk was a cheating bastard like Knox, who was already messing around on his third wife.

Jenk stopped pretending that he wasn't watching Lindsey as she laughed at something Alyssa said. A few more brews, and he'd surely give in. Izzy ordered him another.

"You think that's really what Lindsey wants?" Jenk asked. "No strings?" He frowned slightly, as if he suddenly had an issue with the concept. Or as if he were maybe realizing that a couple of nights wasn't going to be enough to cross everything off his "Want To Do" list, as far as Lindsey was concerned.

"I'm good with body language, and I'm virtually certain that she wants tonight." Izzy stood up. "But there's this really cool new way to find out what other people are thinking," he told Eminem. "You go up to them, and you talk to them. It works almost every time."

Dinner was exquisite.

Tracy had ordered the veal. Lyle had ordered a three-hundred-dollar bottle of wine, most of which she'd single-handedly killed.

Dessert was something called Double Death by Chocolate—mousse in a chocolate-encrusted pyramid, with a cookie crust that was beyond divine.

The entire meal probably cost as much as one month's rent.

For her, not for Lyle, who still lived in Manhattan.

Tracy dabbed at her lips with the fancy cloth napkin. She'd agreed to have dinner with him on the condition that they not speak—at all—about his hopes for a reconciliation until after dessert.

It hadn't left much to discuss, but Lyle could fill hours talking about himself, about his work.

He didn't used to be such a pompous ass.

Well, okay, maybe he did. He'd always loved to hear himself talk. And he'd always considered himself—probably correctly—to be the smartest man in any room. But at least, back when they'd first met, he'd been able to laugh about it.

He'd still been spending his Wednesday evenings doing pro bono work back then, before his ambition to make partner became the driving force behind every breath he took.

He now cleared his throat. Tracy hated the self-important way he did that, signaling a change of subject. But it was time. It was now officially after dessert, and Lyle was getting down to business.

"I want you to come back home. I *need* you to come back, Tracy."

She put down her napkin. "Why would I want to do that?"

"Because you love me," he told her.

Tracy just shook her head, wishing she hadn't had all that wine. "It's not that simple," she insisted. "You know, I've been seeing someone."

That was not quite true, although there had been that night when Weeble—Mark—had kissed her. She'd actually had another man's tongue in her mouth, which was a first for her.

Lyle nodded gravely as if he actually believed her. "And of course there's your job. Your mother told me you've found work that you like? For some kind of company that provides . . . security guards, is it?"

Trust Lyle to make it sound as if she worked dispatch for Rent-a-Cop. And yet he'd always insisted that she have a job, no doubt afraid that if she stayed home all day, she'd start sleeping with the building superintendent. *No, Lyle, it's you who screws everything that moves.* Tracy just flirted. Always and endlessly. She'd gotten so good at it, she hardly knew she was doing it. But she was—passive-aggressively getting back at Lyle for his indiscretions.

"Troubleshooters Incorporated provides personal protection. Personal security. With a focus on counterterrorism. Our assignments take us worldwide. We save lives." Not that the receptionist would do much travel or lifesaving. But still. And now was probably not the time to admit that she was on the verge of being fired.

If she was going back to Lyle, he was going to have to work for it.

"I can see that it's going to take more than promises," he told her, "to convince you—"

"Frankly," Tracy said, "the only thing I'm convinced of, is that if I do come back to New York, it will only be a matter of time before you're fucking your newest paralegal in our bed."

The waiter was right there, refilling their glasses with Tunisian well water, or whatever it was that Lyle drank these days, but he didn't so much as blink.

Lyle wasn't happy about either her language or her lack of discretion—wasn't that hysterical—and he waited until the man had glided away before he spoke. "I give you my word. That won't happen again."

She laughed. "And I'm just supposed to believe you? Last time when you promised, that was just a promise. But now, you've given me your *word* so—"

"I'm giving you more than my word," he told her, reaching into his inside jacket pocket for . . . A jeweler's box. Dear God, had this actually worked? He pushed it across the table. "Tracy, we're so good together. My life doesn't work without you. Marry me."

Had he really just said . . . ? Tracy opened the box, and sure enough, it held a ring with a diamond the size of a small planet.

"I know I'm not perfect," he told her, with, God, real tears in his eyes. "I'll never be perfect. But I love you, and I know we can make this work."

We can make this work. Not, *With a great deal of restraint and therapy and hard work to keep from giving in to constant temptation, I can change and not be a cheating son of a bitch who can't keep his pants zipped.*

But when she saw the inscription engraved on the inside of the ring, *Tracy and Lyle forever,* she found herself nodding, even as she started to cry. This was what she'd wanted for so many years.

It was too late, it was too late . . . How could it be too late? This *was* what she'd wanted. She missed living in New York in Lyle's expensive condo with doormen who knew her name. *How are you today, Miss Shapiro?* She missed dining at expensive restaurants like this one.

And she missed being part of a *we.* God, but she hated living alone.

She must've said yes. Had she really said yes? Because he ordered champagne, a bottle to go, and the check, and his car.

And he kissed her as they waited outside, as only Lyle could kiss her, and she was both laughing and crying as he pulled her with him into the backseat.

He popped the cork right there, telling his driver to get them to the Hotel del Coronado as quickly as possible, and they drank directly from the bottle.

Of course, Lyle being Lyle, he couldn't wait even twenty minutes, and he pulled her so that she was straddling him as she kissed him, never mind the driver watching in the rearview mirror before he closed the privacy partition.

One hand fumbled with his pants, the other reached for the ceiling control to the radio. Loud music came on, then he used both hands to free himself, to slip her panties down her legs. God, God, God, it had been too long.

He thrust, hard, into her, and God help her, but it felt so good.

Lyle may have been a rat-bastard, but he'd become, very rapidly after they'd first hooked up, an exquisite lover, even while delivering a quickie in the backseat of a car.

He remembered just where to touch her to set her on fire, and when he laughed at her response, she knew she'd given away the fact that she hadn't had sex in ages, that she hadn't been with anyone else since she'd packed her bags and left him.

"Ah, Tracy," he breathed, his voice rough.

And she forgot about the driver, forgot about the traffic, forgot about the fact that a diamond ring didn't mean a damned thing—that it wasn't a magic talisman that would keep him either honest or true.

Lindsey had caught the attention of a particularly persistent jarhead.

Jenk just sat at the bar, afraid to jump in and come to her rescue.

Some women didn't like being rescued, and he knew for a fact that Lindsey could take care of herself.

As he watched, she spoke to the man—a Marine corporal—and the smile and nod she gave him as she moved away was clearly a dismissal. Yet still he followed her across the Ladybug's little dance floor, clearly smitten.

He stopped her with a hand on her arm. He was a little too drunk and a little too rough, and Jenk found himself on his feet and halfway across the room before he even knew he was moving.

Of course, Lindsey chose that exact moment to look over at him and . . . "Here's my boyfriend now," she said, turning and pointing to . . . Jenk? "Hi, honey."

"Hi," he said, closing those last few steps between them. "Honey."

She slipped her arm around his waist, which left him with his arm around her shoulder, his hand against the smoothness of her bare shoulder. Eee Gods. She snuggled even closer. "Mark, Frank, Frank, Mark," she introduced them, and Jenk found himself shaking the hand of one very disappointed Marine.

"You're a very lucky man," Frank-the-Marine told Jenk with the super-seriousness of the seriously inebriated. "I, too, have a total thing for hot Asian chicks." He lowered his voice conspiratorially. "LYFMs, you know?"

The son of a bitch wasn't kidding. He wasn't making a joke—an offensive one at that. He was dead serious, and he'd just called Lindsey . . .

"Hey, honey," Jenk asked her. "You want I should beat the crap out of this SWDW for you?"

She got the beginning. "Stupid, white . . . ?"

"Dickless wonder," he finished for her, "which is what he'll be when I send him crawling out of here, crying for his mommy."

Frank wasn't impressed. In fact, he bristled. "I'm not afraid of you, junior."

Oh, no he didn't. Dude was batting a thousand. Jenk could see from Lindsey's face that she expected him to lose it.

Instead, he smiled at her. "Honey, I'm thinking I'll just kill him instead. Do you know, did I already use up my monthly allotment of Marines?"

"Oh," she said. "Yeah, I think, um . . ."

"See," Jenk told Frank, "the military spends so much money training Navy SEALs, we're each given a certain number of, well, they're called Transgression Points."

"You're a Navy SEAL?" Frank was looking a lot less belligerent at that newsflash.

"We get twenty points a month. They're good for everything from running red lights, or getting faced and busting up a bar, to murder—well, manslaughter, because you really can't plan to do it. Well, you can, but . . . Anyway. Twenty points works out to be either two civilians or five Marines. Right? Because Marines are, you know, subhuman?"

"I think you already got your five for December," Lindsey played along beautifully.

"Aw, shit. Already?" Jenk complained.

She nodded, making the most perfect *too bad* face. "The thing at the mall. With the truck?"

It was all he could do not to kiss her, she was that good. "Damn," he said instead. "That's right. I got four in one stomp of the gas pedal. Bad move. And then number five was that other corporal who offended you with that Amy Tan joke."

"You're a Navy SEAL?" Frank asked again.

"Yeah," Jenk said. "But hang on, okay? Don't go anywhere. My friend Izzy's here somewhere. He's a SEAL, too. Maybe he hasn't killed all his December Marines. He probably wouldn't mind killing you for me, considering you called my fiancée a little. Yellow. Fucking. Machine." His last words were through clenched teeth, and Frank actually blanched.

"I'm, like, so not yellow," Lindsey said, a pitch-perfect imitation of a

Valley Girl. "I mean, look at my arms. Yellow? I don't *think* so. I don't know which of the Western explorers is to blame—Marco Polo or what*ever*—but the genius who came up with *yellow*? Seriously color-blind?"

Frank was gone. Out the door. It was going to be a long time before he came back to the Bug.

"I guess you don't have a problem with *little*," Jenk noted.

She laughed, but he could tell she was still pretty pissed off. "I'm sorry about that. Thank you, though, for not killing him and getting yourself in trouble."

"Does that happen a lot?" he asked.

"Well," Lindsey said, "I get *hot Asian chicked* more often than *LYFM'd*. I hear *that* ugliness more near the military base."

He put both arms around her. "I feel like I need to apologize for the entire human race."

"I accept your apology," she said, "but you're not responsible for the Franks of the world. And I do appreciate your nonviolent approach. I once dated this guy, in college, and I'm pretty sure the only reason he went out with me was because he liked getting into fights."

She had her arms around his waist, almost as if they were slow dancing. Man, but it felt good. "I seriously doubt that was the only reason he dated you."

"Spoken like a true gentleman." Amusement danced in her eyes as she stood on her toes and kissed him. On the nose. "I've been wanting to do that for about a week now."

"Thanks," he said, like an idiot. He should have kissed her back—a real kiss. Instead he just stood there, smiling down at her, caught by the sparkle in her eyes. "You want another drink?" he asked. "Or . . . ?"

"I think I'm ready to go," Lindsey told him. "And you don't need to drive me. I'm fine."

She pulled away from him heading toward the bar where she'd left her jacket, and Jenk knew that this was the moment of truth. The next words out of his mouth were going to define exactly how this evening ended. But as he caught her hand and tugged her back to him, as he looked into Lindsey's eyes, he had to smile. Define exactly? Probably not. Despite Izzy's pronouncement, this woman was not a sure thing. She could never be that predictable or mundane.

So he did it. He said it. "In that case, maybe you could drive *me* home." He'd linked their fingers together, and she now looked down at their hands.

"That depends," she said. "Are you going to invite me up to see your collection of *Star Wars* action figures?"

"How did you know—" The words were out of his mouth before he realized that she hadn't known anything. She was, in fact, joking.

Her smile was incredible. "Do you *seriously* have a—"

"No," he said, but it was too late.

"You do." Lindsey's laughter wound around him as she pulled her hand free. "Oh, my God, you're a *Star Wars* nerd."

Sometimes complete honesty was the best approach. "Yes," he said. "Yes, I am. Is that a problem for you?"

"Jar Jar Binks," she said. "Thumbs up or down?"

"Down," he scoffed. "Give me a break. Although I do have a mint Jar Jar, still in the original packaging. It's in storage, though. My entire collection is. Except maybe . . . I think I've got a Darth Vader and an X-wing Fighter or two somewhere in my apartment, but it might take me a while to find them."

"I could help you look," she said, which made his stomach do a slow somersault.

Yeah, he'd definitely gone into free fall. "I'd like that. Very much."

Her smile was swift and beautiful. "Then, yes. I'd love to drive you home."

And there he stood, just smiling foolishly back at her. Except, Jesus, there was more conversation needed. Words that had to be said, even though he had no idea how to broach the topic. God forbid he say anything that would make her change her mind. Although not being completely honest with her would be wrong.

She beat him to it, answering his question of how best to broach the topic. Point-blank, apparently, worked really well.

"That *was* just pickup-joint code, right?" Lindsey asked him. "I did just say yes to you asking me if I wanted to spend the night with you?"

"Yeah," Jenk said, loving her straightforwardness. Man, she was amazing. "Is that what you thought you were saying yes to? Because it doesn't have to be. It could just be a ride home. If that's what you want."

She was just standing there, gazing at him, heat in her bottomless-pit brown eyes. Finally, she spoke. "I like you."

Okay. "Yeah," he said. "I thought maybe you did and . . . I like you, too. Very much."

"I'm not good at this," she told him. "You know, the game, so . . . I just wanted to verify that your invitation was, um . . ."

"It was," he said. "But it doesn't have to be." Shit, why did he keep saying that?

She was wondering the same thing. "Is that code for something else that I should know about—"

"No," he said. "It's not."

Lindsey nodded. "Neither of us are particularly in the right place for a relationship. I'm not. Of course I'm never . . ." She waved away whatever it was she'd been about to say. "But right now, in particular, it's not . . . I've got to bottom line it for you, Mark. I'm not looking for anything heavy."

"That's good information," he said. "I mean, as long as we're on the same page, we should be okay. Right?"

"Yeah," she said. "I figured, you were . . . Well, considering you have a thing for Tracy . . ."

"Yeah," Jenk said. "About that. It's not so much of a thing right now." Considering she was probably with Lyle right this very moment.

Lindsey was looking at him, sympathy in her eyes.

Uh-oh. Was this . . . ?

Jenk picked up her jacket, handed it to her. Finished off the last of his beer, and went point-blank. Why not? If she could do it, he could, too. "So is this, you know, you and me, tonight? Is this like a . . ." He wasn't as good at brutal honesty as she was and he had to clear his throat first. But he spit it out because he had to know. "Pity hookup?"

Lindsey laughed—a mixture of surprise and genuine amusement. "Yes," she said, clearly shitting him. "Because I look at you, and I think, what a shame. He's funny, he smart, he's unbelievably ripped and drop-dead handsome, with the prettiest eyes and these adorable freckles that just make me want to bite his nose. And oh, yeah, he's a Navy SEAL. I feel so, *so* sorry for him."

Okay, now he was blushing. Did she really think . . . ?

Lindsey took her car keys from her pocket, dangling the ring from her index finger, holding it out for him. "Since we're going to your place, you want to drive?"

LOCATION: UNCERTAIN
DATE: UNKNOWN

Number Five remembered her final day of life with remarkable clarity.

She relived it often, sometimes even dreaming about it at night—a temporary escape from the darkness and fear.

Beth—she'd been Beth back then. Beth had slept late, waking at eleven, lazing for another half hour in her bed, in the tiny bedroom that she'd hated since her mother moved into this house nearly twelve years ago, when Beth was fourteen.

She was feeling sorry for herself because John had come into the bar the night before with his new girlfriend. Beth had had to serve them both, which had sucked. She'd started pounding back the gin and tonics herself, and had gotten so drunk she'd ended up leaving her car in the lot. She'd caught a ride home with George Henderson who was cute but married. He'd wanted sex, but she'd been smart enough to say no.

She had let him steal a few kisses, and she was pretty sure he'd had his hand up her shirt at one point. But she'd kept her jeans on.

She finally got out of bed to find some coffee to help her headache, going into the kitchen in her T-shirt and panties, fuzzy slippers on her feet. Her mother had left a note on the kitchen counter. *Make yourself useful*, with a whole list of chores that needed to be done.

Mow the lawn. Yeah. Snowball's chance, Ma.

She made herself some toast to eat with the coffee, then wandered out to the mailbox to get the mail, hoping for a magazine to leaf through.

She'd gotten a far bigger prize. A letter from Bobby, from Iraq. It wasn't more than a few lines, scrawled on a ratty piece of paper, but her brother had sent her a check for a hundred dollars. He'd realized he'd missed her birthday, he wrote. He knew she'd moved back in with Ma, who was garnishing her paychecks to help pay for her car insurance, rent, and groceries while she was living there. This money he'd sent was for Beth to buy something nice for herself.

She'd showered and quickly gotten dressed. Her hair was maintenance free—it would dry by the time she drove over to the mall, except . . . shoot.

Her car was still over at the Lamplight Inn.

Beth called Jenn and Lisa and even Carleen, who was, on a usual day, the last person she'd call for a ride anywhere. But no one was home.

She'd almost called George, who worked over at the Meijers. She had no doubt whatsoever that he'd drive right over and take her wherever she wanted to go.

Instead, she walked—intending to hitchhike when she hit the state road. Mostly because she knew word would get back to her mother. Lord knows she had to give her *some*thing to bitch about. Besides, that is, Beth's failure to mow the lawn and live like a saint and settle for marriage to boring Mitch Jeffers and shave her legs without making a mess in the bathroom.

Beth remembered the heat of the sun on her shoulders as she walked. She remembered the clear blue of the sky, the freshness of the late-spring air.

She remembered the crunch of the ground beneath her feet. The hum of the cars that passed—all going in the wrong direction.

She remembered the silence then as the traffic faded away. The rustle of the breeze in the grass, the buzz of locusts and crickets in the growing heat.

She remembered another car passing, again in the wrong direction. But it slowed.

She turned to watch it. A blue Impala, circa the time of the Pilgrims. Still, it wasn't coughing out black clouds of smoke the way her dying Escort did.

The driver braked to a stop, then did a smooth three-point turn right in the road. And came back toward her.

Well, wasn't that right neighborly?

She could tell from looking through the windshield that the driver was a man. Not a big surprise.

It wasn't until he stopped alongside her and lowered the passenger window, leaning across that big bench seat to talk to her that she saw he wasn't just a man. He was a very well-dressed man.

He wore a business suit and tie, unlike most of the men who lived and worked in this county.

He had dark hair and he wore sunglasses that hid his eyes, but his smile was dazzling. "Need a ride?"

"Just into town." The car was old, but it was cherry, as Bobby would've said. It looked as if it had rolled out of a time tunnel, direct from a dealer's showroom in 1970.

No doubt about it, this man had money. "Hop in." Money, but no wedding ring. Which, of course, didn't mean a thing.

Still, Beth opened the door. Climbed in. Gave him back her best smile. "Thanks."

"Live around here?" he asked, his accent flat. A Yankee. And older than she'd first thought, but very good-looking.

"All my life," she told him. "Where are you from?"

"It seems like a nice little town—what I've seen of it, anyway."

"Thinking about moving here?" she asked. "I have a friend in real estate."

"Is she as pretty as you are?"

Well, well, the Yankee—strange duck that he was—could still bring it. Beth smiled. "Considering she's a he, and his name's Fred . . . no."

He glanced at her. "Your boyfriend?"

"No," she said. "I'm between boyfriends. My name's Beth, by the way."

"No, it's not."

She laughed. "Yeah, okay, you're right, it's Elizabeth."

"No," he said again. But he was smiling, which softened his words. "You're Number Five."

She laughed again, but in truth she was starting to get a little nervous. "And who does that make you? Number Six? No wait, don't tell me—you're Double-Oh-Seven."

"I'm God," he said.

It was then that he slowed down, pulling off into the old Forrester farm road—overgrown with disuse.

"Okay," Beth said. "I don't know what you're thinking, but I have to warn you, I was three years in the Army. I teach a self-defense class here in town on—"

"Tuesday nights," he finished for her. "I know. That's why I chose you."

Okay, now she was a lot nervous. He'd pulled far enough in for his car to be completely hidden by the trees, and he slowed even more.

Beth knew these woods, this old farm, this whole area better than any Yankee possibly could. She slipped off her seat belt, ready to run for it. But when she tried to open the door, it didn't unlatch. It was stuck. Or somehow double locked.

The window wouldn't go down either.

And now she wasn't nervous, she was frightened.

"Look," Beth said, turning to face him as he put the car into park. "I don't want to hurt you."

"Oh, but I do," he said. "I want to hurt you."

She turned, putting her back to the door, pulling her legs up onto the seat to kick him. Legs were a woman's best weapon. The muscles in her thighs packed far more punch than her arms. She knew this. She taught this in her class. She aimed for his head, his face, but he just laughed, telling her awful things he was going to do to her. She screamed as she kicked him. Put voice to your defense—this was something else she taught, along with the need to think, to strategize, to formulate a plan.

Hers was to kick him in the head until he was unconscious, dump him, and take his car to the sheriff's.

She felt his nose break, saw his blood spray the side window, but when she went to kick him again, her leg felt heavy, leaden.

He'd stuck her with some sort of syringe, right through her jeans. It dangled there, and she reached to pull it free, but it was too late. He'd drugged her, and now her hand and her head felt heavy, too, but she still tried to kick him.

Tried and failed.

His face blurred and then faded, as she heard him laughing.

And that was it. Beth's life was over.

And this hell that Number Five endured had just begun.

CHAPTER EIGHT

J enk should have kissed her back in the bar, back when she gave him her car keys. Now here he was, unlocking the door to his apartment—thank God, the place wasn't too much of a mess—and he was freaking out about the fact that he hadn't even kissed her yet.

Lindsey, meanwhile, was looking around, and he tried to see his home from her eyes, even as he surreptitiously kicked his dirty laundry under the sofa.

It was a standard post-1985 American apartment. A box with a cathedral ceiling, since he was on the third floor. The living room elled into the dining area, which had a pass-through to the tiny galley kitchen. The hint of a hall led to the bathroom and single bedroom. He'd decorated the place in standard unmarried Navy SEAL. Blank walls, minimal furnishings, corners filled with unpacked boxes and gear.

"So," Lindsey said, "you're either a serial killer or a Tibetan monk."

Jenk laughed. "Are those my only choices? Maybe I just moved in."

"Did you?"

A year ago February probably no longer qualified as *just*. "No."

She took off her jacket, putting it over the back of one of the two folding chairs that, with his new washing machine's box as table, sat in the dining area.

"Suddenly, I'm terribly nervous."

"I'm not a serial killer." Come to think of it, his washing machine no longer qualified as new, either.

Lindsey looked around his kitchen, peering in at the cereal boxes he kept in his microwave—a habit from his Florida days when he'd had ants. "That's not why I'm nervous," she said.

"Yeah." He opened the fridge, mostly to have something to do. "Beer?"

"Sure, why not? Let's get skunked. Unless . . . Is there a certain time you'll want me to leave?"

He popped the tops with an opener, handing one of the bottles to her. "That was a weird question. Do you want me to try to figure out what you meant by it, or should I just ignore it?"

She made an exasperated sound, clicking her tongue against the roof of her mouth. "It wasn't that weird. Some people have rules or their land-lords don't allow overnight guests or maybe they don't like the idea of their neighbors seeing a strange car in the driveway in the morning . . ."

"We parked in the main lot," Jenk pointed out. There were 240 apart-ments in his complex. Most people living here had one car, some had two. "If my neighbors are keeping track of extra cars, they've got too much time on their hands."

"That was just an example," she said.

"No, there's no time by which you have to leave."

"Good," she said.

"Good." This was about as romantic as returning a rented video late and arguing about the fee.

Lindsey, apparently, was thinking the same thing. "So. That's han-dled. You want to discuss which position we should do it in? Or should we iron out exactly how many more minutes of awkward conversation we have to endure before I can jump you?"

Jenk cracked up. And reached for her.

But she backed away. "No, no, no. First kiss in the kitchen is so junior year of college." She was laughing, too, as she slipped out into the living room and opened the sliding door to his tiny balcony.

He followed her outside.

"This," she decreed, "is a much better place for it." But she still stopped him at arm's length with a hand on his chest. "What do you think? A couple minutes of necking out here in the moonlight, then back inside on the sofa for about fifteen minutes of conversation, topic: intimate se-crets. If we stick to the schedule"—she glanced at her watch—"we could be in the bedroom and naked in twenty minutes. A half hour, tops."

Jenk was still laughing as he kissed her.

She made the softest sound, a mix of surrender and pleasure as he took her mouth with his. Her lips were soft and so sweet, and he found himself sighing, too, as he tried to kiss her gently, tenderly—trying his best to provide the romance that the night thus far had been lacking.

It was, without a doubt, a first kiss for the record books. They were both still holding on to their bottles of beer, and despite that, she melted against him, her body a mix of soft and softer, a perfect fit in so many ways, her fingers in his hair, her back and shoulders so smooth beneath his hand.

But then she pulled back, just slightly, just enough for him to have to let her go, and he did, but all he could think about was kissing her again.

She smiled, and looking into her eyes was like gazing into his immediate future. Heat and passion and laughter. This was going to be one hell of a night.

One of the shoulder straps of her emerald green top had fallen halfway down her arm. He traced it with his finger, anticipating helping her out of it, remembering the way she'd looked just a few nights ago, lying in the moonlight with her shirt undone, in that bra that did little to conceal her.

He should have just kissed her then. He'd wanted to.

And it was more than obvious now that she'd wanted it, too.

"Maybe," she said, "we should rework the schedule. Intimate secrets—only one apiece before getting naked."

Jenk put down his beer, took hers from her hands, put it down, too.

And this time, she kissed him. She was so alive, so vibrant, kissing her back wasn't something he did with only his mouth. He breathed her in—wine and sunblock and even the dust and dirt from the op—on Lindsey it mingled together to smell exotic. He touched her, losing himself in the silkiness of her hair and skin, the softness and power of her body as she pressed herself against him, as if she, too, wanted to be rid of all barriers between them. She was not, by far, the most vocal woman he'd ever kissed, but the sounds of soft approval that she made were electrifying. He tasted her—her mouth, her face, her ears, her neck—she was sweetness and salt.

And Jenk realized, in a flash, that even though she'd made her escape seem easy, she'd worked hard out there tonight. As tired and sore as he was, she had to be even more so.

This time he pulled back.

Lindsey opened her eyes, looking up at him questioningly.

"Do you want to shower?" he whispered.

"Do I smell bad?" she whispered back.

He laughed. "No. I just usually shower when I get home from an exercise, and it suddenly occurred to me that you might like a shower, too. Or that you might want me to . . ."

"I think you smell incredibly sexy," Lindsey told him.

It was impossible not to kiss her again after she said that, deeper this time, harder. This kiss was way more about sex than romance, but she didn't seem to mind. They were both breathing hard when she pulled back.

"But if your shoulder's hurting you . . ." she said.

"To be honest, I haven't really thought about it." Much. He kissed her yet again, damn but he never wanted to stop kissing this woman.

There was real urgency now. She was no longer melting. Instead, she clung to him, no delicate flower, instead a full partner, an equal with a common goal—kissing the breath out of each other. And when she pulled back this time, she was breathing as if she'd sprinted up a flight of stairs.

"A hot shower would help your shoulder," she told him.

"Right now," he told her, "you're all the help my shoulder needs."

"I'm thinking about how you're going to feel tomorrow."

"I'm not," he said.

Lindsey laughed. "No kidding." She kissed him, but it was only a quick caress of her lips against his before she slipped out of his grasp. Grabbing her beer, she went back inside, disappearing down the hall to his bathroom. Sure enough, as he closed and locked the slider, Jenk heard the shower go on. He saw his reflection in the glass—he was grinning like a fool. Life was good. He pulled the blinds.

The bathroom door was closed, so he used the opportunity to check his bedroom, kicking more laundry under his bed, quickly stripping the sheets. He had a clean set on the shelf in the closet and it took less than a minute to put them on the bed.

Okay. He had a ceiling fan—he turned it on low. He adjusted the blinds. There was a streetlight not far from his window that threw a cool pattern on the ceiling. He opened the drawer in the table next to his bed, looking for condoms—check—then kicked more laundry and books and hey, look what he found? A couple of video games that he'd borrowed from Danny Gillman that he'd thought he'd lost. Go figure. He kicked it all into the closet and shut the door.

And then he stood there, listening to the water run.

It was crazy, but his heart was pounding. He was sweating. What was he afraid of? That she'd wash away her desire for him in that shower?

But the water finally went off. And the bathroom door opened. Just a few inches.

"Your turn," Lindsey called.

Jenk stopped just outside the bathroom door. It was possible he was having a heart attack. "May I come in?" Shit, his voice actually squeaked. Way to be cool, Jenkins.

She opened the door wider, wrapped in one of his big blue towels, her hair slicked back from her face. Without makeup, she was even more beautiful. And yes, to anyone who wasn't looking closely, she probably looked fifteen. But when she smiled, the way she was smiling at him right now, there were crinkles around her eyes that revealed years of laughter and life-induced wisdom.

"Sorry, did you say something?" she asked.

"May I come in?" He managed to sound closer to his real age this time. Not that there was space for him in the tiny bathroom. She'd hung her top and bra over his towel rack. Her jeans were in a pile on the white tile floor. Her jeans, and a scrap of black silk that had to be her panties.

"I made an executive decision," Lindsey told him as she opened his medicine cabinet and frowned at the contents. "Showers for everyone. Then a backrub. Don't you have any lotion or oil or . . . ?" There was a bottle of sunblock out on the counter, and she picked it up, squinting to read the ingredients. But then she glanced over at him, still standing out in the hall. "Do you need me to get out of here?"

"No," Jenk said, propelled into action. He unbuttoned his uniform shirt, shrugging out of it and dropping it in the hall. His T-shirt was a little harder to manage with his shoulder as tight as it was.

Lindsey came over. "Keep your elbow down."

She helped him out of his sleeve even as he protested, "I'm okay."

It was a stupid thing to say, because what? Did he really want her to stop touching him? Her hands, her arms were cool as she helped him pull his shirt over his head. She was chilled from her shower, her wet hair almost making her shiver. Without that towel between them, she would slide, cool and clean, against his hot skin.

He reached for her towel—he couldn't help himself—unable to stand that close without kissing her. Her mouth was cool, too, and she tasted like his toothpaste, minty and clean.

But as her towel fell from her, she broke the kiss, dancing down the hall to his bedroom, a brief flash of naked woman. "Shower," she commanded as she pushed the bedroom door mostly closed behind her.

Jenk dropped his pants, his belt buckle clattering on the floor. He had his boots, socks, and shorts off and was under the water in less than three seconds. He soaped himself and washed his hair in record time, catching himself laughing. He was just standing there, all alone in the shower, laughing.

He tried to remember the last time he'd laughed this much after he'd gone home from a bar with a woman. It was possible that the answer was never.

He tried to imagine Tracy saying some of the things Lindsey had said to him tonight, and couldn't do it. It wasn't that he couldn't imagine having sex with Tracy, because he certainly could.

It just wouldn't be this much fun.

The thought made him pause, his hands in his hair.

But the mental image of Lindsey, naked and on his bed, got him moving again. *Tracy who?* He was out of the shower and dripping dry as he ran a comb through his hair, brushed his teeth, sniff-checked his pits. He wrapped Lindsey's towel around his waist, doubling it in the front. But he still had to hold it down as he left the bathroom.

He stopped himself from pushing the door open with so much force that it would have smashed into the wall. Even though Lindsey probably would've laughed at his caveman attitude, he wanted to give her more than immediate gratification. He wanted to do this right.

Whatever the hell that meant. He wasn't quite sure.

"You coming in?" Lindsey asked, and he pushed the door open. Gently. With his fingertips.

She'd turned on the lamp in the corner, but she'd covered the shade with something blue—a pillowcase. It was a nice effect, softening and dimming the light.

She'd also covered herself with a dress shirt from his closet. It totally engulfed her as she knelt, waiting for him, on his bed. She'd rolled the sleeves up, but they still hung to her slender wrists. She'd buttoned only a few of the buttons, leaving a deep V in the front, where he could see the first soft hint of her breasts. As far as outfits went, it wasn't very revealing at all. And yet, it was heart-in-his-throat sexy. Far sexier than any risqué lingerie he'd ever seen, both in catalogs and on adventuresome past girlfriends.

"Does it still feel tight?" she asked, and it took him a moment to realize she was talking about his shoulder.

He rolled his arm. "No, it's okay."

"Are you lying?"

"A little," he admitted.

"I can make you feel better," Lindsey patted the bed. "Lie down. On your stomach."

"I'd rather lie on my back."

"I bet that when Commander Koehl gives you an order," Lindsey said, "you don't argue."

He smiled at her. "You'd win that bet."

"Pretend I'm Koehl."

"No, thank you." But Jenk lay down on the bed. On his stomach.

Lindsey straddled him, sitting on his towel-covered butt. He tried to turn around to look at her, but she took his head and firmly pushed it back down. "Relax." He felt her reach for something, heard the sound of a lotion bottle fart. "I'm using your sunblock," she told him. It was cold against his back, but her hands felt incredible. "Next time you're in the drugstore pick up a bottle of baby oil. Or if you want to go fancy-schmancy, you could get massage oil, but you should give it a sniff first—make sure you like the way it smells. God forbid you open it to use it for the first time and it smells like the perfume your mother wears. Way to kill a mood, you know?"

Whatever she was doing to him, it felt heavenly. She started at his neck and worked her way down his back, her hands strong and sure.

"Did you learn to do this," he asked, "when you were rehabbing your own shoulder?"

"What, you don't assume just because I'm Japanese American, it's hereditary? Like there's a geisha gene?"

Jenk laughed. "That's like assuming I play the bagpipes because my great-grandparents were from Scotland."

Her hands stilled. "Yes," she said. "It is."

"Do people really think . . . ?"

"Yeah," she said. "They do. They also assume that I know all about acupuncture, too. Hello—they call it Chinese Medicine because it's Chinese. China and Japan—two very different countries."

"I hate bagpipes," Jenk told her, "and the idea that I should automatically love them just because two relatives that I never even met used to live in Scotland is pretty stupid, too."

"Yes, it is." She began rubbing his shoulder again, her fingers moving down his arm. She had to shift her weight to do that, her thighs tightening around him, up higher now than his towel. She was naked beneath that shirt, and he could feel her, warm against his back.

It was all he could do to keep talking, to form coherent words. " 'Course, most people don't know I'm Scottish—part Scottish—just from looking at me. You don't have that luxury."

She was silent, just kneading his triceps, so he kept going.

"I can relate," he told her, "a little, anyway. Because I'm short. Shorter. And because I look the way I look."

"Youthful," she said.

"Yeah. People make assumptions."

"Tell me about it," she said. "You know, this body right here?" She smacked his back. "This is a grown-up's body. You should just walk around all the time with your shirt off."

"You should, too," he said.

She laughed. "I'll still look Japanese," she pointed out.

"Yeah, well, I'll still be short."

"Short is relative," she said. "To me, you're tall. Tall, dark, and handsome."

So okay. Every time Jenk was convinced that this night couldn't get any better, Lindsey said or did something to ramp it up another notch. He was getting a presex backrub from an incredible woman who called him tall, dark, and handsome with total conviction in her voice.

But asking her to bear his children was probably not an appropriate response.

Instead, he teased her. "Yeah, well, what do you know? Everyone's taller than a hot Asian chick."

She gasped her outrage, then started tickling him. Holy shit, her fingers were strong. He jerked away, twisting himself beneath her, so he could grab her hands—not an easy thing to do.

But finally he caught her wrists, one in each hand. They were both breathing hard, and she sat, now, straddling his bare stomach. His towel had come off, and the shirt she was wearing had slipped off one shoulder, exposing one exquisitely perfect breast.

Jesus, she was beautiful.

"You do know I was only kidding, right?" He had to make sure, even if he couldn't manage more than a whisper.

Lindsey nodded. "Can I tell you something?"

Now? But he nodded. "Yeah." He released her hands—big mistake, because she reached over and hiked her shirt back up her shoulder. Crap. But then she started rubbing his shoulder again, and leaning forward, she allowed him quite the view. Still, that shirt had to go. The sooner, the better.

"It really bugs me when people make ninja jokes," Lindsey said.

Jenk worked hard to focus. "You mean, like, *Why did the ninja cross the road?*"

She laughed—and kissed him. Yes, *yes* . . . He found the buttons of her shirt, then realized as he fumbled with the first one, that the shirt was loose enough. He could just sweep his hands up the silk of her stomach and rib cage, filling his palms with the softness of her breasts.

The sound she made was all the encouragement he needed. He kept going, pushing the shirt up and over her head. And then she was as naked as he was.

He sat up—he wanted to hold her as he kissed her, as he ran his hands down the softness of her bare skin, as she touched him, too, shifting back so that his erection was pressed against her, trapped—God—between her cheeks.

He touched the hair between her legs, and she reached down to push his fingers lower. She was slick and warm and softer than the petals of a flower, and okay, where the hell had that poetic thought come from? Lindsey was a woman—all woman—not some delicate flower. And she was more than ready for him.

She made that clear by hiking herself up and putting his package in front of her, and—oh yeah!—wrapping her fingers around him like she was never going to let him go.

Jenk leaned back, reaching for the drawer that held his condoms, fumbling to grab one. No sooner did he have it in his hands then she took it from him, tearing open the foil package. Together, they covered him, and he would have lifted her up and pushed himself inside of her, but she stopped him.

"I'm sorry," she said. "Do you mind if we wait a sec? I don't have sex that often, and I don't want to come right away."

Was she serious? "Linds, I'll have sex with you whenever you want."

"Gosh, you are so sweet," she said. "But I know that's asking an *awful* lot, so—"

"What, are you fucking kidding?"

"Yeah." She laughed at him, with him. And she pushed herself down, thrusting him inside of her. "Both."

Pleasure rocked him—it was mind-blowing. It was a moment he was going to have to replay over and over again—later—because his entire universe had shifted and changed. Pleasure had been redefined. Sex itself had just blown past all preassumed parameters.

There was sex, and then there was sex with Lindsey Fontaine.

She kissed him, her body pressed against his, her breasts soft against his chest, even as she strained for more of him, more, even more . . .

He tried to give her all she wanted—it was what he wanted, too. More. *More.*

He kissed her, touched her, clung to her, rocked her, as she laughed and gasped and moved atop him.

"Okay, so this works for me," she breathed into his ear. How could she speak? If he opened his mouth, he'd be able to do no more than make unintelligible sounds. "This working for you?"

"Yuh," he managed, and she laughed.

Laughing during sex was dangerous. It took away a certain amount of self-control. He tried to stop her, to hold her still, to tell her, but he couldn't, and then he didn't want to, because, God, she was coming, just shattering in his arms.

"More," she said, "oh, more . . ." and he gave her all he had, all that he was, all that he could, but then he realized he'd heard her wrong.

She was saying his name. *Mark*. With a catch in her voice, like he was something special, something she wanted. Like he totally turned her on, like just the thought—let alone the sensation—of him, hard inside of her, was making her come and come and come.

And it was over. He came, too, in a hot rush, just *blam*. Just crashing into her, no warning, with a total lack of control.

But Lindsey loved it. "Yes," she breathed, "oh, yes." She pushed him even farther inside of her, kissing him, holding him as tightly as he held on to her, as her laughter wrapped around him.

Tracy had a diamond ring on her finger as she wandered through Lyle's suite at the Hotel del Coronado.

Lyle was on his phone again, talking to someone in Australia about a motion that had to be filed tomorrow. He'd get it done, he promised, before his morning flight to New York.

She was going to have to tell him that she couldn't go back with him. She couldn't just leave Troubleshooters Incorporated in the lurch. She had to give notice, let them have enough time to replace her. Of course, maybe Tom would be so glad that she was leaving that he'd let her clear out her desk and go.

Lyle's room was beautiful—he didn't stay anywhere that wasn't five-star. And yet he left his dirty laundry on the floor. He never bothered to unpack, instead leaving his suitcase out and open on the luggage rack.

Tracy admired her ring as she put his socks and underwear into a plastic laundry bag and tucked it into the inner pocket of his bag.

And that was where she found it. Another jeweler's box. Had Lyle already picked out their wedding rings?

It still felt surreal—an engagement ring, a wedding, maybe even a baby before the end of the new year. A home in Scarsdale—no, strike that. With the hours Lyle put in at work, he'd end up staying over in the city, and there was no way she'd trust him to do that. So instead, they'd make their home on the Upper West Side.

Lyle was still talking on his cell in his important voice. The defendant this, the prosecutor that.

Tracy couldn't resist taking a peek at the rings he'd picked out and . . .

That was odd. Instead of a set of gold bands, the box held another diamond ring, identical to the one already on her finger.

Lyle closed his cell phone, ending his call, so she held it out to him. "What's this?"

He looked at the diamond ring, looked at her, and smiled. But not before she saw an expression that was definitely not happiness in his eyes. He reached for the box. "Believe it or not, I bought the ring in two different sizes. I wanted to be absolutely certain it would fit. I'm going to return that one."

It was possible that she'd imagined that unhappiness. It was possible that he was telling the truth.

Lyle was a perfectionist, and making sure the ring fit properly would matter to him.

Except he'd bought her a ring before. Her birthstone. Surely he still had her ring size in his Palm Pilot.

But it was his choice of words that sent up the biggest flare of mistrust. *Believe it or not . . .*

Heather, Tracy. Tracy, Heather. Heather's a paralegal at the firm. Believe it or not, she just, uh, stopped by to drop off a file . . .

In a choice between *believe it* or *not*, Tracy had learned, the hard way, to select *not*. She held on to that ring box, pulling it out of his reach.

"That is so thoughtful," she said, lying as skillfully as Lyle lied. "This ring *is* a little tight. Maybe this other one will fit better." She forced herself to smile at him, to breathe.

Lyle didn't have much of a choice. He watched Tracy take that second ring from its box.

Tracy held the ring up to the light, so she could read the inscription within. *Heather and Lyle forever.*

Somehow she managed not to throw up. "What, did Heather turn you down?"

"Why don't we have another drink," Lyle said.

"Oh, yes. That will definitely help."

"I can explain," Lyle told her.

How often had she heard him say that? How often would she hear it? Every day for the rest of her miserable life?

Tracy threw the box at him and ran for the door.

"Why *did* the ninja cross the road?" Jenk mused.

Lindsey lifted her head. "You are so funny." She took his lower lip between her teeth, gently tugging it back, and letting go. Fwack. She did it again.

"You having fun?" he asked.

"I love your mouth," she told him as she rolled off of him. "You have a sexy mouth."

She was incredibly good for his ego. Jenk kissed her, making sure she didn't go too far away as he cleaned himself up. She didn't. She snuggled up against him, her head on his shoulder. His good one. Which, he knew, was not by accident.

"What I meant by ninja joke," she told him, "is this: *Hey, Lindsey, what are you some kind of ninja or something? Yo, Lindsey, way to ninja out there.* Six different people made a ninja comment at the Bug tonight."

Jenk interlaced their fingers. "I'm pretty sure it was meant as a compliment."

"Yeah," she said. "I know. It's just . . . It feels wrong. Like people telling Lopez that he'd pulled a Zorro, or saying that Alyssa did an awesome Harriet Tubman."

He had to laugh. "No one would ever dare say that to her."

Lindsey propped herself up on her elbow. "That's my point. Why do they feel it's okay to *ninja* me?"

He kissed the palm of her hand, enjoying the way the covered lamp made her bare skin glow slightly blue. Although she would look beautiful in any light. "Maybe because a ninja is the ultimate. A grand master. We're all good at kicking ass, but a ninja . . . A ninja is something we all secretly want to be. I'd love to be *ninja-ed*. If you want, though, I'll talk to the team about it. Tommy, too. We'll make sure it stops."

"No," she said. "Thanks, but I'll handle it. It just bugs me. Kind of like when anyone has a question about sushi, and everyone looks at me. I hate sushi, and no, I don't know how to use chopsticks or a wok either. No, I don't know kung fu or karate, but I can take a man more than twice my size to the ground if I have to—because, thanks to the LAPD, I've had training. Yes, I speak two languages, but they're English and Spanish. The Spanish came in handy on the job in East LA."

Silence seemed to ring in the room.

"Sorry," she said. "I get a little passionate. I'm as American as you are, and I'm betting you don't get asked recipes for sheep brains or whatever you crazy Scottish people eat. So that's mine. What's yours?"

Jenk knew exactly what she was talking about—or at least he thought he did. He checked to make sure. "You're talking intimate secret, right?"

Lindsey nodded, chin in her hand as she watched him.

"A few months ago," he told her, playing with her hair, pushing it behind her ear. "I thought I was going to die and . . . It was pretty eye-opening."

She nodded again. "I got myself shot a few years ago, so I get it. A near-death experience can trigger major revelations. Mine was to quit the force. But, I'm sorry. Go on. It's your turn. What did you discover?"

"I guess I discovered that there's a lot I haven't done that I still want to do." Jenk touched the scar on Lindsey's back. It was small, but he'd noticed it. "I was wondering what this was from. What'd you do to get back shot? Push someone out of the way?"

She rolled her eyes. "No, it was a . . . misjudgment of character."

"A what?"

"No fair. It's *your* turn."

"Yeah, but that's freaking cryptic. Misjudgment of character—what does that mean? You were shot in the back by a friend?" He'd gotten it right, he could see from her face. "Jesus, Lindsey."

She tried to downplay it, but it was too late. "I thought he was a friend—the perp. He was someone I thought I knew, but apparently didn't. He was going for suicide by cop, and I . . . I couldn't see it."

Oh, man. She was pretending it was nothing, that even talking about it wasn't any kind of big deal. But Jenk knew better. He tried to imagine having to shoot Izzy. Or having Izzy shoot him.

"So he just shot you?" Jenk asked. "Your alleged friend."

She nodded. "He wanted me to shoot him, but I wouldn't even draw on him. I was so wrapped up in talking him down, you know? I was clueless. So he discharged his weapon to get my attention. I dove for cover, he kept shooting and actually hit me. I think he was as surprised as I was. God, talk about spilling secrets. I haven't talked about this with . . . Well, Tom knows, but he doesn't bring it up."

Jenk's heart was in his throat, but he made his voice as matter-of-fact as hers was. "Did you have to kill him?"

"No, I was, you know, too busy bleeding. He settled for suicide by SWAT team. They killed him to get me to the hospital. So what haven't you done that you still want to do?"

For about four seconds, Jenk considered following her lead. He considered just letting the headlines news version of the story she'd told him remain as a matter-of-fact as she'd intended. But he couldn't do it. "If you ever want to talk about it . . . I live in that world, too. I've had friends die. Not like that, but . . . Close enough."

Lindsey gazed at him, searching his eyes. For the first time, probably since he'd met her, amusement wasn't lurking somewhere on her face, ready to slip out through her constant almost-smile, or sparkling in her eyes. She looked wary and vulnerable, and quite possibly even a little afraid.

So he brought her back to her comfort zone. "So what haven't I done that I still want to do? My notepad is around here somewhere." He pretended to look for it. "Have amazing sex with Lindsey Fontaine was pretty high on my list. Where's a pencil? I can cross that one off."

She shoved him. "I'm being serious here. I just told you . . . and now you're making a joke?" She was pretending to be indignant, but he could see her relief.

"I'm being serious, too," he said, grabbing her hands as she started tickling him. He twisted, throwing his leg across her to pin her down. Although he suspected if she hadn't wanted to be pinned, he wouldn't have succeeded. "This whole night has been amazing."

And there it was again. That hint of fear. What was she so afraid of? "It has been, hasn't it?" she whispered.

He kissed her, and, God, she kissed him back so sweetly, he felt his bones melt.

So he told her the truth. "The thing I regretted most—when I thought I was going to die—was that I didn't have a family. You know. Of my own."

"A family," she repeated. "Like, two point five kids, a dog, and a minivan?"

"Yeah," he admitted. "It was . . . weird. I was trying to dig myself free, but . . . fully expecting to be blown into a million pieces, and I was thinking about Charlie. You know, Paoletti."

Lindsey shifted slightly away from him. "It's one thing to babysit. Because you get to go home afterward."

"I know," Jenk said. "I do. It's just . . . Tommy's so . . . satisfied. I've known him for years and . . . I know things aren't perfect for him. Last year, after that sniper attack, when Murphy's wife was killed—that was some serious bad shit. Larry Decker, he was team leader of that op, and he's still running at pucker-factor five thousand. He's being eaten alive by the fact that she died—what was her name?"

"Angelina," Lindsey told him.

"That's right. Deck's still dying from it, still carrying Angelina's death with him every single day. I've seen it happen in the teams, when officers lose men, when guys lose teammates. Some of 'em can't forgive themselves, even though it's not their fault. And it ends up killing them, too. They change—not for the better.

"But Tommy," Jenk continued, "he had Kelly standing beside him. And it wasn't that long after Angelina's funeral that Charlie was born. I know that helped, too. It's not that Tommy didn't mourn or grieve or even feel responsible for any mistakes that were made. But he handled it, he processed it, he implemented some new rules, stepped up your training levels, too. I'm sure he thinks about her every day. Shit, I think about her a lot, and I didn't even know her. But Tommy's found peace, and I know his path was easier because he had Kelly and Charlie to hold on to." He paused. "That's what I want. That's what I realized after Izzy saved my life."

He had no idea what Lindsey was thinking. He only knew that she'd pulled herself free from him, pulled the blanket to cover herself as she curled up, one arm beneath her head, just watching and listening to him talk.

"At the risk of bumming you out," Lindsey finally said, "I've come to know both Tom and Kelly pretty well and . . . I think they're the exception rather than the rule. Most people's relationships don't come close. Take my parents, for example." She shuddered.

"Divorced?" he asked.

"No," she said. "But I'm not sure if they ever really talked." She paused. "My mom lost her fight with cancer, not quite two years ago."

"Wow," Jenk said. "That must've sucked."

Lindsey nodded. "Yeah. She was diagnosed when I was eleven. She fought a good fight, but it kept recurring. She made the decision to have home hospice care about a week before I was shot. That's why I quit the force. I spent all that time in the hospital, and she never left my side. And all I could think was, what if I get hurt again, when she's confined to a bed? And I wanted to take the time, you know, to be with her while I could. It was . . . good. That I did it. I always intended to go back, but then Tom called me and . . ." She shrugged. "Here I am."

She'd had an extremely tough couple of years. Jenk would never have guessed it. She was always so upbeat, so ready with a smile.

Unlike Tracy, who walked around with a list of complaints, ready to rattle them off at the slightest hint of an invitation.

It was the first time he'd even so much as thought of Tracy in hours and, almost as if he'd conjured her, his cell phone rang.

It was her. He'd given her a special ringtone.

Lindsey sat up. "Is your phone really playing 'Here Comes the Bride'?" She started to laugh.

Jenk nearly tripped over the bedcovers as he hurried into the hall, where his phone was blasting majestic organ chords from the pocket of his pants. He silenced it, double-checking the number. Yep, it was definitely Tracy. Holy crap, it was after 0300.

That was the only reason he answered it. "Jenkins."

"Thank God, you're there!" It was Tracy, and she was crying. "I'm so sorry, Mark, but I didn't know who else to call. I just didn't know what to do, I'm sure Lyle's at my apartment and—"

"Whoa, whoa," he said. "Slow down. Where are you? Are you safe?"

"I'm in a cab." She started to cry harder. "Lyle's looking for me. He was *so* upset."

Shit.

Lindsey, meanwhile, had found the towel Jenk had worn out of the shower. She'd wrapped it around herself, apparently not as comfortable as he was to stand there, naked, in his hallway. She met his eyes briefly as she slipped past him and into the bathroom, closing the door tightly behind her.

She was smart. She'd no doubt figured out that it was Tracy on the other end of the phone.

"Tracy," Jenk spoke over her noisy sobs. "Honey, I can't understand what you're saying. You have to slow down and breathe, okay? Where are you? You said you're in a cab—where's the cab?"

"Outside your apartment," she told him, and his entire world tilted.

"You're where?"

"Right outside," she said again. "But I don't have any money to pay the driver. Will you . . . Will you pay the fare so that I can come up?"

Lindsey opened the bathroom door. With her clothes back on. "Where is she?" she asked silently.

"Downstairs," he told her, hating the surprise and then realization that flashed in her eyes. *You're wrong,* he wanted to tell her. *Whatever it is that you're thinking, you're wrong.*

He stepped into his pants, taking his wallet from his pocket. He could fix this quickly by giving Tracy some money to get a hotel room. She'd clearly had too much to drink. Sleeping it off would be a good idea. But, crap. He didn't have that much cash.

"I'll be right down," he said to Tracy, then snapped his phone shut. "I've got to handle this," he told Lindsey. A quick trip to the nearest ATM would solve the problem. Or he could just go with Tracy to that motel over by the Ladybug, use his credit card.

"Of course." Lindsey went to get her jacket from the dining room chair where she'd left it.

"I'm just going to make sure she's somewhere safe, then I'll be back. Twenty minutes, tops." He pulled on his T-shirt. Whoa, was that really what he'd smelled like for most of the evening? He took it back off again.

Lindsey was already halfway out the door. "I have to go."

"Please don't."

She didn't stop. "I have to. Don't worry, I won't let her see me."

"Linds . . ." The hell with it. He put the T-shirt back on, jammed his bare feet into his boots, and clattered down the stairs after her.

But she'd pulled another ninja.

She was already gone.

CHAPTER NINE

S ophia trashed the paper target. It shredded, exploding into confetti as the force of the weapon she was firing jolted her to her very spine.

The ear protectors she was wearing brought the noise level from unbearable to merely hellish. She couldn't imagine firing this thing without them, on a battlefield. It would be insane.

She ran out of ammo—it didn't take very long at all to empty the magazine—and the silence settled around her.

"Excellent," Dave proclaimed, as she set the weapon on the table, following the shooting range's strict rules. "Much better. Do you remember how to reload?"

She took off the headphone-like ear protectors and picked up the clip. "I think so."

"The MP5's much too big for her." Sophia spun around to see Decker standing there. How long had he been watching?

He turned to her, actually meeting her eyes. "You should try the MP4. It's lighter and smaller. Of course, it doesn't have the same range. It's nicknamed the 'room broom' because it's good for indoor situations. But it's definitely more your size."

It shouldn't have been a surprise to see him there. This was the closest range to the Troubleshooters office. And Sophia knew Deck believed in a strict daily practice regimen. It was, he'd told her once, an essential part of staying on top of his game.

"This is the equivalent of the weapon I had last night," she told him. "I wanted to feel what it was like to use it correctly."

He nodded. "You did okay with it. Considering it was your first time."

"I killed Tom, and I killed you," she said. "I don't consider that okay." Was this really happening? Were they actually standing here, having a civil conversation? She glanced at Dave, who was preoccupied with his Palm Pilot.

"That trick you pulled on Lopez and . . . who was it?" Deck actually settled in, leaning slightly against the wall. He was dressed as if he'd come from a meeting, in one of his ill-fitting suits, standard white dress shirt, also a size too large. He'd taken the jacket off, loosened his tie, and rolled up his sleeves. He looked as if he'd worked his entire life in a cubby-divided office, mousy and meek, clothes hanging off his skinny frame.

In truth, he was solid under there. Bumping into him was like running into a brick wall. Sophia knew this from experience. She knew some other things about him from experience, too.

"Gillman," she told him now, hoping he wouldn't be able to tell where her thoughts had gone. "Danny Gillman and Jay Lopez. They're quite a pair, aren't they? It was pretty obvious that they'd fall for the damsel in distress ruse." Which was exactly what she'd tried on Deck, a million years ago. And now she was completely rattled. Had he come here to break the news to her, to tell her he'd already delivered his resignation letter to Tom? "I know I was lucky there were only two of them, and they both fell for it. Although the plan was only to distract them while Dave escaped, and I know it probably wouldn't have worked in real life, because one of the reasons it *did* work was because Danny and Jay know me." She was babbling, she heard herself babbling, and saw that Decker had stopped leaning. He looked ready to run away. "They both sent me flowers today, congratulating me on my success last night." She laughed, and it sounded fake, forced, even to her own ears. "That's a first, huh? Getting flowers from men I've killed? They were nice though, the flowers—"

Dave touched her arm, interrupting her, grounding her, his fingers warm and solid through the sleeve of her blouse. "You did an excellent job last night," he said, then passed the conversational baton back to Decker. "Don't you agree?"

"It was good work," Deck said. He glanced at his watch. And here it came. *I just wanted to tell you that working with you is impossible for me. Gotta go.*

"I had no idea sending flowers to the person who killed you was the proper protocol, post–training-op," Dave commented mildly. "What do you suppose Mark Jenkins likes best? Roses or lilies?"

Sophia laughed.

Deck actually smiled.

"And you owe Sophia a bouquet, Deck," Dave kept going, "although a lunch date would probably be an acceptable substitute."

Sophia shot him a look. What was he doing? But he'd gone back to staring at his Palm Pilot.

"Lopez and Gillman were just . . . They're so young and . . ." She rolled her eyes. "A little too enthusiastic. Besides, I killed Deck by mistake. Which is one of the reasons I'm here today. To try to figure out what I did wrong."

"Killing Tom was your mistake," Decker told her. "As for me . . ." He shook his head. "You had no idea I was in your kill zone. That was my fault. I should have let you know I was there."

"Everything happened so fast," Sophia said. "Although it always does, doesn't it?"

"Yeah," Decker agreed. "Warp speed. Or at least you think it's warp speed until you're in the middle of a firefight. Then you get a real look at what *fast* means. At the same time, adrenaline can make everything seem to slow down, stretch out."

Just standing here talking to her was such hard work for him, he was actually sweating from the effort.

"I don't think I got the adrenaline rush until after it was over," Sophia admitted.

He actually smiled again. It wasn't as genuine as his smile at Dave's flower joke, but it wasn't bad. "Lot of good it did then, huh?"

Sophia managed a smile, too. "Yeah." She also managed to keep her mouth shut when Decker didn't say anything for a moment. Don't babble, don't babble. He didn't like it when she babbled.

So there they were, standing there, smiling at each other, both so tense they were about to snap. Or at least she was smiling at him. Decker's smiles were always much too brief. But he was looking her straight in the eye, as if he were trying to read her mind.

He opened his mouth, as if to speak again, but down the range, someone opened up with an automatic weapon. And Sophia instinctively ducked. She caught herself, turning it into a major flinch rather than a flat-out dive for cover.

Both men—Decker and Dave—took a step toward her, matching concern in their eyes.

"I'm okay," she said. "I just spaced. I forgot I was in a firing range, although this should have been a clue." She held up the ammo clip she was still holding.

"You want to go again?" Dave asked. "Or just head to lunch?" He turned to Decker. "We're going to the Greek place. Want to join us?"

Deck looked at his watch again.

And Sophia just said it. "Or do you have to go write your resignation letter?"

"I guess you didn't talk to Tom yet," he said, and her heart sank. "About going to New Hampshire."

Sophia shook her head, turning to look at Dave. He made a never-heard-it face as he shook his head. "I'm going to New Hampshire?" she asked.

"We all are," Decker told her, told Dave, too. "Along with Team Sixteen. When I left the office, Tom told me it was a go—it happened much faster than he thought, but . . . We're doing more war gaming, and we'll get some winter training in, too. They're having the coldest winter up there in around fifty years. I, uh, requested you—both of you—participate in my squad. I won't be a team leader—we're going to be mixing it up with Sixteen this time, letting their officers lead. But he agreed it would, uh, be a good idea if we continued to . . . Work together. For a while."

Sophia couldn't believe what she was hearing. And then she could, because this was Decker. She'd told him she loved her job, and that was all he'd had to hear. He was going to do whatever he had to do to make sure that she could stay. Sweat was nothing. He would bleed if he had to.

He glanced now at Dave. "I'm hoping you'll accept the assignment."

"Winter in New Hampshire," Dave said with absolutely no inflection. "Whoo-hoo. That's about as good as it gets. I'm in." He turned to Sophia. "You are, too. You can take a day trip into Boston." Back to Deck. "Her father's at Mass General. She's been trying to find the time to go see him. This works out perfectly."

Decker was visibly surprised. "Your father's alive?"

Sophia closed her eyes. *Oh, Dave, wasn't this hard enough?* "Yes," she said aloud. "It turns out I have an aunt—his sister. She tracked me down a few months ago. He's alive, but he's been sick. Last week he went into the hospital, and . . . Aunt Maureen's been calling again."

"You don't have to go," Decker said. He was fierce in his conviction. "You owe him nothing."

"Except he's your father," Dave pointed out. "And after he's gone, you'll never have another chance to talk to him."

"I haven't decided what I'm going to do," Sophia said.

"If there's anything I can do to help . . ." Deck said.

"Thank you," she said. "You've already helped a lot."

He smiled at that. "Yeah, right." Another glance at his watch. "I've got to get moving. You might want to get lunch to go. We're leaving tonight—2100 hours. Pack your warmest clothes."

And with that he was gone.

Sophia stood there, listening to his footsteps fade away. It was only when the outer door closed with a resounding *thunk* that she turned to Dave.

"I hate you," she said.

Dave nodded mildly as he finished locking the weapon back in its case. "I know."

Izzy spotted Marky-Mark just outside the grinder. "Hey, hey, Romeo. How's the view from the top of the world?"

The little dude was on the phone as Iz jogged over. Whoever he was ringing didn't pick up. His mouth tightened, but he didn't leave a message. Probably because Izzy was listening.

"Uh-oh," Izzy said. "Trouble in paradise already?"

Jenkins was seriously pissed. "This is the worst fucking time in the entire history of the world for me to leave town, and we're going to fucking New Hampshire for cold-weather training. Have you heard this? New Hampshire? At 2100? Tonight?" His voice went up about five octaves.

"Yeah," Izzy said. "They want us to practice freezing our balls off. I say we petition to stay here, do the entire op in the warehouse freezer at Stu the Butcher's Wholesale Meats." He followed Jenk into the grinder, where BUD/S class 5000, or whatever number they were up to these days, was doing endless PT. They were still in early phase one of their training. The grind 'em up and ring 'em out phase, hence the name "grinder."

Jenk kept off to the side, but he joined the class as they started their push-ups. He was a maniac. He did this all the time, jumping into whatever torture the SEAL candidates were enduring, and not just keeping up, but making it look effortless.

Izzy sat down on the ground near him, leaning back on his elbows. "So what happened last night?"

Jenk push-upped, eyes on the ground. "Nothing."

"Don't lie to me, Argentina. I saw you leave the Bug with Lindsey."

That one got him a glance, but Izzy wasn't sure if the disbelief Jenk leveled at him was for Lindsey or Argentina.

"She drove me home," Jenk said. He was such a good liar. Izzy studied his technique whenever possible. He'd added just the right amount of *dude, get a grip* with a dash of *don't I wish she'd come inside . . .* Truly brilliant.

"So how was she?" Izzy asked. "Hot or unbelievably hot?"

Point-blank refusal to accept the lie wasn't enough to break the M-ster. "Number one, she drove me home," he said, the fact that he was on his forty-seventh push-up nowhere in his voice. He sounded as if he had his feet up on his desk. "Number two, even if by some miracle I'd *had* intimate relations with her, I wouldn't talk about it."

"Dude, dude, dude," Izzy said. "You better believe she's talking about you right now, with all her friends. Haven't you watched *Sex and the City*? Shit, she's giving a blow-by-blow, complete with exact specifications—length and width—of your physical attributes."

Jenk was unfazed. But he glanced at his phone.

He'd put his cell on the ground next to him, set on silent so it wouldn't disturb the tadpoles, but close enough so he could see it light up if someone called.

Someone important. Izzy wasn't going to try to guess who. Lindsey.

Izzy reached over and picked it up, which—hello!—got a rise out of Marky.

"Give it back, Zanella."

"No worries, Weebs, if it rings, I'll hand it over." He clicked on the outgoing call log. Lindsey, Lindsey, Lindsey, Lindsey, and . . . Lindsey. Starting at 0930 this morning. No, wait. Starting at 0430. "You called her at 0430? No wonder she won't call you back." Or maybe she had. He checked the incoming call log. Nope. Nothing from Lindsey. Except. Whoa, doggies. "Tracy called you at 0314 last night?"

Jenk sat up, wiping the sweat off his face with the bottom of his T-shirt. "Give me that." Izzy surrendered the phone. "You have serious boundary issues, Zanella."

"Holy crap," Izzy said as the lightbulb went on overhead. It was five hundred watts and quite illuminating. "You were with Lindsey last night and Tracy called, begging you to do her."

"Yeah, right." Jenk did crunches now, his phone safely in his pocket.

"No, wait . . ." Izzy was thinking aloud. "Midnight, it's a booty call; 0300, it's *help, I've fallen and I can't get up.* Or the equivalent. A flat tire. Ditched by the ex in some cheap motel. *But he promised me he'd marry me this time . . .*" He imitated Tracy. "Am I warm?"

"No," Jenk grunted.

But Izzy knew he'd discovered why Jenk believed this was the worst time—how had he put it? *The worst fucking time in the entire history of the world to leave town.* "You were banging Lindsey for, what, the second? Third time? When the phone rings. Hello, it's crazy Tracy. *Come save me.* And you were stupid enough to go, which sends a giant message to Lindsey: *You are my second choice.* And maybe she *was* your second choice, until you did a face-to-face with Tracy and it hit you. *She's* the one-night bang. Lindsey's a much better fit in that forever slot that you're suddenly so desperate to fill. Why are you so desperate to fill it? I have no idea. But okay, you handle Tracy, and finally around 0430, she passes out on your couch. You try calling Lindsey, but she won't pick up. You try again today, but she's definitely dodging you. Dude. That's gotta suck."

Jenk had stopped his crunches, and he just lay back on the grinder, arms over his eyes. "Zanella, just give me a break."

"Okay," Izzy said. "How's this for a break? A nonstop transport flight from the air base to New Hampshire. Six uninterrupted hours to pitch your woo, to grovel as charmingly as possible at the fair maiden's feet."

Jenk sat up. "Give me a break as in, I love you like a brother, man, but I can't take any more of your shit today, so *shut* the fuck *up.*"

"So you don't want me to tell you—perhaps more clearly—"

"No."

"That Tommy's Troubleshooters—Lindsey included—are coming with, to Nuevo Hampshire?"

That caught Jenk's attention, but he was still less than happy. "Can't you ever just say what you fucking mean?"

"I did," Izzy said. "What, do you want it like this?" He spoke like a robot, with no inflection. "Lindsey and the other Troubleshooters are coming to New Hampshire. On the troop transport. With us. At 2100 tonight."

Jenk exploded. "Why the fuck didn't you tell me that twenty fucking minutes ago?"

Izzy shrugged. "Hey, you're not banging Lindsey, right? I mean, that's what you told me. I figured you probably didn't care."

Yup. Marky-Mark didn't care so much, he chased Izzy for a good three miles down the beach.

It was after eleven before Tracy got into the office. She was still moving slowly, totally hungover, just tucking her purse into the bottom drawer of the reception desk, when Tom poked his head out of his office.

He didn't call her on the intercom—probably because he thought she wouldn't know how to answer it.

"Good, you're here," he said.

"I'm sorry I'm late—"

"I need you in my office," he said, and vanished. Not his usual *Tracy, when you've got a sec* or *Tracy, can we schedule a time to talk . . .*

She should have just straightened her shoulders and marched on in, ready to face the fire. Or rather the getting fired.

Because that was what this was about. She'd held—and lost—enough jobs to recognize a prefiring glare when she saw one.

Instead, because she was such a ninny, she ran into the ladies' room. *Don't cry, don't cry, don't cry.* If she started to cry, her makeup would run, and her nose would get even redder than it already was from crying last night and this morning, too.

She'd woken up in Mark's apartment, in his bed, and for several dizzying moments had had absolutely no clue where she was. He'd left her a note, though. *I hope you're feeling better. Help yourself to coffee and cereal. Lock the door behind you when you let yourself out.*

As she'd read his neat block handwriting, memories of the night before came surging back. Lyle. A diamond ring—along with a spare engraved with Heather-the-ho's name. *I can explain.* Running to Mark for help.

For more than help—how humiliating *that* had been?

Tracy gazed at herself in the mirror. How could her life have gotten so screwed up? Why, even now, was she considering Lyle's marriage proposal? *I need you,* he'd told her, as he knelt before her in the hallway of the hotel and cried.

He'd *cried.*

He'd insisted that the engagement ring engraved with Heather's name was merely to boost his confidence. He'd been so afraid that Tracy would say no, that he'd pushed her away for good this time, that she wouldn't take him back. He'd bought that other ring—a foolish mistake—as a way to pretend to himself that it didn't matter if Tracy turned him down. He'd told himself that he'd marry Heather instead.

But it was Tracy he loved, Tracy he needed.

She knew she was a fool to think he'd meant all that bullshit—just because he'd cried.

She'd figured it out, too. Lyle had been told that his being married would increase his chances of becoming partner at the firm. When she confronted him with that, he hadn't denied it.

Last night she'd been devastated by that realization.

This morning, though, she'd woken up resigned. It was Tracy who needed Lyle. So what if he was marrying her for ulterior motives? The bottom line was he finally wanted to marry her.

And, God, he'd actually cried.

As usual, she was probably going to cave. But she was unwilling to give in immediately. She'd called, left a message on Lyle's cell phone letting him know that she needed some time—an entire month—to think.

She wanted him to suffer.

Really, truly suffer.

And to sign a prenup that would set her up for life if he ever strayed again. If? When. And wasn't *that* an ugly twist to the end of her Cinderella fairy tale. And she lived wealthily ever after, and never had to work again.

But she needed to work now, especially if she delayed her return to New York for an entire month. She needed a job. Not necessarily this job. But if she got fired, it would be that much harder to find a new one.

She needed a game plan, a strategy. She'd walk in to her boss's office, and say, "Tom, I'm afraid it's just not working out." She'd quit first.

There. She had a plan.

Tracy rinsed her hands in the sink, letting the water run on her wrists, trying to cool herself down, when the door opened.

"There you are." It was Lindsey Fontaine—so petite and perfectly beautiful. She rarely wore makeup because she didn't have to, not with that flawless, smooth skin. Tracy had once kept track—she herself spent over an hour and a half applying and reapplying makeup each day. "Tom's looking for you."

"Oh," Tracy said, turning off the water and drying her hands on a paper towel. "I know. I was just . . . checking my makeup." She forced a smile. "I may be getting fired, but at least I look good."

Lindsey came into the room at that, letting the door close behind her. She was wearing her usual baggy jeans, but instead of the Hawaiian-flavored shirts that she favored, she wore a T-shirt. It should have made her look even more casual, but the shirt was a baby T, with cute little cap sleeves, and it actually fit. It made her look slim and female, but in an athletic, don't-need-a-running-bra-because-I'm-perfect way.

Tracy would have been jealous, except she knew that Lindsey was probably just as envious of Tracy's far more lush figure. That was the way the world worked. You always wanted what you didn't have. American women were so screwed up.

"What makes you think you're getting fired?" Lindsey asked.

"Not only am I late, but I'm a disaster. You don't think I've noticed that we're on day five of *Receptionist Lessons for Dummies,* and you're still here to hold my hand?"

Lindsey smiled, and Tracy realized that she hadn't been smiling when she came in. She was obviously tired this morning, too — not her usual effusive friendly self. "Well, relax. You're not getting fired."

"I'm not?"

"No. We're going to New Hampshire to help Team Sixteen with more training exercises," Lindsey told Tracy. "You know, kind of like the thing we did when I was hostage last night?"

Tracy nodded. Lindsey had spoken of little else but the training exercise earlier in the week.

"How'd that go?" she asked, mostly to be polite. She was jealous, she'd realized a few days ago. Everyone in the office was gearing up to play this massive game of hide-and-seek — except for Tracy.

Lindsey nodded. "Good." She was standing there with her arms crossed, unsmiling, as if she were merely tolerating Tracy's presence today. What was that about? She was usually so warm. In fact, she was everything Tracy wasn't — outgoing and self-confident. She'd actually been a police officer, and she had this ability to pal around with the women and the men in the office alike — to be one of the boys. Tracy had never been one of the boys in her entire life.

"But for this next series of exercises," Lindsey continued, "Tom's looking for a hostage with a little less experience. Even Sophia, who's not field trained, is too . . . familiar, I guess is the right word, with the process. Besides, we want her to play one of the tangos again — she did an amazing job last night."

Tango was the radio call sign for the letter T, which, in this case, stood for terrorist. Everything in this crazy business had a nickname or an acronym or was in some kind of code. SPECWAR. OCONUS. LZ, DZ, SEAL.

"Tom needs to know if you're available to go with us to New Hampshire," Lindsey continued. "To play the part of the hostage."

"Are you serious?" Tracy had to lean back against the row of sinks.

"Yeah," Lindsey said. "But we're working straight through the weekend. There's not going to be any downtime. We'll be staying in a cheap motel, but we won't be there very often. And it's going to be extremely cold."

"I don't care," Tracy said.

Lindsey clearly didn't believe her. "During the exercise we'll be in the woods, probably for days at a time and . . . Have you ever been camping?"

"Not since I was a Girl Scout. And it wasn't really camping," Tracy admitted. "We stayed in cabins, with, you know, flush toilets." When she'd first arrived at the camp, she'd actually been disappointed. And then her group went on a hike and discovered what the word *latrine* really meant.

"This is going to be worse than you can imagine." Lindsey smiled, but it was pretty grim. "You are so going to hate this. I seriously recommend you think hard before you say yes."

"I appreciate your concern, but . . . Things didn't go too well with Lyle last night and I could use a distraction."

A distraction.

Was that what Tracy had been looking for last night, at three o'clock in the morning, when she'd called Mark Jenkins?

Although, truth be told, what Lindsey was really wondering was—had Jenk distracted her?

There was no doubt about it. Lindsey was jealous. Screaming, green-eyed-monster jealous.

She'd tried convincing herself it was just disappointment that she was feeling. Disappointment, after all, was a common reaction to any situation wherein expectations had not been met.

And Lindsey had expected a full fling, not a one-night stand. She'd been looking forward to a week or two spent with a man whose smile could make her heart flutter. But Tracy's late-night phone call had cut that two weeks too short.

It wasn't just Tracy's phone call that had cut it short, but Jenk's reaction to it—his immediate jumping through rings of fire at her teary command.

Which really shouldn't have surprised Lindsey. She'd accepted her Plan B status with her eyes wide open. She really had no right to be hurt or angry or upset or jealous.

But she was.

She tried to tell herself that it was a good thing her time with Mark Jenkins had been terminated. If this was how she was feeling after just one night . . . Well, it was better to be skewered a little now than a whole lot later on.

Still, this current assignment was just about as awful as it could get. Lindsey was going to have to work with both the man and his Plan A girl-friend in close quarters for the next five—count 'em, five—days.

Right now, she stood in the ladies' room, watching Tracy examine her makeup in the mirror over the sinks. The taller woman was wearing pants today, but they were nothing like the pants Lindsey wore. Tracy wore pants the same way Lauren Bacall wore pants. They accentuated her trim waistline and draped around her hips. Made of a soft, expensive fabric, they flowed down her long legs. And, of course, she wore heels, too. On top she wore a sweater—if it could be called that. It had sleeves that ended between her elbows and wrists, and a neckline that was neither low nor high but didn't exactly look as if it would keep her warm. The entire effect was elegant.

Lindsey, on the other hand, looked like an androgynous, rumpled elf. Her short haircut was partly to blame, but only partly.

But there they both were, reflected in that big mirror. Mark Jenkins's Plan A and Plan B.

Were they having fun yet?

Alyssa poked her head into the bathroom. "Everything okay in here?"

It was obvious that Tom had sent her in. He needed immediate answers for their personnel list.

"Yes," Lindsey lied. "Tracy's a go for New Hampshire. She'll be sharing a motel room with Sophia."

Lindsey's escape last night—from the training op, not from Jenk's apartment—had won her a coveted private room. Thank God. There was limited housing in Dark-Side-of-the-Moon, New Hampshire, where they were heading.

"Oh," Tracy said, "I have to share a room?" She must've realized how Paris Hilton that sounded, because she quickly added, "That's fine, of course."

"Good." Alyssa looked at Lindsey. She was clearly picking up on the tension, and her eyes were apologetic. "I'm going to need you to sit down with Tracy, make sure she knows what to pack, luggage limits and so forth."

Oh, boy. Whoo-hoo. Lindsey mustered up a smile from somewhere beneath a ton of resentment. Maybe she'd get some enjoyment out of watching Tracy's face when she informed her she'd only be allowed to bring one small duffel bag on the plane. It would be evil enjoyment, which meant she was a bad, bad person, but right now she didn't care. "Let's go into my office."

Alyssa had been leaving, but now she pushed the bathroom door back open. "Actually . . ." She made an entire apologetic face this time. "Deck's in there today. How about the conference room?"

Decker had stolen Lindsey's office?

Although, okay. Truth was, it was Deck's office, and Lindsey had claimed squatter's rights since he was so rarely around. Still, this was a nice cherry on top of what was turning into a truly shitty day.

Tracy followed Lindsey down the hall. "So my evening was about as awful as it could get. Lyle was . . . God, I so don't want to talk about Lyle."

Call the *San Diego Union-Tribune*. Call channel seven's breaking news hotline. Tracy Shapiro didn't want to talk about Lyle.

"Can I get you some coffee?" Tracy asked. "Because I haven't had any yet, and my head's about to explode."

"Sure, grab me a cup, too." Lindsey opened the supply cabinet, took a legal pad, and went into the conference room. Tossing the pad down onto the big table, she pulled out one of the many chairs. Maybe if she were lucky, Tracy would sit way down at the other end and choke on her coffee. The table was so huge that even though Lindsey would race to her side to try to save her, she'd be too late.

Yeah, she was a bad person. She wrote on the top of the pad in big block letters: LUGGAGE IS LIMITED TO ONE (1) SMALL DUFFEL BAG. On second thought, she added: SMALL = YOU CAN CARRY IT EASILY ON A TWENTY-MILE HIKE. She then put a little caret mark between EASILY and ON and added the word YOURSELF.

Not that they were going on any twenty-mile hikes, but she could just imagine Tracy appearing at the air base with a duffel the size of a Mini Cooper. *You said one small duffel. This is my smallest. I mean, I had to work hard to get everything in it. I thought I was going to have to take the one that's the size of a house. A small house, of course, because you did say small. You know, a two-bedroom ranch. No master bath or swimming pool. Have I mentioned how much Lyle likes to swim?*

Tracy came into the room, carrying two mugs of coffee and clearly trying hard to sound upbeat. "So you will not believe what happened last night." She set Lindsey's favorite mug in front of her. "Milk and just a touch of sugar, right?"

"Thanks," Lindsey said.

"Oh, I also set the phones so that if anyone dials zero, it'll ring in here."

Apparently not getting fired agreed with Tracy. She sat down right next to Lindsey. So much for the choking plan.

"You know Mark Jenkins, right?" Tracy continued. "My Navy SEAL? He's the really cute one, a little short, but he has this giant crush on me?"

Her Navy SEAL. Nice. "Yup, I know him." Lindsey closed her mouth and didn't add, *Had sex with him last night, as a matter of fact.* She so didn't want to hear this. She didn't want to pretend to be Tracy's best friend. She wanted to do her job and go home to pack her own bag. "Look, we really need to—"

"Things went downhill fast with Lyle," Tracy just bulldozed over her. "It was really awful and . . . Anyway, I found myself in a cab without any money, and I didn't know where to go, so I went to Mark's."

La la la la. In her mind, Lindsey plugged her ears and sang loudly. "We're going to get you some cold-weather boots. What size shoe do you wear?"

"Seven," Tracy said. "He was so sweet, just letting me cry on his shoulder. He has amazing shoulders."

Lindsey knew. "We really need to discuss this now," she said, trying hard not to sound desperate. "You're going to have to pack and—"

"I was so drunk," Tracy confided. "I actually hit on him. Oh, my God." She rolled her eyes. "He's a really good kisser. *Really* good."

Yes. Yes, Tracy, she did know that. "I also need your clothing sizes."

"So, okay. We're, like, there, in his apartment, sitting on his sofa and I . . ." Tracy frowned. "What for?"

"Believe it or not, Tom wants you in a nurse's uniform," Lindsey told her.

"Oh, yuck," Tracy made a face. "Like one of those white dresses? Why?"

"It'll probably be pants and a shirt, because of the weather, but yeah," Lindsey informed her, tossing in, "Made of that really thick, nasty polyester. I hate that stuff, too. No one looks good in it." Tracy's dismay only made Lindsey feel like a bitch, and she explained. "Right now there's no snow on the ground, and if you're dressed in white pants, it'll be that much harder for the rescue team to get you out undetected."

"Oh." Tracy forced a smile. "As long as there's a reason for it. I mean, of course, I'd do it anyway. I'm really excited about being able to help. It's like, I'm saving lives. Indirectly, of course, but . . ." She listed her clothing sizes.

As Lindsey wrote them down on a separate piece of paper, she didn't just feel like a bitch. She knew she was one. Tracy had no idea that Mark Jenkins meant anything to Lindsey. Obviously, Jenk hadn't told her. And despite Tracy's attempts to sound upbeat, she was clearly upset about something. She had shadows under her eyes, and when she forgot to force a smile, she looked terribly unhappy.

"Do you have any long underwear?" Lindsey asked, hoping the question would sufficiently distract Tracy from telling the rest of her story.

"Are you serious?" she said.

"Very. There's a sporting goods store three blocks from here," Lindsey told her. "They carry a silk-wool blend that's superlightweight and really warm. You should pick some up as soon as we finish here."

"As long as they take credit cards. I have to finish telling you about last night. I'm just getting to the good part."

Oh, great.

"So we're on Mark's sofa," Tracy said, "and I say to him, *It's really warm in here,* and I start, you know, loosening my clothes and I'm not being at all subtle, and he—"

Lindsey put her pen down rather forcefully onto the table. "I'm sorry, did I somehow give you the impression that I wanted to hear the intimate details of—"

"No, wait. That's the thing. There *are* no intimate details, because do you know what he said?" Tracy was sitting there, amusement and disbelief brimming in her *Sports Illustrated* Swimsuit Issue eyes, like this was going to be the funniest story Lindsey had ever heard. "He said, *I'll open a window.* There I am, giving him a total green light. I mean, I couldn't be any more obvious if I'd said, *Hey, I have a good idea, let's have sex!* So he stands up and actually opens the . . . well, it's not exactly a window. See, there's this sliding glass door that opens onto a little deck off his living room. He opens that, and when he comes back, he doesn't sit on the sofa. He sits *way* across the room." She laughed, but it was suddenly down a notch on the gaiety dial. "It's funny now, but it wasn't that funny then. I think I might've started to cry. I was pretty embarrassed. I mean, what do you do when you throw yourself at someone, and he turns you down?"

Lindsey couldn't stop herself from repeating, "He turned you down."

Tracy nodded. "Totally. But he was so nice about it. From his seat on the other side of the room." She laughed again. "Like he thought I'd jump him if he sat next to me. I probably would've."

"He turned you down because you were too drunk?" Why was Lindsey clarifying this? What did it matter?

"No, he said . . ." Tracy leaned closer and lowered her voice, even though they were the only ones in the room. "Did you know he just started seeing someone?"

Oh, shit. "He told you that?" Lindsey asked.

"Yeah. Can you believe it?" Tracy laughed her amazement. "He kissed me, just last week, so . . . My timing stinks. Anyway, there I am, on a platter, and he's telling me this, going, *She's really special, she's amazing, Trace. It happened fast, but I'm so into her, it's a little scary.*"

Oh, *holy* shit. Jenk had called Lindsey repeatedly today, and she'd assumed he'd wanted to give her the "Wow, we went a little crazy last night, which was a mistake because, really, we're so good together as friends" speech. And while his turning down Tracy's offer of sex didn't surprise her—he didn't really seem the type to be comfortable sleeping with two different women, drunk or not, in the course of one night—the fact that he'd told *Tracy*, of all people, that he was *seeing* someone . . . Someone he was *really into* . . .

Lindsey couldn't find any words, but as usual when conversing with Tracy, a reply was unnecessary.

"I wish I were with someone who thought I was special," Tracy said wistfully. "Lyle would screw your grandmother in her wheelchair if she so much as breathed in his direction."

Both of Lindsey's grandmothers had been dead for years and *She's really special . . . I'm so into her, it's a little scary.*

Yeah. Not just a little scary, a crapload scary. Panic squeezed Lindsey's throat, and she quickly made a list of items Tracy needed to take to New Hampshire. Woolen socks—at least ten pairs. Long underwear. She wrote down the address of the sporting goods store. Turtlenecks. Flannel pajamas. A warm hat. Gloves and mittens.

Tracy had finally fallen silent, but now she mused, "Do you think he's lying? Do you think he's, like, gay?"

No, but she thought it was possible that Jenk had changed Lindsey's ringtone to "Here Comes the Bride."

"Do you know Mark's friend Izzy?" Tracy asked.

"Yeah," Lindsey said tersely as she tried to include everything that Tracy might need. A warm scarf. Winter jacket. Bulky wool sweaters to create layers.

"He's kind of intense, isn't he?" Tracy just would not shut up.

Son of a bitch. Lindsey had told Jenk she didn't want anything heavy. Damnit, she'd let herself have him because he so clearly wasn't looking for that either. Or so she'd mistakenly believed.

What kind of idiot could have one night of sex—and it was great sex, yes, okay, but still . . . What kind of fool could think that one night could be a basis for any kind of real relationship? And he *so* wasn't *seeing* her. One night wasn't *seeing*.

She tore the page off the pad and handed it to Tracy. "Bring only one duffel bag, and make sure it's light enough so you can carry it yourself."

Tracy laughed melodious peals of merriment as Lindsey pushed her chair back and headed for the door. But then the laughter stopped as she hit the hall.

"Oh, my God, you're not kidding, are you?" she heard Tracy say in shock.

Lindsey headed for Tom's office to ask him—beg him if necessary—to let her stay behind.

LOCATION: UNCERTAIN
DATE: UNKNOWN

Beth awoke, disoriented, in a bed that sagged in the middle, in a room she didn't recognize, a room with a window, its shade pulled and curtains closed.

Yet light leaked in around the edges.

This was significant in some way, but she couldn't for the life of her remember why.

The bedroom door was open a crack and a light was on out in the hall. She could see that the walls of the room were a faded yellow, the ceiling white and full of cracks, like a road map of a country where insanity ruled.

Her head was pounding and her mouth was dry and sour-tasting, which was odd because usually after she vomited, the headache from her hangover got much less intense.

One thing was clear—it must've been one hell of a night, because try as she might she could not remember a damn thing. How she got here. Who she went home with. Whether she'd puked before or after they'd gotten it on.

Her mother would love that—if she found out. Of course, her mother would be angry enough over her failure to come home last night. And if Beth couldn't remember exactly who she'd spent the night with, odds were good that she'd also forgotten to give Ma a call.

She was shivering despite blankets pulled up to her chin. The mattress was too soft, her back was killing her. She shifted, trying to get herself out of the center ditch, and . . .

She was tied down. To the cast-iron frame of the bed. Her right ankle and her right wrist. She tried to sit up, tried to pull free, but it wasn't silk scarves or even ropes that bound her. It was chains. Shackles.

She was dressed in ragged, bloodstained clothes that hadn't been properly washed in ages, and her arm had the nastiest-looking gash–Lord, it hurt.

"Feeling better, Number Five?"

The door opened wider, and he was standing there, with the hall light behind him, his face in shadows, and she remembered.

Most of it, but not quite all. How had this happened? Had she fought Number Twenty-One, and lost?

Terror rushed through her, choking her, making sparks appear before her eyes.

How it happened didn't matter. The only thing that mattered was he'd brought her upstairs.

Which meant that now he was going to do to her what he did to Number Four.

CHAPTER
TEN

"Hey."

"Hey."

"Mind if I, uh, sit?"

Well, there was a promising start to a conversation. Dave looked up from his book to see Mark Jenkins standing in the aisle of the plane.

Lindsey Fontaine was sitting in the window seat directly behind Dave. "No," she said. "Please do. This is, um . . . Do you have time to, you know, talk? For more than just a few minutes?"

Jenkins sat next to her. "Yeah, I've pretty much got until we land in New Hampshire. I mean, assuming the commander doesn't need me for anything."

They were talking quietly, but acoustics created some kind of bizarre pocket that made their voices sound as if they were speaking directly into Dave's ear. It was an interesting phenomenon, and it usually only happened on commercial flights, when there was a crying baby sitting behind him. He was about to turn around and comment on it—*Don't get too personal back there, ha-ha-ha* . . . when Lindsey said, "About last night . . ."

And Jenkins said, "I am *so* sorry."

"It was a mistake," Lindsey said.

"I agree. I was wrong to . . . I've been thinking about it all day, and I should have just told her that you were there—"

Dave was gathering up his things—his briefcase, his jacket—when Lindsey cut Jenk off. "I *meant* it was a mistake for us to sleep together. It was a mistake to think that we could have sex without it screwing up our friendship."

Oh, good. Now if Dave stood up and moved to another seat, Lindsey would know that he'd heard her say that. He'd overheard her earlier today, too, in Tom's office, asking to be excused from this op. She didn't want to go to New Hampshire.

Her reasons—she found it hard to handle the cold weather, she needed some time off—apparently hadn't been entirely truthful.

Jenk broke the silence. "Lindsey, look, I know I really messed up, but—"

"You didn't."

"—what we did last night was *not* a mistake. You're incredible—"

"In bed," she said. "You don't know me well enough to know whether I'm incredible at anything besides backrubs and—"

Dave put his fingers in his ears and scrunched down in his seat. This was information that he desperately didn't want to know. But still their voices cut through.

"I think I do." Jenk was certain.

"You have no clue who I am." Lindsey was, too.

Jenk obviously knew he couldn't win this one, that it would rapidly deteriorate to "Do too!" "Do not!" "Do too!" So instead, he said, "Then, let me get to know you. Talk to me. I want to know everything—"

"Do you?" She was pissed. "Or do you only want to know the things about me that fit into your little perfect fantasy? I've actually read the Kama Sutra. I took a course in human sexuality in college that was extremely enlightening—that's one for the double-plus column, huh?"

Dave tried desperately not to listen, but it was no use.

"And I love to camp," Lindsey continued. "Let's see, I've always wanted to learn to white-water raft—as a SEAL those are both probably big thumbs-ups, maybe even bigger than that first item. So, check and check. But oh, wait, I watch a lot of TV. You're not into that. Except, I've got TiVo. That turns it from a minus to a plus, because I'll have something to do all those weeks I'm home alone while you're off jumping out of airplanes."

"Lindsey, I know you're angry. If I were you, I'd be angry, too—"

"Oh, wait, here's something that I've already told you. Let's see what happens when I tell you again. *I'm not looking for anything heavy right now.* Okay, hmmm. That's not a plus, since your goal is two point five kids and a minivan. In fact, it's a pretty major minus, but you know what? Just ignore it. Just keep on ignoring it, Mark."

Now there was silence. Dave held his breath. Was Jenk going to figure it out, or did Lindsey have to put it into even plainer language?

Jenk finally spoke. "You're dumping me."

"No," she said, but this time he cut her off.

"Yeah. You are. Wow."

"Dumping implies—" Lindsey started.

"You honestly don't think we were great together? I'm sorry, but I'm having trouble thinking this isn't about me going to Tracy's rescue, like I failed your test or I'm too human to fit your high standards or—"

"Dumping implies a relationship," she told him hotly. "We had one night, which was, in my opinion, a major mistake. I told you up front that I wasn't looking for a relationship and you said, great, we're on the same page. Well, I'm still on that page. You've gone off into some fairytale somewhere, where you suddenly don't want Tracy anymore, where you've . . . you've . . . photoshopped my face into the wedding photo on some new page that says, *And they lived happily ever after!*"

"What?" He was completely confused.

"She told me what you said," Lindsey was completely indignant. "Tracy. She told me she hit on you and you *turned* her *down*—"

Jenk's voice was incredulous now. "Okay, wait. You're mad at me because I *didn't* sleep with Tracy?"

"Because of me!" Lindsey finished. "You told her you were seeing someone else, but you're not. We had sex, Mark. And the only reason you asked me to go home with you was because you thought Tracy was back with Lyle."

"That's not—" he started.

"Yes," she said firmly. "It is. And you know it."

He was silent for a moment. "So . . . what? I'm not allowed to change my mind?"

"No," Lindsey said. "You are. The same way I'm allowed to *not* change mine."

More silence, then Jenk said, "I thought maybe you . . ." He sighed.

"Would swoon?" she said.

There was more going on here than she was saying, because she was way too angry at Jenkins for . . . not sleeping with Tracy? Yes, there was definitely more to this situation than met the eye. Or the ear, in Dave's case.

"Because suddenly you see me fitting into the little slot you've carved out for your anonymous future wife?" Lindsey continued. "Everything I said must've been bullshit, right? Because everyone knows all women everywhere are really just holding their breath, thinking: Someday my prince will come. Sorry to burst your bubble, but I don't want to marry you, I don't want to move in, I don't want to go steady. I don't even want to *date* you. I wanted to have sex with you. That's all. I thought maybe we could be the kind of friends who hook up for a while and just have a good time. I was wrong. It was a mistake. A big one."

Silence.

"I wasn't asking you to marry me," Jenkins finally said. "What I was gonna say was I thought you liked me as much as I liked you. I guess I got my answer."

"I do like you," Lindsey said. "As a friend."

Those three little words sounded the death knell for that last bit of hope that surely remained in Jenkins's heart. Dave could practically hear the quiet hiss as the faltering flame went out.

"Okay," Jenk said. "It's not what I want, but . . . okay. That's . . . okay."

They were both silent then, but Dave knew the conversation wasn't over. Jenk still had to stand up and walk away.

He finally spoke. "I'm sorry if anything I said or did hurt you."

"I'm sorry if I hurt you, too."

Dave heard the sounds of Jenkins pulling himself to his feet. He pretended to be engrossed in his book, but he could see the young SEAL out of the corner of his eye. Jenk just stood there for a moment, as if he were going to say something more, but then he walked down the aisle to the back of the plane.

Ouch. Dave's stomach hurt. For both of them.

Then Lindsey kicked the back of his seat. "Did you enjoy that?" She was talking to him. Terrific.

He turned around, lifting himself up to look at her. "More than you did, I'm betting."

He'd never seen her so thoroughly miserable. She was always so upbeat, always smiling. Now she looked awful, like she'd just been hit by a bus. It was possible there were tears in her eyes, but she gazed out the window, which made it difficult for him to know for sure. "Please don't tell anyone."

"I won't," Dave said. "I wouldn't." He paused. "Are you sure you—"

"Yes," Lindsey said. "I'm sure. I am very sure," she added, nodding along with her words, as if trying to convince herself.

She was sure, and Jenk was okay.

And Dave regularly had phone sex with the Queen of England.

DARLINGTON, NEW HAMPSHIRE
SATURDAY, DECEMBER 10, 2005

New Hampshire was freaking cold, the morning sun doing little to warm the air.

As they pulled up to their temporary living quarters—an ancient two-

story structure called Motel-a-Rama—Izzy helped the senior chief organize the equipment, while Jenkins ran around making sure everyone had
their room assignments.

"I want to share a room with Tracy and Sophia," Izzy announced,
which started both Lopez and Gillman yammering. *Show a little respect,
Zanella. Christ, Zanella, you're like a fifteen-year-old on a high school
trip. Grow up.*

"A man's allowed to dream, isn't he?" Izzy said to no one in particular
as he lugged a carton of MREs into the motel lobby and *whoa*. Hello,
1976.

Most of the shag had been worn off the avocado green carpet in the
high-traffic areas, but it continued bravely waving under several chairs that
looked as if they'd come direct from a garage sale at Graceland. The ceiling was yellow with exposed beams that had, thirty years ago, been bright
orange. And everything else was covered in cheap paneling.

The woman behind the front desk wore a Harley jacket over about fifteen sweaters, a cloud of cigarette smoke around her head. Her hair was a
shocking shade of red, or maybe it just seemed shocking since it clashed
with the earmuffs she was wearing.

"The entire restaurant's yours for the duration, hon," she croaked at
Izzy in a five-pack-a-day voice as she pointed to a door behind her. "Fastest
way to the kitchen's back through here."

She sounded around five hundred years old, although judging from
her blue eye-shadow, she couldn't be a day over sixty. Still, her smile was
warm, and the Christmas balls she wore, dangling from her ears, were a
hoot.

"Thanks, babe," he said as he humped the MREs past her, winning
both a wink and big brownie points.

It was a good idea to make nice with the locals, considering they were
in the middle of no-oh-oh-oh-where. Darlington, New Hampshire. Or, as
Lindsey called it, the dark side of the moon.

They'd left the airport and driven north. And then north some more.
And then they left the highway and went north on state roads. Then they'd
left those, and went even farther into these frickin' frozen mountains.

"Name's Stella," the redhead told him on his way back out to the
truck.

"No way," he said, stopping to lean on the counter. "You have got to
marry me. My name's Zanella, and Stella Zanella is just too good to pass
up."

She flashed him both a smile and her wedding ring, which of course he'd noticed already. "I'm taken. But feel free to challenge Robert, my husband, to a duel."

"Just out of curiosity, Stell," he said. "Who the fuck owns a motel on Mars?" He'd also noticed a poster pinned up on the wall. A kitten, hanging from a chin-up bar. Someone had crossed out the caption "Hangin' in," and written "Fuck you, very much." He didn't quite get what the new caption had to do with the cat—there was probably a personal joke involved—but he figured the word was in her vocabulary. It was also clear that the Robert she'd mentioned was former military. A display case held his medals, won during Vietnam. Yeah, she'd heard the word before.

Sure enough, Stella laughed. "We do all right. Hunters, snowmobilers, the occasional lost skiers . . . Summer can be slow, but that's okay. More time to work in the garden."

"Come on, Zanella, move it." Jenk was unhappy, and had been ever since sitting down and talking to Lindsey on the plane. Izzy wasn't sure what that was about, but it wasn't good since Marky-Mark obviously bought into the old "misery loves company" adage.

Izzy ignored him. "Stell, if I'm going to be your second husband, you've got to quit smoking," he said. "You're killing yourself, and that's not good. Will you think about doing that for me, babe?"

He didn't hear her answer, because Jenk grabbed him by the back of the jacket and manhandled him outside. "Stop fucking around."

"When the fuck did *you* make chief?" Izzy knocked Jenk's hands away, possibly a little bit harder than necessary. Definitely harder than necessary since he knew that this wasn't about him.

Jenk shoved him back. "I'm tired of doing my work and then yours, too, asshole."

This was about Lindsey.

"She jettisoned you, huh? On the plane?" Izzy asked. "I'm sorry, Mark."

It probably would've been better just to shove him back. As it was, Jenkins didn't know what to do with Izzy's sympathy. He shook his head. "Just do your fucking job," he said, and walked away.

They were sharing a room for the next five days.

Wasn't this going to be great?

Jenk drove the rented SUV as Lopez navigated.

He was tired, he was angry, he was upset, and he was hyperaware that Lindsey was sitting behind him, squeezed in between Izzy and Gillman. If he looked in the rearview, there she was. Looking anywhere but back at him.

He kept his eyes on the narrow road.

"Left up here," Lopez ordered, and Jenk slowed to make the turn onto a dirt trail. "And then it's straight on, as far as you can go."

This could have been way worse. He could've been alone in this vehicle, with only Lindsey beside him, peering at the map.

"Jenkins!" He'd been helping to unload their supplies when Tommy Paoletti had shouted for him.

He'd made a dash for Tommy, who was in the motel restaurant. He'd had to smile because he'd moved instinctively—temporarily transported back in time a few years, to when Paoletti was the commanding officer of Team Sixteen. Damn, but he missed the man. Their current CO, Lew Koehl, had probably never bellowed in his life.

Jenk had slowed to a jog and his smile faded as he realized Lindsey was standing next to Tom. But okay. He had five full days of this. He was going to come face-to-face with her many times throughout the op, that was a given. It might as well happen for the first time right here and now.

Tommy, as usual, didn't wait for him to *yes, sir* or otherwise say hello. He just jumped in. He knew Jenk could keep up.

"It's colder than we thought," Tom said, "and we've got weather moving in. I'm thinking about setting up a camp, just outside the perimeter of the area where we'll be running tomorrow night's training op. We've gotten permission to use an old hunting lodge—well the property, anyway. The lodge burned years ago, but there're still a number of other structures on-site. I have no idea their condition or suitability. I want you to go check the place out."

And yes, that had been a plural *you*, aimed also at Lindsey, who was clutching a map. She silently passed it to Jenk, who pretended to look at it in the wan midday light that was streaming in through the restaurant windows, all the while thinking, *shit*.

"Ideal location is close to the top of a hillside," Tom continued. "I'm going to want a homing beacon broadcast to as large an area as possible, in case visibility becomes an issue."

"Wait," Lindsey said. Even though they were inside, and the heaters were groaning and hissing, it was cold enough for her to keep her hat and gloves on, her arms wrapped around herself as she tried to retain body heat. "You lost me, boss. Visibility? Are we expecting fog?"

That's right—she was a Southern California girl.

"Snow. Blizzard conditions can create total whiteouts," Jenk explained. "The homing beacon will allow us to find this base camp if we get into trouble during the exercise. It's a safety precaution." He turned back to Tom. "Sir, we should probably check with your team, see who else may not have had extensive winter survival experience—make sure they're teamed up with someone who has."

"Good idea," Tom nodded. "I'll get Tracy working on that."

And so much for Jenk's next suggestion, which was that Lindsey stay behind, here where the windchill wasn't a factor, and handle it.

"There used to be a road all the way in to the lodge," Tom told them. "I want a report on its condition. I want to know where it becomes impassable— which is how the property owner described it—as well as exactly how impassable it really is. I want recommendations on the best way to get a generator and supplies in there. And I'm assuming we'll have to set up some temporary sat towers, too, but check out cell reception while you're out there."

"Excuse me, sir," Johnny O. ran up. "If you've got a sec, Commander Koehl would like to talk to you. He's in the kitchen."

"I'm on my way," Tommy said, but he wasn't quite done giving orders to Lindsey and Jenk. "Take one of the rental vehicles. And make sure you grab some MREs. There're no Mickey-Ds where you're heading."

"You mean to hell?" Jenk may actually have said that aloud. Lindsey didn't look offended, though. She, too, did not look happy at the prospect of this little road trip. "Okay," he told her. "I'll get the food, you get more layers on, because we're going to be hiking."

She nodded. "Thanks for trying. You know, to make it so I could stay here where it's slightly less freezing."

"That wasn't entirely for you," Jenk admitted. "Meet you by the rental cars."

Lindsey had shown up with Dave and Sophia in tow, both of whom were apparently willing to spend their precious downtime playing chaperone. Jenk had been trying to do something similar—to talk Izzy, Lopez, and Gillman into riding along. They'd resisted his efforts—this was, after all, supposed to be one of their few breaks—until they saw that Sophia was going. Then they pretty much begged him for a seat in that SUV.

He should have charged them each fifty bucks.

"Is this really a road?" Dave now asked. He and Sophia were sitting in a rear-facing seat, but he'd twisted around to face front.

"It was, back when the lodge was in its heyday," Jenk reported. He'd stopped to gather as much info as possible from Izzy's married fiancée, Stella, after he'd packed up a delightful assortment of MREs. That was her word. *Heyday.* "It was originally a trail—a trapper's route from Canada to Boston. Apparently it got a lot of use during the French and Indian War, too."

"Marky-Mark, you are better than a Fodor's travel guide," Izzy said. "How do you know this shit? Okay, let's see if he can answer this one. For twenty thousand points: How did the hunting lodge burn down, and . . . drumroll please! Is it haunted?"

"Generator malfunction plus a very dry summer and fall," Jenk answered. "And no, despite rumors, it is *not* haunted."

"Nuh-nuh na-net, na-net," Izzy sang the opening bars to the *Ghostbusters'* theme. "*I ain't afraid of no ghosts.* Okay, so for those who weren't aware, Jenkins has this unswerving lack of belief in the supernatural. There's no such thing as ghosts; therefore, it can't be haunted. Just out of curiosity, M, what exactly are these rumors?"

"Typical boogeyman stuff," Jenk said as the SUV lurched and bounced along the pitted trail. He slowed even more as the underbrush scratched against the side of the vehicle like hundreds of bony fingers.

Gillman leaned forward. "Such as?"

"The gardener-gets-unjustly-arrested-and-comes-back-to-wreak-vengeance story," Jenk said.

"*Give me back my leg!*" Izzy intoned in a quavering voice. "I love that shit."

"Yeah," Lopez said. "I want to hear this."

"Come on, Unca Jenk, tell us kids a scary-ass story."

Jesus, he shouldn't have brought Izzy along. Jenk glanced in the rearview—shit, why did he keep doing that?—and saw that Lindsey was smiling. Fuck, that was worse than when she'd been sitting there, obviously wishing she were anywhere else on the planet. Because she was smiling at Izzy.

"I don't know if you should tell it," she said. "Izzy might have nightmares."

Oh, good. Don't just sit next to him. Flirt with him, too. Of course, some might interpret her words merely as friendly banter. Still, it pissed Jenk off.

But telling them all to shut the fuck up would clearly raise some eyebrows. Not to mention that it would reveal to Lindsey just how badly he'd let her burn him.

He was gripping the steering wheel so tightly, his knuckles were white.

"I'm sharing a room with Jenk," Izzy told Lindsey. "If I get scared I'll just climb in with him. I've heard he's good in bed. Gentle yet strong. Can anyone here verify that?"

Okay, now Lindsey was back to looking like she'd rather be wrestling alligators.

Izzy, of course, wasn't done. "Fishboy, you've shared close quarters with the Markster. Is he as talented as they all say?"

"Homophobic jokes are *so* funny," Dave remarked from the back, in his mild voice. "Oh, wait. No, they're not funny at all."

"Dave, why do you always get to sit next to Sophia?" Izzy turned his attention to the back of the SUV, but then added, "No offense, Lindsey. You're hot, too."

"Jenkins, will you please just tell the ghost story?" Dave implored.

"All right," Jenk said. "Okay. Jesus." The road was so overgrown, they were moving just slightly faster than they could've done on a brisk hike. At this pace, they weren't going to get back until after dark. Which, at this time of year, this far north, would probably happen at 1500 hours. "It all starts in the 1940s, right after the Second World War. The gardener's some local kid, home from the fighting in France. He's working at the lodge, he's got a beautiful fiancée–"

"There's always a beautiful fiancée," Lopez said. "She works there, too, right?"

"As a maid," Jenk said. "Life is good. But then this rich family comes to the lodge. They've got this son who served by taking some cushy desk job in DC during the war, totally entitled. He points at what he wants, and he gets it. But this time, he points at the maid, and he gets nothing. And he's pissed, because he's seen her with the gardener."

"Doing the deed with the war hero, in the arbor, au naturel," Izzy chimed in. "She's exotic in her beauty. He's strong, yet gentle . . ."

"A hunting lodge doesn't have an arbor," Gillman scoffed, saving Jenk from having to drive into a tree to shut Izzy up.

Not that Gillman managed to do more than change the subject, but it was enough.

"Yeah, well, in the movies they're always gettin' it on in the arbor. Or in the gazebo. There was probably a gazebo," Izzy decided.

"It's a hunting lodge," Gillman said as if that would explain everything, the *Stupid* silent but intensely implied.

"Yeah, well, my name's not Daniel Peckerfart Gillman the Third," Izzy said. "Mumsy and Pop-Pop never took me to a hunting lodge."

"I've never been to a hunting lodge either," Gillman said, "but I do read."

"You do?" Izzy was incredulous, and Lindsey was laughing again. "Marky-Mark, did you know that Fishboy knows how to read? Maybe he'll teach the rest of us kids someday."

"Let Jenk finish the story," Lindsey said.

Jenk. He was back to being Jenk. Apparently she only called him Mark when they were having sex. Which they were never going to do again.

"Was there a stable, oh great expert on hunting lodges?" Izzy leaned across Lindsey to ask Gillman.

Jenk went over a fallen branch a little too fast, which bounced everyone around and pushed Izzy back into his seat.

"There could've been a stable." Gillman gave him that but only grudgingly.

"Stable works for me," Izzy said. "Okay. I'm picturing it. I'm good. He sees her with the gardener in the stable. Go on, M."

Jenk sighed. "Aren't we tired of this yet?"

"No," was chorused back to him.

"Right. A piece of jewelry—a necklace—goes missing from this rich family's suite, and the gardener's accused of taking it. He swears he's innocent, that the son set him up, but no one believes him and they haul him off to jail."

"Time-out," Izzy proclaimed. "Can we not give these people names? The rich family is Horace and Prudence Peckerfart and their son Dick. No relation to Gillman—or is there? Say this for us, Daniel: *Zounds! That scoundrel stole Mumsy's necklace!*"

Lindsey laughed again, and Jenk glanced in the rearview to see Gillman covering her eyes while he silently mouthed a completely different and far more concise collection of words to Zanella.

"Not going to say it?" Izzy said. "Understandable. You don't want to incriminate yourself. But we still need a name for the gardener. How about Bill Jones, all-American boy, former GI, nephew to his Uncle Sam. And his fiancée, Lydia McDoomed. You'd think she'd change her name. So okay, Bill is in jail for stealing Dick's mumsy's necklace, which creates anxiety for fair Lydia. Take it away, Marky-Mark."

Jenk rolled his eyes. "*Dick* goes to see *Lydia,* and promises her he'll 'look for' the necklace if she sleeps with him, so she does. Why? Who knows. She's an idiot to trust him."

"She's a McDoomed," Izzy pointed out. "Bad choices run in the family."

"Of course, when the gardener—Bill—goes to trial, Dick never steps forward to clear him. Bill's about to be sentenced to twenty years in prison, so Lydia goes all the way to Boston to see this son of a bitch, who just laughs at her. He looked for the necklace, but he didn't find it. What can he do?

"Several months later, Lydia dies, pregnant and alone in the snow."

"Man, I hate when that happens," Izzy said.

"No one hears from the gardener again," Jenk continued, "except twenty years later, the same family—"

"The Peckerfarts," Izzy interjected.

Right. "They come back to the lodge—"

"Except for Horace, whose heart exploded years ago," Izzy said.

Jenk didn't stop the SUV, pull Izzy out into the cold, and beat him senseless. Instead, he very calmly asked, "Do you want me to tell the story, or do you want to?"

"Well, I would, but I don't know it. It amazes me how you always seem to know everything," Izzy said. "Isn't Mark amazing, Linds?"

Jenk focused on the road, forcing himself not to glance into the mirror and see her embarrassment. "Dick's got his own family now—a whole pack of daughters," he said loudly, just plowing over any hemming and hawing she might have started. "I think Stella said there were five of them."

"My Stella?" Izzy was delighted, completely clueless to the fact that even if he survived this day, he was going to be murdered in his sleep. And not by the ghost of the hunting lodge, either.

"Her kids used to camp up here."

"They probably came on a dare," Gillman said. "We used to do that—me and my brothers. Up by Bloody Creek. Scared ourselves to death. My mom was always, like, *It's two* A.M., *what are you doing back home? Is it raining?* And we were like, *Yeah, Mom, uh, yeah, it's, uh, raining, yeah.*"

"My older brothers once ditched me in a graveyard," Izzy contributed to the discussion. "I got the last laugh—when they came back, looking for me, I pretended I turned into a zombie. I scared the bejeezus out of them. Of course they retaliated by beating the living Christ out of me. Broke my collarbone and two ribs."

There was silence for a moment, which Lindsey broke by saying, "Suddenly being an only child doesn't seem so bad."

Lopez turned to look back at her. "You too, huh?"

And now she was bonding with freaking Lopez, smiling into his eyes. Jenk smacked the map. "I need you looking at this."

Lopez faced forward. "Sorry, man. I'm on it—we're moving pretty slowly." He must've noticed the steam coming out of Jenk's ears, and he lowered his voice to ask, "You okay?"

But he didn't have to answer because Gillman spoke over him. "Dick and his daughters are at the lodge. Come on, Jenkins. Don't leave us hanging."

"Not just his daughters, but his wife and mother are there, too," Jenk continued the story. "The men all go out hunting, and it's the first cold day of the season, so the women stay inside. They're all in the lodge when the generator explodes. Everything's so dry, the place goes up like a torch.

"Dick's family is trapped—they're all killed in the fire. Except, mysteriously of course, their bodies were never recovered. No bones, no teeth, no wedding rings, no jewelry—except . . . The necklace that was missing all those years is discovered in the search through the rubble. It was hidden under a floorboard in the room where Dick had stayed, twenty years earlier.

"Dick vanishes, mad with grief, into the mountains," Jenk told them. "Or so everyone thinks. What really happens—yeah, right—is that the gardener, Bill, came back and kidnapped Dick's entire family, using the fire as a diversion. He lured Dick into the woods with a note, promising to free his wife and children, but of course, he breaks that promise, the same way Dick had broken his promise to Lydia, years before.

"So Bill the crazy gardener keeps Dick locked up, torturing him for the same number of years that Bill spent in prison, killing Dick's mother and wife and daughters slowly in front of him, carving them up, before finally slashing and hacking them into a hundred pieces, all in retribution for Lydia's death. By the time he lets him go, Dick's completely insane. He still wanders this area at night. You know, cannibalizing little children who don't brush their teeth before going to bed."

"You suck at telling ghost stories, dude," Izzy complained. "Couldn't you, like, throw in a part right before the fire, where all those women at the hunting lodge hear this scary voice going, *Give me back my leg*."

Jenk looked at Izzy in the rearview. Of course that meant he looked at Lindsey, too. She was laughing again.

"Whose leg and what does it have to do with anything?" Lindsey asked.

"I don't know," Iz said. "It's just creepy. Like this leg is somewhere in the lodge."

"Hopping around by itself?" Lindsey asked. She met Jenk's eyes in the mirror, a big smile on her face, but then quickly looked away, her smile instantly dimmed.

"Another skeptic." Izzy turned to the backseat. "How about you, Sophia? Ghost stories—thumbs-up or thumbs-down?"

"Down," Sophia said. "I'm not a fan of stories that include carving and slashing and hacking innocent people into a hundred pieces."

"But they're not innocent," Izzy pointed out. "They're Peckerfarts."

"So what are you saying?" Lopez asked. "That children are responsible for the sins of their fathers? No one subscribes to that anymore."

"My father does," Lindsey said, as Jenk focused on the road ahead. It looked blocked.

"Really?" Again, Lopez found Lindsey more fascinating than his map.

It *was* blocked. Jenk turned the headlights on a tree that had fallen across the road, illuminating it in the afternoon gloom as he braked to a stop.

Before Jenk put the SUV in park, Izzy was already out of the vehicle, examining the barrier. "We're not going to be able to move this," he reported. "You know, by dragging it. It's huge."

"Maybe if we bring in some chain saws." Jenk joined him in the freezing afternoon. The air was unbelievably cold. Frozen-nose-hair cold.

"Maybe if we bring in a Caterpillar," Dave had left the comfort of the car, too. "Not in our budget, huh?" he added, as Jenk and Izzy just looked at him.

There was another tree across the road, just a short distance away. It was even bigger than this one.

Lopez and Gillman followed Lindsey and Sophia out of the vehicle. The two SEALs were quite a pair. Gillman wore his jacket unzipped, no hat, no gloves. Lopez, on the other hand, had winter gear that was practically outer-space ready. Hood up over a ski mask, he looked like Kenny from *South Park*.

"What?" he said, as Izzy laughed at him. "I don't like the cold. Is that all right with you?"

He was carrying the map, but how he could read it was anyone's guess. Lindsey gently took it from him. "Where are we?"

He pointed with one overstuffed-glove finger. "About a mile from the lodge."

Lindsey looked at Jenk. "We don't all have to go."

He nodded. "Good idea. Izzy and I'll—"

"Tom asked *me* to check the place out," Lindsey interrupted him.

He tried to explain. "But it'll take less time if—"

"Do *you* want to stay behind?" she asked him.

"I don't want to stay behind," Gillman said. "To come all this way, and then not see, you know, the scene of the crime?"

Jenk turned to him. "There was no crime. It's a story, a myth, an urban legend."

"Urban?" Izzy asked, looking around at all the trees.

"A mile's not that far," Sophia said. "I'd like to go."

"Me, too," Dave chimed in.

Jenk looked at Lopez. "You could stay with the car."

"All by yourself," Izzy pointed out. He made his voice quaver. *"Give me back my leg!"*

"Now that I'm out here, it's not really that cold," Lopez said, hurrying to catch up with the others, who'd already humped it over the fallen tree.

"Wow," Izzy said. "He's either a chicken, or he thinks he's got a chance with Sophia. Or Lindsey. He's actually doing better with Linds—" He realized what he was saying and who he was saying it to. "Sorry, dude."

Jenk turned off the car, grabbing both the bag with the MREs as well as the pack that traveled with the SUV. It contained a flashlight, a compass, and a hunting knife, along with other essentials like a first-aid kit and a rope. He locked the vehicle and pocketed the keys.

"This'll be over in three hours," Izzy said, taking the pack from him and shouldering it. "Tops." It was clearly meant to be encouragement, but he ruined it by snickering. "Three hours. That always makes me think, *a three-hour tour.*" He sang the phrase from the *Gilligan's Island* theme song, and then made the sound of thunder crashing. "We'd make great castaways. You could be the skipper. He was kind of short, too. Sophia and Lindsey are both a little bit Mary Ann, a little bit Ginger. And Dave is so obviously the professor. Gillman's got the idiot thing down, and his nickname is even Gilligan, I mean, along with Fishboy and Fuckhead and—"

"Not helping," Jenk informed him as he circumnavigated the second fallen tree.

"Not even the thought of Lopez cross-dressing and playing Mrs. Howell?" Izzy tried.

"Silence would be nice right now."

They walked for a moment with only the sound of their feet crunching leaves and fallen branches and frozen mud. The sky was a uniform white, and the bare trees stood out stark and black against it. Even the evergreens seemed gray. It was beautiful in a bleak way, as if the world had become a subtly lit black-and-white art film, filled with angst and despair.

But the sound of laughter carried back from up the trail, and as Jenk rounded a curve he saw Lindsey's red hat, her blue jacket.

Izzy ran to catch up with the others, leaving Jenk with more silence and frozen mud than he could ever possibly want in an entire lifetime.

CHAPTER
ELEVEN

The view from the ruins of the hunting lodge was incredible.

Sophia picked her way down what had once been a broad, sloping expanse of lawn, toward the two outbuildings. Danny Gillman came out of the more squat of the two.

"I think this was probably some kind of smokehouse," he said. "And see, look, over here. I'm pretty sure this is where the lodge owners set up their summer kitchen. The tables for the guests probably went here."

He'd moved to a patch of ground that was relatively flat. And, sure enough, there looked to be the remains of a grill made from stones and bricks. It was reminiscent of the ones used by refugees in Kazbekistan in *their* summer kitchens, which were also usually their winter kitchens, considering their homes were tents.

"I'm pretty sure we can modify the smokehouse so the smoke actually exits the structure." Danny started for the second building. "This other one looks a little too big to be an icehouse," he said, "although it would make sense for them to keep it tucked back in the woods, in the shade."

Sophia hesitated before following him, glancing back toward the ruins of the lodge. Izzy and Jay Lopez were racing each other up to the rise of the hill, where Tom Paoletti would no doubt want to put his communications tower—if he decided he wanted one. She spotted Dave near the last remaining walls of the burned-out main building, deep in discussion with Jenk and Lindsey. He was making good on the promise he'd made to Lindsey before they'd left the motel. *Please, please, please don't let me be alone with Mark Jenkins.*

Something had happened between Jenk and Lindsey over the past few days, something that put them at odds, which was a real shame. Sophia had thought that the spark she'd noticed whenever they were together was mutual, despite the SEAL's silly infatuation with Tracy Shapiro. She'd felt glad for Lindsey, who spent far too much of her off time at home watching television and pretending her life was peachy keen just the way it was, thanks.

Sophia could relate.

And watching Lindsey with Jenk, she'd even felt a little envious.

But now, for the first time, she could finally appreciate the noninclusiveness of the SEALs, with their men-only teams. There would be no unhappy romantic entanglements there.

At least none to which anyone would admit.

"Still, the smokehouse is a little small," Danny was saying. "As of right now, if this one's in the same condition . . . Of course, we could always use tents, but . . ." He realized Sophia wasn't right behind him and waited for her to catch up.

"An icehouse wouldn't have a fireplace," she pointed toward the chimney. That roof had definitely seen better days. There were saplings growing on it, like it was some kind of living fairyland cottage.

Danny laughed. "Yeah, that's kind of oxymoronic, huh? Maybe this was a servant's cottage. Maybe the gardener lived here. Maybe his spirit lives here still." He shot her a look filled with such little boy pleasure and anticipation, she had to laugh.

The ancient, rusting padlock didn't stop him. He had a picklock that he put to good use, and soon pushed the door open with a squeak of rusty hinges that was pure B-grade horror movie. And again, she laughed. Instead of going inside, he turned to face her.

"Hey, you know, I just wanted to tell you that Zanella's totally wrong about me," he said earnestly. "Yeah, I'm the third Dan Gillman, but there's no trust fund or . . . I mean, I heard your ex-husband was some kind of millionaire so . . ."

He seemed to want some kind of response—a confirmation or maybe encouragement of some kind. But Sophia wasn't sure where to start, with the fact checking—her husband Dimitri was dead, not an ex, and he had only played at being a millionaire—or some sort of personal mission statement to stem the tide, which was roaring to a place she didn't want to go. A place where his next words would be, *How about we get together for dinner after we get back to California? I know this great little Thai restaurant . . .*

I don't date Navy SEALs. Except she would date a Navy SEAL—a former one—if Decker would only ask her. She didn't want to lie.

I don't date children. Except Jay Lopez was older, closer to her own age. She'd have to come up with a separate excuse for when *he* asked her out. And he would. She had no doubt about that.

Besides, what exactly did the reference to Dimitri have to do with Danny's trust fund—or lack thereof? Was she supposed to conclude that he was looking for more than just a dinner date? Was he implying that he was interested in filling out an application to be Sophia's second husband?

Third husband, really. Even though her sham of a marriage to Padsha Bashir, the warlord who'd killed Dimitri and locked her away in his palace, probably wouldn't be upheld as legal here in the United States, Sophia found those particular months of her life impossible to forget.

Try as she might.

"I just wanted to be honest," Danny continued when she stood there staring at him, mired in her uncertainty as to how to respond. "That's really important to me. Honesty. I like everything out on the table—no secrets, no guessing. At least where I'm coming from. I mean, I like you. A lot. Why shouldn't I be up front about that, right?"

He was like the hero in a Disney movie. Drawn with clean, clear lines—honorable, and upstanding and true.

Sophia didn't want to hurt his feelings, so she started with, "Danny, I like you, too."

He didn't let her get to the *but.* "Great, let's have dinner. How's tonight? Why wait to get back to—"

She clarified. "I like you as a friend."

He didn't so much as blink. "Even better. Friendship is the perfect place to start. I like you as a friend, too."

"Seriously, there are too many reasons why I really can't—"

He interrupted her. "I can give you just as many reasons—more—why you can and you should." He smiled. "It's the Navy SEAL way. We're not easily scared off."

"I prefer men who are more mature," Sophia chose her words carefully. "I'm sorry, but you're just not my type."

He was undaunted. "I'm very mature."

"I meant older, and you know it."

He looked at his watch, frowning slightly. And when she tried to speak he held up one finger. "Wait . . . Okay, I'm older now."

The smile he gave her was so mischievous, she laughed, which was a mistake. Because clearly he took it as encouragement. She forced her face into a more serious expression. "I *meant,* older than me. It's just a preference, please don't take it personally."

"Oh, I don't. I get it. But it's all the more reason to have dinner with me—see if maybe you're wrong."

"I'm not."

"People are known to change their minds. My argument stands."

"I have a ton of baggage," she tried.

"I'm strong," he countered. "I'll carry it for a while, if you want."

Oh, God. He meant it, too. "I won't ever talk about any of it, about where I've been and what I've . . . been through, and you just said you hated secrets."

Danny shook his head. "You misunderstood. I don't hate them. I just don't like having any myself. You want to know something about me? I'll tell you. Anything. And I'll be honest. You have my word. But if you want to hide yourself from me? That's okay. I'd prefer you didn't, and I like to think you won't." He reached out to touch her, a gentle caress of his thumb down her cheek. He wasn't wearing gloves, and yet his hands were somehow warm. "I'm a nice guy," he told her. "Maybe it's time to make nice guys be your type."

She stepped back, and blurted, "I'm in love with someone else."

That one finally stopped him. He didn't have an immediate comeback. In fact, he just gazed at her for several long seconds.

"I'm sorry," she started, but he cut her off.

"Okay, I'm definitely stupid for saying this, but whoever he is, have you *told* him? Because I can't think of anyone who wouldn't turn cartwheels at that news. I mean, unless he's married."

"He's not," Sophia said. "He's just . . . an idiot."

"So he knows? And . . . Is he, like, gay?"

"No. At least I don't think so." How did this conversation get so completely out of hand?

"Not that it really matters," Danny pointed out. "It doesn't change how *you* feel. But okay. Okay. What are you going to do? Are you going to sit home alone for the rest of your life? No, right? Say it. No."

"No," she echoed, rolling her eyes.

"Very good." His smile was contagious. "That's step one. Step two's just as easy. Give me one night. Just one. And I'll make you forget you ever met him." The look in his melted-chocolate eyes was now completely non-Disney.

Sophia laughed, even as her heart sank. *The Navy SEAL way*, he'd called it. She'd seen the Navy SEAL way before, plenty of times, with Tom Paoletti, with Mark Jenkins during their last training op, and with all the other SEALs who'd worked with Troubleshooters Incorporated. They were unstoppable when it came to achieving their goals.

The pathetic truth was that if Decker had truly wanted to overcome the plethora of obstacles between them, if he'd really wanted to establish a relationship with Sophia, he surely would have found a way by now.

"Soph! Sophia!"

That was Dave's voice. She was out of his line of sight, and he was making sure she was okay.

"Here comes your guard dog." Danny took her hand, and pulled her with him into the cabin.

"Don't be disrespectful," Sophia said, freeing her hand. "And don't underestimate Dave—whoa." The roof on the cabin had definitely seen better days. She could see the overcast sky through a gaping hole.

There was only one large room, its corners deep in shadow. The walls were made from logs, their bark roughly removed. Mud and moss had been used to block the cracks between them, but most of it had long since dried up and fallen out. There were no windows, just the door and a massive stone fireplace. There was no true ceiling, just exposed beams that supported the remains of the roof.

"Is it Dave?" Danny asked. "You know, your idiot? We could make him jealous. He could find us in here, making out." He pulled her close, his arms around her, his eyes sparkling.

The floor was wood—wide, rough planks. It was covered with leaves and debris, and it groaned under their combined weight.

"Careful," Sophia said. It came out little louder than a whisper. "I'm not . . . I don't . . ."

"I've got you," he said, choosing to interpret her warning as being about the floor. Years of rain had come pouring in through that hole in the roof. The wood beneath their feet was already old and surely decaying. "No worries. There's probably not a basement in a cabin like this. At most there's a twelve-inch space between the dirt and these floorboards."

He smelled good. Even his breath. He must've popped a mint along with that padlock on the door. He was so different from the last man who'd put his heavy hands all over her. He was different, too, from Dimitri, who was actually about the same height, yet not as solidly built.

Sophia didn't move. She couldn't move. She didn't want to move. Because *she* was the idiot, not Decker. The truth was, she'd never told him how she felt. She hadn't called him up and left a message on his voice mail. *Hi, yes, it's Sophia, how are you? I'm fine. In fact, I'm so much better these days. I've started rebuilding my life, but I've realized there's something missing, and I'm pretty sure it's you. I'm in love with you so . . . call me back, okay?*

Because what if he did call her back—or better yet, what if he showed up at her apartment? And what if, during the big romantic moment, when he took her into his arms and declared his undying love for her . . . what if she froze?

What if the traumas of her past made her start to shake and sweat and need to push him away?

She usually hated being touched by anyone. A hand on her shoulder could make her flinch. Yet here was Danny Gillman, leaning in for a kiss—no doubt because she was standing there gawking up at him, as if she wanted him to kiss her.

For the first time in forever she could imagine that, if he were Decker, she would close her eyes and lift her mouth . . .

He kissed her so sweetly, his mouth soft and warm, but when she opened her eyes, it was Danny who'd just kissed her.

She pulled free from his arms—not because she was on the verge of panic, but because the look on his face was of having just found heaven. What on earth was she doing? She jumped backwards, and the floor gave, as if she were stepping onto a sponge, and then her foot went through and her leg went even farther down.

"Danny!"

"I've got you!" His mistake was lunging forward to try to grab her.

Sophia felt the entire floor go.

It was not twelve inches to the ground at the most. It was much farther, and she was falling. She heard herself scream, not for Danny who was falling with her, but for Dave.

She hit something—glass?—that shattered upon impact—ice!—then plunged into water with a splash. Deep water—*cold* water. The shock drove the air from her, and she gasped, but her head was submerged and she felt herself choke.

Which way was up? Her eyes were open, but it was so dark.

She tried to swim toward what had to be the surface, but felt a hand on her jacket, pulling on her. Why was Danny pulling her down? She fought but he didn't let go, and she realized he was somehow hooked to her hood.

He was a deadweight, unmoving, and she knew with a frightening certainty that he must've hit his head.

She couldn't let go of him. If she did, he would die.

If she didn't, she would probably die, too.

She grabbed him under the arms, her lungs nearly exploding with her need for air, and she kicked for what she prayed was the surface.

After hearing Sophia scream, Dave ran, full sprint, for the cabin, Jenkins and Lindsey right behind him.

The door was open and it was dim inside, but he could see well enough to know what had happened. "Don't go in!" The floor had given way. "Sophia!"

Nothing. There was silence, with the exception of the oddest sound. Like water lapping against a seawall.

"What's down there?" Lindsey asked. "Some kind of swimming pool? But why isn't it frozen solid?"

"I don't know." Dave peeled off his coat, handed it to her along with his hat and scarf. There looked to be a set of stairs heading downward, in the gloom of the far corner. How was he going to get over there without going through the floor? "But I'm going to find out."

"Warm springs." Jenk was a fountain of information. He, too, had taken off his jacket and even the sweater he wore. "There are several in this area." He stopped Dave. "I'm going first. I'm lighter."

"Do we have a rope?" Lindsey asked.

"Izzy's carrying the pack," Jenk said as he started around the edge of the cabin's single room. He moved much faster than Dave dared. "There's one in there."

"What we really need is light," Dave said, even as Lindsey started shouting, "Zanella!"

Her voice suddenly seemed to be coming from above them. "Zanella! He's coming," she called to Dave and Jenk. "Lopez, too."

"What are you doing—Be careful!" Jenk was looking up at the roof above them, but he didn't let it slow him down. He was almost near the stairs when his foot slipped and the bit of floor he was standing on gave way. Somehow he managed to cling to the wall. "Don't you fall, too!"

"I'm good," Lindsey told the SEAL, as suddenly there was more light.

She was peeling away the roof, making one of the holes bigger, hacking at the opening.

And then Dave heard it. From below. The sound of splashing, of coughing, of a huge, ragged breath being drawn in.

"Sophia!" he shouted. With the additional light, even dim as the afternoon was, he could see through the broken floor, down a full story beneath them to where, yes, there was water. It was some kind of man-made pool, no doubt constructed on the site of a natural spring, with this structure built around it. He could see Sophia's blond hair, plastered against her head, her face pale as she looked up, searching for him.

"Dave." It was barely a word, more like a gasp. She was holding on to Dan Gillman, his head lolled back, blood on his face.

Dave gripped the log walls with his fingertips. "We're coming! Hold on!" He kept talking to her. He may not have been able to throw her a rope, but he could use his voice as a lifeline. "Jenk's almost at the stairs. We're moving as fast as we can. We're coming. Sophia, hold on. Jenk's almost there."

"It's solid here," Jenkins called. "You should be able to jump over."

Yeah, maybe if he were Spider-Man or a freaking Navy SEAL, then he could jump all that way from a stationary position.

But Dave didn't have time for either a radioactive mutation or BUD/S training, so he just did it. He flung himself forward and miraculously landed without killing himself. He could hear Lindsey shouting orders to Izzy and Lopez. Start a fire. Not in here, in the other structure. Go, go, go!

Yes, there was rope that they could use to pull Sophia and Gillman up, but they were going to need to widen the hole in the floor, remove some of that rotting wood. No, the roof wasn't stable enough to brace the weight of one person, let alone two. Time was of the essence. It was paramount to get Sophia and Gillman dry and warm as quickly as possible.

"I need Lopez!" Jenk shouted from below. Lopez had, among all of them, the most medical training. "Now! Gillman's not breathing!"

The stairs down were made of thicker boards than the floor. Dave stopped testing them in his haste to get down. But then the floor beneath his feet was concrete, and he ran to where Jenkins was pulling Gillman out of the pool.

Sophia had somehow managed to push him halfway out, and she now clung to the side with fingers that were white.

"Lopez!" Jenk shouted again. "Get Sophia," he ordered Dave, who was already doing just that.

"Nuh-nuh-nuh-t . . ." Sophia was trying to speak, but she gave up and touched her mouth and nose, shaking her head, as Dave grabbed her.

"Gillman's not breathing," he interpreted as he pulled Sophia from the water with one enormous heave. "Jenk knows. He's working on him, Soph."

She was freezing to death. Literally. Her lips were already blue.

"I'm helping Izzy rig the rope," Lopez shouted down to Jenkins. "Check for a pulse, man. You know what to do."

"Come on, come on, Danny," Jenk muttered, already fumbling with the prone SEAL's jacket and scarf, trying to get to his throat. "Got a pulse, thank you, Jesus. Starting mouth to mouth."

"Lindsey, status of that fire!" Dave shouted up to the roof as he tried to peel Sophia's wet clothes off of her.

But Sophia pushed him away. She crawled over to Jenk who was breathing into the mouth of his unconscious teammate. Gillman must've knocked himself out on his way through the floor. He had a nasty gash on his forehead.

"Come on, come on, come on, come on," Jenk muttered in between breaths.

"Watch your heads!" Izzy shouted as, holding on to a rope that was somehow anchored outside the cabin, he used himself as a wrecking ball, stomping in the rest of the rotting floorboards.

Jenk shielded Gillman with his back, as Dave tried to do the same for Sophia. Chunks of wood fell into the water, breaking through the thin sheet of ice that had already formed. Splinters and leaves showered onto them.

As Dave looked up, he could see Lopez peering down at them from the doorway. "Fire's started," he reported, as Dave brushed the debris from Sophia's head. "Lindsey's getting it good and hot. Jenk, keep it going. Don't stop. Sophia, can you hear me?"

She didn't look up, her full focus on Gillman.

"She's pretty out of it," Dave called back to Lopez. He had to wrestle her out of those freezing, wet clothes. "Come on, Soph, you can't help Jenkins, but you can help me."

But Lopez stopped him. "Wait, Dave, if she's wearing wool, she'll be warmer with her clothes on, even soaked."

Sophia was shaking. "She's wearing flannel-lined jeans and a down jacket, a coupla sweaters," Dave told the SEAL. He touched her sodden sweater, reaching beneath to what felt like a turtleneck shirt. Her skin beneath was icy. "Definitely not wool. Cotton maybe."

"Get 'em off her," Lopez commanded. "Why isn't she wearing wool?"

She heard that, which was a good sign, wasn't it? "I'm . . . aller . . . aller . . ." Still, she couldn't even pronounce the word *allergic*. She barely even had her eyes open as Dave struggled to pull her wet jacket off of her.

"Yes!" Jenk shouted his triumph. Sure enough, Danny Gillman gurgled and coughed and spit out what seemed like gallons of water as Jenkins rolled him onto his side.

Alleluia. Maybe now Sophia would focus on saving her own life. She may have been out of the water, but she wasn't out of the woods. Neither of them were. Not in this cold. Not yet.

"Come on, Sophia, help me," Dave told her again, working on getting her out of her jeans. He had to peel them off, one leg at a time—not an easy task, since they stuck to her wet skin. "Gillman's okay. Jenk's got him breathing. Let's do some work on you. Can you help me?"

But she was shivering so hard, she couldn't even hold her head up.

And there came Lopez, sliding like Tarzan down that rope through the wider hole in the floor that Izzy had cleared. He was carrying Dave's and Jenk's jackets. But Dave was already ahead of him. He'd pulled off his own wool sweater—too bad if it made Sophia itch—and was ready to step out of his pants.

Lopez swore in Spanish at the sight of her, but he didn't slow down. "Mark, help Dave," he ordered, and then it was Jenkins who was gaping at Sophia's nearly naked body.

"Shit, are those scars?" he asked, but like Lopez, he didn't stop moving. He helped Dave feed her limp arms into the dry sweater.

"Yeah," Dave said tersely.

"What happened to her?" Jenk asked. "Did she, like, go through a plate glass window a few years ago?"

"No." Dave was wearing long johns, and he kicked off his boots to strip down to them, giving Jenkins his socks to put on Sophia's pale feet.

In the time it took him to put his pants and his boots back on his now much colder legs and feet, Jenk had wrestled Sophia into the long johns, wrapped her in Dave's jacket, put her over his back in a fireman's carry, and taken her up the rope.

Lopez had done not quite the same with Gillman because he *was* wearing wool, but they were gone, too.

"Hurry up," Izzy admonished in the fading light at the edge of the hole.

Dave had barely grabbed the rope before Izzy, using plain brute strength, just hauled him straight up. Dave hit the frozen ground like a landed fish, the wind temporarily knocked out of him. As he caught his breath, he smelled the sharpness of smoke from a wood fire.

It was terribly cold without his many layers. He could only imagine how Sophia must've felt.

"Let's go," Izzy said, coiling the rope as he hurried toward the smaller structure.

Dave followed.

Location: Uncertain
Date: Unknown

The first thing he'd do to her was cut off her eyelids.

He'd told Beth that, back when he'd trapped her inside of his car.

Her eyes felt gritty and hot, but only from her fever. She could still blink, still close her eyes. He hadn't cut her.

Not yet.

He was coming toward her, though, the hall light behind him making it hard in the room's dimness to see his face. Or to see what he was carrying in his hands.

"Unchain me, you son of a bitch," she rasped, pulling with all her might against the iron bedframe to which she was tethered. Lord, she was weak.

She knew where he kept the key that would release her. It was on a hook on the wall in the kitchen, right by the basement door. He'd told her where it was nearly every time he left the house, laughing because he knew how much it frustrated her to hear about a key that she could never use, never reach.

The chain that bound her now was too short for her to wrap around his neck.

Although she did have one hand free. One arm and one leg.

Beth lay still. Best to let him think she was helpless. To let him come closer.

"You don't really want me to unchain you, do you, Number Five?" he asked. "To bring you into my kitchen? Wouldn't you rather stay and fight?"

He wasn't holding his carving knife. He was holding a glass with a straw. He'd brought her something to drink. He held it out to her, putting the straw against her dry, chapped lips.

Was it drugged? Possibly. Sometimes the food and water he gave her made the world fade away. She'd awaken to find herself chained up again. Sometimes he stripped her naked and posed her in provocative positions. She'd wake up chilled, with a stiff neck or back. She didn't think he'd ever had sex with her, though—she didn't think he was capable.

She suspected he was afraid of disease. Or maybe he got everything he needed from the power he held over her, combined with his own practiced hand.

"You'll never get better if you don't drink something," he coaxed her, and she took a sip.

It could have been anything in that glass. Blood. Urine. Her own vomit. But it wasn't. It was water, cool and fresh.

She drank more.

"That's my girl." He actually reached out to stroke her hair. Her horribly dirty, matted hair. His hands were gentle—hands that cut and mutilated, but didn't kill.

Hers were the hands that did the killing.

He smiled a gentle smile, a loving smile, as if she were a child or a favorite pet.

He might've been considered handsome—if it weren't for his eyes. His eyes were cold. Empty. Dead.

And very blue.

DARLINGTON, NEW HAMPSHIRE
SATURDAY, DECEMBER 10, 2005

"You were great back there."

Jenk glanced at Lindsey. "We don't have to talk."

"Yeah, I know," she said as she easily kept up with him on the overgrown and potholed road leading back to the SUV. He'd made it more than clear, with his body language and swift pace, that he didn't want to have a conversation.

They'd been given the relatively simple task of going to get blankets and warm, dry clothes for Sophia and Danny. It was matter of height and weight. As the two smallest members of the group, they were not particularly helpful in providing either extra body heat or spare clothing. Although Jenk *had* given up his jacket to the cause. He was out here, in the growing darkness, in just a sweater.

"I just . . . thought you were great back there," Lindsey told him.

"Thanks," he said. He didn't seem cold, but his voice wasn't very warm. "You were, too."

And *that* was quite possibly the least-sincere-sounding compliment she'd ever received.

"It was good teamwork," Lindsey acknowledged. "Dave was impressive, wasn't he? And Izzy and Lopez were pretty amazing with that rope."

"Yeah, will you do me a favor?" Jenk said. "If you're planning on screwing them, too, will you please not do it in the next five days? You know, at least not until we leave New Hampshire?"

If the rudeness of his words hadn't stopped her short, the anger and hurt in his voice would have.

Jenk's hurt stung her more than anger or rudeness ever could. The idea that *she'd* hurt *him* . . . ? How had she hurt him? He was the one who ran off to save Tracy, with his bed still warm from Lindsey's body heat.

Yet *she'd* hurt *him* because, why? Because she didn't want to be his generic bride? Because even though she was lower maintenance than Tracy and damn good in bed, she wasn't willing to help him achieve a headache-free substitute version of some planned-out perfect life?

Because he wanted a minivan, and he'd thought Lindsey would look good behind the wheel?

She ran to catch up. "That was totally uncalled for."

"Was it? Like you said, I don't really know you. Maybe that's how you get your kicks. One-night stands—a new guy every night?"

Yeah, right. It was more like a new guy every few years, with long, dry periods in between. Because usually after she made the mistake of becoming intimate with some fool, it took her months to recover, and then many months more to be willing to take such a risk again.

Still, even though he was far from right, his holier-than-thou implication pissed her off.

"So what if it is?" she countered. "Look me in the eye and tell me you've never had sex with someone, and then decided right then and there that that was enough."

He skidded to a stop. "So that's what happened? You decided enough was enough? Despite the incredible sex, I'm just, what? Too annoying?"

Oh, my God. "No," she said.

"Or maybe I got it completely wrong, and you were just faking it—"

Men could be so predictable. "Yeah." Lindsey let sarcasm drip from her voice. "You're not man enough for me. Come on, Jenkins, what's up with the childish insecurity? I *told* you what happened—*nothing* happened. I'm just not looking for a heavy relationship right now, period, the end. It has nothing to do with . . . with . . . penis size, or endurance, or lack of originality in bed. And no, you have no problem with any of those things. God! It's also not about my insatiable man-eating appetite. Any longing looks I've been casting toward Izzy or Lopez or freaking Dave Malkoff are completely your own craziness. For your information, I'm not scheduled to have sex again until 2008, although after this fiasco, it's going to be 2010!"

Jenk was standing there, his cheeks pink, shivering from the cold. The reason he'd been moving at such a brisk pace was to keep warm.

There was no real haste needed in their quest to get blankets and dry clothing. After Izzy and Dave had sandwiched Sophia between them, sharing body heat, skin to skin, her dangerously low temperature had finally begun to rise. She was going to be okay.

"Come on," Lindsey told Jenk. "You're freezing."

But he didn't move. "I don't believe you."

She rolled her eyes. "Of course you don't. Okay. You want a troglodyte reason for why I don't want to be with you? You're too short for me. Happy, or do you need more? You're too short, and I'm a slut—I'll never be satisfied with just one man. Is that what you want me to say? Does that fit your narrow little worldview?"

"I think I scared you," Jenk said.

Lindsey started down the road at a jog. "Believe whatever you want. Just . . . Let's keep moving."

He caught up with her easily. "I'm right, aren't I?"

"Look," Lindsey said. "I know you're disappointed. I know it's a hard concept for you to grasp—the idea that I'm not secretly waiting for true love to ride up on a white stallion and sweep me away to a life of casseroles, PTA meetings, and sitting in traffic as I go to pick up the dry cleaning. Maybe I don't fit with your antiquated idea of how women should behave. I suspect your struggle comes from the fact that I actually managed to have sex like a man. Like you, as a matter of fact. You didn't invite me home because you thought I was great—"

"Yeah, actually, I did."

She rephrased. "But it wasn't because you thought I would make a great life partner. You wanted to have sex, and you thought it might be fun to have sex with me. Look me in the eye and tell me that if I'd turned into some kind of nightmare—a crying drunk, or some kind of high-maintenance perfectionist—you wouldn't have just faded into the night afterwards and never called me again."

"I would, too, have called you," he insisted. "Considering we're working together . . ."

"Yeah, but at the time you didn't know we'd be working together again, so soon," she pointed out. "But that's not the point. You keep focusing on the tangents. The point is, when we hooked up, you wanted exactly what I did. You can't accuse me of being a slut unless you admit that you're one, too."

"I never said you were a slut," he said. "That was your word."

"Hello, you're doing it again," Lindsey said. "Let me make it simple. On the night we had sex, did you or did you not have Tracy's ringtone set to 'Here Comes the Bride'?"

"We keep coming back to this," he said. "Obviously it matters to you a great deal—"

"Hey! I asked you a simple yes/no question. So, yes or no?"

"Yes, but—"

Lindsey spoke loudly over him. "So what were you doing with me, if you wanted to marry Tracy?"

Jenk shook his head. "That was just a stupid fantasy."

"Oh, yeah? I saw you sitting with her on the plane—it didn't look like you thought it was a fantasy, even then." Great, now he had her doing it—getting totally off point.

And he was looking back at her as if she were nuts. "I only sat with her because you dumped me."

"The point is, damnit, that you were supposedly in love with her—*while* you were in bed with me. What exactly does that say about you, huh?"

"You're jealous that I was sitting with Tracy even though you dumped me," Jenk said slowly, realization in his eyes. "That's crazy, unless . . . you dumped me because I scare you. And I scare you because . . . you like me too much."

"Yeah, right," Lindsey scoffed. "I dump you because I like you. What am I, a total head case? And hello. I didn't even dump you. You can't be dumped after only one night. There was no dumping. We had a thing, and it ended. A little early, but it was always going to end."

"You like me too much," Jenk said again. "You're afraid that I'm going to screw up *your* carefully planned life, spent all alone with your TiVo, doing penance for your guilt about your dead mother and your dead partner—he *was* your partner, right, when you were with the LAPD? The friend who nearly killed you? Not to mention all the other dead people in your past that you didn't get around to telling me about."

How dare he . . . ? Lindsey stopped, and he jogged back toward her, moving in a circle around her to stay warm.

"How'd I do? Close, huh?"

She couldn't speak. It was as if he'd hit her with a two-by-four, square in the gut.

"You've figured out what you deserve," Jenk told her with a jab of his finger in her direction, "because of some bullshit that you've brainwashed yourself to believe, and since you don't think you deserve to be happy, you dumped me."

She stopped herself from saying the words she desperately wanted to say. The anatomically impossible directive, or even a less obscene request that he take up permanent residence in the underworld. She wanted to instruct him to take his overinflated ego with him and never darken her door again.

And why on earth had she told him anything about Dale and the shooting? And shame on Jenk for using that against her. She'd told him things she never told anyone, and this was what he did with it. That would teach her. God, she wanted to cry.

Instead, she made herself laugh. "Believe what you want, if it helps you cope."

"Back at you, babe. Although I wouldn't have pegged you as a coward."

Them was fightin' words, but she knew that her nonchalant shrugs pissed him off more than any angry outburst ever could. "Whatever."

"You know what, Lindsey? It turns out you're right. You *don't* deserve me." Jenk jogged away from her. "You're not worth my time."

She had to lean over, pretending to catch her breath, trying to regain her equilibrium. *Good riddance, good riddance . . .*

They were almost at the SUV, almost done with this nightmare. Back at the motel, she'd go see Tom. She'd tell him she had a family emergency, and she'd catch a bus down to Boston. Fly home to California from there.

She just got the first season of *Rescue Me* on DVD. She'd marathon it. Ten straight hours of Dennis Leary, popcorn, and ice cream would make her feel better. And then she'd go visit her father so the family emergency excuse wouldn't be a total lie.

Lindsey straightened up and made herself follow Jenk down the road, one foot at a time, picking up speed as the cold numbed her face.

And then there it was, the SUV, the last of the daylight gleaming off its front windshield.

Jenkins didn't say anything to her as he unlocked the doors, as they climbed inside, as he turned over the engine. He couldn't manage turning at that point in the narrow road, so he ran the vehicle in reverse until he could maneuver it around.

It took several moments for the heat to come up, and when it did, Lindsey blasted it.

It was possible, though, that she was too numb ever to feel completely warm again.

CHAPTER
TWELVE

This was pretty durn weird.

It wasn't as if Izzy had never helped warm up a teammate with hypothermia before.

It was a lot like hugging an ice cube.

Since a tub of warm water wasn't available, skin-to-skin contact had been the only available way to increase Sophia's body temperature.

Her proximity to the fire hadn't helped, so Izzy and Dave had stripped to their briefs and crawled under a pile of jackets and clothes to cradle Sophia between them.

Maybe the fact that made it so weird was that his SEAL teammates who'd suffered hypothermia in the past tended not to have breasts.

Or perhaps it was the Arabic writing carved into the small of Sophia's back that was freaking him out.

She had about a half a dozen thin, fading scars on the trunk of her body that had at first shocked him because he'd thought they were self-inflicted.

Izzy had once picked up this Goth chick at a Renaissance fair. It turned out that she had some serious issues that she'd tried to handle by taking a razor blade to her arms and stomach. Coming face-to-face with *that* had been an instant soft-on. He'd made some lame excuse—he was coming down with the flu—and boogied out of her ramshackle RV. He'd kicked himself for his cowardice though, for not being honest and telling her that he had issues with her method of dealing, so to speak, with *her* issues. He'd even gone back to find her several days later, to urge her to get help, but the entire fair was gone, leaving an empty, trampled field.

Here in the haunted hunting lodge's former smokehouse, Izzy had seen that none of Sophia's cuts were recent. But as he'd gotten closer, he'd realized that there were more than six of them, but most were almost entirely faded. Those would, eventually, become all but invisible. There *was* one, though, that she'd carry with her to her grave.

Izzy's Arabic was limited to barely more than the standard phrases in the talkee-pointee booklets he'd found in a Marine camp in Iraq. *Put down your weapons, and no one will get hurt.* Or *Would you like some chocolate for your son?* Still, he knew enough to recognize not just that Sophia had Arabic writing carved into her very flesh, but also that it was in a spot that she could not have reached by herself. Even if she were a very nimble ballet dancer.

And he wasn't sure, but he was pretty sure it said *slave.*

Sophia had finally stopped shivering. She no longer felt like an ice cube—with breasts—but more like a side of beef.

With breasts.

Dave Malkoff frowned across the top of Sophia's head, as if he could read Izzy's mind.

Like, what? Izzy was going to cop a feel? Well, okay, so he already had, but it was totally by accident. There wasn't a lot of wiggle room here, wedged in between the stone wall and the fire, jammed in tight against Sophia and Dave, beneath a pile of clothing and jackets.

For the record, he'd also managed to grab Dave's ass during the past few hours. And that was absolutely not on purpose.

But then he realized that Dave's glare had been to warn him that Sophia was waking up. She'd fallen asleep, but now she stirred.

"You're okay, you're safe," Dave murmured to her. "We're just here with you like this to keep you warm. I know it must seem inappropriate, but, really, this was the only way to get your temperature back up."

She tensed, as if the close contact was more than she could handle.

Izzy tried to imagine someone having the word *slave* carved into the small of their back for shits and giggles. But he couldn't. Whoever had written that there hadn't had Sophia's permission. No doubt about it, those memories were not fond ones.

"It's okay," Dave told her again and again, his voice calm, reassuring. "You're safe."

And she slowly relaxed as Izzy pretended he was a warming brick—nonthreatening and purely functional.

Lopez came over wearing only his long underwear. The rest of his clothes were either on top of them or beneath them. He tried to hide the fact that he was shivering despite the fire. "How you doing, Sophia? You want to try to get something warm inside of you?"

Izzy was on his best behavior, so all he did was close his eyes. But oh, how he could have commented. Instead, he just silently let Lopez continue.

"I've got some MREs heating up. I've also purified some of the water from that spring you and Dan found. I've got tea brewing."

"Is Danny okay?" Sophia asked.

Danny-Danny-Bo-Banny was over on the other side of the fire, no doubt steaming like a fresh yak turd as his wet clothes dried. Izzy had been there, done that, a time or two. Wearing wet wool wasn't on his top ten list of fun ways to spend an evening. The fragrance, at least that of his own sweaters, was decidedly barnyard-like. Still, Izzy was willing to bet that Dan Gillman was warmer than Lopez, thanks to his multiple layers.

"I'm fine," Gillman called. He pushed himself to his feet and came to stand looking down at them. Lopez had cleaned up the gash on his forehead, but it was developing into quite the egg-shaped bruise. His eye was starting to rainbow, too. "Sophia, I am so sorry. This was all my fault. My actions were inappropriate—"

Lopez was getting Sophia some of that tea, pouring it into an MRE wrapper, for lack of a hot cup. "This isn't the time or place for recriminations or—"

"What actions?" Dave asked Gillman, clearly not climbing into Lopez's boat floating gently on the sea of tranquillity. In fact, the ship he was boarding was the U.S.S. *Pop-a-Vein*, despite his deceptively mild voice.

Izzy was close enough to hear the sound of Dave's teeth grinding together.

"Or accusations." Lopez surely knew that he was talking to himself, and he sighed.

"I came on too strong. I didn't realize . . ." Gillman didn't notice Dave's displeasure. He was wrapped up in his own ball of guilt, no doubt feeling bad for treating Sophia like a normal woman, when it was clear to all of them, after eyeballing those freaky scars, that she was anything but.

"It's not your fault," Sophia tried to reassure him.

Dave wasn't convinced. Still, he kept his voice even. Calm. Deceptively matter-of-fact. "So you were, what? Groping her? She tries to get away, you give chase and take her with you through the floor and into the water?" He climbed out from beneath the pile of clothing.

"Pretty much," Gillman admitted. "Although groping is a little strong."

Dressed only in his briefs, Dave was not a formidable-looking man.

He was one of those guys who managed to be both skinny and fat, and Izzy was betting he'd been rope-thin until recently. He'd probably crossed that invisible age line where his metabolism changed and, much to his dismay, he suddenly had love handles. That had to suck.

"Dave," Sophia said. "It wasn't—"

"Nearly killing both you and Sophia." Dave clarified as he sauntered over to Gillman.

Sophia turned to Izzy. "Give me some space. Please."

He didn't respond. He was just an inanimate object, a warming brick that could only be moved by Lopez. But Lopez was elsewhere, ready to intercede should Dave start throwing punches instead of words.

"Guys," Lopez said, as Dave crossed well into Gillman's personal space.

And kept going.

Fighting in a small space that also contained a pit fire was Darwinism in action. Getting one's nuts seared off made procreation highly unlikely. Of course, there was also the element of Darwinism that suggested that the fittest who survived probably didn't hang around with monkey-minded morons who fought in a small space that contained a pit fire.

Instead of shifting away from Sophia, Izzy shifted toward her. Away from the fire.

"You want to hit me?" Gillman asked Dave, not at all belligerently. He actually sounded hopeful. "Go ahead."

"How about taking this outside?" Izzy suggested. So okay, he was now a warming brick that talked.

But apparently Dave wasn't the hitting kind. He was the threatening kind. "If you ever touch her again," he told Gillman, right up in his face, "I'll kill you."

Izzy couldn't see Dave's eyes from his position on the floor, but he had a clear shot of Gillman. The SEAL would have stood there, absorbing a blow without retaliation, but words like that could not be ignored. So he bristled. And he started to get back in Dave's face, with one of the snappiest comebacks known to mankind. "Oh, yeah?"

Sophia was wriggling around beside Izzy, which was about as distracting as anything he'd ever experienced, except maybe the thought of getting his nuts seared off.

Aha, she was getting dressed. She'd been rummaging around, apparently searching for something, anything to put on, and now she was doing just that. "Zanella, get your hands off me!"

For the record, Izzy's hands had been nowhere near her. She, in her wiggling, had connected with him. She'd nearly kneed him in the groin, and he'd executed evasive maneuvers, period, the end.

Of course, both Dave and Gillman combined their anger and turned, aiming it now at Izzy. Except it had morphed into disgust. "Zanella . . ." Even Lopez joined in on the familiar chorus, adding a descant of "Izzy, come on."

Sophia, meanwhile, scrambled to her feet. She was wearing one of his sweaters, and what looked like Dave's pants, holding them up with one hand. But then she swayed, as if she'd stood too fast, and everyone—Izzy included—jumped to support her, helping her sit on the remaining pile of clothing.

Lopez leaped to get his tea, helping her take a sip from the MRE wrapper. "It's not too hot," he told her. "I couldn't heat it too much or I wouldn't've been able to pour it into this. But it should be warm enough."

"Thanks," Sophia said. Her eyes met Izzy's, and he knew she was no more wobbly-legged than he was. Her goal—skillfully achieved—had been to distract and refocus, starting with her mention of his allegedly way-ward hands. It was masterful—she had the poor little blond waif role down perfectly.

And he was king of the miscreants. "So that was a fun way to spend the afternoon," he said. "Although—no offense Dave—I would've preferred the third in our little hypothermia-be-gone party be Lindsey."

He got *Zanella-ed* again, as expected.

Dave and Gillman were now bonding in their revulsion of him. Well, not quite. But they no longer looked ready to get their calendars out, to schedule their impending duel to the death.

Sophia frowned. "Where *is* Lindsey?"

Dave looked at his watch. "Probably reentering radio range right about . . . now."

Tracy had just gotten out of the shower when someone knocked loudly on the bathroom door.

There was no exhaust fan—probably because they hadn't invented them back in the dark ages when this motel was built—and the mirror was completely fogged. So she opened the door, both to let the steam out and to greet her roomie, who had surely returned from her hike.

"I'll be out in a sec, Sophia," she said, only to find herself face-to-face with Lawrence Decker. She was so surprised to see him, she just stood there, gaping.

"Sorry to intrude," he said. "But I need some help."

She had a towel wrapped around herself, but the thin motel towels weren't exactly generous. Certainly not as generous as her backside. She moved behind the door, peering out at him.

Had Sophia actually given Decker a key to their room? There was something going on between them—or there had been at one time. Tracy had thought, however, that the key-sharing phase of their relationship was over and done. But maybe not. Maybe they were as messed up as she and Lyle were.

Terrific. It would give her something to talk about with Sophia later tonight. God, she hated sharing a room, and wished, for the thousandth time, that her roommate could've been Lindsey. At least Lindsey liked her. Sophia was distant, reserved, mysterious, and a natural blond.

But really, out of everyone she'd met from Troubleshooters Incorporated, Lawrence Decker had to be the biggest mystery. From what Tracy had heard from nearly everyone in the office, Decker was like some kind of mythical warrior god. From the way they'd all talked about him, with awe and reverence in their voices, she'd expected someone like Sam Starrett, only taller, bigger, and ten times more handsome and charismatic.

Instead, Decker was one of those utterly forgettable men who blended into the background at parties or in bars. He was the guy whose name she'd forget ten minutes after he'd been introduced. With medium brown eyes, medium brown hair cut medium short, and a medium build, he was neither handsome nor not handsome. He just . . . was.

"Sophia's not here," she told him now.

"Yeah, I know," he said in his mediumly modulated voice. "That's why I need your help. There was an accident up at the hunting lodge."

"Oh, my God," Tracy said. Lindsey had gone up there. Mark and Izzy, too. "Was anyone hurt?"

"Everyone's okay," he reassured her. "But Sophia and one of the SEALs fell into some water. It's cold out there, and getting colder."

"No kidding," Tracy said. "Which SEAL?"

"Dan Gillman. They need dry clothes as quickly as possible. Which drawers are Sophia's?"

He wasn't here because he was stalking Sophia. He was here to get some of her clothes. Of course, maybe he was here both to get her clothes and to stalk her. Stalkers were clever that way.

"The ones on the left," Tracy told him. "No, right." She closed her eyes, trying to picture the dresser.

"Just show me," Decker said.

Tracy hadn't brought her bathrobe, mostly because if she had, she wouldn't have had room to pack anything else. But now, instead of taking the time to pull on her clothes, she pointed out the bathroom door to her winter coat that was hanging on the open closet rack. "Hand me that, will you?"

He did, and she slipped it on, letting her towel fall to the bathroom floor as she fastened the coat. Earlier that same afternoon, one of the buttons had come off, and she'd yet to find a sewing kit to reattach it. But she would be okay, as long as she didn't lean over too far.

She came out of the bathroom and opened the drawers. She'd been right the first time. Sophia's things were to the left. "What exactly does she need?"

"Everything," he told her, just reaching in and taking two sweaters, a long-sleeved T-shirt, and a pair of jeans. He didn't hesitate until he got to Sophia's underwear drawer, and even then his pause was only infinitesimal. He went for white, both bra and panties, but he was just a little too businesslike. Tracy knew he really wanted to check out the more colorful selections, maybe take a moment, remembering what Sophia had looked like with them on. Or off.

"When did you two break up?" she asked, and he looked up at her. It was weird. In this light, his eyes were more green than brown. And the intensity of his gaze was startling. And in no way forgettable.

"What makes you think we were together?" he asked.

"Oh, please." Tracy made a face at him. "It's pretty obvious. I mean, after the thing with Dave? Also, no one in the office will talk about the two of you. There's lots of gossip about other things, but you're definitely off-limits. So whatever happened, it must've been ugly."

"Or maybe just no one's business," he said, taking an extra pair of Sophia's socks.

"Like that would stop people from gossiping?" she asked, as he went through the drawers again, searching for something. "Or maybe they're all just in awe of you."

That got her another look, this one amusement sharpened with disbelief.

"What are you looking for?" she asked.

"Long underwear," Decker said.

"It's under the nonlong underwear," she told him, letting him open that top drawer and rummage some more. "You're friends with Tess Bailey and Jim Nash, right?"

"Yeah." He added one of Sophia's neatly rolled pairs of long underwear to his pile. "Boots?"

"Did you know they were having problems? Probably not, because no one talks about *that* either. But their on-again, off-again wedding plans aren't just about scheduling issues." Tracy handed him Sophia's spare pair of boots. "I thought you might like to know."

"Thanks," he said, and now his eyes looked almost blue. Was it possible he could change their color at will? "Although that's not your business either." He started for the door. "Sorry to bother you."

"Wait." She had a daypack, and she emptied it onto one of the beds. Ah, this was where she'd put her other book. As well as her Tae Bo exercise DVD—like she was going to use that, here in the land of no technology— and her iPod and headphones. And oh, yes, hemorrhoid ointment, the athlete's foot spray she'd needed after taking antibiotics for that annoying bladder infection, her pink fuzzy mittens, a variety of feminine products including panty liners for thongs, her—ahem—personal massager she'd named George, and the Ziploc baggie that held her supply of emergency condoms.

The baggie seemed to gleam, shiny in the overhead fluorescent light. But it wasn't quite as attention-sucking as her massager. George's on/off switch had somehow been flipped in its dive from her daypack, and it lay there in its neon green phallic glory shivering and whirring.

She sat down on top of it, an attempt to hide it, because maybe Decker hadn't seen it yet—yeah, right. His eyes had actually widened at the sight. She held the daypack out to him with a forced smile. "You don't want to drop Sophia's underwear in a puddle, right?"

"It's too cold for puddles." He was trying not to smile, but then he frowned. He shook the bag slightly. "There's something else in here. Maybe you should . . ." He handed it back to her, clearly afraid of what he might find.

Tracy opened the front zipper pocket. Altoids, No-Doz and . . . a tube of K-Y jelly. Great. She tucked it away beneath her winter coat, taking the opportunity while her hand was down there to silence George. "Good call," she said, handing the now completely empty pack back to him.

Decker laughed, and just like that she understood why Sophia still gave him a key to her room. The man had an incredible smile.

As she watched, he put Sophia's boots in at the bottom, the rest of the clothes on top. He was still grinning as he zipped it shut and met her gaze again.

"Thanks for your help," he said.

"Before you go," she started.

He cut her off. "Don't worry, I'm good at minding my own business, too."

It took her a moment to realize he was talking about George. She rolled her eyes. "No—thank you, but . . ." She held out her hand. "I'd prefer it if you didn't have a key to my room."

"I don't have a key."

"You don't have a key. You just came in without a key?"

Decker laughed again. "Honey, think about who we both work for."

Tom Paoletti. Who probably didn't need keys either. "I don't think I'm cut out for this," Tracy admitted.

"It takes getting used to," he told her. "It's a different world."

"I'll say."

"It's an important job," he told her. "Doing what you do."

Said the warrior god to the inept receptionist.

"It's not easy to help run an office like TS Inc," he continued. "There are things you can't hear or see—even if you do. You've got to spend your days submerged in that different world, with no promise of ever fitting in. Always on the outside, looking in."

He sounded as if he knew exactly what that felt like.

"Is that why you spend most of your time out in the field?" Tracy asked. "Because *you* don't fit in, in the world where people still use keys?"

Decker glanced at his watch, and when he spoke, she expected an excuse. He had to go. Instead, he answered her. "I haven't lived in your world in a long time."

"That's right," Tracy said. "Someone told me you don't even go on vacation. Although, shh, don't tell anyone you heard it from me—there was talk of forcing you to take one."

"Thanks for the heads-up," he said. "Jesus, that'll be fun."

"Maybe it will be," Tracy said. "You know, if you let it. You could take Sophia to Cancún."

"Cancún," he repeated.

"Or somewhere more exotic," she suggested. "Athens or . . . Rome." She herself had always wanted to visit Rome.

That made him even more bemused. "You don't know Sophia very well, do you?"

"I really don't," she admitted.

"She grew up overseas," Decker told her. "She'd probably prefer a trip to the Grand Canyon."

"Well, there's your answer," Tracy said. "Take her to the Grand Canyon."

For a half a second, the look on his face was almost wistful. But then

Decker shook his head. "I'm not taking her anywhere." He hefted the bag. "I'm bringing her a change of clothes. Thanks again. I'm sorry if I scared you before."

He opened the door and was halfway out before she asked, "Was that just *your* world we were in? Because, to be honest, it felt like it morphed into mine. I mean, considering what I'm sitting on, I'm pretty sure, by the end there at least, it *was* mine."

He turned to look at her with eyes that were once again plain brown. How *did* he do that?

"And I thought you fit in just fine," Tracy told him.

Decker gave her one last smile and shut the door behind him.

The headlights coming toward them could mean only one thing.

The current level of hell that Jenk found himself in was moments from ending.

Lindsey hadn't spoken since they'd gotten into the SUV, but now she cleared her throat. "Do you, by any chance, know Arabic?"

Jenk glanced at her. She was watching him in the dim light from the dashboard, her eyes little more than a gleam in the darkness. "Some," he said.

"Enough to know if that was—"

"Yes," he said. She was talking about Sophia's biggest scar. "It was."

"God." She exhaled the word with a heartfelt emotion.

"Yeah," he agreed.

"I don't have anything to complain about," Lindsey told him. "I mean, compared to Sophia."

He would have replied that some scars weren't quite as visible, but that would have sounded as if he'd started to forgive her, so he didn't say anything at all.

"Could you read what it said?" she asked, after the silence stretched on.

"It wasn't very nice." Jenk was pretty sure that the word he'd caught a glimpse of carved into Sophia's lower back was in a Kazbekistani dialect. It looked like slang for female slave, which usually meant a woman who was used for sex.

Lindsey got the drift. "What, some kind of scarlet letter?"

"Yeah. Although I'm betting her alleged transgressions weren't by choice. Kazbekistan's a harsh place."

"Have you been there?" she asked.

Jenk slowed down, but the approaching vehicle didn't. Crap, it was some kind of delivery truck, not the relief team from the motel. It zoomed past them, probably on its way to Maine.

"Or maybe I should ask how many times you've been there," Lindsey said.

"You know I can't tell you that."

"I'd like to go there someday," Lindsey said. "The pictures I've seen are—"

"You wouldn't like it," Jenk interrupted her. "Trust me. It's called 'the Pit' for a reason." Kazbekistan was a nightmare, its central government replaced by tribal warlords who spent most of their time fighting with each other. Outlaws roamed free, terrorizing the general population. The chaos had made the small country an even more popular site for al Qaeda training camps than it had been in the past. And it had always been very popular. "It's no place for a woman, particularly not an American."

"Tess Bailey was sent there. Sophia, too, apparently."

"And look at how well that worked out for her."

"Yeah," Lindsey agreed. "That had to suck. Still, the information they acquired was vital."

Jenk was well aware of the op to which Lindsey was referring. He'd been thinking about it ever since seeing Sophia's scars. He'd been connected to it, as part of a SEAL team sent via helo on a rescue mission to pull some Troubleshooters' operatives out of a warlord's palace. Sophia was one of them. And yes, freckle-faced computer specialist Tess Bailey had been there, too.

Decker had been the Troubleshooters' leader, sent with his team into the Pit to retrieve a terrorist's laptop—and whatever secrets it contained on its hard drive.

They'd succeeded. But at what price?

For a while now, there had been rumors floating around the SpecOp community of some kind of modern Mata Hari, an American operative who'd managed to become a concubine of a powerful K-stani warlord. She was, people were saying, instrumental in providing vital information about al Qaeda to the U.S.

Jenk was beginning to believe that the operative in question was Sophia, and the information she'd provided had been on that laptop.

Lindsey had apparently heard the rumors, too. She was thinking along the exact same lines. "Is it possible that Sophia is this M-2000 everyone's talking about?"

He glanced at her. "Is that really what they're calling her?"

"Yeah, technically it should be M-2004. I think that's when she first appeared. But I think it's also supposed to be a Terminator reference. A vague one."

"M-2000," Jenk repeated. "Like she's some kind of robot?"

"It couldn't be Sophia, could it? I mean, it doesn't make sense. She's not an operator. You saw her on that exercise. She's had virtually no weapons training. No U.S. agency would send someone on such a dangerous mission with no training."

Jenk wasn't so sure about that. "She was pretty good at deception, though," he pointed out. "And she's got balls. She saved Gillman's life today."

"She's also incredibly proper," Lindsey argued. She'd turned to face him, her arm along the back of the seat. "She dresses kind of like a . . . well, not a nun, but maybe a lawyer. A real one. More Harriet Miers than Ally McBeal. Knee-length skirts. Blouses with scarves—nothing low-cut. Two-inch heels at the most. The idea of her willingly working undercover as a prostitute? I just don't see it."

"Maybe it wasn't something she did willingly," Jenk said.

She wasn't convinced, leaning closer from her intensity. "It's just so outlandish. The whole story reeks of urban legend." She laughed. "And you know how true those turn out to be, camouflage man."

If this had been a few days ago, Jenk would've laughed, too. If this had been just two nights ago, he would've laughed and kissed her. God damn it.

Instead, he gritted his teeth, and prayed that the headlights that flickered into view as he rounded a curve were Decker's.

The silence that had fallen over them cast a total chill, and Lindsey became aware of the way she was sitting. She pulled her arm back, straightened her legs so she was facing front again. Adjusted her red hat so that it more completely covered her ears.

Jenk slowed as the oncoming car slowed, too.

And Lindsey spoke. "I've done the one thing I absolutely didn't want to do. I've lost you as a friend. I can't tell you how sorry I am about that."

Yes, that was definitely Decker driving the other vehicle. Jenk did a youie, pulling over to the side of the road, behind him. "Yeah, well, when you're a coward, you lose things."

"Sometimes," she said quietly, "you lose them even when you're not."

She got out and approached the other car. Jenk rolled his window down, as did Decker.

"Jenk's going to lead you back," Lindsey told the former SEAL chief. "The road in is clear until about a mile from the lodge."

"Let's go," Decker said, as always a man of action.

"Is there room in there?" Lindsey asked. "Jenk's a little tired of me."

He was tired of her. Nice. "Way to make me sound like an asshole," he called.

It was possible that she didn't hear him—she was too busy getting into the back and already laughing with whoever was in there.

Decker waved him ahead, and Jenk took off, burning a patch of rubber on the mountain road.

Decker, of course, came to save the day.

Dave was sitting with Sophia, sharing some of Lopez's tea, when Deck arrived. He didn't come crashing in, kicking down the door like an action hero. He called out when he was still some distance away. And then he knocked when he was closer.

Gillman was waiting, and he pulled open the little door.

Deck had to duck as he came in, but his gaze fell immediately upon Sophia, and his relief was obvious.

Dave could practically see the list Deck was mentally checking off. She was conscious—sitting up, wearing Jenk's jacket with Dave's sweater around her head like a hood, and Lopez's sweater wrapped around her feet. Her color was good and her hair was dry if slightly messy. She was holding that MRE wrapper filled with tea in her hands, and her eyes were bright and alert.

"Everyone okay?" Decker asked, as Lindsey and two SEALs—an officer and a senior chief—squeezed their way in behind him.

There was a chorus of affirmatives, from Sophia, too. Still Decker came right over to her. He pulled off his gloves as he hunkered down, reaching into that makeshift hood to touch her, his hand against her neck so he could check her temperature for himself.

She saw it coming and tensed, which, of course, Decker noticed. How could he not? And instead of pulling her close and greeting her more properly with a soul kiss, he let her go.

Of course, maybe the soul kiss thing had never been his intention. It was, however, what Dave would have given her, had Dave been Decker.

Or at least he would have said something along the lines of, "Thank God you're okay. I was so worried."

Instead, Deck swung a daypack off his shoulder. He gave it to Sophia. "Dry clothes and boots," he told her, then straightened up, moving over to check on that asshole, Gillman.

The SEAL officer, a burly lieutenant name of MacInnough, was carrying a duffel. "Coats and blankets and plenty of flashlights," he announced. He smiled at Sophia. "Glad to see you're feeling better, ma'am."

Decker and the senior chief were over talking to Lopez, checking Gillman out as carefully as Deck had looked at Sophia.

"Where's Jenk?" Sophia asked Lindsey.

"His jacket was back here, so he stayed with the vehicles."

"All by himself?" Izzy asked. "Man, he really doesn't get spooked easily, does he?"

"It was a direct order from the lieutenant," Lindsey said. "He didn't stay behind by choice."

"Okay," Izzy said. "This is too good to pass up. First one back has to kill their light, sneak up on Marky-Mark, and say, *Give me back my leg!*"

Sophia laughed, but Dave could tell she was distracted by Decker's presence. He knew with certainty that she, too, had expected Deck to do more with his mouth than utter the words "Dry clothes and boots," as he'd crouched there in front of her.

Or maybe expected was too strong a word. Maybe she'd only hoped.

Because even though Decker hadn't said "thank God you're all right," it had been there, in his eyes, clear as day.

"Let's get coats and boots on so Sophia can get dressed in privacy," Decker ordered now. "Lindsey, stay and assist."

He led the way out into the sharp coldness of the night. Dave followed more slowly, putting on the sweater that Sophia gave back to him. It smelled like her hair. He breathed in deeply as he pulled it over his head.

As he shrugged into his jacket, he realized that he himself might well have been guilty of the very thing Decker had done, so he went back inside.

"Have I told you how thankful I am that you're okay?" he asked Sophia. "I treasure your friendship more than you will ever know. And I'm so proud of you. Your strength and courage awe me on an average day, but today . . . You were incredible. You *are* incredible. There's no doubt in my mind that you saved Dan's life."

"Thanks, Dave," Sophia whispered. The smile she gave him was so wistful, it broke his heart. She wasn't just brave and strong, she was smart, too. She knew he was trying to make up for everything that Decker hadn't said.

It probably only made it worse.

CHAPTER
THIRTEEN

Dinner was destined to suck.

Since everyone else had eaten earlier, and someone had noticed that it was significantly warmer in the restaurant kitchen, they'd moved a few tables in for the group that had been out at the hunting lodge. In theory, it was nice, especially since Lindsey still hadn't completely warmed up yet.

But the price to be paid for the warmth was that the space in the kitchen was limited. The tables had to be pushed together, so that the Troubleshooters and SEALs were forced to eat in one big group. Like one big, happy family.

Lindsey sat at one end. If she were lucky, Jenk would arrive while there were still plenty of empty seats available. Her hope was for him to sit as far away from her as possible.

His harsh words rang in her head quite nicely on their own. She didn't need to look at him and see an echo of his accusations in his eyes.

One of his words in particular had lodged like an arrow in her gut.

Penance. Used in the same sentence as *your dead mother.*

Just thinking about it still hurt a little too much. So much so that Lindsey was beginning to believe that Mark Jenkins might be right.

Dave plopped into the seat next to her. Lopez claimed the chair on her other side, and she was mostly safe. All she needed now was someone who wasn't Jenk to sit directly across from her, and she might make it through the meal without massive heartburn.

Izzy didn't save the day, the bastard. He sat next to Lopez.

It was then that Lindsey spotted Jenk, still helping himself to the food—spaghetti with meat sauce—kept hot in warmers over on the other side of the kitchen. Tom Paoletti was with him, and the two men were deep in conversation.

Clearly the best thing for her to do was to eat fast and get out of here.

She put her head down, dug in and, whoa. She'd expected military rations or school cafeteria food at best, but this sauce was delicious. The salad dressing was excellent, too. She hadn't realized just how hungry she was.

"Stella told me her husband Rob cooked dinner," Izzy announced. "I begin to understand why she hasn't left him for me. This shit *rocks.*"

Decker sat down across from Lopez. Two of the SEALs Lindsey didn't know that well—their names were Stan and Mac—sat next to Izzy and immediately began arguing the pros and cons of setting up that bad-weather shelter out at the hunting lodge. Apparently, the storm they were expecting had slowed down over Chicago, and Tom still hadn't decided if the precaution was necessary.

There were only three empty seats available at the table now, and Lindsey knew without a doubt that Jenk would end up seated across from her. It had been that kind of day.

"I've been meaning to ask you for a coupla days now," Lopez said, and she looked up to find that he was talking to her. "You made a toast back at the Bug to your grandfather, Henry. Was he your father's father?"

Lindsey nodded, her mouth full.

"Oh, man," he interrupted himself to say, "this is good, isn't it?"

She nodded again.

"Stella told me Rob's back is out again," Izzy reported. "He got out of bed to cook for us. Dude deserves a medal."

Across the table, Dave asked Decker, "Is Sophia having dinner in her room?"

"Yeah," Deck said. "We thought it was smart for her to get into a warm bath. Tracy came and got her something to eat."

Dave laughed. "Tracy did." He opened his mouth, as if to say something else, but then just shook his head, obviously disgusted.

One thing about military personnel—they ate unbelievably fast. Faster even than cops.

Lopez turned to her again as he mopped up the last of the sauce on his plate with a crust of bread. "So was your grandfather by any chance the same Henry Fontaine who was a guerilla fighter in the Philippines during the Second World War?" he asked.

And suddenly the entire table's attention was focused directly on

Lindsey. Including Jenk, who was juggling his dinner, a salad, and a mug of coffee as he approached. Tom was right behind him.

Lindsey considered lying, but Tom knew the truth. Or at least the version of it that she'd chosen to share with him.

She tried to make light of it. "Yeah, although he wasn't my biological grandfather. He married my grandmother when she was already pregnant with my father, so . . ."

"Yeah, but you knew him." Dan Gillman slid into one of the few remaining chairs. He had a bandage just below his hairline and was starting to develop one heck of a shiner. He must've hit his head terribly hard, and yet here he was, having dinner with the rest of them. "That's very cool."

"Everyone who's been through BUD/S has studied Henry Fontaine's jungle warfare techniques," Dave told her. "He was amazing. What was he, nineteen, when the Japanese invaded the Philippines?"

"He didn't talk much about the war," Lindsey admitted. She'd found out about her grandfather's heroic part in World War II through books, the year after he'd died.

"My great-uncle was OSS, in France," Tom sat down, leaving Jenk, yes, the seat across from her. "Medal of Honor winner. Try getting him to talk about it."

"*We did what we had to,*" Gillman said. "That's what my grandmother always said right before she changed the subject. She was an Army nurse in North Africa. Incredible lady."

"So what was he like?" Lopez asked her, bringing the focus back to Lindsey.

"He was quiet," she told them. "He never had much to say." And when her grandfather did speak, he never wasted a single word. "He was . . . tall. Solid. With this thick shock of white hair."

And those blue eyes that were so different from her own. He had a face that was leathery from years spent outdoors. Big, gentle hands, warm and reassuring, resting briefly on the crown of her head—she could feel him still if she closed her eyes, infusing her with some of his peace and calm. The smell of cinnamon, of Red Hots. Although come to think of it, he'd liked chocolate, too. He'd offer her a piece of a Hershey's bar, warm from his pocket, as they sat and watched his vegetable garden grow in the peace of a lazy afternoon.

Lindsey had spent an entire summer with him when her mother was first diagnosed with cancer, when the chemo made it impossible for her to do so much as get out of bed. Grandpa had taken Lindsey camping. He'd also taken her to visit her mother as often as she wanted, battling the freeway traffic in his old truck as if the five-hour round-trip was nothing for a sixty-plus-year-old.

Of course five hours in a car *was* nothing compared to what her grandfather had endured during the war. He was one of only a handful of men who'd managed to escape during the Bataan death march—the Japanese transport of seventy thousand malaria-ridden American and Filipino POWs over sixty miles in the tropical sun. Sixteen thousand men had died, not just from the grueling heat and lack of water, but also from the brutality of the guards and their commanding officers.

One of whom had been her biological grandfather.

"He ate Wheaties for breakfast," Lindsey continued, because it was clear they wanted more. "Every morning. At least whenever I was visiting. He had these forearms that were like Popeye's—solid muscle. He read a lot, and he loved doing jigsaw puzzles and playing Monopoly. He played to win, too. None of this 'let the kid have Boardwalk' crap. He was quiet and kind and . . . I don't know what else to say."

Henry Fontaine kept his house immaculately clean. And he'd kept a photo of his Japanese wife on the table beside his bed. Perpetually twenty-two years old, she smiled unblinking through the years, her hair and clothes that of a typical 1950s American housewife. She was the grandmother that Lindsey had never known, as well as the reason Henry had never returned to his little hometown in Iowa after the war.

One of the reasons. The other was her father, who'd been only five when his mother had died.

Lindsey had asked Grandpa once why he didn't move back home after her father was grown. He'd answered her after careful consideration, as he always did, never talking down to her because she was a child. "California is my home now." Hours later, while they sat on the back porch in the twilight, he'd told her, "I still see Keiko's hands at work in this garden."

"He died when I was fourteen," Lindsey told them. "He just . . . didn't wake up one morning."

It was then, while getting his father's papers in order, that her own father had made the rude discovery of his true paternity. Henry had told him that he was the son of a lowly lieutenant in the Japanese army, a former student at the university in Tokyo, who served his country dutifully, but in truth preferred a quiet evening spent reading to the art of war. Instead, the blood that flowed through his veins was that of a far-higher-ranking officer. His real father was career army—and one of the bloody right hands of the Japanese commander who'd gone down in history known forevermore as "the Butcher of Bataan."

Lindsey's father had freaked. Quietly, of course, since he never did anything loudly. But she'd overheard him, talking with her mother. *He should
have told me.* He meaning Henry senior. *If I'd known, I would have . . .*

What would you have done differently? her mother gently asked.

I would never have had a child. Words to make a fourteen-year-old's
head snap back. *It's an insult—all those men who died, men he killed.
Thousands of them. Most of them never had families. They never had the
chance. Yet this monster's lineage is allowed to live on.*

Lindsey was descended from a monster. It wasn't the best news to receive, especially since, in her innocence and naivety she hadn't even realized
that her father, Henry Fontaine Junior, wasn't truly her grandfather's son.

Along with her grief and confusion, worry and fear consumed her.
Her beloved grandfather was dead, having slipped away in his sleep. To
her knowledge he hadn't even been ill. If *he* could just suddenly die, what
was to keep her mother, who still fought her cancer, from doing the very
same thing?

Lindsey took to sitting outside her parents' bedroom late at night, after
they'd gone to sleep. She'd kept her ear pressed to the door, listening for
the quiet sound of her mother's breathing. If she stopped, Lindsey would
hear her, rush in, and revive her.

At least that was her plan.

It wasn't until years later that she truly understood. Her grandfather
had had a massive heart attack. Even if she'd been by his side when it had
happened, she wouldn't have been able to keep him from dying.

Much in the same way she hadn't been able to keep her mother alive.

Around the table, the men were silent, still watching her expectantly,
still wanting to hear more about the man who was a legend in the military
community.

Jenk, however, was looking at her with almost tender understanding—
as if he'd been able to see into her mind and follow exactly where her
thoughts had gone.

She forced a smile, forced herself to look anywhere else but at him.
She smiled particularly sunnily at Izzy—what was wrong with her? That
was just plain childish. Was she trying to piss Jenk off? "What else can I tell
you? He was . . . *really* good at hide-and-seek," she told them, which of
course got the laugh she'd hoped for.

From everyone, that is, but Jenkins. He just watched her, his dinner
ignored.

The way he was looking at her was making her feel more exposed than
when she'd been with him and naked.

So she pushed back her chair and got to her feet. "I hear a hot shower calling my name. I'll see you guys later. Or tomorrow. Whichever comes first." Hardy-har-har. It wasn't even funny, but she laughed, so they did, too.

Except, of course, Jenk.

She took her plate to the sink, feeling his thoughtful gaze following her all the way out the door.

Tracy had failed to pack her sleeping pills.

Or her hip flask filled with tequila.

Who knew that their destination would be outside the reaches of civilization, and that their rustic motel would be sans attached top-line-liquor-filled lounge?

She sure hadn't.

Feigning an oncoming case of sniffles, she'd grabbed her purse and told Sophia she was going to see if she could score some NyQuil, which contained both alcohol and sleep aids.

Wearing only her sneakers and her flannel pjs, a zippered hoodie on top, Tracy braved the arctic cold. She jammed her hands in her sweatshirt's pocket and hurried along the outside corridor and down the stairs, toward the motel lobby. Her hair was back in a ponytail and she'd long since taken off her makeup. She wasn't exactly dressed for human contact, but her luck was good. Stella was at the front desk.

And she had some NyQuil that Tracy could have, no charge.

She rummaged through a drawer and came up with a small foil-and-plastic packet that she put into Tracy's hand.

Tracy stared down at it. Two shiny green gel capsules stared back at her, like some alien creature's unblinking eyes.

"Oh," she said. "No, I was hoping for a bottle, you know, the kind that comes in a liquid?"

"That's all we've got," Stella said.

"Are you sure?" Tracy said. "Sometimes people have it in the back of their medicine cabinets and don't even know—"

"I'm sure," Stella said. "Honey, we're dry. We don't have any alcohol here. But we do hold a sunrise meeting. Of course, if you need one tonight, you'll have to drive into Happy Hills. There's a nine o'clock at the Congregational Church. Rob would be heading over to it himself if his back wasn't hurting."

"Meeting?" Tracy echoed even as she understood. AA meeting, as in

Alcoholics Anonymous. She laughed. "No, see, I'm just coming down with a cold."

"Those pills work fine," Stella told her. "And they're alcohol-free."

"Great," Tracy said, backing away. "Thanks. Is there, by any chance a store—"

"Nearest store is in Happy Hills, too," Stella told her. "Although the only thing open at this hour is the Criminal, attached to the gas station. But it closes at nine. There's a twenty-four hour pharmacy, but it's much farther away."

"What's a Criminal?"

"Convenience store." The older woman leaned on the counter with an elbow, chin in her hand. With her crazy hair, she looked like a character from a zany sitcom. "You know, you go in and pick up one of those little half-sized boxes of Lorna Doones, and they're so expensive, you practically drop them. But you get them anyway, because you're hungry, and nothing else is open. But as you're paying, you're thinking, *This is highway robbery. It's criminal.*"

"Cute. How far is Happy Hills?" It sounded like a final resting place for cocker spaniels. But if Happy Hills had a store, and that store was open until nine . . .

"It's a haul and a half," Stella told her.

"Okay, now, you're purposely being evasive," Tracy accused her.

"I am," Stella agreed, straightening up. "Because you have that same look in your eye that Robert used to have when he—"

"Excuse me, I'm a paying customer," Tracy said. What a total bitch. "And I certainly didn't request a psychology guessing game with an uneducated amateur, along with your third-world towels, the fourteen-thread-count sheets, cigarette-burned blankets, and that spider the size of Staten Island that was in the bathtub!"

"What's going on?" A blast of cold air from outside hit Tracy, and she turned to see Izzy standing just inside the door. He stamped his feet and smacked his hands together to get them warm. "I get back from the gas station to see the two top candidates for the role of Mrs. Irving Zanella doing everything but pulling out their switchblades and slashing each other's throats."

"Shoot, you were just at the gas station?" Tracy couldn't believe her bad timing. "In Happy Hills?"

"Shoot," he said. "Yes. But I'm going back. I'm gassing up the trucks we took out to the lodge. Why? You need some pork rinds? Or one of those little teddy bears holding a flag that says *Live free or die?*"

"The princess needs a drink," Stella tossed over her shoulder as she waddled into the back room.

Izzy turned to look at Tracy. There was heat in his eyes tonight. The same kind of heat that she'd thought she'd seen when he'd first walked into the Troubleshooters' office, the first time she saw him. Heat that she'd glimpsed from time to time since then. Heat that he'd tried to hide.

He wasn't trying to hide it now.

It was as if she were face-to-face with an entirely different man than the one who'd turned down her clumsy invitation in the parking lot of the Ladybug Lounge.

"I need some cold medicine," Tracy said, her mouth suddenly dry. The more times she repeated the lie, the more her throat hurt, as if she really did have a postnasal drip. "And, yes, okay, I could use a drink." She raised her voice so that it would carry into the back. "It doesn't mean I need a meeting!"

"Hmm," Izzy said, his gaze skimming down her, taking in her shapeless sweatshirt, her baggy pj pants. "You want to tag along, gorgeous? Round-trip takes a minimum of fifty minutes. Longer if we stop on the side of the road to neck."

If he'd said that to her a few days ago, she would have responded with, As if. The Izzy Zanella she knew then talked a big game, but that's all it was. Talk.

But this man was looking at her right now as if she were a piece of cheesecake that he wanted to devour.

His smile made her heart pound, and when she spoke, her voice sounded breathless. "I'm not exactly dressed for travel." She didn't want to sound too eager. "And tomorrow's an early morning . . ."

"It'll take longer still if we stop for a beer at Hooters. Well, I'll only have a Coke. The Navy's funny about the whole drinking and driving thing."

"Happy Hills has a Hooters?"

"I'm pretty sure it was a prerequisite to the registration of their town name. I mean, Happy Hills. How could there *not* be a Hooters?" He grinned at her.

"I should get my coat."

"I got a jacket you can borrow," Izzy told her. "It's already in the truck. Shall we?" He held the door for her, and with only the briefest hesitation, she went outside.

"Damn," he added. "How do you do it? How do you manage to make plaid look sexy?"

Lyle would have berated her for looking so slovenly in public. He would have insisted she go back to her room to change. God, Tracy hated him. And she hated herself for being stupid enough to want him anyway.

As the cold air slapped her face and stung her lungs, she knew in the sharp clarity of the winter night that she was going to take Lyle back. She always did, always would. She was going to say yes to his marriage proposal. Because as much as she hated Lyle right now, she hated being alone even more. It was stupid. *She* was stupid.

Because, worst of all, she actually hoped that their marriage license would make a difference. She actually dared to believe that by making their relationship legal, Lyle would become faithful and true.

But before she called him to tell him that she'd be his wife — his ticket to making partner at the law firm — she was going to play Lyle's game.

By Lyle's rules.

Izzy opened the passenger door of the SUV, holding it for her as she got in. It was like climbing into a freezer on wheels.

"That extra jacket's in the backseat," he told her. "Although, if you want, you can scoot over close to me. I'm good at sharing body heat."

Tall and solid, with his lean face, charismatic smile, and inscrutable dark eyes, Izzy Zanella — this new, bold Izzy Zanella — was finally Tracy's chance to even the score.

LOCATION: UNCERTAIN
DATE: UNKNOWN

Just because the water tasted fresh didn't mean it wasn't drugged.

Beth drank more, pulling the cool liquid through the straw, waiting for that familiar feeling of lethargy to descend upon her. The heaviness of limbs and head. The sense of time and space being altered. The feeling of floating, of leaving her body behind . . .

But the pain in her arm throbbed with each beat of her heart.

Of course, sometimes the drug he gave her didn't kick in right away.

He was still petting her tangled mass of hair, still crooning nonsensical endearments. "That's my girl." She was neither a girl nor his. In theory, anyway. In practical application, she was chained to this bed. He held the power, which made her anything he wanted her to be.

Including clean and healthy, if he so desired it.

There was no doubt about it, her arm, slashed in the fight with Number Twenty, was infected.

He was being careful, holding tightly to the glass that held the water, even as she held its base, as if to keep it steady. It was thick and heavy, but there was no way she could muscle it away from him. Not as weak as she currently was.

Still, she made a plan. Take the glass from him. Smash it back against the cast-iron frame of the bed. Kick her free leg over him, holding him down, as she plunged a sharp fragment into his carotid artery.

Plunged and slashed.

He smiled. "You'd like to kill me, Five, wouldn't you?"

Beth's stomach churned, and instinctively she pulled back from the straw. No more, or she'd get sick. But then she knew what to do.

She sucked harder on the straw, and it gurgled and burped as she drained the glass.

Her stomach heaved, and her vision tunneled, but she focused only on the glass. Hold on to that glass.

"You bitch!" He let go of the glass as she emptied her stomach all over him. But his cursing and anger were barely audible background noise. Her world shrank down to only the glass, the glass, the glass.

She thrust it back, as hard as she could, felt it shatter. It was now a knife without a handle, cutting her as well, but she didn't feel it, couldn't feel it.

Her legs were pinned by the blankets, so she couldn't hold him down, but she swung at him anyway, her own blood dripping down her arm. It was her one chance, and she couldn't blow it, except she knew she already had.

She heard him laughing, and she knew it was over. She'd tried, and failed. Probably for the last time.

And sure enough, although she connected with him, it was a glancing blow. Barely hard enough to cut him, let alone kill.

Still, his laughter stopped as he cursed. He hit her—a blow meant to torment—on her injured arm.

The pain was incredible. She heard herself scream, and he hit her again.

Mercifully, the world went black.

DARLINGTON, NEW HAMPSHIRE
SATURDAY NIGHT, DECEMBER 10, 2005

As they slid onto the bench seats on either side of the table, Tracy checked herself in the mirrored wall at the end of the booth. She'd actually put makeup on in the truck, as Izzy drove through the freezing night, giving her the details on the day's misadventure.

He now caught the bartender's eye. "You can just bring us a tequila IV. As soon as possible, okay?"

Tracy leaned in closer to stare into her own eyes.

"Yup," Izzy said. "Your invisibility cloak is still malfunctioning."

She pulled off a clump of mascara, then moved on to an examination of her mouth. Rubbing her lips together, then pursing them, she checked for imperfections, turning her head this way and that. "Have you ever tried putting on makeup in the dark?"

"Generally, I don't wear very much unless I'm going to a party," he told her.

She frowned at herself, then let her hair out of her ponytail, shaking her head to distribute it more evenly around her shoulders. But that needed a closer visual confirmation, too.

She moved it around a bit, adjusted it, fluffed it. Izzy couldn't really tell the difference. But whatever she did, she seemed satisfied that she was now totally and undeniably fuckable. The smile she sent him proved it. She'd set her flirtatiousness on kill, heavy on the eye contact.

This was going to be interesting, because despite that smile, her body language was, once again, a twisted mix of signals. Shoulders tight and defensive. Hands tucked in close.

Of course, maybe she was just cold.

But probably not. Izzy had watched her on the flight to New Hampshire and thought he'd picked up a pattern. When she was in a large group, she flirted shamelessly, without hesitation.

When she was one-on-one, though, *that* was where her signals started to get weird.

But okay. He was willing to play this game. Especially since Jenkie's close encounter with Lindsey had forfeited any claim he had on Tracy. Izzy's rules of engagement had changed.

"Personally, I thought the ponytail was cute," Izzy told Tracy, deliberately holding her gaze. "And I find the no-makeup thing sexy. It's very *roommate's girlfriend just out of the shower*. Makes me all hot and bothered."

She looked away, pretending to be fascinated with a grimy cardboard ad for Sam Adams Winter Lager at the wall end of the table. Was that real shyness suddenly kicking in, or was she just being coy and playing him like a cheap violin? With crazy Tracy, it was hard to tell.

Across the room, the bartender put the tequila bottle and two shot glasses on the bar. Apparently this was a self-service joint.

"I thought we were going to Hooters," Tracy explained, as Izzy slid back out of the booth. "No self-respecting woman on earth would walk into a Hooters without makeup on."

They'd found this little roadhouse right on the outskirts of town. It was fifteen minutes closer than the gas station, so they'd stopped. Izzy'd parked at the edge of the unlit lot, along with two mangy-looking pickup trucks and a scorched Toyota Corolla that appeared to have survived the apocalypse. Assuming the apocalypse had happened without him noticing.

He grabbed the bottle and one of the glasses from the bar.

"We could still go to Hooters," he said as he sat back down, fully knowing what Tracy's response would be, since she was eyeballing that tequila bottle as if it were the Second Coming. Hooters only served beer and wine. "It seems a shame to go to all that effort for nothing."

She took the bottle from him and poured herself a shot. Downed it like a pro. Poured again, and—whoa—again bottomed up. She was like a woman on a mission.

"Are you nervous about tomorrow?" Izzy asked. "Because you shouldn't be. No one expects anything from you. You just have to show up."

She didn't look convinced, so he kept going. "I'll be with you the whole time. I'm part of the Red Cell—the terrorists who'll be holding you hostage."

"So, in other words, I shouldn't trust you or believe a word that you say," Tracy countered. She poured another shot. Waved the bottle at him. "Sure you don't want some?"

"I do, but I can't," he said.

"Maybe just one to take the edge off?" She pushed the glass toward him. "I won't tell." She was already feeling the effects of those first two shots. Her tension level had dropped from a ten to a nine point five. She was still tightly wound, but Izzy was no longer concerned that her face was going to crack.

He pushed the glass back. "It doesn't work that way."

She shrugged. Drained the glass. Refilled it.

Damn, maybe Stella had been right about Tracy having a drinking problem. "So. Is this your usual nightcap regimen?"

She laughed. Toasted him. "Liquid courage."

"I'm telling you," Izzy said. "Tomorrow's going to be fun. You don't have to be afraid."

"What's the hardest thing you've ever done?"

He didn't have to think about it. "Doing nothing," he said.

Tracy didn't get it. She was in the process of seriously stewing her brain cells, but even fully sober, she probably would have struggled with the concept. "Nothing has ever been hard?" she asked, frowning at him.

There was a time and place for dick jokes, but sitting in this drafty little roadhouse with Tracy Shapiro and her weird mixed signals was not one of them.

"What I meant," Izzy said, "was that the hardest thing I've ever done was to do nothing. Kind of like stepping away from you the other night when you invited me to follow you home."

Whatever she saw in his eyes made her lift that glass and pour that tequila down her throat.

Just like the night she'd returned to the Ladybug for her allegedly missing jacket, Tracy's body language was a curious mix of fear and hope. And bravado.

"That's the hardest thing you've ever done." Skepticism tinged her voice. "Not following me home?"

Izzy smiled. "No, but the concept's the same. There's something that you want really badly, but you know if you do it, you'll be in an even worse situation. Frying pan to fire, you know? I was once in a bind that I can't go into in too much detail. But it was recon—which means you're there just to watch and listen. You don't engage the enemy. Usually you're seriously outnumbered, and that was the case this time, so . . . I stumbled into this really bad scene. About a dozen hostages had just been murdered in the middle of this field, their bodies left to rot—at least that's what I thought. I should've stayed hidden, but I didn't. I wanted to be able to identify them—see if they included this pair of American doctors who'd been grabbed." They had definitely been among the dead. "I was taking pictures when the enemy returned."

Pictures as well as DNA samples, using his pant leg as a petri dish. But she didn't have to know that.

"There was nowhere to hide," Izzy continued, "so I had to pull the bodies on top of me and play dead. That was absolutely the hardest thing I've ever done—to lie there and not move. To listen to them congratulate themselves for killing these two doctors who were completely dedicated to saving lives—who wouldn't have hesitated to treat them if they were wounded."

But lie there he had. With the already swelling bodies of Drs. Mary

Ullright and Charlotte Weston covering him. Gagging from the smell was not an option. He was beyond lucky that none of the enemy had taken a closer look or done a head count.

"Another thing that saved me was the enemy's shortage of ammo," he told Tracy, who was clearly both grossed out and impressed. "If there'd been enough bullets, some hot dog prolly would have drilled all the bodies one more time—including mine. One thing I've learned through the years is that luck plays an important part in survival."

"How many—" Tracy stopped herself, taking a moment to gnaw on her lush lower lip. She rephrased. "Do you keep track of things, like, how many lives you've saved, or . . . taken?"

"Absolutely," he said. "I've got a kill belt. Actually, I've got three of 'em. I make a notch for—Look at you—you're buying this shit. Do *you* keep track?"

"I've never killed anyone," she pointed out. "And what are my chances of ever saving anyone's life? I'm the Lieutenant Uhura of Troubleshooters Incorporated. *Hailing frequencies open, Captain!* Maybe if I try really hard, I can save someone from a paper cut."

"Do you keep track of guys you've slept with?" Izzy asked. "Hearts you've broken?"

He'd said it to make her bristle defensively, but she took it totally in stride.

"Doesn't everybody keep score to some degree?" she countered, pouring herself more tequila. "It's human nature. Don't you think? To keep rankings, too. Was it yawnable, or total screaming monkey sex?"

"So, what are you saying? You have a belt with notches? Color-coded? Gray for *yawnable*. Vermilion for—"

"If I did, it wouldn't be a very colorful belt," Tracy admitted. "Or a very long one. Only two notches, one of them gray."

Was she serious? If she was shitting him, she was doing an incredible job of it. She was no longer meeting his gaze, and she tossed back that shot as if she needed it desperately.

"That's . . . actually pretty admirable," Izzy told her. "I mean, in a world where people treat sex casually, that's . . . I'm impressed."

She looked up at him. And again, if the shy thing was an act, she deserved an Oscar. God, she had the prettiest eyes. "Really?"

"Yeah," he said.

"You don't think it's pathetic? Considering Lyle would probably have a belt that he could wrap around him three times?" She rolled those eyes at the mention of her ex. "God, I'm such a loser."

She was on the verge of sliding into full-steam pity-party mode. So he sang to her. "*Well, I lay my head on the railroad track waiting on the Double E.*"

She gave him her *what the fuck?* look. "Why do you do that? Just randomly start to sing?"

"Because each of the thousands of people I've killed had a favorite song, and since part of them lives inside me now—"

"Sometimes I think you're completely crazy," Tracy told him. "I never know when you're serious or when you're kidding."

"Usually I start kidding when people get serious. Too much serious gives me a rash. Can I give you some advice?"

She poured herself another shot, some of which missed the glass and hit the table. "Can I stop you?"

Izzy laughed as he claimed possession of the bottle. "Not a chance. Here's the deal. Asking for stats on personal body counts is extremely uncool. It implies a certain morbid fascination with violent death. Some guys find that to be a turnoff."

"Oh, come on. Isn't everyone fascinated by violent death?" she asked, finally taking just a sip from the glass. Apparently the shot part of the evening was over. Which was a good thing. As it was, he was probably going to have to carry her out of here. "I mean, why else are horror movies so popular?"

"So what are you saying?" Izzy asked. "You'd like me more if you knew for sure that I'd killed people? And if I tell you exactly how many, you'll be unable to keep yourself from pulling me out to the car, tearing off my clothes, and joining me in a rousing chorus of 'She'll Be Coming Round the Mountain'?"

"Of course not." She didn't get the joke. Or maybe she did, and she was just ignoring it. And he was wrong about the shot part of the evening being over, because she tipped her head back and drained her glass. She really did have a lovely throat and neck. Come to think of it, she had a lovely everything.

He couldn't help but wonder if he would find her as enchanting after he cut her off, when she started screaming obscenities at him.

But this time, when she set her glass on the table, she turned it upside down, cutting herself off. How sweet was that?

"So here's the deal," Tracy said. She didn't look or sound drunk, but she had to be. No one could drink that much and not feel it. "I'm going to marry Lyle."

"Now's probably not the time to make that kind of decision," Izzy started, but she waved him off.

"This is not the tequila talking. This is . . . fact facing. Facing the facts. I'm going to marry Vile." She cracked up. "Vile Lyle, the man-ho."

Izzy stood to return the bottle to the bar and settle up their bill, but she caught his arm.

"Wait, please?"

He waited.

"I need to ask you a favor." She closed her eyes. "Will you please sit back down so I don't have to shout it?"

"Don't tell me," he said. "You want me to be flower girl at the wedding?"

Tracy laughed. "You're funnier when I'm drunk."

"That's what all the girls tell me."

She leaned forward, gesturing for him to do the same. So he leaned forward, too. At this proximity, her eyes were unbelievable. Tomorrow, however, they were going to be unbelievably bloodshot.

"I'm just going to say it," she said. "Okay?"

"Best way to say anything," he agreed, "is to just say it."

"I'm just going to ask," she said.

"Good plan," Izzy said.

She was looking into his eyes, as if she were searching for something. But then she sat back, her head hitting the back of the booth with a thud. "I can't do this." But then she sat forward again. "Do you have paper? Maybe I could write it."

There must've been a pen in the pocket of the olive drab jacket he'd loaned her, because she put it on the table now.

"There's always paper in a bar," he told her. "I'll be right back."

This time she let him leave, and he took the bottle with him, setting it on the bar with a twenty. Sure enough, there were napkins there in a little pile. He took a few back to the table. "Here."

Tracy made a barricade with her hand so he couldn't see what she was writing, like a middle school student taking a test. He sat back down across from her, glancing at his watch. This had been amusing when it first started, but it was quickly becoming old.

She was going to marry Lyle, which meant the odds of Izzy actually getting laid tonight had dipped into negative numbers. Not that the odds had ever been all that strong. Still . . .

Tracy was finally finished writing, and she folded the napkin in half and then in half again. He stopped her before she attempted to turn it into an origami swan, taking it out of her hands.

"Oh, my God," she said, slumping back, one arm holding on to herself, the other hand covering her eyes, as if she were too embarrassed to look at him.

Izzy unfolded the napkin and . . . Whoa.

Will you have sex with me?

Her handwriting wasn't helped by the tequila or the porous nature of the napkin, but those were definitely the words she'd written there. And, yup, they were still there when he read them again.

Was she serious?

"Oh, my God," she said again, peeking out at him from under her hand. "You're gay, right? Because I am *so* bad at this, it would be just like me to ask someone who was—"

"I'm not gay," he said. "I'm just . . . like . . ." He laughed, because what the hell? She'd managed to surprise him completely. "You mean, you want to right *now?*"

"Not in here," she said, as if she actually thought he was about to throw her across the table.

"Yeah, no," Izzy said. "I meant now, like, tonight."

She met his eyes for the briefest of moments, and there it was again. Fear. And hope. "If you don't want to—"

"Wait," Izzy said. "You did not hear me say that. I'm just trying to clarify. And work out the logistics. I've got a roommate at the motel. You do, too."

"We've got the SUV," she pointed out, almost shyly.

Indeed they did. And it didn't take much imagination for him to picture them, parked somewhere dark and private, steaming up the windows as they removed just enough of their clothes for her to straddle him.

She held his gaze for slightly longer now. It was possible, though, that she was blushing.

Damn, he was having one weird day. "Tracy, are you sure you—"

"Yes." *So here's the deal. I'm going to marry Lyle.*

"So what is this," Izzy asked. "Some kind of revenge fuck?"

Tracy winced. "That sounds so awful. But . . ." She took a deep breath, exhaled hard. "Yes. It is. Is that okay with you?"

"Hey, I'm not judging you," Izzy said.

But she felt compelled to explain. "I walked in on him and his research assistant. Practically in our bed. How can I just take him back without at least—"

"I'm also not trying to talk you out of it," he added.

"I want him to wonder what I'm smiling about when he catches me daydreaming." This time she held his gaze.

Dear Penthouse, *Was this really happening?*

Yes, it was. "Don't get me wrong," Izzy said. "But I just sat here and watched you consume a crapload of tequila. I remember doing something similar once, and having what seemed like a truly genius idea of how to handle a problem I was having with this asshole neighbor who never cleaned up after his dog. But believe me, approaching him in a crowded bar, surrounded by his asshole friends, and insulting his mother was *so* not the way to go. If I'd stepped back, and waited until the next morning—"

"You don't understand," Tracy told him. "This isn't . . . I didn't . . . The tequila was so I could get up the nerve to ask. You know, flat out, like . . ." She pointed to the napkin. "I tried asking more suttelbly . . . More subtly"—she took her time with the word, making sure she got it all out—"but you didn't get it, so . . . And then I was so desperate I tried Mark, except *he's* suddenly all in love with someone else. God. That was embarrassing."

And so much for his ego. She was so desperate she'd tried asking Mark, who'd turned her down. So now she was back to Izzy. Who would she approach if he said no? Lopez, maybe. Or Gillman. Apparently she found them all interchangeable.

"You do understand, right?" Tracy told him with the earnestness of the inebriated. "That this is just sex. This is me thinking you're attractive and wanting to hook up with you without having to be afraid of anyone getting hurt."

"Except Lyle," Izzy pointed out.

She laughed at that. "God, I hope so."

This was definitely crazier than anything he'd fantasized. He had to be honest with himself. He'd imagined getting busy with Tracy in her attempt to exorcise Lyle from her life. He'd imagined her using him as an exclamation point at the end of that dead relationship. But he'd also imagined her choosing him because she was drawn to him, because she found him irresistible. Not just because he was mildly attractive and conveniently available.

But okay. What, was *he* now the crazy one? He was going to sit here and pout because she wanted to use him to punish Lyle?

A gorgeous, sexy woman wanted to have no-strings, no-guilt sex with him. Tonight. Probably as soon as they went outside and got the SUV warmed up.

Izzy reached across the table for her pen. Holding her gaze, he uncapped it. Only then did he look down, and only briefly, as he spread the napkin on the table, holding it taut so he could write on it.

Three little words.

He spun the napkin so that she could read them.

I'd love to.

CHAPTER
FOURTEEN

Lindsey was the first to arrive.

Blanket wrapped around her shoulder, Sophia opened the door to see her smiling face.

"How are you?" Lindsey said, slipping inside and closing the door tightly behind her. "I won't stay long. I just wanted to make sure you didn't need anything."

"I'm okay." The burst of cold air that accompanied her into the room made Sophia sit directly on the wall heater. "But thank you."

And this was where it would happen. If Lindsey was going to say anything, she was going to say it now, while they were alone.

Unless, of course, she didn't realize that they were alone.

Sure enough, Lindsey leaned forward slightly, to see if the bathroom door was closed.

It wasn't. The bathroom was dark, the light off. "Where's Tracy?"

Sophia wasn't exactly sure. "She went out to get some cold medicine."

"Is she sick?" Lindsey asked.

"I didn't think so," Sophia said. "She's been gone for a while, so . . ."

It would have been typical of Lindsey to make a joke about Tracy's alleged illness being nothing that a Navy SEAL injection wouldn't cure, but instead she was silent, her smile suddenly gone.

"I'm sure she's just inventorying everyone's pharmaceuticals," Sophia said quickly, realizing with a flash of clarity that Lindsey was imagining Tracy off somewhere with Mark Jenkins. "Or she's hanging out with Danny Gillman and Jay Lopez. Or Izzy. He's a riot, isn't he?"

"Izzy's out, getting gas," Lindsey informed her.

Which meant that Jenk was alone in the motel room that the two men shared. Or maybe he wasn't alone. Maybe that *was* where Tracy had gone.

"Shit," Lindsey said. "*Shit.* Do you think I'm a coward?"

"Absolutely not," Sophia said, but before she could ask why Lindsey would question that, someone knocked on the door.

And there it was. Their last few seconds of privacy. Lindsey proved Sophia right. "I saw your scars," she said fearlessly. "I wasn't trying to, but—"

"I know," Sophia said. Everyone who'd gone out to the lodge in Jenk and Lindsey's little recon party had seen them—her souvenirs from her former nightmare of a life. "They're hard to miss."

"If you ever want to talk . . . I'm here. No pressure, though. I don't need to know. I mean, I figured you already knew that you've got an entire team of people here who love and respect you, people you can talk to about anything at all. So what I'm really trying to say is that you *don't* have to talk to me. That whatever you do or don't tell me isn't going to change our friendship. I'm not going to feel as if you don't trust me or—anything like that. I just didn't want you to feel awkward around me, like I'm always going to be wondering what happened to you. Because I won't. I'm not. Sure, those scars are part of you, but no way are they all of you. Does that make any sense?"

Sophia nodded, unable to speak. Her tentative friendship with Tess Bailey had all but faded away because Tess's concern for Sophia had been such a palpable thing. And Sophia knew that her own failure to talk about her past had frustrated Tess. It had become easier simply to make up excuses not to socialize.

"Soph, you okay in there?" It was Dave outside the door. He knocked again, more loudly.

"Just a minute," Lindsey called. She lowered her voice even more. "I also wanted to say . . . Please don't take this the wrong way, but . . . I have some money saved. I know you've been working to pay off a loan, but . . . You wouldn't have to pay *me* back for a long time, until you were done with that, and . . . I'm talking zero interest, it's just, I know this really great cosmetic surgeon."

And Lindsey actually thought she was a coward. No one, not even Dave, had ever dared to suggest such a thing to Sophia.

"I know it's none of my business," Lindsey said. "But—"

"No," Sophia said. "It's okay. I guess I was hoping they were just going to fade away. I mean, they mostly have." Hadn't they?

From the look on Lindsey's face, it was clear she didn't agree.

"I try not to notice," Sophia admitted. "I guess I'm used to it. I didn't realize it was that disturbing."

"It's not," Lindsey said, but then opted for honesty. "It's just . . . to have that kind of constant reminder . . . ? It occurred to me that it might be a financial issue for you, and if that's the case, I can help. That's all."

"Thanks," Sophia said. She ended the conversation by opening the door. "Sorry, Dave."

"It's freezing out." He came into the room, looking from her to Lindsey and back, no doubt wondering what they'd been talking about. "I can't stay—I'm just checking in. Did you get enough to eat?"

"I'm good," Sophia said, back on her heated perch. Was she ever going to be completely warm again? "Thanks."

"How's the roommate thing working out?" he asked, clearly noting that Tracy wasn't there. "Any additional boundary issues?"

"She unpacked for me," Sophia told Lindsey. She was pretty sure Tracy just wanted to go through her stuff. Not that Sophia had anything to hide. Not so far as her clothes went, anyway. "Other than that, it's been okay. I was picturing the TV on twenty-four/seven, but she brought a book. She's been reading."

There was another knock on the door.

"Where is she?" Dave asked, opening it. Jay Lopez and Danny Gillman were standing outside, huddled against the wind.

"Where's who?" Danny responded.

"Tracy. If you're coming in, come in," Dave said. "This is not weather for an open-door chat."

They came in. Clearly, they'd come to see Sophia together, both feeling the need to make sure she was okay, but far too uncomfortable to face her solo. She wondered if they'd discussed it, discussed her. They were close friends—why wouldn't they?

"How's your head?" she asked Danny.

"I'm okay," he said. "How about you? I heard Tommy's benching you."

"Just for a few days," Sophia said. She'd been given a direct order from the boss to take it easy. "At the risk of being thought a wimp, I'm admitting that I'm actually okay with that."

"No one thinks you're a wimp." Dave, as always, was ready to defend her—even from herself.

And there they all were. Standing there. Crowded together near the door to the room. No one sat down, probably because the room was so small there was nowhere to sit besides on the beds.

The dynamic was that of tension. Dave was carefully ignoring Danny, whom he still clearly blamed for the accident out at the lodge. Danny and Lopez obviously felt obligated to drop in, but clearly wished they were anywhere else on the planet. And Lindsey . . .

It was obvious to Sophia that Lindsey could no longer pretend that Tracy was off amusing herself by hanging out with these two young SEALs. With Izzy out of the picture, it was more and more likely that Tracy was, indeed, with her old friend Jenk.

Although, maybe they were just sharing high school memories. Or playing Monopoly.

"Can we get you anything?" Lopez asked.

She looked at Lindsey. "Actually, yes," Sophia said. "Have you seen Mark Jenkins? I need to talk to him."

Lindsey made a *what?* face at Sophia.

Sophia gave her a shrug in return. *Why not?* This was a quick and easy way to find out where Jenk was, and if Tracy was or was not with him. "Since I'm not part of the exercise tomorrow, Tom asked me to help with the scheduling," she fabricated. "I need to get some information from him—"

Lindsey cut her off. "No, you don't. I can help you with whatever you need." She shook her head at Sophia.

"Are you sure?" Sophia said.

"Yes," Lindsey said. "I am. Very sure." She sidled toward the door. "My notes are in my room. I'll . . . call you. Later."

"Let us know if you need anything," Danny said, and he and Lopez made their escape with Lindsey.

Dave alone remained. He scratched his ear. "You gonna tell me what *that* was about?"

Sophia shook her head no. "Do you think I should go see a cosmetic surgeon?"

She'd surprised him. He tried to hide it, but couldn't. He actually sat down on her bed. "Wow," he said, giving her one of his try-to-read-her-mind looks. "Do you want to go? Because if you do, I'll—"

"No," she said. "Actually, I don't. I've already hurt enough. The thought of enduring more pain . . ."

"Then absolutely not." Dave didn't hesitate. "You shouldn't go. There's no reason—"

"Isn't there?" She put her mug of tea down on the table next to the bed, took the blanket off her shoulders. She turned her back to him, lifting her sweatshirt, lowering the already low-riding elastic waistband of her yoga pants.

She heard him draw in his breath, which should have been answer enough.

But he tried to bluff. "So what? People get tattoos to cover scars, and women have tattoos in that particular spot all the time. Even if you felt compelled to hide it, which I don't think you need to do—"

"Pretend you're Decker," Sophia said.

He was silent.

"Yeah," Sophia said, covering herself back up. She picked up the blanket, wrapped it around her shoulders again. "That's what I thought. He can't even handle looking at my face. There's no way . . ."

"He's a fool," Dave whispered. "Have you ever considered the possibility that he's not good enough for you?"

Sophia sat down next to him. "I'm kind of in love with him."

Dave sighed. "I know," he said. "But I'm starting to be pretty certain that he's not in love with you. He could be, but he just won't let himself."

"You always know just what to say to cheer me up," Sophia said.

He laughed, but his smile faded as he met and held her gaze. "No more pain," he told her. "Promise me, Sophia."

"I promise," she said, "that I'll talk to you about it first."

Dave nodded. "Fair enough."

"As long as we're in the no-pain department," Sophia told him, "I had another call from my aunt. My father's been moved into a nursing home. He's doing much better and . . . I've decided not to visit him. Not on this trip. I just can't. I know you disapprove, but . . ." She shook her head.

"I don't," Dave said. "I'll support any decision you make, a hundred percent. I just don't want you to regret a missed opportunity." He stood up. "You look exhausted." Kissed her on the top of the head. "Call me if you need anything." Opened the door. "Try to get some sleep. Whoa."

"Hey." It was Decker, standing there, about to knock. He'd actually come to see her.

"Come on in," Dave said.

"No," she heard Deck say. "If she's going to bed . . ."

"She hasn't yet," Dave said.

"I just wanted to make sure she was okay," Decker said. He leaned in. Waved at her. "Hey. Just checking in."

"I'm okay," Sophia said, wrapping the blanket more tightly around her as a wave of cold air swept into the room.

"Come in," Dave said. "Please. Just because I was leaving, doesn't mean—"

"It's good if she sleeps," Decker said. "I'll check in later. Don't leave the door open."

Dave looked at her in exasperation as Deck pulled him outside and closed the door behind them both.

Frustration mingled with relief. It was odd, actually, how relieved she was that Deck hadn't come in. If he had, it would have been the perfect opportunity to lay a little honesty out in front of him. *I'm still a little chilled and I think I might've pulled a muscle when I tried to push Danny out of the water and despite the months of separation, I think of you constantly and I'm pretty convinced that I'm in love with you.*

In her fantasies, he would look at her the same way he'd looked at her this afternoon in the smokehouse, and he'd tell her he loved her, too. She'd fall into his arms and . . .

After kissing Danny, she was no longer quite as concerned that physical intimacy would make her run, sweating and shaking, to hide in the bathroom.

No, now it was Decker she pictured on his knees in front of the toilet, sickened by the sight of her scars.

Sophia climbed into bed and pulled the covers around her, switching off the light. But as soon as the room was dark, her phone rang.

She reached for it, picked it up. "Hello?"

"*Jesus.*" It was Dave. "That's all," he said. "Just . . . *Jesus.*"

She laughed.

"I am *so* sorry," he said.

"It's okay. Really."

"I thought you might appreciate knowing that I managed not to kick him down the stairs, despite desperately wanting to."

Sophia laughed again. "I really love you, you know."

"Yeah," Dave said. "I know."

"So what's your biggest fantasy?" Izzy asked.

That was easy. "Well, I just told you that when I was little my favorite movie was *The Little Mermaid*," Tracy told him. "So . . ."

"So . . . being abducted by a giant sea witch and having your voice stolen makes you hot?"

She laughed. "Being swept off my feet by a handsome prince, thank you very much."

Tracy had been on edge as they'd left the bar, Izzy's hand warm against her back as he'd helped her navigate the potholes and broken tarmac of the parking lot. She'd definitely begun feeling the alcohol.

But as he'd helped her into the SUV, even as he handed her the packs of condoms he'd gotten from the machine in the men's room, he'd suggested that they gas up first.

At first she'd gotten even more nervous at the delay, her stomach churning with anxiety and too much tequila.

But as they drove through the darkness, Izzy had kept up a constant stream of conversation: favorite books, favorite movies, favorite parts of Manhattan. Eventually she'd started to relax. They had so much in common, not the least being that they were dog people. They'd actually both had golden labs, growing up. His was named Dyno-mite, hers Nathaniel.

Lyle was allergic.

"Ah," Izzy said now. "Someday my prince will come, love at first sight—am I right? You're a traditionalist, heavy on the romance—and maybe the high drama, too?"

She didn't understand.

"*Casablanca*," he said. "Thumbs-up or thumbs-down?"

"I've never seen it," she admitted. "Not the whole thing."

"Wow. Okay. How about . . . *Moulin Rouge*," Izzy said. "*Shakespeare in Love, The Last of the Mohicans?*" He glanced at her. "*Stay alive, whatever you do . . .*"

Tracy nodded. His Daniel Day-Lewis imitation was rather good, right down to the super-intense eyes. "Big favorites. All of them."

"Good," Izzy said. "Okay. Give me a second, I can do this . . ." He was silent for another moment, but then he said, "You know, you remind me of her. Of Ariel." He glanced at her, and in the light from the dashboard, his smile was warm and charmingly crooked. "It's your eyes."

"Really?"

When Izzy smiled, his face was transformed from merely dangerously attractive, with all its planes and hard edges and angles, to extremely handsome. His eyes crinkled at the edges, sparking and dancing with that offbeat, devilish amusement he brought to everything he did or said.

"Absolutely," he told her. "Big and blue and . . ." He glanced at her again, and this time, it was the tenderness she saw on his face that took her breath away. "Just a little bit sad." He pulled his gaze back to the road, a muscle jumping in the side of his jaw. "God, I could fall for you so easily."

Tracy sat up, her heart in her throat. "You could?"

The smile he sent her now was forced. "I don't know if I can do this,

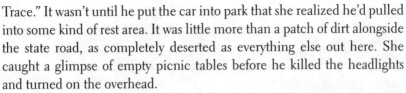

Trace." It wasn't until he put the car into park that she realized he'd pulled into some kind of rest area. It was little more than a patch of dirt alongside the state road, as completely deserted as everything else out here. She caught a glimpse of empty picnic tables before he killed the headlights and turned on the overhead.

It was glaringly bright, as if he didn't trust himself to sit with her in the dark.

"I'm afraid," he whispered, his eyes tormented as he turned in his seat, toward her, "that if we make love . . . my fate will be sealed." He touched her, though, his hand warm against her cheek. "But if you don't kiss me right now, I may not survive."

It was unreal—as if he'd somehow changed, again, into someone else. Someone gallant and romantic and . . . perfect.

Tracy kissed him. How could she not?

It was like a kiss from a movie about star-crossed lovers, starving for one another's touch. This was incredible—she'd never been kissed with such passion before. Not by Lyle, not by anyone.

She hadn't expected it to be like this, to actually *want* to be with another man. Whenever she'd thought about paying Lyle back, she'd imagined it would happen fast. With her closing her eyes and turning her head away.

And faking it.

But when Izzy finally pulled back, she was breathing hard, her heart pounding.

He held on to the steering wheel with both hands. "This is going to kill me," he gasped. "Having you like this, then letting you go . . ."

"Maybe we should stop." The last thing she wanted to do was hurt him, but oh, dear God help her, she was praying he wouldn't let her shut this down.

"No," he said—thank God. His voice was rough, his eyes those of a man possessed. It was the way Lyle had once looked at her. As if she were everything—and then some. "I want you too badly. I need you—God, I need you so much, Tracy. Just . . . I'm going to have to live on my memories of this one night. Only one night—in a lousy car." He kissed her again. "I wish I could make love to you in a bed—no, on a bed covered in rose petals. I wish I could see you lying there, the most beautiful woman in the world—all mine, even if just for one too-short night."

He'd unzipped her sweatshirt, and she helped him peel it down her arms, helped him pull off the T-shirt she wore as a pajama top.

"Whoa," he breathed, because she was naked beneath it. "Hello, hot mama—I mean, oh, my darling, you're so beautiful, it takes my breath away."

The look in his eyes was pure worship and heat. But he didn't reach for her. He just sat back and looked, as if in his mind she were on that romantic petal-strewn bed.

Except she had on plaid pajama pants. She kicked off her sneakers and skimmed her pjs down her legs. And there she was. Completely naked, even though the car was lit up like a fishbowl in the darkness.

"I know it's not the same as being in a bed," she started.

"So not caring," he said, and reached for her.

To her surprise, he was gentle, almost unbearably so. As he skimmed his hands across her bare skin, she had to close her eyes. And then, yes, he was kissing her, licking, touching and tasting, his lips and mouth soft, in such contrast with the scratchiness from his chin against her throat, her breasts, lower. . . . Except there wasn't enough room, despite the fact that he'd somehow reached around her and completely reclined her seat. The car horn went off, a sharp blast as he bumped it, and he lifted his head, laughing into her eyes. "Whoops. Sorry."

He still had most of his clothes on—he'd only managed to shed his jacket, and she touched his belt buckle. But he shifted back, out of reach. "What, don't you like surprises?" he teased.

Tracy laughed, smiling back at him. "What, do you want me to beg or something?"

"Yeah, actually, that would work well for me," he said, his fingers exploring between her legs, finding her hot and slick with desire. "Ah, Tracy . . ."

He was being so brave, smiling and laughing, when in truth his heart had to be breaking. She kissed him, long and deep. How could she not?

"Please," she whispered, between kisses. "I'm begging you. Please, baby. I need you inside me. Now."

Somehow, while she was kissing him, he'd maneuvered himself beneath her. Somehow he'd unbuckled his belt and unfastened his pants and covered himself with one of those condoms she'd put in the cup holder.

He lifted her up, way up, his hands on her hips, and she felt him, hard and large, against her.

"Oh, dear God," she said, as he started to fill her, but then he stopped, halfway. She tried to move closer, but his grip on her was unrelenting. She opened her eyes and found him laughing up at her.

"Ooh, the eye contact is nice, but I'm looking for something more," he told her.

"Please," she said. "Please, baby . . ."

"Please, *who?*" he asked.

"Izzy," she said, and he smiled.

"Much better," he said, holding her gaze as he lowered her all the way down.

"Izzy," she said again, as he pushed himself impossibly deeply inside of her, as he finally let her move on top of him. "Oh, Izzy . . ."

"Oh, yeah," he said, his voice hoarse. "Fucking A, you are so incredibly sexy . . . I mean, I know I can only have you for this one night, my dearest. If only wishes could come true . . . But I'll remember this . . . I'll remember you forever—giving yourself so completely to me."

"Izzy . . ."

He moved with her now, catching her hips to slow her down, pulling her close to capture her mouth with his, even as he murmured, "Oh, yeah. This is amazing."

It was. She was on top and should have been in control, but she wasn't. He dictated the slow slide of their bodies, the tempo of their movement, just how far she could go, holding her back unless she breathed his name.

He still had his sweater on, and his scarf, too, but when she tugged at them, trying to get to his bare skin beneath, he gently pulled her hands away. "No, no, no," he said, "that's part of *my* fantasy."

Tracy didn't understand. His fantasy? But she stopped wondering as he pushed himself all the way inside of her, as she cried out, and he laughed up at her.

He was finally letting her move without any restrictions, and so she did as he gazed at her, his eyes half-closed, his pleasure clearly etched on his face. "Damn, you are beautiful. And I *am* going to remember tonight forever. That part wasn't just bullshit."

Bullshit?

But he was looking at her with such hunger. "Kiss me."

She met him halfway, and, almost as if they'd planned it in advance, they both hesitated. It was only for a second or two, with their lips a whisper apart. But Tracy opened her eyes to find Izzy's eyes open, too.

He smiled—she may have smiled back. But then he kissed her, and she kissed him, and the world exploded in a barrage of amazing sensations. His sweater-clad arms wrapped tightly around her bare back. The rasp of his chin against hers. His tongue in her mouth, her fingers in his hair, her knee against the hard plastic of the seat belt lock, the overhead light so bright that the windows revealed only pitch-black, their bodies straining to get closer, even closer.

Izzy made a sound low in his throat, and she felt him tighten beneath her through the powerful waves of her own release.

How could this feel so good, so right, so . . .

Perfect.

And still he kissed her.

But sweetly now, as if he were kissing her good-bye.

And Tracy burst into tears.

Jenk turned off the TV, frustrated with Izzy for dropping off the edge of the earth.

He was frustrated with himself, too—with his goddamn overly creative imagination. It had come up with this scenario where, coming back from putting gas in the two SUVs they'd used today, Izzy wandered over to Lindsey's room. Just to say hi.

Right.

Jenk threw on his jacket, telling himself that as long as he couldn't sleep, he might as well see who was awake and hanging in the restaurant, over by the bottomless supply of coffee.

Sure, that's where he was going. Which was why he ended up standing outside of Lindsey's room, shoulders hunched against that bitch of a north wind.

A light was on inside. He could see it through the curtains that covered the window. It was nothing too bright, and he found himself thinking of the way she'd covered that lamp on his bedside table with a pillowcase, creating a soft, romantic glow. He could hear the murmur of her voice. The musical sound of her laughter.

Fuck it. He knocked, jamming his hand back into his pocket as he stood and waited for the door to open.

Which it did, almost immediately.

She'd changed out of the clothes she'd worn to dinner. Instead she wore workout gear—gym pants and one of those form-fitting bra tops that left her arms and most of her shoulders completely bare.

And there they were, standing and staring at each other. For a moment, it was as if all the harsh words and hurt and disappointment of the past few days had vanished. She was looking at him much in the same way she had when he'd first brought her into his apartment.

"I'm looking for Izzy," Jenk said, because they weren't back there. They were here. In the Land of Suck. A journey for which she'd been on point.

"Damn, Izzy," she called in a voice that would have reached the tiny bathroom. "Jenk's onto us. Better put your clothes back on, stud." She turned back to Jenk, jerking the door wider open. "No, he's not here, but by all means, come in and search."

"There's no need to get hostile." Jenk started to back away, but she grabbed his arm and pulled him into the room, slamming the door behind him. "I was just looking for him and thought—"

"Lindsey's a slut, maybe he's in her room," she said, lifting the bedspread so he could see beneath it.

"You don't like yourself very much, do you?" he said.

Her laptop was out on the bed, along with the room phone. She'd been calling the members of the TS Inc team, making sure everyone knew the revised start time for tomorrow's exercise. Jenk had gotten a similar call from the senior chief.

Instead of answering, Lindsey marched over to the bathroom, slapping on the light and pulling the shower curtain back with a screech. "Of course, Izzy's a SEAL. He might be hiding in the toilet tank. Izzy, are you in there?"

"Look, he's been gone too long," Jenk foolishly tried to explain. "It was nice for a while, you know, to have the privacy—"

"Yeah, how *is* Tracy?" Lindsey came back out of the bathroom to ask. "What'd you two do all evening? Watch Animal Planet?"

"What?" Jenk couldn't believe what he was hearing. Lindsey actually thought that . . . "Privacy as in solitude. God *damn* it, are you *really*—" This was not going to help. He took a deep breath. "Can we hit pause for a second here?" The jealousy they were both guilty of feeling was surely a sign that the relationship they'd had was more than friendship and casual sex. Why couldn't she see that?

But Lindsey was still stuck on the details. "Tracy wasn't with you?" she clarified. "Starting around eight?"

"No."

"Not at all?"

Jesus. "*No.*"

Any jealousy she might have been feeling had been completely replaced with concern. "Because I just spoke to Sophia, and Tracy's still not back in their room."

"Aw, come on, Tracy. It's going to be all right, I promise," Izzy said as the wicked-ass fun part of the evening morphed seamlessly into the far soggier regrets and recriminations part. He tried to cheer himself up by thinking that it could have been way worse. At least *both* of them weren't shit-faced and crying.

To her credit, Tracy was trying hard to stanch the flow, searching for her clothes, scrambling with them into the backseat where she got dressed. "I'm sorry," she kept saying, as he zipped his pants.

He'd spotted a trash container out by a picnic table when he'd first pulled off the road, and he turned up the heat and defroster before he opened the car door and stepped into the bracing night air. Shit, it was cold. He dashed to the trash can, ditched the condom they'd used, and . . .

Something made him pause. Was someone actually out there, in the woods?

He listened for a moment, but the night was silent. It was just his over-active imagination. *Give me back my leg.* Yeah, right. If he and Tracy were going to be killed by a deranged ghoul, it would've happened well before they'd climaxed.

Izzy dashed back to the car, climbing in behind the wheel. He hit the lock button though. Why not?

Tracy's sneakers were still on the floor in the front, so he picked them up. When he turned to hand them to her, she actually managed to give him a shaky smile.

"I was thinking," she said, almost shyly, "about that only one night thing . . . ?"

Ding, ding, ding-ity ding. Izzy's notch in her belt was clearly vermil-ion. Thank you. Thank you very much. And he'd been wrong about the evening going south fast. It was, perchance, turning into a night for his "Best of" list. As in Best Unexpected Sex of His Life.

Tracy Shapiro wanted a replay. Or four. Or nineteen. Hello, hello, the places they could go.

Izzy played it casually, nodding instead of grinning at her like a fool. "Makes sense to me," he said. After all, payback was a tricky thing. It could take a while to really set. To take hold. Besides, Tracy had said Lyle had cheated on her way more than one time. "I mean, why *shouldn't* you have some fun, right?"

She was frowning at him, a furrow of confusion on her gorgeous brow. "Fun?"

"Or, it doesn't have to be fun at all," he quickly backpedaled. "It could be very, very hard work. A strenuous schedule works well for me. Three, four times a day. Twice each night. I'm ready and able and extremely will-ing."

Now she was staring at him as if he were a hypnotist, or speaking Japanese.

"I'm quite the conscientious worker," Izzy continued, resisting the urge to snap his fingers in her face, to see if maybe that would make her blink. Clearly, she was not in a joking mood, or maybe the tequila was clouding the issue, so he brought it to the bottom line. "Just tell me where and when, and I'll be there." He sang it for emphasis. *"Don't you know, baby, yeah, yeah, I'll be there . . ."*

That was obviously the right thing to do, because she finally smiled. "Sometimes I don't get your jokes at all," she told him.

No shit.

Izzy patted the front seat. "Come on, Sherlock, let's get back to the motel, where I'll climb into my lonely bed and dream of you."

He was on a roll with the saying-the-right-thing thing, because after Tracy scrambled into the front, she kissed him. It was the kind of kiss that made him glance at his watch and calculate just how late they'd return to the motel if they got supercrazy and took another condom out for a test run.

But all of his numbers jumped immediately to zero, as if Tracy hit his recalibration button by whispering, "I think I've totally fallen for you, too."

Come again?

Okay, she'd probably meant that in a *sex with you puts the va-va-voom in vermilion, so let's fuck like bunnies until I return to New York to marry Lyle* way.

But Izzy found himself looking into Tracy's Disney-blue eyes as she smiled almost shyly up at him.

"I think I've been willing to settle for Lyle," she said, "because, well, you know that expression—the devil you know?"

Izzy nodded.

"Lyle's the devil I knew," Tracy said. "But now, God, I can't believe I found you."

Um.

"I can't believe how perfect we are together. It was like . . . magic."

He'd put the car into gear, but now he put it back to park and turned slightly in his seat to face her. "The sex, you mean."

Tracy nodded. Some people got way too intense when they were drunk. Clearly she was in that subset. "The sex is definitely part of it, but I'm talking about all of it. The way you feel about me."

"The way I feel about . . . ?"

She kissed him again, her fingers in his hair, which really felt very nice despite his unease. And then she said, "Your fate is sealed."

He'd told her if they made love, his fate would be sealed, and . . . She'd *believed* him?

Oh, fuck. Izzy caught her hands. "Tracy, whoa. Time out. When I said that, I was, you know, trying to special-deliver your personal fantasy— heavy on the fairy-tale romance with a little tragedy thrown in? Remember when we talked about that? *Moulin Rouge* and *Stay alive whatever you . . .*" He frantically tried to remember all that he'd said to her. *God, I could fall for you so easily. This is going to kill me . . . letting you go . . .* Oh, double fuck. "Babe, none of that was real. It was just a game."

She struggled to understand. "A game?"

"We were playacting." At least he had been. "Prince Charming and Princess Tracy. You know. Haven't you ever done that before? The divorcee and the pool boy? Or the prom queen and the . . . the cowboy? A little role-playing to make the encounter more exciting?"

"More exciting," she repeated. She looked as if he'd just killed her puppy.

"You were so tense," he said, even though he knew he was totally screwed. "I guess I was trying to get you outside of your own head. I mean, shit, I was up for anything, but I thought it would be better for both of us if Lyle wasn't sitting directly on your shoulder." There was nothing Izzy could say now to make her think of him as anything but the most loathsome villain. From her perspective, he'd lied to her. Repeatedly. "Tracy, seriously, I thought you understood. I thought . . ."

How could he not have known that she was taking him seriously? Except, damn, how *could* he have known? The things she'd said back to him had been so totally cornball, he'd been certain she was role-playing merrily along.

"Bullshit," she said. She had tears in her eyes, but she was fighting to keep them back. "*That's* what you meant when you said that it wasn't just bullshit—that you'd remember tonight forever. Unlike the rest of what you told me, which *was* bullshit. Oh, my God."

"Tracy, I am so, so sorry—"

"What was your fantasy?" she asked. "You said something about it . . . It was something about me not taking off your sweater, right?"

"You naked, me not," Izzy admitted. "You know, full-service treatment from an incredibly hot naked woman. I think it's probably got elements of love slave and master."

Tracy nodded. "Of course. Silly me for not realizing. Although, you know, I suspect it's also got *elements* of you not wanting me to see your horrible rash."

His laughter was clearly not welcome.

"Or your two-inch toothpick of a penis."

He shot her a look. "Hey, now."

She wouldn't look at him, focusing on tying her sneakers, her movements jerky with anger. But anger was good. It was better than those big blue eyes brimming with tears and hurt. "God, I'm stupid. I actually thought I'd done something right for a change, that I'd found someone special, but you're not. You're just like Lyle. Only with way less money." She glared at him. "If you so much as breathe a word about any of this to anyone, I will—"

"I won't," he said. "I promise."

She snorted at that—clearly his promises weren't worth much to her anymore. "And if you think you're *ever* touching me again," she told him, "you are *so* delusional." She fastened her seat belt. "I have to go back to my room now."

Good idea. Izzy put the SUV in gear.

"We've got to wake up Tom," Lindsey said, following Jenk into the motel parking lot.

"It was somewhere over here," Jenk said, holding his cell phone out and open, like Mr. Spock with his tricorder on *Star Trek*, exploring the class-M planet Nocellzonius. "I actually got a signal this morning. When we first arrived."

After discovering Tracy was MIA, Lindsey had gone to the room that the receptionist shared with Sophia, while Jenk had knocked on the doors of some of the usual suspects among SEAL Team Sixteen.

Going through Tracy's personal belongings had been somewhat . . . interesting. But she and Sophia had found nothing obvious cluing them in to Tracy's whereabouts, such as a journal entry with the words, *I can't take this anymore. I'm going back to New York* underscored, with four exclamation points.

Tracy didn't have a journal.

She did, apparently, have a slight fungal problem. As well as questionable taste in music, and a brightly colored shower-safe aid to assist her in self-entertainment.

And yet she'd gone to seek entertainment elsewhere. With Izzy Zanella, apparently, who was also still conspicuously absent.

That conclusion, taken straight from the Detecting 101 textbook—if two people were missing late at night from a low-budget New Hampshire

motel, chances that they were together were high—made Jenk extremely
pissy.

He had been jealous at the thought of Lindsey with Izzy, but he was
mondo-mega-jealous of *Tracy* and Izzy.

Every time he opened his mouth it was Tracy this, Tracy that. Tracy,
Tracy, Tracy.

"I understand the reasons why we train for situations in places where
phone and radio coverage is nonexistent, but why do we actually have to
go to the fucking dark side of the moon?" Jenk now vented his frustration
as his cell phone continued not to work. "Can't we just hand over our radios and cell phones and promise not to use them? I mean, yeah, okay,
when it's just the team, fine. But when civilians are involved . . . ?"

"I'm getting concerned that Izzy might've had some trouble on the
road," Lindsey said. Tracy had left her room without her winter coat, wearing little more than a sweatshirt over her pajamas. "If Tracy's with him,
and they broke down—"

"If Tracy's with him," Jenk said, "I'm going to fucking kill him."

Apparently, he was no longer self-censoring his language around her.
"You know," she said, her own temper sparking, "nothing quite says *I love
you* like *I'm going to fucking kill him,* so frankly, I don't know why you
bothered to come pounding on *my* door before, oozing with jealousy. Unless it's Izzy you're obsessed with . . ."

Jenk laughed. "Yeah, Linds, I'm gay. That's our big problem here."

"*Our problem,*" she said, "would probably be solved if we just got the
keys to one of the other trucks, and—"

"*Our* problem," he said, snapping his phone shut, "is that you care
about me. I've been watching you grind your teeth every time I mention
Tracy's name. I've been doing it on purpose, you know. Just to watch you
squirm. You *are* jealous."

"Oh, yeah, right," she said, "like you're completely fine with the idea
of Tracy and Izzy—"

"No, you're right, I'm not fine," he fired back at her. "Have you talked
to Tracy? Because she's going back to Lyle—it's not a question of if, but
when. Izzy acts like he's a player, but I really don't think he is. I mean, he
pretends to be an asshole, but I've seen the way he looks at Tracy. If he
hooks up with her, she's going to do to him what you did to me, and he's
going to get his heart broken."

"I didn't break your heart," Lindsey said, and as the words left her lips,
she realized how stupid she sounded.

"Oh, well, good," Jenk said. "I was worried that you might have. I'm glad to get a more accurate read on what *I'm* feeling—from someone who's too terrified to feel anything at all."

"Hey, I'm not the only one with intimacy issues," Lindsey countered hotly. "If I broke your heart, well then, you're guilty of giving it away much too soon. What are you, fourteen? *Dear Burger King cashier girl, I know we've only spoken once, but when you told me '$4.68 please,' I knew you felt it, too—this bond that ties us together. A love to last throughout all time.*"

"Great, Lindsey. Make a joke. *That's* real mature."

And there it was. Salvation in the form of headlights out on the road.

"I'm sorry I broke your heart," she told him, as what looked to be the SUV with their missing teammates pulled into the motel parking lot. "I'm sorry that an incredible night of great sex wasn't enough for you."

"And *I'm* sorry that it *was* enough for you."

The sliver of moon wasn't bright enough to light his face, but the neon Motel-A-Rama sign took up the slack. Jenk was standing there, in that pink-and-green glow, with his pretty eyes filled with frustration and regret. There was probably pity and disdain in there, too, but Lindsey chose not to search for it. Instead, she turned her back on him, heading toward the row of parked cars and trucks.

Where, yes, both Izzy and Tracy were getting out of that SUV.

Izzy went around to help Tracy, his voice carrying even though he didn't speak loudly. "Careful, it's slippery."

She said something back to him that Lindsey couldn't hear, but it sure looked as if she jerked her arm away. The end result was that they both went down.

They were hidden behind the hood, but as Lindsey rushed to help, she could hear Izzy again. "Oh, that's just perfect."

She reached the end of the line of cars to see that . . . Oh, dear. Tracy had booted, right in Izzy's lap.

"God, I'm sorry," she mumbled, pushing her hair back from her face far too late.

"Did she hit her head?" Jenk was right behind Lindsey. But then he, too, caught the unmistakable and extremely unpleasant whiff of previously-used alcohol. "Zanella, what the hell?"

Tracy was fried on both sides, as Grandpa Henry used to say.

"Come on, Trace. Can you stand?" With Jenk's assistance, Izzy helped her up. "I know what you're thinking," he told Jenk, "but she just wanted a drink."

"Or twenty. Jesus, Iz, what were *you* thinking?"

"I was thinking . . . give her what she wants?"

With her chunkified hair and glistening chin, this was not Tracy's finest hour. Apparently she wasn't too drunk not to know it, because she started to cry.

Lindsey sighed. She might as well take charge now. "Help me get her to her room." This was going to fall on her anyway. There was no way Lindsey was simply going to let Jenk or Izzy walk Tracy to her door, push her in, and wave good-bye. Sophia was in no condition to hose down an inebriated roommate.

"I just want to state for the record," Tracy announced, as they started to move across the parking lot, "that I didn't do that on purpose."

"Yeah, I know," Izzy said. "And hey, snaps for waiting until you were out of the car. I do appreciate that."

The stairs were trickier to negotiate, but they finally all made it up to the second level.

"I need a shower," Tracy said.

"I got it from here," Lindsey told the two men, neither of whom hesitated to hang back—thanks a million, brave Navy SEALs.

Izzy did, however, call after them. "Tracy, I'm sorry, too. Linds, put her clothes outside the door. I'll run a load of laundry, and, you know, throw her stuff in with mine."

"What did you do to her, asshole?" Lindsey heard Jenk ask the other SEAL as she helped Tracy into her room. "What are you so sorry about?"

"Nothing. Weebs, I swear. I mean, come on. Dude, Tracy Shapiro? Only in my dreams."

Tracy cried even harder.

In the motel room, Sophia was back under the blankets of her bed, wearing a ski cap on her head, reading a book. Her eyes widened as she saw Tracy, but to her credit she didn't make a horrified face.

"I smell," Tracy sobbed. "I'm so sorry."

It was the refrain of the evening.

Tracy was sorry, Izzy was sorry, Jenk was sorry, Lindsey was sorry. Everyone was sorry. She was certain that Sophia, although she'd yet to speak, was pretty damn sorry, too.

Lindsey closed the door behind her and got to work.

CHAPTER
FIFTEEN

In the morning, Jenk found Lindsey out in the parking lot, in the area where his cell phone had worked when they'd first arrived yesterday. She had obviously managed to get a signal, because she was talking on her phone, and he slowed his steps slightly, not wanting to intrude.

But he only had a few minutes, and he needed to thank her.

Sophia had told him that Lindsey had swapped rooms with her last night. Sophia had gone to Lindsey's room to sleep, while Lindsey stayed and babysat Tracy.

"No," he heard Lindsey say. "No, Dad, it's okay. Really."

She was talking to her father. Jenk was on the verge of clearing his throat to get her attention, when she forced a laugh.

"Christmas is just another day to a writer on deadline, right?" she said into her phone. "Don't worry, I've got lots of friends, I'll . . . draw names from a hat." She laughed again, but to Jenk it sounded so brittle. "That's right and . . . Oh, you do? Oh. Okay, then I'll talk to you next week, if not . . . Yeah, I'm great, yeah . . . Okay. Love you, too."

She shut her phone, but she didn't move. She just stood there, breathing, her back both to him and the hotel.

"Everything okay?" Jenk finally asked.

Lindsey jumped, looking over her shoulder at him, but then turned away again, to wipe her eyes. "Yeah." She hadn't been breathing; she'd been trying not to cry.

Holy shit. Jenk took a step toward her.

"It didn't sound okay," he said. "I mean, from what I overheard."

When she turned around again, she'd actually managed to fabricate a smile. "Just my weekly phone call to my father."

"During which he canceled your plans for Christmas?" Jenk guessed.

She shrugged, an exaggerated sitcom actor move, complete with *what-you-gonna-do-about-it* face. "It's not like I wasn't expecting it," she lied.

"That's crap, and you know it," he said. "Because this is, what? Only the second Christmas since your mother died?"

Her smile didn't falter. "Wow, you really pay attention when people talk to you, don't you?"

Lindsey had told him she was just a kid when her mother first got sick. "How many years did you do that?" he asked her now. "Keep smiling for your mother's sake?" Putting a positive face on a bad situation, always being cheerful and upbeat, must've become her default mode.

But she just laughed.

"Lindsey, you don't have to do it anymore," Jenk told her. "She's gone. You're allowed to look sad when someone asks you about her passing."

"Wow, Dr. Mark, isn't it a little early in the day for psychoanalysis?"

She started to walk away, shaking her head, but his temper flared. She was still fucking smiling, and he just could not let this or her go.

Jenk blocked her path. "Hide what you feel—or better yet, don't acknowledge that you feel anything at all. That's much easier, huh?"

She gave him a big, exaggerated sigh. "I had a long night. Will you please just . . . back off?"

"Last Christmas must've really sucked, huh?" Jenk said. "Your first holiday without your mother? And now your dad's hiding—probably because he can't stand to be near you and your *everything's okay, we can just pretend Mom's gone to Bermuda* attitude." He snapped his fingers at her. "Come on, Linds, let's hear you make a joke now. Where's the snappy comeback? Make it a good one—don't disappoint me."

But her smile had finally vanished. "That was an awful thing to say," she whispered.

He'd pushed too hard and gone too far. It was obvious that she actually believed it might be true, that her father couldn't stand having her around, and Jenk's anger instantly evaporated.

"Look, I was just trying to hit a nerve, which I've obviously done," he told her. "I'm sure it's not about you—his canceling your plans. I mean, she wasn't just your mother, she was his wife and lover, and it's gotta be incredibly hard for him, too." The look on her face made his stomach hurt, and he couldn't help himself. He reached for her. "My point is that you're allowed to feel sad. When your mother dies, you're allowed to—"

Lindsey sidestepped. "You must really hate me," she said as she hurried back toward the motel.

"I don't," he said, following. "Will you just wait? Come on, slow down."

"Just stay away from me."

He caught her arm. "Lindsey—"

She spun to face him. "Stay *away* from me!"

And, terrific, there Commander Koehl was, out by the SUVs, putting on his gloves. Lindsey's shout had most definitely caught the commanding officer's attention.

She ran for the motel, and this time, as Koehl watched, Jenk stayed put. "You're allowed to grieve," he called after her again, "and you're allowed to show it."

Lindsey didn't look back as she dashed up the stairs and unlocked the door to her room.

"Oh, yeah," Jenk said, in a voice she couldn't possibly hear, particularly after she'd slammed the door behind her. "And thanks for helping Tracy last night."

This was supposed to be fun.

Scrambling around in the woods, playing the terrorist equivalent of the big bad wolf, kidnapping their own little Florence Nightingale, and creating challenges for the rescue team was supposed to be amusing.

Yet Dave had never seen Izzy Zanella as quiet and subdued as he was this evening. During their drive to this cabin—part of what had once been a thriving Girl Scout camp a dozen miles north of the haunted hunting lodge—Izzy had been positively silent.

There was trouble brewing in Afghanistan. Team Sixteen's CO had received a heads-up phone call earlier in the day, advising him as to the impending likelihood of the SEALs being called in. It was possible that that news had created Izzy's extra-crunchy coating of grim.

Their exercise had been delayed while several temporary sat towers were installed. Despite the fact that they'd come to this remote part of New England to train without any communication devices, they'd all come out tonight with radios or—for the civilians among them—their cell phones in their pockets. The alternative was to cancel the exercise, hang at the motel, and wait for the phone to ring and the SEALs to deploy.

Still, Dave was betting Izzy's mood was less than effervescent for other reasons.

"Can I get you anything?" Izzy asked Tracy now, as she sat in a straight-backed chair near the cabin's roaring fire, pink mittens still on her hands, her arms belligerently crossed.

She shook her head as she continued to study her sturdy white nurse's shoes—part of her costume, intended to make her escape more difficult through the darkness of the woods. "No, thank you."

Izzy stood there for several long moments, glancing over to where Dave was listening to the rest of their mock terrorist cell—Decker, Gillman, and Lopez—trying to second-guess when and where and how the rescue attempt would come.

Izzy lowered his voice, but Dave's ears were quite good. "Look, we're not going to have a chance to talk when—"

"Thank God," Tracy said.

"I just wanted to say that I'm really sorry—"

"*Don't*, okay?"

Izzy turned away, but then turned back, his voice sharper now. "You know, I tried my best to deliver exactly what you wanted—exactly what you asked for. I'm sorry I was too good for you."

Tracy made an insulted sound, and probably would have said far more than he wanted to hear if Dave hadn't stopped her. "Prisoner! No talking."

She closed her mouth, attempting to incinerate Izzy with her eyes, as he slammed out the door. "Checking the perimeter," he announced.

Decker looked at Lopez. "Go with him."

Lopez followed.

There was going to be no better time than this, so . . .

Dave wandered toward Tracy. "You warm enough?" he asked, as Decker glanced over at them.

She was, quite obviously, still steamed from whatever she and Izzy had been discussing.

"My feet are cold," she told him curtly, and he put down his weapon so he could throw another log onto the fire.

But Gillman stopped him. "Will you please just move her closer? I'm dying here."

Their jackets were cold-weather versions of the cammie-print BDUs they'd worn during their last exercise in California. There were sensors in them that would register their status as living or dead, and they were required not only to keep them on, but to keep them zipped. This was a definite problem for Dan Gillman, who must've been descended from Himalayan Sherpas or maybe Eskimos. The man was never cold.

"Switch with Lopez," Decker ordered, as Dave gestured for Tracy to stand up.

As Gillman clattered out the door into what for him must have been the refreshing coolness of the subzero evening, Dave leaned closer to Tracy. "The door to the left of the fireplace is unlocked. When I give you the signal, go straight behind the cabin—toward the road." A rescue team would be back there, but there was no way to tell her that as Gillman's footsteps faded.

Because Dave knew that Decker had very good ears, too.

Tracy's eyes were wide as Dave moved her chair closer to the fire. "Sit," he ordered, and she sat.

A squad of SEALs, led by Lieutenant Jacquette, was getting ready to approach the cabin where the hostage—Tracy—was being held.

Lindsey's team—led by Commander Koehl himself—was on the verge of moving into another position at the rear of the cabin.

They'd all dug in a little deeper a few minutes ago, when Izzy and then Lopez and Gillman had come out for an evening stroll. Both the SEALs and Koehl's team were well out of range, but they all still kept their heads down.

It wasn't long, though, before all three "terrorists" went back inside, the cabin buttoned tightly shut again.

"Lindsey, got a sec?"

It was, of course, Mark Jenkins. She'd been avoiding him successfully all day, ever since his attempt at playing pop psychologist outside the motel.

"No," she told him now, "and neither do you."

It was ridiculously close to go-time, and he glanced over his shoulder at Lieutenant Jacquette, who was having one last conversation with Tom and Koehl.

"Look," Jenk said, "I just wanted to—"

"You need to go," Lindsey said.

"—see if you maybe wanted to come home with me for Christmas," he finished, then dashed off to join his squad.

Lindsey stood there, staring after him. What on earth . . . ?

"Linds."

She looked up to see Alyssa Locke gesturing at her. Great, caught with her thumb up her butt by Tom's second-in-command.

They were on the move, so Lindsey shouldered her weapon and followed, focusing all of her thoughts and energy on the task at hand.

She could not think about Mark Jenkins—or his invitation home for Christmas. Instead, she took it and compartmentalized it. It was what she'd trained herself to do—to push unwanted thoughts and feelings away and focus only on the problem she was currently facing.

If there was one thing she was very good at, it was compartmentalizing.

With all distractions locked away, Lindsey became the night, breathing with it, moving silently, soundlessly.

Shots were fired. Two separate bursts from an automatic weapon.

She dropped to the ground along with the rest of her team, which was probably unnecessary, considering those gunshots came from inside that cabin.

Crazy Dave Malkoff went postal.

He swung his weapon around and blew Decker, their Red Cell leader, away. Just *rat-a-tat-tat*.

"I heard Decker talking to Tracy," Dave shouted as he did it. "He's a plant, a mole. He's working for the enemy!"

Tracy made squeaking sounds, mittens up over her ears. She'd probably never heard a weapon being fired at such close range before, and Izzy found himself standing stupidly in front of her. Like he was going to protect her from the pretend bullets or something.

Although chances were that, even if he did save her life, she'd be pissed off at him for getting too close to her in the process.

"What are you looking at?" Dave was screaming at Gillman, like some kind of serious sociopath. "Are you working with him?"

"No," the fishboy said, but damned if Dave didn't just, *blam*, shoot him, too.

Izzy looked at Lopez, who looked over at Izzy. Both of their weapons were up and trained on Dave's back. Not that he seemed to care, but he *did* put his arms up, his weapon now loosely held in one hand.

Izzy knew exactly what Lopez was thinking. They'd just lost two-fifths of their team. They could pull their triggers and make it three-fifths.

Danny, meanwhile, was making WTF noises, despite being dead.

"Yeah," Dave said, much calmer now. "I knew you weren't working with him. I just don't like you, Dan."

Decker was already sitting down, his back against the wall, his eyes closed, and Gillman went to join him, making a big show of unfastening his jacket, taking it off, and tossing it onto the floor at Tracy's feet.

"At least I don't have to worry about heatstroke anymore," he said, as she gratefully wrapped it around her ankles.

"You boys make up your mind yet about whether or not to shoot me?" Dave asked Izzy and Lopez, "or would you rather listen to my plan for winning this whole thing first?"

"I don't understand what's happening," Tracy said.

"Silence," Dave ordered, turning to glance at her but being careful not to turn too far.

Izzy shook his head. This was pathetic. "Dude, you know what's *really* not going to happen? Us winning. What, are you gonna drag Tracy to Canada or something stupid like that? It's freezing out there. We're seriously outnumbered, and she's completely unskilled—"

"I'm now moving, gentlemen," Dave said as he did just that, heading away from them, "toward my rucksack by the front door."

Izzy exchanged a glance with Lopez again. Was Dave trying to sound like some James Bondian villain on purpose, or had a screw really come loose? They both shifted automatically, keeping him in their faux-kill zones.

Although knowing Tommy Paoletti, this was probably just another one of his mind games. Provide the rescue squad with intel on the five tangos who'd kidnapped a hostage, and then make sure the tangos self-reduced their ranks, providing confusion and an opportunity for the good guys to kill said hostage by accident.

"I'm putting down my weapon," Dave said, again narrating his action, "so I can reach into my bag and show you—"

Someone's cell phone rang.

It was Decker's. It was joined by someone else's—probably Dave's. And then, simultaneously, Izzy's, Lopez's, and Gillman's radios chirped.

And just like that, the game was over. No doubt about it, SEAL Team Sixteen was going wheels up.

Lights went on. Training equipment was piled on the floor. SEALs who had, moments before, been sneaking up on the cabin now Avonladied right up to the front door.

There was no word on where Team Sixteen was going. If they were going to be briefed, it would happen on the plane. Still, from the furrow that Izzy had seen in Commander Koehl's forehead this morning, it seemed likely Team Sixteen was heading to either A-stan or Iraq.

Izzy turned to Tracy, to say—what? *I just wanted you to know that if something happens to me over there, I will die with a smile on my face, thanks to you.* Nah, probably not the way to go. Besides, he was bulletproof. Death was not an option. He should probably just say, *I really* am *sorry, and I hope your life works out just the way you want it to.* And then ride off into the sunset.

So to speak, considering the sun had set hours ago.

But none of it mattered, because Tracy was gone, her chair empty.

Izzy went outside to wave to her from afar, to let her know that it was safe to go back in and sit next to the fire, where she wouldn't have to worry about running into him again for a good long time.

Everyone who didn't have to rush down to the airport in Manchester—as in Tommy's team—was gathering in the cabin.

The plan was to get the SEALs on the road as quickly as possible. They didn't even have to pick up their stuff from the motel—they'd planned for that in advance, loading all their duffels and gear into one of the trucks.

Nevertheless, Jenk risked the senior chief's wrath by looking for Lindsey after he'd put both his training weapon and his jacket onto the piles on the cabin floor.

She was standing by the fireplace, talking to Dave.

"Excuse me," Jenk said. "May I have a moment with Lindsey?"

She didn't give Dave a chance to depart. "You hate me." She just jumped right into the conversation that would have happened earlier, had Jenk not had to run away. "Why would you ask me to come home with you for Christmas when you hate me?"

Dave gave him an *oh really?* look as he drifted out of earshot.

"I don't hate you," Jenk said. "I'm upset with you. I'm angry. I'm very angry, yeah, but I don't hate you."

"So you figure, what, you'll bring me home for Festivus?" she asked.

Jenk shook his head. "I don't know what that is."

"Of course you don't," she said. "You don't watch much TV." Like that was a bad thing.

"I just don't want you to be alone for Christmas," he told her.

Lindsey just looked at him. Silent. Unsmiling. He had no idea what she was thinking, what she was feeling. He took it as a good sign that she didn't *whatever* him or try to make a joke.

"It's not meant as some kind of trick," he felt compelled to explain. "Like, I'm still secretly in love with you or something, so I invite you home to meet my folks, with hopes of brainwashing you into . . ." Jenk rolled his eyes. "I just figured that by Christmas the anger I'm feeling will be down to a dull mad, and I'll be able to handle the idea of being your friend again. I've been thinking about what you said yesterday, and bottom line, I don't want to lose you, either."

"I hate that you're so nice," she finally said. "Can't you be more . . . awful?"

"What, just never talk to you again? I considered it, but . . . I like you. I think you're really messed up, but I still like you."

"You like me just the way I am, huh?" she said. "That's from *Bridget Jones's Diary.*"

"Yeah, I know," Jenk said. "I actually saw that one. And no. I *don't* like you just the way you are. I think you need, I don't know, a mental tune-up, or a reality check or *some*thing. I know you didn't purposely set out to hurt me, but I wish you would open your eyes and see how you're sabotaging yourself. But what can I do?"

"Jenkins!" The shout came from outside.

"Shit," he said. "I gotta go." He held out his hand, because friends shook when they said good-bye.

Lindsey took his hand, her fingers cold. "Mark, I—"

"Jenkins. Have you seen Tracy?" Izzy nearly barreled into them—perfectly terrible timing, because Lindsey was clearly about to say something heartfelt for a change and maybe even accept his Christmas invitation.

"No," Jenk said as, crap, she pulled her hand away.

"Linds?" Izzy asked.

"I haven't seen her either. Sorry."

"Okay," Izzy said, "this is starting to freak me out. She's gone. She's not in here, she's not in the yard, she's not by the trucks. Unless she's hiding from me, because she's, like, embarrassed about last night—" He looked at Jenk. "You know, about ralphing on me? Dude, do me a favor and just take a quick look around."

Jenk had one, maybe two minutes left to let Lindsey tell him whatever it was that she was going to tell him, but instead he was going to go chasing after Tracy? The irony of that was not lost on him.

"She's got her cell phone with her," Lindsey pointed out. "I'll just call her." She opened her own phone. "What's her number?" She looked at Jenk.

He, of course, knew Tracy's number by heart—another strike against him. He rattled it off, and she dialed, holding the phone to her ear.

"Come on, pick it up," Izzy muttered.

Lindsey shook her head. "I'm going right to voice mail. Tracy, this is

Lindsey. I'm betting your phone is set on silent. When you get this message, call me. Right away." She hung up.

"Shit," Izzy said.

But then, over on the other side of the room, a phone let out a voice mail beep.

Okay, that probably wasn't a good thing.

Izzy loped over, kicking aside Dave's knapsack and some other equipment. He bent down and held it up—the phone he'd found was bright pink. And if there was still any doubt that it was Tracy's, he opened it, hit a few buttons, and Lindsey's phone rang.

"I hit redial," he said into it, as she answered. "I guess she doesn't have her phone with her."

"I guess not," Lindsey agreed, hanging up. "But that's gotta mean she can't be too far." She looked at Jenk, as over in the corner Izzy flagged down Dave Malkoff. "Why don't you go check by the trucks. And take Izzy, because if she is avoiding him, then she'll surely come back in here once he leaves. For obvious reasons." She gestured toward the fire.

Jenk hesitated, and she misunderstood. "Before you go getting all jealous," she continued, "I really doubt she's hiding from Izzy for any reason other than the puking incident. I was with her all night, and although she railed against men in general and Lyle in particular, she didn't mention Izzy once."

"I'm not jealous," he said.

"What are you, crazy?" Izzy exclaimed from across the room. "Damnit, Dave!"

"Lindsey," Dave called, stepping over the pile of jackets, "you were in Commander Koehl's team, right?"

She nodded. "Yeah?"

"Damnit!" Izzy followed Dave across the room, clearly irked.

"So you connected with Tracy in the woods behind the cabin." Dave said. "Right?"

Uh-oh. Jenk looked at Lindsey. This wasn't going to be good.

Lindsey met his eyes, then looked from Izzy to Dave. "That was one of the potential plans, yeah, but . . . No, we never even got into position."

"Shit!" Izzy said. "Fucking *shit!*"

"When those shots were fired," Lindsey continued, "we hunkered down, intending to investigate, but before we could, we got the game over notice. At which point we immediately moved back toward Jacquette's squad. They were at the front of the cabin."

"*What* was one of the potential plans?" Jenk asked her. For Tracy to go into the woods . . . ?

"Dave here was working for the good guys," Izzy told him. "He told Tracy to leave by the back door while he created a diversion."

"So Tracy went out the back door." Jenk repeated. Fucking shit, indeed. "But no one was there to collect her."

"She must've left right before we got the call," Dave said. "Or maybe even during it? I was reaching for my phone, I didn't see her."

Lindsey crossed to the door in question. "This is the door she was supposed to use?" she asked, even as she opened it and scanned the ground outside.

"Guys, we've got to go." Gillman appeared, like the angel of doom.

"There's a clear trail," Lindsey announced. "Leading due north, back toward the state road."

"It's cold out there," Dave said, ever the voice of reason. "How far is she going to go before she realizes something's wrong and turns around?"

"Yeah, but this girl's not a camper," Izzy said.

"Even someone experienced could turn around, shift to the right or left a few degrees and miss the cabin by a mile," Jenk pointed out. He couldn't believe this. "How did this happen? After the lessons we all allegedly learned from Lindsey?"

"Guys," Gilligan said. He tapped his watch.

Izzy lit into him. "Do you not understand that Tracy is missing?" He quickly shifted gears. "Yo, you were in the cabin with us. Did *you* see her leave?"

"I didn't," Gillman admitted. "But weren't you standing right next to her?"

"I was in front of her," Izzy said. "I was focused on Crazy-Ass Dave."

"Nice to know I'm so well respected." Dave sniffed.

Lindsey knocked on the door to get their attention. "Dave, please go and find Tom. And Decker, too. And all the flashlights you can round up." She looked at Izzy and Jenk. "Go. We'll find her. I promise. I'll call you when we do. It'll probably be before you even hit the airfield."

"I'm going to make sure Koehl knows about this." Izzy bounded off.

"Come on," Gillman said.

But still Jenk hesitated.

Lindsey lifted her right hand. "I swear, I won't go to sleep tonight until I'm sure Tracy is safe and secure. Go save the world."

Jenk nodded. "Call me."

"Better yet, I'll have Tracy call you herself," Lindsey told him, then turned to meet Tom, who was coming into the cabin. "Sir, we've got a little problem."

"I don't know Tracy that well," Gillman said, as he and Jenk headed at a jog back toward the waiting trucks. "But seriously, how far could she have gone?"

Tracy finally reached the road.

There was no one there to meet her, and the little bit of scared she'd been harboring ever since she'd left the cabin turned into a serious dose of frightened.

She tried to bolster her sagging spirits by remembering Izzy's insulting words. *She's completely unskilled.* Sure, he'd meant it in terms of counterterrorism, but it was also very clearly a personal dig, obviously referring to last night's total fiasco.

God, she was still so embarrassed. Mortified. Yeah, she'd had a lot of tequila, but how could she have been so totally stupid and naive as to believe all those things Izzy'd said?

She'd believed him because she'd wanted to. Because she'd never had sex before with someone she didn't love. Because she'd been temporarily blinded by the hormones rushing through her system.

Then reality had reared its ugly head. And it wasn't just her own stupidity that stared back at her. She realized this morning that she was willing to marry Lyle simply so she wouldn't have to be alone anymore. She'd thought it was his money she wanted—the financial security. But apparently it wasn't—since she'd been so instantly willing to give that up for some sailor who'd said words she'd wanted to hear.

He'd said words she was starving to hear.

God, Izzy must think she was an idiot.

And yet, she'd managed to walk right out of that cabin, right out from under his enormously unattractive nose. He was probably being taken to task for it right this very moment.

Which was nice to consider, but not as nice as sitting in front of a fireplace with a mug of hot chocolate would've been.

It was unbelievably cold, and Tracy wrapped the jacket more tightly around her, covering her ears with her mittened hands. She had no idea which way to walk, since the road was deserted and there were no lights in either direction and . . .

Wait, what was that?

Tracy squinted and . . .

Yes, hello, those *were* headlights coming toward her. She most definitely was on the verge of being saved.

She'd get back to the motel, hours ahead of them all. They'd rush in, terrified that she was still out on the mountain, frozen to death, and she'd be all like, "Oh, you thought I was unskilled? Really? You must be so cold, would you like some of the chicken soup that I made from scratch while I was waiting . . . ?"

She jumped up and down, waving her arms, and sure enough, the car slowed to a stop. It was similar to the other cars she'd seen here in the wilderness of New Hampshire—ancient, but still seeming to run well. Not that she cared, as long as the heater worked.

The window went down to reveal a man, alone behind the wheel. "What are you doing out here," he said, in that weird twangy accent that marked some people as being from Maine. Not all of them, though. Her college roommate, Mindy, had been from Bangor, and she'd talked like a normal person. But her father sounded as if someone had tried to clone a Kennedy, and the experiment had gone terribly, horribly wrong. *Yuh cahn't get thah from he-yah* instead of *you can't get there from here.*

"I was out hiking," Tracy said now, which was not entirely untrue, "and I got separated from my friends. We're staying at the Motel-A-Rama in Darlington. Are you going anywhere even remotely near there?"

"There's a bus station that isn't too far out of my way," the man in the car told her. "Hop on in."

The sound of someone pounding on the door woke Sophia from a restless sleep.

"Sophia! Open up!" It was Dave.

The clock radio said it was barely ten. It felt more like 3:00 A.M.

She threw back the blankets, which knocked a pile of books onto the floor, and staggered to the door. It was about a million degrees in the room, and the heater was still cranking.

She opened the door. For the first time since she'd gotten soaked out at the hunting lodge she was grateful for the blast of frigid air.

Dave pushed past her. "Is Tracy here?"

"No," she said, fanning herself with the door as she turned to look at him as he strode purposefully into her bathroom. "Well, I don't think so. I was asleep."

"Shit," Dave said. "*Shit.*"

Apparently Tracy was AWOL again. "Have you tried the bar that's half-way between here and Happy Hills? I'm not sure exactly where it is, but Izzy probably knows." As she closed the door, she caught a glimpse of herself in the mirror. Her hair was doing its Bride of Frankenstein thing, and she tried to tame it, pulling it back and searching on the dresser for a scrunchee.

"Is it possible she came back while you were sleeping?" Dave asked. "Maybe she came in quietly and—"

"Not a chance," she said, because on the dresser were two room keys. Her own and Tracy's. She held them up for him to see.

"Terrific," he said, heading for the door.

Sophia stopped him, one hand still holding back her hair. "Wait," she said. "What's going on?"

"Tracy's missing," he told her. "She left the cabin, and Lindsey tracked her all the way to the road. But that was it. End of trail."

"Are you sure this isn't just another one of Tom's games?" she asked.

"Absolutely," he told her. "The SEALs got the call—they're already gone. And if the rest of us mobilized right now, we could catch a flight to California before the bad weather hits."

Sophia had spent some time this evening watching the Weather Channel. There was a huge storm heading directly for them. It was expected to hit the coast and stall. The airports were going to start to close, probably as early as tomorrow morning. If the Troubleshooters were delayed, they'd be snowed in. Possibly for days.

Being snowed in was one thing if they were training, another entirely if they were sitting in cheap motel rooms, twirling their thumbs.

Tom was not a thumb twirler—getting home to his wife and baby son would be a priority for him.

"Tracy probably got a ride," Sophia deduced. "Someone stopped and picked her up."

"I hope so." Dave didn't sound convinced. "Lindsey and Decker walked the road, looking for signs of her in either direction. Ninety minutes, and there wasn't a single car. We're afraid she went back into the woods, to try to return to the cabin." He gently pushed her aside and opened the door. "I've got to go talk to Stella and Rob, see if they've seen her. Maybe she came back here and didn't want to disturb you."

"Dave, wait—"

But he closed the door behind him.

Sophia quickly threw on clothes and her boots—which were finally dry. Her jacket was, too, but she couldn't find her hat, so she borrowed one of Tracy's and pocketed her key.

The night was bitterly cold. If Tracy were in the woods, if she'd gotten lost . . . Sophia hurried down to the restaurant, but Dave was already coming back out.

"This is a total nightmare," he told her. "I'm the one who told Tracy to leave the cabin. But I didn't have time to give her the complete instructions, tell her to look for Koehl's team . . ."

Dave had told her earlier that Tom had given him an additional role to play—that of undercover operative who'd infiltrated the terrorist cell.

"I was trying to be a hotshot," he admitted now. "Get the hostage to safety and single-handedly wipe out the terrorists. Instead, I put Tracy into danger. If she doesn't keep moving . . . In this cold . . . If she fell or hurt herself . . ." His eyes were anguished. "She'll freeze to death before dawn."

"I'll go with you," Sophia said. "We'll find that bar. I bet you anything she's there."

But before they reached Dave's vehicle, the rest of the team's SUVs and trucks pulled into the parking lot, stones crunching beneath their tires. Everyone was driving just a little too fast.

And Tom and Decker both hopped out before their vehicles came to a complete stop. Tess Bailey, Troubleshooters' computer specialist, was right behind them. "I've got my computer set up in my room," she told them. "Do you want me to bring it down to the restaurant?"

"Did you find her?" Sophia called.

"It'll take less time if we go up there," Tom said. "If you don't mind."

"Of course not," Tess said, running up the stairs to the second floor. "Just let me make sure Jimmy's dressed."

Decker answered Sophia. "Haven't found her yet," he said. "But we will very shortly."

"Of course," Dave said, slapping his forehead. "The sensors in the jackets. Tracy was wearing one, so . . ."

Sophia understood. The sensors that identified participants as dead or alive were part of a computer program. Apparently they could use that same program as something of a tracking device, to pinpoint Tracy.

Or at least her jacket.

"Thank God someone's thinking clearly." Dave was so excited, he actually started to dance. He grabbed her and swung her around.

As Sophia laughed at his exuberance, she kept her thoughts to herself. She didn't want to take away his hope, but she'd had lunch while Tess had organized the team that put up all those temporary satellite towers earlier today. Apparently, even with the additional towers, there were still large areas of what she'd called "dead zones."

"What are you doing out here?" Decker asked Sophia. "Dave, what the hell . . . ? Get her inside. Now." He followed Tom up the stairs.

Dave let her go, but still danced in a circle around her.

Up on the second level, Tess had unlocked the door to her room. "Great," she said, sounding as if it were anything but. "He's not even here. Okay, come on in—please ignore the dirty laundry."

Down in the parking lot, Alyssa Locke had opened up the back of the van, revealing piles of their training equipment.

"I need help getting this unloaded," Alyssa called, motioning them over. She put a pile of jackets similar to the one Tracy was wearing into Sophia's arms. "This should go into the storage room, off the kitchen. We'll organize it and pack it up later." She gave another armload to Dave, whose relief was still making him grin.

"Some people say *I love you*," he whispered to Sophia as they headed inside. "Others say *Dave, what the hell . . . ?*"

Sophia rolled her eyes. "Please don't start."

"I'm just saying," Dave said, holding the door for her. "Just making note of what sure felt to me like, oh . . . I don't know . . . jealousy? Maybe we should dance together more often."

"Oh, was that what that was?" she asked him. "Dancing?"

Dave laughed. "That's so mean. I'm a good dancer. All those exotic embassy parties. All those exotic ambassadors' wives? Decker should be worried. You might want to mention to him, just in passing, that I actually know how to tango. Or maybe if you start sighing"—he demonstrated—"every time you say my name."

"How much coffee have you had tonight?" She led the way into the kitchen.

"Too much," he admitted, as she turned on the light in the storage room. He waited while she put her load of jackets onto the floor, then added his to the top. "I'm just really glad we're going to find her. Tracy."

What if we don't?

But Sophia couldn't bring herself to ask him that as they headed up to Tess's room, to watch the miracle of the computer tracking system at work.

"Thank you *so* much," Tracy said as the car pulled into the store parking lot.

"Now, it's the nine-thirty bus to Concord that you want," the man reminded her. "Not Lewiston or Burlington."

"Got it," she said. There was a pay phone on the wall out front, thank goodness. The trip back to civilization—if this run-down, dimly lit, squat little store in the middle of nowhere could qualify as such—had taken far longer than she'd expected.

Of course, with Crazy God-Man behind the wheel, it was a wonder they'd ever gotten here at all. He'd delivered bags of food to what he called "neighbors in need," ringing their doorbells and running away—giggling like some prank-playing teenager—before they saw him or his car. They'd made twenty different stops since he'd picked her up. That wasn't what made their trip so relentlessly endless, though. No, it was the praying over each bag that took the most time.

Tracy's suggestion that they simply say one big prayer over all the bags at once had not been well received.

Now he frowned at the store, which, according to the signage, was also a FedEx pickup point, a Dunkin' Donuts, a convenience store, and a twenty-four-hour pharmacy. "Place looks like it's closing. I wonder if Stephen's having septic system troubles again. Last time he was shut down tight for days."

There was another car in the lot, and she could see at least one person inside through the window.

"I'm sure it's open. These places are always open," Tracy said. It was time to go—before he decided to pray for her. She tried to open the door, but it was locked. "Is there . . . ?"

He hit a button, and it still wouldn't unlatch. "Oopsie. I always push it the wrong way." He giggled.

Mere fractions of a second before full panic hit, there was a click and Tracy was able to open the door. Trying not to appear too freaked, she jumped out. "Thanks again."

With a wave and a honk, he went on his merry way.

Tracy turned, heading for the phone, and nearly ran right into the man she'd seen through the store window. "Oh, my God," she said.

Up close like that, her first thought was that he was Izzy—that he'd somehow followed her here. But he wasn't. He may have been tall and lean and good-looking, but his eyes were electric blue.

Any disappointment she was feeling was only because she hated the idea of having to take a bus. If she never saw Izzy Zanella again, it would be fine with her.

"Are you a nurse?" the un-Izzy asked. On him, the R-less Maine accent was kind of cute. He was carrying two big plastic shopping bags in each hand.

"What? Oh." She looked down at her pants and shoes. "Yeah," she said, because there was something in his eyes that was a little off. Like he'd come to the—what had Stella called it?—the *criminal* because he had the munchies from being stoned. It would have taken too many brain cells for him to understand the concept of her pretending to be a nurse for a Navy SEAL training operation.

Out here, in the natural habitat of Crazy God-Man and Hot Guy on Dope, the concept was a little difficult even for *her* to comprehend.

Tracy inched away, a little afraid to turn her back on him. But he finally nodded and headed for his car.

She picked up the pay phone and punched in the numbers of Lyle's calling card—a number he'd made her memorize after 9/11, when their cell phones hadn't worked due to an overloaded system.

"Now enter the number of the party you are calling," a voice instructed her. Okay, this was the tricky part. She wanted to call Lindsey, but she wasn't sure she remembered her phone number. She was good with memorization, though, and she'd seen it on the list of Troubleshooters personnel that was taped to her desk in San Diego. She'd stared at it for hours as she'd answered the phones. Area code 619. Just do it. If it was wrong, she'd try again. Big whoop.

Across the parking lot, the hot druggie had gotten into his car. He started it, and was just sitting there, watching her, which was a little weird.

The phone rang only twice, and a machine picked up. "Hi, you've reached Lindsey, I can't come to the phone right now. If this is an emergency, try my cell phone—"

Tracy scrambled for something to write with. She'd remembered Lindsey's number all right—but that of her home phone, not her cell. There was actually a pen in the pocket of her jacket, so she uncapped it and quickly scribbled the number on a flyer for a lost dog that was taped to the side of the phone's so-called wind barrier. She'd only been out here for a few minutes, but God, her ears were already frozen. And she seemed to have lost one of her mittens.

"... or leave a message at the beep." Lindsey's recorded voice finished.

"Yeah, hi, it's me, Tracy." She didn't want to hang up, not with stoned-man still watching her like that. Better to let him think she was talking to someone. Like her police-trooper, former-Marine boyfriend, whose jacket she was obviously wearing. "I'm calling from some pay phone on the freaking North Pole. I just got your cell number, so I'll call you right back in a sec. See, there's this guy who's kind of hot, but kind of not—think if Ralph Fiennes sniffed glue—and he's ... Shoot, he's getting out of his car. I feel like I should give you the license plate number, in case I drop off the face of the earth. Except it's dark and ... I think there's a nine ... That's all I can see. There's mud or pig poop on it, or whatever animal they farm up here. It's got New Hampshire plates. Except, okay. He's just refilling his windshield wiper fluid. Silly me. I'll call you back on your cell."

She hung up, which was stupid, because she could have just pushed one of the numbers—was it the eight?—and dialed Lindsey's cell. Now, though, she had to go through the whole long calling card thing again.

Drug guy closed his hood. The sound made her look over at him, which was a mistake, because he took that as an invitation to communicate.

"I need you to hang up now," he said, as he strolled toward her.

Okay, it was probably time to get inside the store, but she only had a few more numbers to dial. "I'm sorry, I didn't realize you needed to use the phone." Tracy forced a smile. "I'll be quick. I just need to finish telling my boyfriend about my latest outbreak of herpes."

He reached over and pushed the hang-up button, taking the phone out of her hands and replacing it in the cradle. "Get into the car."

"I don't need a ride. Thanks, though." There was something seriously wrong with this guy, and she was really frightened now, but she knew she shouldn't show it. "I *do* need some coffee. Excuse me."

He shifted, blocking her. "I don't care what you need. Get in the car."

Dear God, he actually had a gun.

Tracy looked up from the barrel, into his eyes. And she knew with a certainty that was terrifying that if she got into this man's car, it would be the last thing she ever did.

It wasn't bravery that made her run for it, despite the instant death that could come pouring out of that tiny little hole. Running was the only option. She bolted for the entrance to the store, and sure enough, he didn't shoot her.

He did, however, give chase.

She flung open the door. "Call 911, call 911!"

But there was no one behind the counter. She ran for the back, searching for someone, anyone.

And found the store clerk in front of the door to the bathroom. Lying facedown in a pool of blood, eyes open and staring, the back of his head caved in.

There was nothing to grab and swing, nothing to use to fight back, and she tried to open the ladies' room door, tried to lock herself in, when the stoner hit her, hard.

Pain mixed with disbelief. This couldn't be real. Things like this didn't actually happen. Not to her. Please God, no.

But her chin smashed into the floor, and the overhead light seemed to short and spark. He hit her again, and the world disappeared.

CHAPTER
SIXTEEN

"So . . . provided we can get this program to work," Lindsey said, "we'll just . . . what? See a little blip on a map, and that'll be where Tracy is?"

"That's correct," Tess said, her fingers flying across her computer keyboard. She had hands like a concert pianist or a surgeon—with long, elegant fingers. At least compared to Lindsey's.

Please God, let this work . . .

"Did we find her?" Dave asked, as he and Sophia joined the crowd in the tiny motel room.

"Not yet," Decker said. He was the only one besides Lindsey who glanced up from the computer. Everyone else—including Tess's fiancé, Jim Nash, who'd sheepishly turned up smelling almost as much like a distillery as Tracy had last night—was glued to the screen.

Scanning for signal, was flashing there. Followed by the message, *downloading map of sector 817.*

Slowly a map appeared, starting at the top of the computer screen, and filling in down through the bottom. It included most of New Hampshire.

They all leaned closer.

"Come on, Tracy," Dave murmured. "Be in Manchester, at some four-star hotel."

"Have we called her ex?" Decker asked. "Lyle—is it Anderson?"

"Andrews," Lindsey said. "And yes. We did."

"He hasn't heard from her, doesn't seem particularly worried," Tom told them.

The map was just about completely downloaded.

"I don't see any blip," Lindsey said. "Isn't there supposed to be a blip?"

"Yes, there is," Tom said. But there wasn't.

"Is something wrong with the computer?" Dave asked. His voice was tight and as Lindsey glanced up, Sophia put her hand on his shoulder.

"The program seems to be working," Tess reported. Again, her hands flew, and info flashed across the screen at lightning speeds. "Yeah, the codes are all correct. I'm sorry." She turned and looked up at Tom. "There's no signal from the jacket."

Lindsey swore. "I *so* wanted this to work." Disappointment made her stomach hurt.

Dave, too, looked as if he might hurl.

"Is it possible she's left the sector?" Tom asked.

Again Tess's fingers made the keys clack. This time, instead of a map, what looked like programmer's code filled the screen. "There's no signal from anywhere in the hemisphere. Is she in China? I could access other satellites to look. But we'd risk catching the attention of someone at the Pentagon. If they're alert, they might also notice that Team Sixteen is supposed to be in transit to Germany, and cut us off. See, we're kind of borrowing their access codes."

"Oh, good," Tom said. "I love hearing things like that."

"What would keep the satellite from picking up the signal from the jacket?" Lindsey asked. "Something like putting it in a lead box, or . . . what?"

"It's far more likely that Tracy's in a dead zone." Tess not only looked like a sweet, cheerful second grade teacher, but she had a tendency to try to educate. She couldn't help herself. "You know how it's impossible to talk on your cell on the stretch of road near the Krispy Kreme, if you're heading east past the Troubleshooters office in San Diego? It's some kind of weird no-signal area, probably due to cell towers that aren't spaced closely enough together. This sensor system that we're using for training relies on cell towers, just like your phone. The signal goes from the jacket to a nearby tower to the satellite, then back to the tower nearest to this computer, then to the computer. If the jacket's in a dead zone, we're not going to see it here."

"So what we have to do," Lindsey said, "is map the dead zones and focus our search to those areas."

"Or put up more cell towers," Tess said.

"Or move the towers we have," Dave suggested.

Tess nodded. "That's if we can assume Tracy's stationary—that she's not going to be on the move. If we move the towers, and she moves . . ." She shrugged.

Tom stood. "I'll make some calls."

"Is there a way to access the history of the jacket's movement?" Lindsey asked, desperate for some good news. Dave looked like he could use some, too. He was rubbing his forehead as if he had a killer headache. "I mean, Tracy put the jacket on, hours ago, starting here at the motel. Is there a record that will allow us to track her past movements out to the cabin—and beyond? Even if we can't see where Tracy is right now, can't we at least see where she *was*, at least until she entered whatever dead zone she's currently in?"

"Good thinking." Dave perked up. "That'll help us narrow our search efforts."

Tess took a deep breath, blew it out hard. "The short answer is yes. The long answer is . . . I don't know how long it'll take me to find that information. Since I'm going to have to hack into the system . . ."

"Just do the best you can," Decker told her. "We don't have much else to go on."

She glanced at him. "Yeah. In the meantime, I'll keep the program running. Maybe we'll get lucky, and she'll move back out of whatever dead zone she's in."

"What are the odds of Tracy still having the jacket on? It's not exactly high fashion," Dave pointed out, his brief burst of hope obviously already deflated. "That's assuming she's not lying somewhere, in some dead zone, literally dead."

"Thanks, Dave. We can always count on your unflagging optimism." Lindsey put her hat and gloves back on. "I'm heading back to the cabin," she announced. Maybe there was something there that they'd all missed. "Please call me as soon as anyone knows anything."

This was ridiculous.

Jenk paced the worn carpeting of the airport's terminal as he waited for the senior chief to finish speaking with Commander Koehl.

The news had come down that the C-5 troop transport that was due to take them to Germany had, once again, been delayed.

Apparently, it was snowing rather hard in Illinois.

To add insult to injury, Team Sixteen's little transatlantic journey was only a drill. It was a test of their ability to be available, immediately, on the other side of the world. They were also, Jenk suspected, putting in an appearance as part of America's "big stick" on the international stage at Ramstein Air Base. Someone was sending a message to anyone who might be monitoring U.S. troop movement that SEAL Team Sixteen was in the house.

Now, if only the seriously disconnected top brass would use them for that which they'd been trained, instead of outsourcing the big jobs—like the capture of bin Laden—to people whose loyalty was for sale to the highest bidder.

And as long as Jenk was wishing for the impossible, he willed his phone to ring. He was desperate for Lindsey to call, telling him that Tracy had been found, safe and sound.

Tommy Paoletti had kept Commander Koehl updated throughout the night. The news that both Lindsey and Decker had tracked Tracy all the way to the road without finding her had landed like a punch to the gut.

Team Sixteen should have been out there, helping to beat the bushes, setting up search patterns from both the cabin and the point on the road where Lindsey had lost Tracy's trail.

The senior chief had told Jenk, over and over, that there was nothing they could do that Tommy wasn't already doing—except provide more manpower. More eyes to search. More boots on the ground.

Izzy had been sitting on the floor, leaning back against the wall, head in his hands. But now he stood up. "Where's the senior chief?"

"Finally talking to Koehl," Jenk told him.

"Oh, good," Izzy said. "That'll give me the opportunity to let Lew know what I think of commanders who care so much about their own career advancement that they'd turn their back on a missing woman."

"Jesus, Izzy . . ."

But Izzy was already moving, like a heat-seeking missile, on a path of mutually assured destruction, although in this case the mutual parties were Izzy and Jenk.

"Zanella, don't. I've already spoken to the senior—" Jenk caught the bigger man's arm, but the idiot shook him off.

It took a full body slam, sideways into the wall, to stop him, and even then, it was only a temporary delay.

It also ratcheted up the goatfuck potential by catching both Koehl's and the senior chief's attention.

"Get off me, Jenkins!" Izzy may have grabbed the front of Jenk's jacket to keep from being knocked off his feet, but he quickly shifted from defense to offense as he roughly yanked Jenk away from him.

Or rather, tried to.

Because Jenk had an equally good grasp on Izzy, and he didn't let go. Which resulted in Izzy losing his balance.

Jenk wrapped his legs around the bigger man as they both hit the floor, which was unfortunate but necessary. Necessary because he didn't want to hurt Izzy, and their differences in size and weight didn't leave him with many options. Unfortunate, because to the rest of the world, it no doubt looked as if they were having a very public private moment.

Apparently, Izzy wasn't feeling the need to not hurt Jenk as he tried to shake him off by crushing him between his own body and the wall.

"Senior's trying to clear the way for us both to head back to help Tommy," Jenk grunted into Izzy's ear. "I told him my shoulder was hurting, and you desperately needed to go to the dentist."

"What the *fuck* are you idiots doing?"

Jenk turned to find the senior's boots planted inches from his face.

"Ow," Izzy said, too little, too late. "My tooth. My God, what happened? Mark, is that you? How did I get here? I must be having tooth-decay-induced madness."

Way, way up there, the senior chief was shaking his head in disgust. "Sure looks to me like the shoulder's okay, Jenkins."

Great. "It's definitely not, senior chief." As Jenk untangled himself from Izzy, his wince was not an act. "Izzy was helping me test my ability to extend my—"

"Save your breath, you're good to go," he said, holding up a hand to stop Izzy. "Not you. There're dentists at Ramstein."

Those were not the words Izzy wanted to hear. "Jesus Christ," he said. "Senior, come on. When do I ever ask for anything?"

"Other than all the time?" The senior crossed his arms.

"God! You know damn well that if this son of a bitch were *half* the CO that Tommy was, we'd already be back there by now, helping look for Tracy!"

The senior chief glanced at Jenk, since it was pretty obvious that this was the reason he'd wrestled Izzy to the ground. He turned to give Izzy his dead-eye glare. "I'm going to pretend I didn't hear that. Why don't you go and try to be very invisible and very silent for a very long time."

"Sorry," Jenk told Izzy, as the senior chief walked away.

"Dude, you tried." Izzy forced a tight smile. "Find her, okay? And no, nothing happened the other night. Tracy's a nice girl. A stupid girl, but a nice one. I just don't want to see anything bad happen to her."

The more Izzy protested, the less Jenk believed him. Still, he let it go. "I'll call you."

"Do that. And throw Lindsey another bang while you're at it."

Jenk shook his head as he headed for the rental car counter. He felt his shoulders tightening as he walked away, certain that Izzy wasn't quite ready to be silent or invisible yet.

He was halfway there when Izzy shouted, "Jenkins! I wish I could quit yew!"

Of course. The obligatory *Brokeback Mountain* reference. Jenk flipped Zanella a double bird without bothering to look back.

Cold slapped Tracy's face and cut off her air, making her gag and cough. She woke up spitting, with her hair dripping down her face and into her eyes. She lifted her head, and the movement made it feel as if it were splitting in half. Oh God, she was hungover again.

But she wasn't in her own bed. She wasn't on her bathroom floor either.

This floor was carpeted in a patterned shade of green. Squinting against the light, she realized she was both wet and fully clothed.

Water hit her again, directly in the face, and she sputtered and choked, and turned to see . . .

"Help her." Whoever had doused her with those buckets of water was tall and male and . . .

It all came rushing back. The man she'd thought was stoned because his eyes were so flat and lifeless. The clerk in the puddle of blood. *Get into the car.*

Tracy started to cry. "Please don't hurt me."

"If you don't get off your ugly ass and help her, I'll kill you right now."

Ugly ass? Her ass wasn't ugly.

It was an amazingly stupid thing to be focusing on when he'd just threatened to kill her, but her burst of disbelieving indignation was far better than the mind-numbing fear. She could either lie there sobbing and be killed now, or push herself off her *ugly ass* and maybe live through this.

Tracy wiped her eyes. There'd be plenty of time to cry when she was dead.

"Help who?" As she sat up, she saw that the carpeting wasn't patterned. It was just blotchy with dirt and ancient stains. She also saw a bed. A woman lay upon it, cuffed by at least one wrist to the cast-iron frame.

The smell was horrific, the woman lying on her side because she'd tried—unsuccessfully—not to puke all over herself. She had a nasty-looking gash on her arm, like someone had taken a steak knife to it.

It was all Tracy could do not to add to the mess on the floor and bedcovers. With her head pounding and stomach churning, she was at a serious disadvantage, made worse by the fact that when she touched her hair, her fingers came away streaked with blood. Still, she'd had experience dealing with the pain and nausea of hangovers. She'd coped with cleaning up messes like this one with a throbbing head plenty of times before. Although it was probably easier when the vomit was her own.

"Which of these will help her?" her own personal Ted Bundy asked, dumping two big bags of drugs on the floor. Some were in pharmacy-sized containers, others were in little bags, with information about the prescription and dosage stapled to them.

How should I know, I'm not a doctor was on the tip of her tongue, but she stopped herself from speaking just in time.

Are you a nurse?

Tracy had told him yes. She was here, living this nightmare because she'd told him yes, she was a nurse. Of course if she'd said no, he probably would've killed her right then and there.

As long as he thought she was a nurse, and that she could save his . . . girlfriend or whoever the freak-show was that he'd chained to his bed, she would stay alive.

"Which of these will help her?" he repeated much more loudly.

"I'll need to examine her first," Tracy said, trying to sound as nurse-ish as possible. Stern. Disapproving. Just like the nurse in the ER had been that time she'd gotten drunk out on the beach and cut her foot on a broken bottle. They'd given her something after stitching her up, something to prevent infection. An antibiotic. But what had it been called? Zithro-something. No, that's what she'd had for that sinus infection last year.

"I'll need clean sheets, clean towels, clean clothes for her to wear," she told him, taking off her sodden jackets, and rolling up her sleeves. "Clean, warm water. Lots of it."

Was that blood encrusted on the buttons on the ill woman's shirt? She was gaunt, clearly starving, the bones on her face standing out in sharp relief. Tracy forced herself to touch her. A nurse would not be squeamish.

Her skin was hot—she was burning up. "Something for her to drink, too," Tracy added, since he hadn't killed her yet for being overly strident. "She's clearly dehydrated. Ginger ale." She turned toward him, as impatiently as she could manage, considering he had a gun and wasn't afraid to use it. "What are you waiting for? If you want me to help her, you've got to help me."

For a moment, he just stood there, looking at her, and she was instantly terrified that she'd pushed too hard, that he was going to decide she was too demanding and shoot her right where she stood.

But then he turned and left the room.

He didn't go far—just down the hall to a bathroom. He left the door open, so sneaking past in search of the front door was not an option. Tracy did make it around the bed, though, and over to that window. Please dear God, let her peek out from behind that grimy shade to find other houses nearby—somewhere to run to for help.

But all she could see was darkness.

Over on the bed, the woman groaned, waking up, and Tracy went toward her. There were so many questions to ask, she wasn't sure where to start. "Where are we—"

The woman's uncuffed hand grabbed the front of Tracy's shirt, pulling her close with surprising strength for someone so thin and so ill.

"Finish me," the woman whispered through lips that were cracked and dry. "Kill me. Please. Don't let him take me upstairs while I'm still alive!"

Dear God . . .

"Promise me," the woman begged. Her eyes were an almost golden shade of brown. Once upon a time, she'd been truly beautiful.

"Who are you?" Tracy asked. "Why are you handcuffed? And who is this guy who—"

But her eyes closed, her head lolled back, and her grip on Tracy's shirt went limp.

"Her name is Five."

Tracy turned to see that her kidnapper had come back into the room, carrying a pile of dingy-looking towels.

"Your name is Twenty-One," he continued. "And me? I'm your lord and master. If I catch you talking to her again, I'll kill you. Slowly. I'll start by slicing off your eyelids—"

"I get it," Tracy said. Dear God, dear God . . . "No talking, just saving her life. I still need water to do it. And something for her to drink."

He left the room again, and she started shaking—so hard that she had to sit down.

Jenk had just backed out of the parking spot in the rental lot when someone banged on the roof of the car.

Izzy's face appeared out of the darkness. He tried the passenger-side door, but it was locked. "Open up, Eminem. Let me in."

Jenk popped the lock. "Zanella, what the fuck?"

"Oh, sweet," Izzy said with a heavy layer of indignation as he swung his bag into the back seat and climbed in. "You think I'm going UA. Thanks for the vote of confidence, bro."

"So what are you saying," Jenk said. "That you cleared this with the senior chief, that you have it in writing?"

"Think of this as a variation of don't ask, don't tell. Don't ask, don't know, don't get into trouble," Izzy said. "Do, however, drive."

"Iz. Think about what you're doing."

"You think I fucking haven't?" Zanella finally stopped trying to bullshit him. "I can't just sit here anymore, doing nothing." He met Jenk's gaze with a mix of anger and misery. "And yeah, I've been lying to you about me and Tracy hooking up. Mostly because she made me swear not to tell anyone. But partly because I know you've liked her since forever, and it makes me feel like double the dickhead."

Jenk put the car into gear a tad too forcefully and drove. "This happened . . . last night?" he asked. Had it really only been last night that Tracy had come back to the motel, drunk? It felt more like last year.

"Yes," Izzy admitted. "Barely twenty-four hours ago. It was stupid, and if I could do it again . . . Well, shoot me, I'm human, I'd definitely do it again, but . . . I'd do it differently."

"You are such an asshole."

"I don't mean, like, in a different position, like the *Cosmo Girl's Guide to Sex*, page twelve. I mean, I'd do it so that she wouldn't end up mad at me afterward." Izzy sighed, leaning back against the headrest. "I'm responsible for her leaving. You know, boogying out of the cabin like that? She didn't want to talk to me."

"Like I said. You are such an asshole."

"She came to me, all like, *I'm going to marry Lyle, but I want him to pay*. What was I supposed to say, no?"

"I did," Jenk pointed out.

"Yeah, well, I'm neither Jesus nor in love with Lindsey," Izzy said.

And that was a statement that was meant to distract. Izzy expected Jenk to deny it. *I'm not in love with Lindsey.*

An argument would ensue. *I've seen the way you look at her, bro. Even now, after she dumped you.*

Seriously, we're just friends.

Yeah, that's what she wants, right? Dude, she can't make you not feel it if it's there. And I think it's there. I mean, I just told you I've done the deed with Tracy, and you didn't even flinch. I think we both know that if I'd given you the same newsflash about me and Lindsey, my broken and bloody body would already be stashed in the trunk.

Izzy would be right about that. About all of it. Jenk drove in silence for a long time. "Are you . . . you know. With Tracy? In love?" he finally asked.

Izzy laughed. "Uh, no."

Jenk glanced at him. "Are you lying?"

"No, man, seriously," Izzy told him. "Would I do her again? Oh, yeah. But . . . I'm not even sure I like her. I mean, I thought I did, and then she went all weird on me. I mean, come on. It was a revenge fuck. She was very clear about that. And yeah, the sex was unbelievable, but then she's suddenly discussing future plans? That's crazy."

Was it? It sounded a little too familiar. "Maybe it's not," Jenk suggested. "Maybe she really fell for you." Izzy started to make protesting noises, but he spoke over him. "It's not completely impossible. Maybe she just didn't know how else to tell you that she wants to get to know you better."

"Me?" Izzy asked. "Or the tragic hero I was pretending to be? See, we were doing this role-playing thing and—"

Jenk stopped him. "I really don't want to know."

"Most of the time Tracy looks at me like I'm from another planet," Izzy said. "She doesn't get my jokes and . . . Dude, this isn't anything like you and Lindsey. I know you're thinking that it is, but it's not. You guys click out of bed, too. I'm not asking for details, but I've got to assume that when you get it on it's—"

"I'm not having this conversation," Jenk said.

"I'm not either," Izzy said, "but I can imagine—"

"Don't."

"What I'm trying to say is, if you really want Lindsey, go and get her. Stick around long enough, sooner or later she'll cave. She likes you, M. She does. And I know you're totally in love with her, so stop pretending you're not. But me and Tracy?" Izzy laughed. "She doesn't like *me*, she likes—"

"I get it," Jenk said.

"Plus, she made it very clear she was going back to Lyle. I'd be stupid to believe her, or want to start something with her that wasn't . . . I mean, Christ, I don't exactly earn six hundred dollars an hour, do I? Besides, there's something seriously wrong with a girl who'll marry a guy who treats her like shit."

"So you're risking your career for someone you allegedly don't even like."

Izzy nodded. "Yeah, pretty fucked, huh? But if something happens to her while I'm sitting around on my ass . . . I'd rather spend the rest of my life living with the consequences of an unauthorized absence. Shit, I'd rather be arrested than spend the rest of my life thinking, *maybe I could've been the one who found her before she froze to death.*"

He turned away, looking out into the darkness of the night. His concern for Tracy was palpable. Jenk could practically smell it on him. And yet he didn't even like her? Didn't *want* to like her was more like it.

They drove in silence for quite a few miles before Izzy spoke again.

"Can I just say that she was unbelievably hot? Like, smoking."

Typical Izzy—acting like an asshole to hide any hint of vulnerability.

"Not unless you want to walk from here," Jenk said.

"Can't say that I do," Izzy said with a sigh. "I can't say that I do."

What would Lindsey do?

Tracy fought the panic that kept creeping in and overwhelming her by imagining Lindsey caught in this terrible situation.

She'd approve of the whole pretending-to-be-a-nurse thing, that much was for certain.

Stall, she'd tell Tracy if she were here. *It's not like we won't notice that you're missing. You left that message on my answering machine—of course it was my home number. But hey, I'm a professional. Surely I call home on a regular basis to pick up messages. Right?*

Tracy had no idea.

But God, what she wouldn't give for Lindsey and the rest of the Troubleshooters Incorporated team to come crashing through that little window, weapons blazing. She'd even welcome Izzy Zanella with open arms.

She'd looked at the window again. It wasn't just painted shut, it was locked, with shiny new hardware that required a key. There also appeared to be some kind of security system. An alarm would go off if the window were opened.

If Mr. Slice-off-your-eyelids got pissed at Tracy talking to the bedwoman, imagine how less than thrilled he'd be at her setting off his alarm.

She'd gotten the woman—she refused to use his name for her, Five—

cleaned up. Aside from a seriously infected cut on her arm, Tracy found no other injuries. Bruises and scrapes, sure, but nothing life-threatening.

Of course her illness could have been a case of the good old flu, on top of that nasty wound. But something contagious, something that would take her kidnapper to the floor, was too much to hope for. Tracy's luck just wasn't that good. Still, that wasn't going to keep her from watching him for any little sign of weakness.

She'd also keep trying to get him to leave the house, so she could attempt an escape.

"She needs nourishment," she told him one of the times he came into the room. "The medication I'm going to try first needs to be taken with food. But it's not going to be easy for her to keep anything down, so it's got to be something simple. Chicken broth. If you don't have any, I can make some. If, you know, you have chicken."

He didn't say anything, and she couldn't stop herself from babbling.

"Of course, you'll have to let me use your kitchen."

That made him smile, for some reason. "You want to go into my kitchen?"

"No." The woman from the bed spoke, her voice weak, but the word still forceful.

Tracy nearly crapped her pants. Even Eyelid-man was startled. But then he laughed.

Still laughing, he left the room. He laughed his way down the hall and clattered in what was probably his kitchen.

"I'm Tracy," she quietly told the woman, her heart in her throat, because she was particularly attached to her eyelids. "How long have you been here, locked up like this?"

"I'm Beth," the woman whispered. "And I don't know." She shook her head sharply then, holding a finger to her lips and warning Tracy with eyes bright with fever.

Yes, Tracy heard his footsteps growing louder. He was coming back.

"Did you think I was kidding?" he asked. He threw three slices of white bread, of the Wonder variety, onto Beth's bed before turning to Tracy. He had a Ziploc bag, one of those larger, pink-colored ones, and he shook it, emptying it out onto the floor.

At first she thought it was pieces of dried fruit, dried apricots maybe, as a whole pile of them spilled out, but then she realized . . .

Some of the smaller ones had a fringe of . . . lashes?

Eyelashes.

Tracy lunged for the bucket she'd placed beside the bed in case Beth got sick again, but the sound of her own violent retching didn't drown out his voice.

"After a while, the lashes fall out," he said. "There's no way to prevent it, which is a shame."

Almighty God.

"Pick them up," he ordered her. "And don't speak to Number Five again."

DARLINGTON, NEW HAMPSHIRE
MONDAY, DECEMBER 12, 2005

As the very first streaks of dawn lit the winter sky, Lindsey stood outside the cabin where Tracy had last been seen, hoping . . . what? That she'd find some vital clue that they'd all previously missed?

Like maybe burn marks from the landing craft that the aliens had used when they'd abducted her?

But why not? In the past hours since Tracy had disappeared, Tom had sent teams to check the bus stations and local airports. They'd visited hospitals and even police station drunk tanks. But no one had seen their missing receptionist. She was gone without a trace.

Headlights swept across the black-and-gray skeletons of the bare trees. Lindsey went to see who else had come back here because they, too, were out of ideas.

"Hey."

It was Mark Jenkins—the last person she'd expected to see today. Izzy also climbed out of the car and into the glow from her flashlight.

"Is the entire team back?" she asked them.

"Just us," Jenk told her. "I called in some favors and came back as quickly as I could." He exchanged a glance with Izzy. "As we could."

Izzy pointed in the direction that Tracy had disappeared. "I'm gonna go and . . ." He vanished into the trees, no doubt to see for himself that she had, indeed, headed directly for the road.

His doing so left Lindsey alone with Jenk.

"I'm sorry I didn't call you." She tried, but she couldn't hold his gaze. "I was waiting until we found her and . . ." Unable to stand still, she went up onto the cabin's little porch. She was running on pure caffeine. "Tracy left a clear trail. I know it was dark, but . . . She didn't stop, she didn't turn around, she moved at a brisk, even pace. It couldn't have been easier to follow if she'd left a trail of bread crumbs."

Unless Lindsey, in her arrogance, had missed something.

Jenk followed her into the cabin.

The fire that had been burning merrily mere hours ago had been doused when Tom pulled the remaining search teams from these woods. This area was in one of the computer system's hot zones. It was twenty miles—at least—to the nearest dead zone. Unless Tracy had suddenly started running fourteen-minute miles—for five hours straight—it seemed likely that she had gotten a ride from someone.

Comspesh Tess Bailey was working, among other things, on establishing a clear map of those areas where cell signals were nonexistent or even patchy—assuming the reason they weren't picking up the signal from Tracy's jacket was because she was in one of those zones.

But right here and now, Jenk's attention was drawn to the fireplace.

Lindsey had set kindling there. She'd built a ready-to-burn fire, complete with wads of paper to make it easier for an inexperienced person to light. She'd tried to make it idiot-proof, putting a box of matches on top of a nearby pile of blankets. A cell phone—one of those disposable ones—was next to the matches.

"In case she finds her way back here," she told Jenk. "I wanted to make it as easy as possible for her to get warm, get a fire started."

He turned to face her. "You think she's still out there, somewhere in the woods."

He'd left out the most important words—*lying dead, frozen to death.*

"What if the jacket's malfunctioning?" Lindsey asked. "The technology's not infallible. Yet everyone's acting as if it is. Besides, if someone gave her a ride, then where is she? Why didn't she come back to the motel?"

"I'm assuming Lyle was called," he said.

Lindsey nodded. "He claims he hasn't heard from her. But Tom's got a friend in the Manhattan DA's office who's verified that Lyle's in the middle of some relatively high-profile criminal case. If there's been foul play—"

Just saying those words made her sick. Not because she believed someone had intentionally killed Tracy. No, if Tracy were dead—and as each hour ticked past it was looking more and more likely that she was—then she'd died from exposure. From being lost in the woods. From falling and hurting herself and being unable to keep moving. The temperature was still well below freezing. A person lying unconscious and unprotected would have frozen to death in mere hours. As a SEAL, Jenk had surely had cold-weather training. He had to know that.

She forced herself to look at him, to hold his gaze despite the tears that were welling in her eyes. "I'm so sorry. I was sure I'd be able to find her."

"Lindsey, this isn't your fault."

"But maybe if Team Sixteen hadn't left . . ." Her voice broke, and she felt all the emotion of the past few grueling days hit her square in the chest. "Maybe we could have found her right away."

"Hey," he said, reaching for her as—damnit—she actually started to cry. "Hey, come on." This time she didn't sidestep him or pull away. She couldn't. She didn't want to. She just went into his arms, just closed her eyes and leaned into him, her head tucked beneath his chin.

"The team didn't leave because of anything you said or didn't say," Jenk told her, his voice as warm and solid as his body. "You know that. We get called, we go. That's how it works in SpecOps. We don't put in a call to SOCOM and say *Sorry, it's inconvenient. Try us next week.* The only reason I'm here right now is because it was all just another drill. If it were the real deal, I'd be on that plane."

He paused, and she knew she should take a deep breath and pull away from him. Force a smile and acknowledge his words—it wasn't her fault—as being true. Instead, she'd turned into a little crying girl. But now that she'd started, she couldn't seem to stop.

And it wasn't just Tracy being lost. It was everything.

Her father's phone call. And not just that one where he'd canceled their holiday plans, but all of them. He was so distant, so remote—and even more so since her mother had died.

Her mother's death. The relief Lindsey had felt that her mother's pain had finally ended, mixing unpalatably with the looming sense of total loss. Her mother was *gone.*

It was Jenk being so kind and inviting her home for Christmas when she wouldn't have blamed him for never speaking to her again. Jenk, naked amidst the rumpled sheets of his bed, smiling at her, his eyes sparking with amusement and attraction and . . .

Satisfaction. He'd found what he was looking for—or so he'd thought.

Of course, she'd had to go and prove him wrong.

"Dan Gillman's sister lived in New Orleans," he told her now, clearly just talking to fill the space so that they didn't have to stand there awkwardly—more awkwardly—listening only to the sounds of her ragged breathing. "His dad died a few years ago, and his mom moved down to live with his sister and her family. When Katrina hit, we were in Iraq. News started coming in that New Orleans had flooded, that people were literally dying of thirst, their homes destroyed, that nobody was helping them—the whole FEMA goatfuck, remember that?"

He didn't bother to pause, as if he knew that even a nod was too much for her right now. He just kept going. "Dan was frantic. He had no idea if his family was even alive, if they'd gotten out of their house in time, if they were trapped in their attic, if they were dying right that moment, while he was an entire world away. There was no word for two whole weeks, but we were fighting insurgents. It's what we do. He couldn't just pack up and leave.

"Turns out they all survived," he continued, "but it was a nightmare for a while. They made it to the Superdome, which was twice as terrifying after the storm ended. The kids finally got put on a bus to Houston, but by the time Sandy and her husband and mom got out, *they* ended up in San Antonio. Then they spent all their energy finding the kids. Getting to a computer to e-mail Danny just didn't happen." He paused. "Maybe something's going on with Tracy that's taking all of her attention. Or maybe she walked until she reached a house, knocked on their door . . . Maybe she's sleeping on someone's couch, and she'll call when she wakes up. Or maybe she's somewhere safe and warm, but she's waiting to call because she's pissed at . . . us."

"She wouldn't not call on purpose," Lindsey told him. "If she hasn't called, it's because she can't." He let her turn away, so she could wipe her eyes, her face, blow her nose.

"I wouldn't have expected her to go out and get ripped the other night, either," Jenk pointed out. "I respect your opinion. You know I do. But I just don't think any of us knows her well enough to rule out the possibility that she's purposely hiding. I think we're going to find her—well, really I think she'll just turn up, call in for a ride, whatever. I also think she's going to be really disappointed that Lyle isn't up here, helping with the search, wringing his hands." He smiled ruefully. "Actually, hand-wringing probably wouldn't cut it. Tracy'll be disappointed with anything less than hair tearing and rending of clothes."

Lindsey had once believed that Jenk didn't really know Tracy, that he couldn't see the true person behind her *Girls Gone Wild* body type, pretty face, and perfect hair. Apparently, he'd been taking a closer look.

He'd also come to this cabin not only because this was where Tracy had last been seen, but because he knew Lindsey would be here. He'd come because he knew how upset she was. He'd come to offer support and comfort. And a solid shoulder to cry on.

"I *was* jealous," Lindsey admitted, as much to herself as to him. "Of

Tracy. When she called that night, and you just . . . were ready to leave, like I didn't matter . . ."

"Ah, Linds, I'm so sorry." He stepped toward her, but she stepped away.

"It scared me," she said. "That I should care so much. And then you scared me even more by doing a complete one-eighty, by suddenly being so into me when, God, you don't even know me and . . . But I can't stop thinking about you. About us, about the sex," she admitted.

"The sex was great," he agreed. "It's kind of hard not to think about."

"But I don't want to hurt you more than I already have," she told him. And she really didn't want to put herself in a position where he would end up hurting her. Except wasn't that exactly what they'd been doing, pretty much continuously since that night? Hurting each other?

Jenk was looking at her with what she thought of as his Navy SEAL face—an unwavering gaze, steady determination in the set of his jaw. "Maybe I should be the one to decide when and if I'm being hurt."

Her cell phone rang, saving her from having to respond to the quiet reasonableness of his words. Lindsey took off her glove with her teeth so she could dig in her pocket. "It's Sophia," she told Jenk as she pulled it free.

"Maybe it's good news," he said, as she opened it.

"Fontaine." At this point, any news would be good.

"Are you still up at the cabin?" Sophia asked. "Are Jenk and Izzy with you?"

"Yes and yes," Lindsey told her. "What's going on?"

She could hear Sophia relaying the information, probably to Tom. "They're there," she said. Her voice got louder as she spoke directly into the phone. "We've got a blip. It just entered your area. According to the computer, Tracy's moving southwest, about eight miles east of you."

CHAPTER
SEVENTEEN

B eth woke up slowly, gradually, with the awful realization that the house was still silent.

She lay in the bed, just listening—automatically testing each of the restraints that held her prisoner there.

They were all still secure. All and then some. He'd cuffed her other ankle, now, too.

"Hello?" Beth called, her voice as weak as her body. Still, the sound had to carry. If he were here, he'd hear her.

Nothing moved. Floorboards didn't creak. No one so much as breathed.

She knew the sensation of being alone in this house quite well. Of course, she was used to being down in the basement.

"Tracy?" she called, but of course, there was no answer.

Tracy, who'd dared to stand up to him, was gone.

She'd given Beth an antibiotic to fight the infected cut on her arm. She'd washed and bandaged it, too—using some of the ointment he'd brought back from the pharmacy.

Her makeup had been streaked from crying and her face pale, but as she'd sat bandaging Beth's arm, she'd dared defy him.

Can you read my lips? she silently asked Beth, as she kept giving him reasons to leave the room. The water he'd brought was too cold. She needed a needle and thread to stitch up the wound. Both had to be sterilized. Ice to numb the raw edges of Beth's skin. No, never mind, now that she'd cleaned it up, she could see it would be better to leave it open to allow it to drain.

That sounded like bull to Beth, who'd taken first aid in the army, but he didn't question her.

Squeeze my hand once for yes, twice for no, Tracy told her silently. *Did he kidnap you, too?*

Beth squeezed once.

If we scream, will anyone hear us?

She squeezed twice. With the amount of screaming that she alone had done in this house, it was clear there was no one around to hear and come to the rescue.

Were those really eyelids?

Beth squeezed once, and Tracy's eyes filled with tears.

Is he going to kill me?

Two squeezes, as Beth felt herself start to cry, too. *I am,* she told Tracy silently. But she could tell Tracy didn't understand. *He'll make me do it. He'll make us fight until one of us is dead.*

And then Tracy did understand, horror on her pretty face.

He came back then, his footsteps heavy in the hall.

But Tracy dared to say one more thing: *Two against one . . .*

She wiped her tears and faced him. "Beth's in agony. I'm going to give her something for the pain."

He hit Tracy, backhanding her across her face, sending her flying into the wall.

"Five," Beth said frantically. "I'm Five!"

"Five," Tracy sobbed. "I meant Five."

"Give her what she needs."

Tracy crawled to the piles of medicine bottles on the floor, searching through them. She found what she was looking for, opened the bottle, brought it to Beth.

Her lip had split—it was bloody and already swollen, and her face was wet with tears and snot. She handed Beth a plastic tumbler that held water, and put the pill into her mouth.

Except . . . there was no pill.

"Swallow," Tracy had told her, then turned back to him. "I've given her Percodan. It'll knock her out for quite a few hours. I suggest you help improve her circulation by unlocking her during that time."

It had been a valiant try.

"What did you give her for her arm?" he'd asked then.

Tracy had shook her head, chin high in defiance. "If I tell you, you won't need me. You're just going to have to keep me around to give her the next dose, in eight hours. Although I'll be surprised if she keeps it down, with only bread in her stomach. She needs soup."

It was then that he grabbed her. He just pulled her, kicking and screaming, out of the room.

"What are you doing?" Tracy had shrieked, over and over again. And then, "Oh, my God! Oh, my God!"

And then she'd just screamed. And screamed. And screamed.

Until she'd stopped.

Izzy heard the distant sound of a car horn and ran back toward the cabin.

Sure enough, it was Jenkins making all that noise. Lindsey was in the front with him, so Izzy scrambled into the back.

"The computer picked up the signal from Tracy's jacket." Jenk took off like a rocket, even before Izzy got the door shut.

"About freaking time." He slid into the middle of the backseat, pushing aside a bag of Lindsey's gear, so he could see both of them. "So why the double grim?"

Lindsey was on her phone, but Jenk glanced at him in the rearview mirror and Izzy knew the news wasn't going to be good. "Tommy also just got a call from the local police," Jenk said. "There's been a robbery/murder at a twenty-four-hour pharmacy about twenty miles north of here."

Oh, please, no. "Tracy?" Izzy managed to ask. The computer had picked up the signal from Tracy's jacket, they'd said. Not Tracy, her jacket.

Lindsey turned to look at him, her phone still to her ear. "We don't think so. We don't know much, though," she told him. "Apparently the store's owner—he's also the local pharmacist . . . He was bludgeoned to death, about nine o'clock last night."

Mere hours after Tracy had left the cabin.

"Yeah, Tess, I'm still here," Lindsey said into her phone. She was talking to Tess Bailey, Troubleshooters' computer expert. "We're moving though, and the signal's not too good. What's the road we're looking for?"

"The police think the crime's drug-related," Jenk reported. "The store's entire supply of prescription meds was stolen. If Tracy stumbled in there, in the middle of the robbery . . ."

"Wellington Mountain Road," Lindsey said. She was peering at a map. "It's a left? Okay, I found it on the map."

"But there's only one body?" Izzy asked.

"As far as we know," Lindsey said—words to offer little comfort. "Tom literally just got the call. He's sending a team to the crime scene. He himself is heading in our direction. He's aware that we're not armed."

"Fuck that," Izzy muttered. "I don't need a weapon to rip off some motherfucker's arm and use it to fucking bludgeon *him.*"

Jenk just shook his head, but Lindsey felt the need to issue words of warning. "We've been given a direct order to proceed with extreme caution."

She'd been given one. He and Jenk, however, didn't take orders from Tommy Paoletti. "Was there any sign of a struggle? I mean, other than the . . . bludgeoning." Jesus Christ.

"We don't know that either." Lindsey was apologetic. "Damnit, the cell signal's gone. Great—we're supposed to be in a hot zone."

Last but not least was the question of the hour. "Do you really think Tracy's with the killer?" Izzy asked.

"Tom seems to think so."

"What do *you* think?" Izzy persisted. Lindsey had clocked a lot of hours with the LAPD.

She glanced at Jenk before looking back at Izzy. "Honestly?"

"No, make something up for us. Yes, honestly. Christ."

"In the law enforcement realm," she said, "when a person goes missing—mysteriously—on the exact same night as a murder, in a rural area where most people don't lock their doors, yes, odds are the two are linked."

Izzy sat back. It was possible he was going to be sick.

"Oh, one thing we *do* know . . ." Lindsey looked at Jenk. "I don't think I told you this either. The killer took the time not just to lock the door behind him, but he also put up a sign saying that the septic system wasn't working again. Left up here, remember—it's a fork. Wellington Mountain Road, but there's probably not a street sign."

Lindsey turned on her flashlight so she could read the map she was holding. Even though it was dawn, the sky was overcast, with clouds that were heavy and dark. It was only a matter of time—hours—before the snow started.

"Got it," Jenk said, as he made the turn.

"We'll take this to the end, and then take a right." Lindsey turned off the torch. "The store was open twenty-four hours," she continued. "Apparently the owner was an insomniac. Kind of eccentric, but a longtime local—a favorite son."

"What's your take on this sign that was put on the door?" Jenk asked.

Lindsey didn't need any time to consider the question. "It's the *again* that's key. Perp knew there'd been a sewage problem in the past," she said. "Perp's a local boy."

"Boy?" he repeated. "Isn't that sexist?"

"Bludgeoning," Lindsey said, as her phone rang. "According to the LAPD homicide handbook, it's generally not something people do while singing 'I Feel Pretty.' Good timing," she said into the phone.

Jenk was slowing as the road ended in a T. "Right?"

"Right," Lindsey confirmed. "Tess, we're pulling onto the state road, and there's a car approaching us. What's Tracy's status?" She paused as she listened, but then immediately reported to the two SEALs, "Tess says Tracy's been mostly stationary for about five minutes now, about two kilometers due west. We'll need to take another right onto Quarry Road, about a kilometer from here."

The approaching car passed them—an older-model American car, possibly an Impala. Izzy turned, trying to see the plates, but it was moving too fast. "We're sure she's in front of us?"

"What is *mostly stationary?*" Lindsey asked into her phone. She frowned as she listened to Tess's response, then looked from Jenk to Izzy. "The computer is giving them some weird data."

Freaking perfect. "If she's not there," Izzy started. "If it turns out she was in that car . . ." But another zipped past—a pickup truck this time, followed closely by a beat-up Volvo. It was rush hour in Dogbutt, New Hampshire.

"A variation in altitude?" Lindsey was saying to Tess, skepticism heavy in her voice. She turned to Jenk. "Is it possible she's . . . skiing?"

They all looked more closely out the windows. The terrain was hilly enough for someone to set up a low-level beginner slope, sure, but everything Izzy could see was covered with a dense growth of trees.

"On what snow?" he asked.

"At dawn after being missing all night?" Jenk asked. "Is this my right?"

"Right here?" Lindsey asked Tess through the phone. "Yeah," she relayed back to Jenk. "She says we're close."

How did Tess know where they were? Izzy was about to ask, but then he realized that one of the training op jackets was among Lindsey's gear. Tess was picking up their signal, too, and monitoring their movement. Someone had put on their thinking cap this morning. Lindsey.

"How close?" Izzy asked instead.

"One point two three kilometers," Lindsey reported. "According to Tess, the strange movement has stopped. Tracy's now fully stationary. Let's hope she's inside of a house or some other shelter. Maybe she went into the basement."

Jenk, who was driving, had to slow down. The road was little more than broken rocks and frozen mud, similar to the seldom-used path they'd taken to the hunting lodge. If there was a house out here, it was owned by a hermit who'd gone off the grid.

The next few tenths of a kilometer took forever, but finally they moved into what should have been visual range. But there were no other cars, no one standing in the road, nothing but trees, trees, and more trees.

"Where is she?" Izzy asked. And what would she be doing, out here in the middle of the woods?

"Still a quarter kilometer west of us. Stop here," Lindsey ordered Jenk.

Izzy got out of the car. "Which way?"

"Wait for Jenkins," she told him.

But he didn't. He couldn't. West could only be one direction.

He started to run, and the sky lightened because the trees thinned and no, no, please God no.

A pond stretched in front of him, desolate and frozen.

Except for the hole someone had cut into the ice. The opening had already frozen over, but he cracked it easily with his heel. He took off his jacket, his sweater. His boots.

He felt Jenk's hand on his arm. "Zanella, don't. If she's in there . . ."

"We're on top of the signal," Lindsey reported, her face drawn.

"How many feet down is she?" Izzy asked, shaking off Jenk's hand to unfasten his belt. He took off his pants and put them on top of his boots.

"Izzy, God, she's been underwater for more than twenty minutes," Lindsey told him. "That's assuming she was still alive when she was dumped in there."

"Well, fuck that," Izzy said sharply. "I didn't ask you that. I asked how many fucking feet down is she."

"Watch your mouth," Jenk snapped back. "You're not the only one who's upset here, okay? So just back the fuck off."

"Guys," Lindsey said. "Please." She stepped between Izzy and the hole in the ice. "You're not seriously going to—"

"I'm getting her out of there," Izzy said.

Something in his eyes must've convinced her he wasn't going to be talked out of it, so she nodded. "There's rope in the car." She looked at Jenk. "Why don't you go get that? It's in the pack." He hesitated, and she added, "Izzy's not going in without the rope." She looked at him. "Right?"

Sometimes people who drowned in the winter were able to be resuscitated after longer-than-usual amounts of time, with little or no brain damage. It had something to do with the freezing temperature of the water. But twenty minutes . . . ?

Izzy nodded, and Jenk ran for the car.

"We're also figuring out how far down she is. Tess'll have that info for us, in just a sec," Lindsey told him, as Jenk sprinted back to them with the rope—a length of blue mountain-climbing cord. She listened to Tess on the other end of the phone, then added, "The best guess is that she's about thirty feet down."

"It's really that deep?" Izzy asked as he tied the end of the rope securely around his chest. Just beneath his arms. He should have been freezing, but he couldn't feel anything—just an absolute need to get Tracy out of that water.

"Deeper," Lindsey told him. "It's a flooded quarry. It's more than a hundred feet in places. We think that she's . . . snagged on something." It was clear that she didn't find that a particularly pretty thought, so she kept talking. "Tess has already notified Tom. He'll get the equipment we need to get her out, so. . . ."

Jenk double-checked his knots. "You don't have to do this, Iz."

"Yeah, I do," Izzy said. He took a deep breath and plunged into the icy water.

Sophia found Dave by the store's Dumpster, sitting on the frozen dirt, his back against the building's brick wall. "Are you all right?"

"Oh, yeah," he said. "I'm great. I'm super."

He'd seen dead bodies plenty of times before. Too many times. And he hadn't batted an eye at the store owner with his head caved in. So why did he find the sight of one of Tracy's unmistakable pink mittens so incredibly disturbing? It was on the floor in the ladies' room, along with mere smatters of what DNA tests would no doubt reveal to be her blood.

The sight had made him sick—because he was the one who'd told Tracy to leave the cabin.

His stomach clenched again, and he had to close his eyes to keep from embarrassing himself even further, this time in front of Sophia.

He'd set the wheels in motion. Clearly Tracy had gotten into a car with a person capable of brutal murder, and he, Dave Malkoff, was at least partly responsible.

Hence his early-morning version of the twist and shout.

He was a total and utter wimp.

"If it's any consolation," Sophia told him, her hands in her pockets, shoulders hunched against the cold, "Alyssa says Sam sometimes has a similar . . . how did she put it? Intense physical reaction. So you're in good company."

Yeah. Right. A big, tough-guy former SEAL—especially one with a very sexy wife—could get away with puking his guts up every time he encountered violent death. *He* never would be thought of as a wimp. His weakness would be endearing. People would smile fondly as they thought about his sensitive—yet masculine—nature.

They would snicker, though, when they heard about Dave.

"This, by the way, is what happens when I'm a team leader," he told Sophia as he pushed himself to his feet. It was freezing out here, and he knew she wouldn't go back inside until he did, too.

"You weren't team leader," she pointed out. "Decker was."

"Yeah, well, I killed Decker. Intentionally. So that made me team leader."

She caught his arm, her face serious beneath her ridiculous fuzzy hat. "You're determined to hold yourself responsible for this, aren't you? But you're not, you know."

He gently pulled himself free. "Take the time to try to convince me *after* we've found Tracy, okay?"

"No one could have foreseen this," she persisted, following him back around to the front of the building, where Decker was deep in discussion with the police chief.

A car was pulling into the now-crowded lot. It parked and Gillman, Lopez, and a SEAL officer nicknamed Big Mac all climbed out.

"Oh, good," Dave said. "It's your fan club. Things aren't exciting enough around here with a mere robbery homicide and kidnapping."

"They're not exactly my fan club anymore," Sophia said. "They've been avoiding me. Especially Danny. Ever since . . ."

The hunting lodge incident. What a jerk. "You want me to kill him for you?"

"Not funny," she said.

"Hey, Sophia," the officer—Mac—waved to her with a wide grin.

"This is how people avoid you?" Dave asked, as she gave the SEAL a somewhat pathetic attempt at a smile.

"Mac's not avoiding me. He's suddenly been coming on so strong, it gives me the creeps," Sophia admitted as she turned away. "Why the sudden interest? Unless he's been talking to Danny and Jay and . . ." This time her forced smile was for his benefit. "Sometimes it's hard not to wonder what people think of me."

"I'm pretty sure most of them think, *Wow, she's so beautiful,*" Dave said. "And then they meet you and think, *Wow, she's smart and funny and nice, too.*"

"And then they run and hide," Sophia said.

"Probably because they think your seven-foot-tall bruiser of a boyfriend is going to come and kill them just for thinking lascivious thoughts about you."

"Either that, or they see me naked," she said. She took a deep breath. "I've pretty much decided to do the plastic surgery thing."

Which would subject her to more pain. His stomach lurched again. "I think you should think about it some more," Dave said evenly. "But if you do decide it's what you want to do, I'm here to help, with whatever you need. Rides to the doctor's, pizza delivery . . . I can even help change bandages. I'm normally not squeamish at all." Of course, he had to close his eyes as he said it, which discounted his words.

"Are you okay?" Sophia asked. "You look a little green again."

"Yes," he said. "I'm feeling a little green again, thanks." Apparently he'd come out from his Dumpster hiding place a little too soon.

Dave turned and headed toward the pay phone, pretending to be interested in checking it out. What he really needed was the wall to help hold himself up, along with the privacy shield to hide behind. And yeah, having a clear path back to the Dumpster didn't hurt.

Sophia, of course, followed him, concern in her eyes. There was amusement there, too—not much, due to the seriousness of the crime scene. But there was definitely a trace. "Can I get you anything?"

Dave nodded a mix of both yes and no. "Please," he managed. "A little space. Please?"

She backed off, joining the others. Alyssa had come out of the store, too.

As Dave closed his eyes and breathed, he could hear Deck telling the new arrivals that an FBI forensics team was on its way. The local police were more than happy to put their first murder investigation in twenty years into the hands of the feds.

Were they sure that Tracy had really been here?

The consensus was that the mitten on the ladies' room floor was indeed hers. But until they did a DNA test on the blood, they couldn't be absolutely positive.

They were certain, however, that the weapon used to murder store owner Stephen Syta had been his very own baseball bat. According to family members, he'd kept it just inside the room where he'd locked up the pharmacy's prescription drugs. The going theory was that the perp—the perpetrator—had threatened Syta with a weapon—probably a knife—forcing him to unlock the door. At which point, Syta had grabbed that bat. There'd been a struggle, whereupon the perp had gained possession and used it to end the struggle with brutal finality.

Forensics would confirm this, but Alyssa and the police chief were both pretty certain from the amount of damage to the victim's skull that the killer had landed far more than one blow. Death had been the intended outcome of such viciousness.

Wouldn't a place like this—a pharmacy in the middle of nowhere— have a security camera?

It did. It had been disabled at 8:30 P.M.

Dave kept on breathing as the pounding in his head slowly subsided.

All of the prescription drugs locked in that back room had been taken, but the perp hadn't touched the cash that was in the register. That was an important detail.

Also important was the fact that the killer had both put up a sign and locked the door behind him. He'd been trying to buy himself getaway time.

The body probably wouldn't have been discovered as quickly as it had if the victim's own brother-in-law hadn't stopped to pick up cigarettes and found the store closed. As an employee of the local septic tank pumping company, the b-i-l knew that if the victim were having sewage problems, as it said in that note taped to the door, he would've been the first person called.

The consensus was that the killer lived, if not nearby, then at least in this general area.

Dave opened his eyes and found himself staring at the side of the pay phone. He straightened up, testing to see if his legs would hold him. They would.

The phone was an older model that still took coins, although anyone using it would need a double handful.

The FBI would check records, to see if any calls were made from this phone—part of turning over every stone. They'd find nothing of course. It would take time and manpower, and bring them nowhere closer to Tracy, who was in the company of someone who had crushed another man's skull with a baseball bat.

Still, it had to be done.

"We should get some crime-scene tape over here," Dave called to Decker. "They're going to want to fingerprint the phone."

Deck acknowledged him with a nod.

"We got the order to stand down a few hours ago," Danny Gillman was telling Deck. "Everyone's pretty much on their way back here, to help look for Tracy. Although . . . Have you seen Izzy?"

Lopez wandered over to Dave. "You okay there, Dr. Malkoff?"

Great. So much for assuming he didn't look quite as terrible. "Yeah."

"You got a handkerchief, sir?"

"Yes," Dave said, "I do. But, trust me, you don't want to borrow it."

"No, sir, not for me. You got a little . . ." Lopez pointed to his own chin.

Even better. Dave turned around to try to clean himself up more thoroughly, and found himself face-to-face with a flyer advertising a reward for a lost lab-spaniel mix named Dixie. But it wasn't the badly photocopied picture of Dixie and her sad brown eyes that caught his attention.

Directly above the photo was a phone number, scribbled in blue pen.

"Hey," Dave shouted, even as he took out his cell phone. "Over here!" He flipped it open. There was no signal here—they were in one of Tess Bailey's famous dead zones—but he only needed to access his phone book and . . . Sure enough. "This must be Tracy's handwriting, because this is Lindsey's cell phone number."

No one else was excited at the news. No one even appeared to have heard him. They were all tuned in to something that the police chief was saying, his voice too low for Dave to hear. Whatever it was, though, it wasn't good news.

"I'm sorry," the chief said. That much Dave heard.

"What happened? I missed that," Dave said, moving toward them.

Sophia looked up, tears in her eyes.

"What just happened?" he asked again.

"Tom just called the police chief," she told him. "Izzy, Jenk, and Lindsey found a body. They think it's Tracy's."

"Think?" he repeated.

Sophia nodded. "They're unable to identify her—she's been too badly mutilated."

"Is Izzy okay?" Lindsey asked.

Jenk looked up at her from his perch on a fallen log. He was sitting near their car, its engine running. Izzy was in the front seat, heat blasting, recovering from his hellish swim.

Hellish in more ways than one. The body Lindsey had helped pull out of the quarry pond was . . . Awful.

Scalped. Eyeless, earless, a hole where the nose had once been. Mouth sewed shut with thick black thread. The rest of the body had been equally horrifyingly mutilated, with Frankenstein stitches suturing shut a slit throat, like someone's sick art project.

"I don't know," Jenk admitted. "Are you okay, because I'm sure as hell not." He couldn't hold her gaze. His eyes were red—it was clear he'd been crying.

Lindsey sat down next to him, all those hours without sleep making her legs as heavy as her heart. "We don't know for sure that it's Tracy."

"Izzy thinks it is."

"I understand that. But until we check dental records or DNA—"

"The alternative is that she's with this guy. Right now," Jenk said, his head in his hands. "Jesus, in some ways that's worse."

"Mark." She put her arms around him.

"What am I going to tell her parents?" he whispered as he clung to her.

"The truth," Lindsey said, her heart aching.

"The truth?" He pulled back to look into her eyes.

"That we're going to find whoever did this," she promised him. "That we're not going let him do this ever again, not to anyone else."

"Do I also tell them the truth about what I thought, what I felt when Izzy pushed Tracy out of the water?"

It had been awful. All of it.

Waiting, fearful for Izzy's safety, while he swam down into that freezing water, deeper and deeper. Watching that rope sliding between Jenk's fingers as he fed Izzy slack.

Lindsey had been certain that if Tracy were in there, she was dead. There was no hope of resuscitation. As soon as she'd seen that hole in the ice, she knew their mission had changed from one of rescue to recovery.

And when Izzy yanked twice on the rope—their predetermined signal to start hauling him up—Lindsey prayed not that they'd be able to revive her, but for a different sort of miracle. That Izzy would find only Tracy's jacket, wrapped around something that needed discarding. Someone's collection of Duran Duran records. A pillowcase filled with porn. A weapon used in a crime.

Instead, Izzy'd surfaced with a splash, with an enormous gasp for air, and with what was quite obviously a body—much smaller than he was, slighter. A woman. And she was definitely wearing Tracy's jacket.

Jenk leaped to help him.

Tracy's hood was up around her head as Jenk grabbed her beneath the arms. He didn't have time to do more than haul her onto the ice before turning back to help Lindsey with Izzy.

"Start CPR," Izzy was roaring, and God, it seemed so unlikely that anyone could save her, but Lindsey scrambled over to the awkwardly sprawled form, turning her onto her back and . . .

At first she thought it was some kind of mask, left over from Halloween. And then she knew that it wasn't.

"What are you waiting for?" Izzy shouted. He knocked her aside.

"Aw, Jesus," Jenk breathed as he, too, saw what was left of that face.

Izzy lost it. He either didn't see, or he couldn't. Maybe his brain had started to freeze. He was shaking from the cold, his own lips blue, as he pushed the body more completely onto her back, as he actually started trying to pound life back into her heart.

Jenk pulled him off her. He'd held Izzy back. "She's dead," he'd said over and over. "You can't help her, man. She's dead."

Somehow they'd gotten Izzy into the car, heat turned high. Then Tom and his team had arrived.

It was only now that they had the luxury of time to react to this nightmare.

And as Lindsey watched, emotion welled in Jenk's eyes. "When I saw her, when I saw she was dead, I thanked God it wasn't you. I thanked Christ, Lindsey, that you weren't playing the hostage last night," he whispered, and then, oh God, he kissed her.

His mouth was hard and hot, the heat they generated instantaneous, and all she wanted was to be close to him, closer. But just as suddenly as it started, it stopped. He pulled away. First to arm's length, and then farther, jumping to his feet to get away from her.

"Don't," he said, turning his back to her as he wiped his face. Clearly, he didn't want her to see him cry.

Don't? "You're the one who kissed me," she said.

"No, *you* kissed *me*. I should know when I'm being kissed." He turned toward her, but it soon became obvious that he was unable to stop his tears. "*Shit.*"

"Mark . . ." She reached for him, but he yanked his arm away.

"Just leave me alone!"

Her temper flared. "What, it's okay if I cry, but not you? You're allowed to comfort me, but when I try to do the same—"

"Was *that* what that was? Comfort?" He savagely wiped his eyes with his hands. "I thought it was your tongue in my mouth, but okay."

"I know you're angry," Lindsey told him, her voice shaking. "With yourself, with the entire world. And with me. I get that—loud and clear. I even deserve it, but—"

"Lindsey!" Tom Paoletti was shouting for her.

"Are you going to be okay to drive?" she asked Jenk. "Because Tom needs me to go over to the pharmacy with him."

Her boss hadn't been impressed by the FBI agent in charge of the investigation. He'd made a few phone calls, and a replacement—a bigwig from DC—was on his way. But it would be hours before he arrived. Until then, Tom was convinced that Lindsey had more experience working homicide than anyone currently in the county. He'd asked her to pay a visit to the crime scene.

"I'm fine," Jenk said. "Just go. Be careful."

"FYI, Koehl and rest of the SEALs are back," Lindsey told him. "In case you don't know it—which is stupid because you know everything— Izzy's UA." She took her room key from her pocket and held it out to him. "I don't know what's up, what happened between him and Tracy, why he felt it was so important to get back here. All I know is that we're on the verge of a massive manhunt, and I can't imagine that he wouldn't want to be part of that. From what Tom told me, Izzy's facing some serious consequences. If he wants to stay off Koehl's radar so he can help catch this twisted bastard, he's welcome to use my room."

Jenk took the key and put it into his pocket as he shook his head. He made a sound that might have been laughter on a different day. "You always make it hard for me to stay mad at you."

With a whine from the transmission, Tom started backing his SUV toward Lindsey.

"Will you wait for me at the motel?" she asked Jenk. "I'd like a chance to finish the conversation we started, because . . . I didn't kiss you."

He made that same almost laughter sound and closed his eyes. "It probably was my fault. I apologize. So it's not necessary to—"

"Yes, it is necessary," Lindsey said. "You were like, all, *don't* and *get away from me.* You didn't stop to ask if maybe, after saying something incredibly honest and . . . Terrifying." She met his eyes and nodded. "It was terrifying. For me. To hear that you feel that way, even after . . . everything.

But you didn't stop to think that maybe after you said what you said, I was okay with you, you know. Kissing me."

She stood on her toes, wrapped her arms around his neck, and kissed him. Right in front of Tom, who had just braked to a stop and started to roll down his window. He immediately rolled it back up.

"*That* was me kissing you," she told Jenk. "Just so there's no confusion."

Jenk laughed. His smile didn't stay for long, but it didn't have to. She could see his very heart and soul in his eyes. He nodded. "I'll see you at the motel," he said.

"Well," Tom said, as Lindsey climbed into the SUV.

"Please don't say anything," she warned her boss as she fastened her seat belt. "I have absolutely no idea what I'm doing. None at all."

Tom put the car into gear. "Am I allowed to say thank you?"

"For what?" Lindsey tried not to be too obvious about turning to watch Jenk as they drove away. He was watching her, too. He lifted his hand in a wave.

"For reminding me," Tom told her, "that even in the face of sheer ugliness and evil, there's still a lot in life that's hopeful and good."

Chapter
Eighteen

I zzy didn't give a shit.

Jenk had offered him Lindsey's room key, but he just shook his head. He walked right into the motel restaurant—still shivering from the freezing water. He just marched over to the senior chief.

Word of the recovery of Tracy's body—what was left of it—had obviously made it back here. The entire team was quiet, subdued. And the senior didn't ream him a new one upon first contact. "Sit down over there, Zanella." His voice was almost gentle as he gestured with his chin toward the tables by the window. "I'll be right with you."

No one came over to talk to Izzy—it was clear they didn't know what to say. Or maybe they thought he was an asshole, because really, that was what he was. Hell of a lot of good his taking unauthorized leave had done for Tracy, though.

Sophia was the only person who approached. She brought him a blanket, which she put around his shoulders, and a cup of hot chocolate. She even sat down across from him. "You really will warm up faster if you drink something hot."

So he took a sip. Not that he gave a shit whether or not he stopped shivering. It was just the path of least resistance with her sitting there watching him.

Her buddy Dave was watching him, too. Or rather, he was watching over Sophia. As usual, he was never too far from her. He stood at the next table, collating what looked like computer-generated maps, pretending not to listen in.

"Are you up to speed?" Sophia asked Izzy. "Tom's got a phone call scheduled, in about thirty minutes, with Jules Cassidy—the FBI agent from DC. He's going to put it on speakerphone."

A phone call. They were all sitting around waiting for a phone call from some geek in a suit. Like that was going to make any of this better.

"Cassidy's flight was canceled due to the weather," Sophia continued, "but he's still taking charge of the investigation. I don't know if you know him, but I do, and he's very good. Apparently he's got some information that he wants to share with all of us."

At which time . . . what? They'd all hold hands and sing empowerment songs? Unless Mr. Very Good had information that would lead them directly to the motherfucker who had killed Tracy, this was just a waste of time.

"Do you know about the phone call Tracy made to Lindsey?" Sophia asked him, nudging the mug of chocolate closer to him.

"Yeah," he told her as he took another sip. Tracy had ended up leaving a message on Lindsey's home answering machine. Apparently she had known she was in trouble and managed to give a brief description of her killer, as well as a partial license plate number. Maybe. She herself had admitted that it was dark and hard for her to read.

"Tess Bailey—our comspesh—has managed to map the routes of Tracy and her jacket. After leaving the cabin, she went in and out of zones that had signal. We now have a pretty clear picture of where she was for at least some of last night. But, unfortunately, not where her abductor is right now."

"Yeah, I heard that, too," Izzy said. They'd narrowed Tracy's killer's suspected location down to something like a hundred square miles. Give or take a few dozen. And that was assuming their man hadn't gone over the state lines into Maine or Vermont. "Fuck of a lot of good it's going to do us."

Dave bristled at his language. Fuck him, too.

Sophia didn't seem to care about Izzy's word choices. "It must've been awful," she said, sympathy in her eyes. "Seeing her like that."

"It might not be her," Izzy said, because that's what everyone else was saying. But if it wasn't Tracy, then the bastard who did that to her might well be carving her into pieces right this very moment. The thought of that was almost too hard to bear when the chances they would find her were slim to none. All they had to go on was a vague description—who the hell was Ralph Fiennes, anyway?—and possibly incorrect information, along with those dozens of huge chunks of New Hampshire that made up Tess Bailey's aptly named dead zones.

The current genius plan was to canvass those areas. Knock on doors and politely ask if anyone had seen Tracy, and hope that someone came to the door with blood on their Nikes. But if he didn't, they could conceivably knock on the motherfucker's door, have a conversation, *No, I haven't seen her, but I'll keep my eyes open,* then drive away, while he tromped back into the basement and blithely went back to sewing her mouth shut with a leather needle.

Izzy put his head down on the table.

"Even if it wasn't Tracy, it's still somebody," Sophia gently pointed out. "It might make it less personal, but it doesn't make it less awful." She touched his hand, her fingers warm. "It might not be over, Irving. Don't just quit."

It might not be over. The sewing-the-mouth-shut part might still be in Tracy's future.

"I don't know what to pray for," he admitted, lifting his head to look at Sophia.

She understood that he meant whether to pray that the body came back identified as Tracy—which would mean her suffering was over, or . . .

"I always prayed to stay alive," she told him, and Izzy knew from Dave's reaction that she was talking about her own ordeal as a prisoner of some sadistic warlord in some godforsaken country—the ordeal that had left her so badly scarred. He also knew from both her own and Dave's body language that this was something she didn't often discuss.

"I prayed that someone would rescue me, and I vowed to still be breathing when they came," she continued quietly. "As long as there's life, there's hope. If Tracy's still alive, she knows we're out here, looking for her. So don't quit on her, okay? Get yourself warmed up and ready to help. And talk to whoever you need to and convince them that you'll turn yourself back in—*after* we find Tracy. Otherwise, not only will you not be able to help us, but someone else will be forced to stay behind to guard you."

He hadn't thought of that. It was completely unacceptable.

Sophia stood up. She got him another mug of hot chocolate and set it down on the table in front of him. "Drink," she told him.

Izzy drank.

By the time she got back to the motel, the snow had started falling. Lightly at first, with big fluffy flakes.

It was beautiful. Or it could have been, if Lindsey had been able to erase the memory of that horrible face from her mind.

She knocked on Jenk's motel room door, and he opened it right away, as if he'd been waiting for her. He seemed alert, but she suspected he'd been sleeping. He had total bedhead, as if he'd showered but then immediately crashed for a nap.

He didn't say a word. No *hello*, no nothing. He just grabbed her and pulled her inside.

And kissed her.

It was quite the kiss. His tongue was hot as he filled her mouth—no warm-up, no foreplay, just wham. Instant soul kiss. His entire body was radiating heat, his T-shirt warm and soft beneath her hands and against her body—he'd definitely been asleep just moments earlier.

Lindsey kissed him, too, harder, deeper, tightly closing her eyes, her fingers in the softness of his hair, banishing all thoughts but those of his mouth, his hands, his body, his solid heat.

He had his hand up her shirt, her back pressed against the wall, before she realized he'd somehow managed to get her jacket unzipped and off of her.

And still he kissed her.

Lindsey felt his fingers at the waist of her pants, fumbling with the button. He got it on his second try, and she knew, even without her help, she'd be out of them in an another instant.

"We should probably talk," she pulled away to gasp.

He captured her mouth again, kissing her just as thoroughly, stopping only to breathe, "I need you," as he kissed her face, her throat.

Oh, God. "I need you, too." Enough said.

He kissed her again as he wrapped her legs around him and carried her to the back of the room, where he had a leather case on the sink counter. He set her down only for a moment as he rummaged in it, during which time she managed to kick off one of her boots. He found what he was looking for and covered himself, then pulled her closer to kiss her again, even as she tried to lose her second boot. It was impossible to pry it off with her other foot in only a sock—no traction—but he ignored it, focusing on removing her jeans.

Having one of her legs free was sufficient for what he wanted, and he didn't try for more. His own pants were already down around his thighs, and he picked her up and pushed her against the wall by the thermostat, filling her just as unceremoniously and completely as that very first kiss.

She caught a glimpse of them both in the mirror above the sink—his broad back straining, butt pumping—round cheeks bare and gleaming. It would have been comical, with her one boot off and one boot on, jeans flapping from one ankle, her head visible above his shoulder, bouncing with each thrust, occasionally bumping the wall.

It would have been, if it weren't for the expression on her face.

Eyes half-closed, mouth open as she gasped her pleasure, she looked like somebody else. Like somebody who knew what she wanted and wasn't afraid to grab it with both hands and hold on tight. Like somebody who was doing just that.

She watched him kiss her throat, his mouth so warm and soft, his eyes closed, lashes long and dark against his freshly shaved cheeks. He was so sweet. So solid and strong.

And she was what he wanted, even though she'd tried her best to chase him away.

"Linds," he breathed. "God . . ."

Yeah, he'd seen her at her worst, and he still wanted her. Needed her. Loved her.

Lindsey watched herself start to come, and then she didn't watch because her eyes closed as he kissed her, as she felt his own release, as together they crashed past the point of no return.

They would not be mere friends after this. This time, there would be no going back. Only forward.

If she dared.

Lindsey opened her eyes.

In the mirror, Mark's reflection panted for breath, his head against the wall.

She saw her own hands, twisted tightly in the cotton of his T-shirt, as if, were it up to them, they would never let him go.

Sophia went looking for Tom, but found Decker instead.

He was scrutinizing the maps that someone had tacked up on the restaurant wall, just staring at them as if, were he only to look hard enough, he'd figure out where Tracy was being held.

As usual, he knew Sophia was standing behind him, without even turning around. "Tom's on the phone with the police chief," he told her. "Is there something I can help you with?"

"Yes," she said. "I hope so. I was getting nudgy, just sitting around waiting for this meeting to start, a little cabin feverish . . ."

Decker finally looked away from the maps. He had this way of looking at her sometimes, as if they were barely acquaintances. As if he couldn't quite remember her name. Polite, yet distant. She hated when he did that. "Tom still doesn't want you spending much time outside, and I'm sorry, but I've got to agree."

"No," she said, "that's not . . . Trust me, I'm not in any hurry to go hiking again. In Hawaii, sure, but . . ."

He smiled, but again it was loaded with politeness.

Getting to the point would be good. "I started organizing the training equipment we were using the other night. Packing it up. But I've counted three times, and I'm still short a jacket. In addition to Tracy's. If she somehow managed to take a second jacket with her . . ."

Then they could conceivably still track it via the computer. Sure, it would require some effort. They'd need additional sat towers, or teams to move the temporary ones that had been set up . . .

Suddenly the look in Decker's eyes was anything but polite and reserved. He advanced on her, intense to the point of ferocity. "Show me."

Jenk's watch alarm sounded and, because he was still holding Lindsey, he shifted her to one arm and shut it off with his teeth.

He could feel her watching him, and he turned to meet her gaze.

"Hi," she said. "I mean, that was kind of like a giant, extraspecial hi, no words necessary, but I just felt it needed to be said."

He smiled. "Hi."

"Is your shoulder okay?"

"Never better."

"So was your watch set for a five- or a ten-minute warning?" Lindsey asked, smoothing down the part of his T-shirt that she'd grabbed onto toward the end there.

"Fifteen," Jenk told her, searching her eyes, aware that they were having this conversation as if they hadn't just made love, as if he weren't still inside of her. "It's really twenty minutes before the meeting officially starts, but I wanted to get there early."

"Wow," she said. "We've got time to get some food and coffee. Unless . . . we're just going to stay here like this forever . . . ?"

He pulled out, letting her slide down, feet on the floor, and instantly missed her warmth.

Lindsey immediately went about turning her jeans right side out and getting herself cleaned up, so he did the same. Now was apparently not the time to discuss what it all meant—that kiss she'd given him in front of

Tommy, and this latest, yes, very special greeting. She was either going to get scared and run again, or not. There was little he could do until it happened.

Although this time, if she left, he was going to go with her. It was definitely much harder to walk away from someone who insisted upon tagging along.

"So did it work for you, too?" Lindsey asked, and Jenk didn't understand until she added, "For a few minutes, I actually stopped seeing . . . you know. That face."

Ah, crap. Jenk nodded. "Yeah, it worked. But yeah, she's going to haunt me for a long time, too." Whoever she was. He'd made up his mind that the woman they'd pulled out of the quarry wasn't Tracy. It was possible that dental records would prove otherwise, at which time he'd have to deal, but until then . . . Not Tracy.

"She's going to haunt me forever," Lindsey said, as she went into the separate room that held the toilet and bathtub. She closed the door only partway, leaving it open a crack so they could continue to talk. "I've got a bunch of things already in that file. You know, the one labeled *Nightmare Material, to be reviewed regularly over the next eighty-plus years, including when upon deathbed.*"

"Oh, yeah?" He worked hard to make his voice come out sounding casual and relaxed, as if his heart wasn't in his throat, since by introducing the topic, she'd given him permission to ask questions. "You mean, like when your partner shot you?"

She was silent for a moment. "Yes," she finally said. "Like that." She paused again. "His name was Dale. He was . . . We were friends. I mean, I knew he was having problems with his wife, but he always talked about winning her back, like it was a given. She just needed some time, he said." Another pause. "I had no idea she'd gotten remarried. I had no clue he was using drugs—I mean *no* clue. One day, he didn't show up for work, so I went to his apartment and . . . He drew on me. I thought he was kidding at first. I mean, he was standing there, aiming his sidearm at me and . . . Then I thought he was drunk. I tried to talk him down, but . . . He shot me. I hear myself say it, and I still can't believe it. I mean, it would be like *you* shooting me."

"That would never happen," Jenk told her. "Never."

"I know," she said. "I didn't mean to imply . . . It was just . . . such a surprise. Why didn't I know he was so desperate?"

"I used to spend a lot of time replaying situations where I made mistakes," Jenk told her through that crack in the door. "Trying to figure out what I could've done differently, to change the outcome."

"Yeah," she agreed. Maybe it was easier for her to talk when they weren't face-to-face. "Although it's a real bitch when you realize that doing just about *anything* other than what you did might've made the situation end differently." She made a frustrated noise. "The thing that I beat myself up for the most is that I didn't see it coming. I should have. I should have known. Instead, it just blindsided me."

"Probably similar to when your grandfather died, huh?" Jenk said. "His just not waking up one day? That had to suck."

"Oh, yeah," she agreed.

"Because you were used to a big, looming, impending doom," he guessed. "All those years, living with your mother's cancer . . ."

Lindsey flushed the toilet. She came out and washed her hands in the sink, splashing water up and onto her face, too. "The hardest part of *that* nightmare," she told him, after drying herself on one of the hand towels, "was actually when she was given a clean bill of health. Statistically, people who made it that far in their treatment tended to live cancer-free, but . . . Hers recurred, much sooner than anyone expected." She met his eyes in the mirror. "That was it for me. She lived another twelve years, but she was sick almost all that time. It wasn't really living. It felt more like she took twelve years to die. It was like living with a death sentence."

Which she'd done while working hard to hide all of her fear and grief and anger and frustration from her mother.

"You once accused me of having a plan for my life," Lindsey told Jenk now. "Watching TiVo and—"

"I know what I said," he interrupted. "I was angry and—"

"Truth is, I don't have a plan," she said. "I'm unable to plan. I trained myself not to when my mother first got sick. Projecting myself into the future meant . . ." She shook her head.

It meant imagining a time when her mother was gone. Jenk reached for her, but she deftly sidestepped him.

"I mean, sure, I can do it for work. You know, set schedules and strategize how to get the bad guy, or how to evade capture. I can do that. But when it comes to my personal life . . ." She shook her head. "I have no long-term career plan. And I never take vacations—I mean, I take time off, but I don't go anywhere."

How do you plan for tomorrow, when tomorrow might not come? Jenk reached for her again, this time with the pretense of pulling her over to the bed, so she could sit down. She hadn't had the luxury of a nap and was obviously exhausted. He tugged her down beside him, their fingers interlaced.

"I know people who have one-year, five-year, ten-year plans for their lives," she said. "Look at you. You joined the Navy to become a SEAL, right?"

"Yeah," he said, wishing they had more time, hoping this conversation was just one of many to come. "That was my goal, right from high school."

"What's next?" she asked. "Are you staying in, or . . . ?"

"I'm in for another few years," Jenk told her. "And then . . . Well, Tommy's made it clear he wants me. It would definitely be fun to work with you again—and get paid what you're getting."

But she was shaking her head. "See, *you* know what you're doing, where you'll be. I don't have plans for two years from now. I don't have plans for next weekend."

"You could spend the weekend with me," Jenk offered. "That is, if you're up for two in a row, because the one after that is Christmas."

She pulled her hand away. Stood up. "I don't know, Mark."

He'd scared her. Okay. "This isn't a marriage proposal, Lindsey. This is just about spending time together. I love being with you. It's that simple."

She managed a smile. "The sex is great."

"The sex," he agreed, "*is* great." If she wanted to pretend that sex was all this was, he was willing to let her. At least for now.

But then she turned away. "God, I'm really screwed up."

"No, you're not," he said. "Well, a little, maybe, but who's not?"

"You're not," she countered.

"Hello," he said. "I'm the one who thought using his fourteen-year-old self's criteria for selecting a wife was a good idea."

"That was just testosterone talking." Her smile faded far too soon. "Seriously, I don't want to hurt you."

"You keep saying that," he said. "So just don't hurt me."

"I'm afraid of everything. Plus, I've got this totally messed-up relationship with my father, who wishes I'd never been born."

"You've talked to him about this?" Jenk asked.

"Well, no, but—"

"Linds. Then how do you know—"

"I overheard him talking to my mother. After my grandfather died, he found out his biological father was responsible for terrible war crimes—genocide—in China before the U.S. even got into World War II. And then in the Philippines . . . So many Allied prisoners died because of him. He was a monster. It was like finding out my real grandfather was Joseph Goebbels. I can't believe I'm telling you this!" She found her jacket. "We really need to go."

Jenk didn't stand up. "So let me see if I've got this right. Because his father was a monster, *your* father felt as if he shouldn't have had a child, as what? Some kind of punishment or penance? Like his lineage should die out or something?"

Lindsey nodded.

"That's crazy," he said. "Because your father didn't spring forth from his father's thigh. He's just as much his mother's child."

She put on her jacket. "Look, it's *his* craziness. I don't—"

"But you believe it, too."

"No, I don't."

He didn't push. "Well, good." He also didn't believe her. "Because that *is* crazy. I mean, if your father really does feel that way. If this wasn't just something he said in a knee-jerk reaction. God knows no one in your family's ever had a knee-jerk reaction before."

That got the smile he was hoping for, along with an eye roll. "Yeah, but I'm nothing like him. My father is an economics professor. He talks reeeeally slowly. I don't think he's ever said anything he didn't mean."

"To you," Jenk pointed out. "But he wasn't talking to you, right? He was talking to your mother. And he'd just found out that his father lied— and Henry was his *real* father, biology be damned. Henry lied to him. That had to have hurt."

She nodded, acknowledging that. "We should go."

Jenk put on his jacket, pocketed his room key, and followed her outside. They were halfway down the stairs before he said, "You know, sometimes, when people hear stuff when they're kids, they believe it without questioning. And they hang on to those beliefs as adults, and they don't stop to think, *is this really true?* And sometimes when you stop and really think about those beliefs, you realize, *wow, that's really wrong.* Or *believing that doesn't help me.*"

Lindsey wasn't running away, but she wasn't exactly hanging on his every word. Still, Jenk kept going—both talking and following her through the gently falling snow.

"I was afraid of heights for the longest time," he told her. "I had a total fear of falling, like I really believed if I fell, I'd be in a wheelchair for the rest of my life. I almost didn't make it through BUD/S because of it. And I sat down with it, and I thought about, and I realized it was probably something my mom had drilled into me when I was, like, two years old, so I wouldn't climb the trees in our yard or play on the roof or something. But it didn't apply to me anymore. As an adult, I could learn to climb, learn how to do it as safely as possible. I really went after it, to knock the fear—the belief—out of my system. I did a lot of rope work at first, and purposely took falls. It was scary, but I wanted to be a SEAL. I wanted it badly enough."

She'd stopped, but now she pushed through the door to the motel lobby. "I don't know what I want," she admitted.

Ouch.

She must've realized how harsh that sounded, considering that the rather obvious subtext of his words were *if she wanted* him *badly enough she, too, could face down her fears.* Because she added, "Please don't take that personally. It's not about you."

Yeah, right.

"It's about . . . me." Lindsey struggled to find the words. "I really don't know . . . anything. For me, tomorrow is this . . . gray shadow of a doorway that I know I'll step through. It's coming—it's unavoidable. But I can't see through to the other side. For such a long time, I didn't want to see. And now, no matter how hard I try, I just *can't* see."

On one side of the lobby, someone—probably Stella—had set up a little Christmas tree. It was only about four feet tall, but it was alive, its roots in a big container. It was covered with ornaments of all different shapes and sizes, and lights that flashed off and on.

"Check this out," Jenk said, taking Lindsey's hand and pulling her over to it. "My mother is so totally into Christmas, she added a room onto our house that she calls the Christmas Tree Room. It's really the playroom, but she insisted on cathedral ceilings, so she could have a twelve-foot-tall tree. It's got a ceramic tile floor, because back when they built it, Chewie was a hundred and ten in dog years, and he got so upset when he had an accident—"

"Your dog was named after Chewbacca?"

"He was an awesome dog," he told her. "Now they've got Threepio, who's a little high-strung. Anyway, picture this: The tree's at one end of the room, and it's like this one—smothered in ornaments, and each one has its own history. In fact, the trimming of the tree, which always happens on Christmas Eve, is all about telling the stories. Like, the year I was born, there was a fire in the attic, and all but three ornaments were destroyed. You'll know my mother likes you if she lets you hold one of them. She's in the no-flashing school as far as the lights go. But multicolored. None of that monochromatic crap on her tree. Her words. There'll be a fire in the fire-place, and a crèche on the mantel, but don't put Jesus in the manger until Christmas morning or there'll be trouble. And don't be freaked out by the tiny Santa-head mugs. They're antiques, and they need to be out on dis-play, even if seeing them makes you realize that the difference between Santa and Satan is the placement of a single N.

"My dad is into the ritual watching of *The Christmas Story*—you know, the kid who wants a BB gun—'*It'll put your eye out*,' and the *Char-lie Brown Christmas Special*. But the best part about Christmas at my house is that you never know who's going to show up for dinner. Foreign exchange students, coworkers whose families lived too far away, kids from the teen shelter . . . One year it was a trio of drag queens who'd gotten snowed in and stranded at the train station." He laughed. "From that year on, there's been mandatory tiara wearing at dinner. We draw straws to see who gets the honor. My mother swears it's all fair, but it's usually always me or my dad. Can you picture me sitting at the table in pink rhinestones? *Please pass the gravy . . .*"

Lindsey was laughing. "Actually, yes."

"Good," Jenk said. "Now picture yourself sitting next to me." And then, because wariness leaped back into her eyes, he pulled her close, and added, "My hand on your leg, signaling for you to pretend to help clear the table, but in truth to meet me in the upstairs bathroom for a quickie, be-cause my mother has her house rules, so we'll be sleeping in separate bed-rooms. By dinnertime, I'll be so freaking crazy from wanting you, I'll actually have eaten the turnips that my mother insists are traditional, but oh, my God. They look like winter squash, but don't take too large of a spoonful, because like I said, oh, my God."

Lindsey was laughing again by the time his watch beeped.

"Come on." Jenk kissed her neck. "Let's go find out that the body we recovered wasn't Tracy's."

But she stopped him. "Mark."

He turned, bracing himself for God knows what. Something that started with, *I know the sex is great, but . . .*

Instead, she said, "I think we should be prepared for the worst."

She was talking about Tracy. Jenk nodded. "I know you do. But the more I think about it, I don't think it was her. She hasn't been missing that long. Whoever did that . . . It had to take time." He shrugged. "Maybe I'm a fool, but I'd rather hope for the best. That we can find her. That we *will* find her."

He could see her disbelief. "She could be anywhere," Lindsey pointed out. "And we're about to be smacked with what they're calling the biggest snowstorm of the decade."

Most of the SEALs and members of Tom's team were already in the motel restaurant, waiting for the meeting to start. Jenk opened the door, letting her go first, determined to stick with her. She could run, but this time he was going to keep pace.

"Maybe that's good," he said. "It'll keep this bastard from leaving the state."

She laughed. "Okay, that's a little too optimistically over the top, even for you, Little Marky Sunshine."

"Too bad," he said. "My glass is not only half-full, it holds five-hundred-dollar-a-bottle Dom Pérignon champagne."

It was then, as she took a seat near Izzy, that he knew just how totally screwed he was. He got a clear measurement of just how much he cared for Lindsey, and how badly he wanted her in his life.

Because she said, "I'll think about it. About Christmas."

And there he sat, happy as a pig in shit because, although she hadn't said yes, she hadn't said no.

"Good," Jenk said, but there was no time to say anything more because the meeting started.

The body Izzy had pulled from the quarry had yet to be identified.

Tommy Paoletti started the meeting with that no-news-is-good-news-flash. Apparently they were having trouble finding Tracy's dental records. IDing her through fingerprints was not an option—the body they'd recovered didn't have fingers.

Jesus.

They were waiting on DNA test results which, Tom reported, would probably be in within the next few hours, possibly as early as minutes from now, when they connected via speakerphone to Jules Cassidy, the FBI agent in charge of the investigation.

In the real good-news department, however, it appeared highly likely that Tracy had taken a second sensor-equipped training jacket with her when she'd left the cabin.

"Each jacket has an ID number," Sophia announced, "and it's definitely Dan Gillman's jacket that's missing. He remembers taking it off, right after he was 'killed,' during the exercise. He gave it to Tracy to put over her legs because her feet were cold."

Two tables over from Izzy, the fishboy was nodding his head.

Lindsey raised her hand. "You're taking into account the jacket I bor-rowed, right? I took one out to the cabin, which was allegedly a non–dead zone. I wanted to see if the computer really did pick up its signal."

"For the record, it did," Tess Bailey reported. "And yes, Mark Jenkins returned that jacket a few hours ago."

Izzy couldn't keep his mouth shut a moment longer. "So all we have to do is shuffle the temporary sat dishes around, resurrecting the dead zones until the computer program picks up the signal from Gillman's missing jacket. What are we sitting around here for?"

"Have you looked out the window?" Gillman said.

Izzy looked. The wind was blowing, and the snow was coming down so fast and heavy, he could barely see the SUVs parked in the lot, three feet away. But a little ice and snow was nothing compared to what some freak job might be doing to Tracy right that very moment.

"Again," Tess, the cute little comspesh, was saying. "It would be better to set up additional sat dishes, rather than simply redistricting the dead zones. If Tracy's killer moves the jacket—"

"For now, we're limited to the equipment we have," Tom interrupted. "And I think it's safe to assume that wherever Tracy is, she's going to re-main there, at least until the storm passes. Also, listen up, people. Until the body is identified, we're going with the assumption that Tracy's still alive. Is that clear?" He looked around the room, at the SEALs and Trou-bleshooters alike, at Lew Koehl, who was clearly letting him take com-mand. "We've got to start somewhere. We may as well start here. We'll be breaking into teams. We've got five temporary sat dishes out there. The goal will be to locate them, dismantle them, transport them to new locations— coordinating with Tess and the computer. Sophia and Lindsey, you'll assist Tess."

Lindsey clearly couldn't stand the thought of not being in the thick of the action, because she raised her hand. "Sir, as a person with perhaps the most experience in homicide investigations—"

"I want you here," Tom interrupted again, "studying satellite maps. I want you to identify the areas where you think it's most likely a killer like this one could live, undetected. We don't have the luxury of doing a grid-by-grid search. If Tracy's alive, she's running out of time. I want you to use your experience to help us find her."

"Yes, sir."

"In addition to the five teams who'll be moving the sat dishes, we'll also have teams canvassing these areas, going door-to-door with pictures of Tracy. The local police have done some of this, but again, I want to focus on some of the more remote areas."

Alyssa Locke spoke up. "Excuse me, Tom, we've got Jules Cassidy on the phone."

Tom nodded. "Plug him in."

She did. "Jules, you're on the speaker," she said.

"Any news on the DNA tests?" Tom asked, because he knew that was what they all desperately wanted to know.

"Sorry, not yet," came the voice from the speakerphone. "As soon as I hear anything, I'll let you know."

"Where are you?" Tom asked.

"I actually caught a flight to Hartford," the FBI agent said. "I'm in a rental car, heading north on 91. It's slow going, but I've been assigned my very own snowplow. He's going to drive in front of me, all the way to Darlington if necessary."

Tom exchanged a look with Commander Koehl.

"And, yeah, I know that you're wondering how one missing receptionist warrants the expense of all those taxpayer dollars," Cassidy continued, "and, well, do you want the good news or the bad news?"

"Good news," Tom said, at the exact same time that Koehl said, "Bad news."

"That was actually a trick question, because the good news is also the bad news," Cassidy told them. "We believe the killer is a man by the name of Richard Eulie, who the Bureau's been actively looking for, for about six years now. He's a sociopath. A serial killer. The mutilations to the body that you recovered are similar to some of his work in the past. And it is clear that he thinks of it as work—artwork, even."

Holy crap.

"Even though it's been three years since we've recovered a body, he hasn't been shy about letting us know whom he's abducted," the FBI agent continued. "His MO is to leave behind a full handprint—in his victim's blood. I've got a list here of twenty of his abductees, all from the last three years. All women, from pretty much all over the country. But one of the states he's never hit is New Hampshire. Needless to say, we now believe his home base is somewhere in the Darlington/Happy Hills area. We also suspect the quarry where you found the body has been his dumping ground. As soon as the weather clears, we'll drag it, in hopes of finding more of his victims."

Holy shit. Holy, holy shit. Izzy sat, listening to the FBI agent rattle off this information. A freaking serial killer . . .

"But there was no handprint in the convenience store ladies' room," Lindsey spoke up. "Where Tracy's mitten was found."

"Yeah, the store was wiped of fingerprints, which is counter to his pattern," Cassidy agreed. "As was the murder of the store owner—male, unmutilated. But we think this plays into the theory that Eulie lives and works—so to speak—in this area. His goal was to steal the drugs from the pharmacy—the murder was incidental. It's clear he didn't want to be discovered. And yet, he slipped. He left a bunch of big, fat prints on the pay phone outside the store. Tracy's prints were on that same phone."

"So . . . Eulie stole the drugs," Dave Malkoff wondered aloud, "because . . . he's ill?"

"Eulie or someone he cares about," Cassidy said. "That's our best guess."

"Are serial killers capable of caring about other people?" Sophia asked. She was clearly as horrified by this as Izzy was.

"The BTK was married with kids," Dave told her.

"Nurse's uniform," Lindsey reminded them. "Tracy was wearing a nurse's uniform."

"Yeah," Cassidy responded to her. "We think that might be why he took her. But she's not a nurse, right? Has she had any significant medical training?"

Everyone looked at Jenk. "Not that I know of," he said. He looked at Izzy.

Who couldn't do more than shake his head. He didn't know, either. But he did have a question for the FBI agent. "Do you think, if the body we found turns out to be someone else, that Tracy's still alive?"

"I don't know," the man replied honestly.

"I do," Sophia said. She stood up. "I think she's still alive, and I think we should go find her."

CHAPTER
NINETEEN

"Sophia, wait up."

Dave looked up from the table that held the maps and photos of Tracy to see the brawny red-haired SEAL officer named MacInnough—nicknamed Big Mac—chasing Sophia down. She turned to face him, clutching the file she was holding to her chest. *He comes on so strong, it gives me the creeps.*

Dave began wandering in their direction.

"I just wanted to let you know that we'll do our best to find your friend," Mac told her.

"Thanks," she said.

"You seem to have survived your arctic swim the other day," he said. "Quite a shock to the system, huh? You know, I actually do that sort of thing on purpose. Back home, in Buffalo, I'm part of a polar bear club. We all go for a swim every New Year's Day."

"That's crazy," she said.

He laughed. "No, it's a fun tradition. My dad and his dad used to do it. Someday my kids'll watch me, and hopefully want to be like their old man, too. Not that I have any kids. We're talking a far-into-the-future someday."

Sophia gave him a smile that was definitely strained. "We both have things to do."

"Yeah," he said. "Onward, into the storm. I just wanted to check up on you, make sure you were okay."

"I am."

"And see where you wanted to go for a celebration dinner after we find

Tracy," Mac said. He wasn't asking her out, he was *telling* her that they were going out.

Dave didn't know whether to be impressed or disgusted. The man had stones the size of China.

"I've got some time off coming," Mac continued. "We could go to Boston, or even New York—really get to know each other. I know this great place on Seventh Avenue and . . . Well, think about it, okay?" he added. "I'll catch up with you later."

Sophia had been in the process of escaping, but now she turned back, stopping him. "Alex, wait."

"Um, actually it's Alec," he told her. "C instead of X."

Sophia winced. "Sorry."

"So much for my fantasy that you've been doodling my name on your notepad," he said. "Shucks."

"I can't have dinner with you," she said. "Not in New York, not even here."

"Sure you can." He *was* persistent.

"My husband died only a few years ago. It's just too soon to think about dating. I'm just not ready."

Dave turned to see Decker standing next to him.

"We're canvassing the south sector," he informed Dave, one eye on Sophia. "You and I are going out together."

Oh, joy. "Do we have to?" Dave asked.

Decker ignored the question, instead holding out the car keys. "You want to drive?"

It was clearly a peace offering.

But across the room, Sophia pretended to stop to get some coffee. It was obvious, though, that her real reason for turning her back on the rest of the room was to wipe her eyes.

Mac had vanished, but what had that son of a bitch said to her to make her almost cry?

Dave went to find out. "Hey."

She forced a smile. "Heading out?"

"Yeah," Dave said. "Are you all right? I saw you talking to Mac. If he said something inappropriate . . ."

"No. He just . . ." Her brave face suddenly crumbled. "Dave," she whispered, "do you think everyone knows?"

"Knows that you're a great person?" he countered, even though he knew she was referring to the nightmare she'd lived through as a prisoner and concubine of a vicious man. "Absolutely."

But Sophia shook her head. "Doesn't it seem too coincidental? That Alec should hit on me now? After hanging out with Gillman and Lopez, who saw my scars . . ." Her voice trailed off as she looked over his shoulder, and Dave realized Deck was standing right behind him.

The look in his eyes was pure *I'll fucking kill them.* "I'll meet you at the car," Deck told Dave, and it was clear he was going to go kick some Navy SEAL ass. Sophia was too busy trying to hide her upset from Decker to notice.

Dave's choice was between defusing the Decker-bomb or trying to set Sophia straight, and he let Deck disappear.

"Soph," he said. "Come on. I've worked with these mega-mondo-alpha types before. Mac wasn't hitting on you because he thinks you're easy, or that you'll put out. I mean, obviously, he's hoping you'll put out. You're beautiful and extremely sexy and he wants you—both on his arm and in his bed. How could he not? But I've never heard him or anyone else talking about you with anything less than respect. In fact, it's usually reverence. Worshipful, even."

That got him a disbelieving smile. "Okay, that's laying it on a little thick," she said.

"It's the truth," he told her. "You're a goddess, and they're all over-achievers. If they're gossiping about you, I'd bet it's about the fact that you keep saying no. These are men who take *no* as a challenge. You said no to Gillman, which probably made Mac more determined than ever to get you to say yes to him. Make sense?"

Sophia nodded. And hugged him. "You always say the right thing. I don't know if it's true, but, okay. It might be."

"It is." He closed his eyes as he hugged her, too, his cheek against the silkiness of her sweet-smelling hair.

"Be careful out there," she told him.

"You be careful, too."

She pulled away. "Careful not to burn my mouth on hot coffee? I'll be here, safe and warm, while you're—"

"Seriously," he said. "Until we catch this guy, I want you to stay close to Lindsey or Tess."

"Wait, haven't I heard this story before?" she teased. "The men leave the women behind at the hunting lodge—or in this case, the Motel-A-Rama. Where's Izzy with his *Give me back my leg?*" She laughed at his expression. "I'm kidding. Now *you* come on. Lindsey and Tess are both armed. And Stella and Robert are here. We're ridiculously safe."

"Those sound like such famous last words," Dave said, glad, though, that her smile seemed more genuine. "Cut to scene of you, tied to railroad tracks."

Her laughter was warm. "Go," she said, pushing him away. "Find Tracy and bring her back here, healthy and alive. Then we'll all have a celebration dinner."

Those were much better last words. Cut to scene of bedroom, where the hero and the fairy-goddess blond heroine finally kiss, and fade to black.

Provided the hero ever got his head out of his ass.

"Go," Sophia said again.

Dave bowed, just very slightly. "As you wish."

It was then, as if punctuating his words, that the power went out.

In the dim light from the overworked generator, Lindsey had the full attention of all of the personnel, both SEALs and Troubleshooters, who were going out in groups of two, three, and four, to canvass the area.

She'd already pored over the maps, looking for isolated houses that were in relatively close—but not too close—proximity to both the quarry and the pharmacy that had been robbed, and had identified quite a few starting places.

She'd also played them the message Tracy had left on Lindsey's home answering machine. God, it was weird to hear her voice. Tom had ordered them to assume she was still alive, but Lindsey could see from their eyes that many of them doubted it.

Yeah, hi, it's me, Tracy. I'm calling from some pay phone on the freaking North Pole. I just got your cell number, so I'll call you right back in a sec. See, there's this guy who's kind of hot, but kind of not—think if Ralph Fiennes sniffed glue—and he's . . . Shoot, he's getting out of his car. I feel like I should give you the license plate number, in case I drop off the face of the earth. Except it's dark and . . . I think there's a nine . . . That's all I can see. There's mud or pig poop on it, or whatever animal they farm up here. It's got New Hampshire plates. Except, okay. He's just refilling his windshield wiper fluid. Silly me. I'll call you back on your cell.

Lindsey had shown the teams—thanks to the motel generator, Tess's computer, and imdb.com—a photo of Ralph Fiennes, the handsome English actor who'd starred in *The English Patient* and *The Constant Gardener*. She'd also shown them photos of glue-sniffers—of their glazed and vacant eyes. It was probable that Tracy had been exaggerating in her description of the man who'd abducted her, but Lindsey wanted to arm them as thoroughly as possible.

"When they answer the door, be friendly," Lindsey reminded them. Alyssa was going out with Sam and a SEAL officer named John Nilsson. Dave was with Decker, although Deck was conspicuously absent from this briefing. A group of SEALs she didn't know very well were actually taking notes. Good for them. "Ask for their help in finding a missing woman — don't mention serial killers or the murder of the pharmacist. Ask to come inside. Use small talk — the flu's been going around, ask if anyone in the house has been ill. Notice the smell. You can smell sickness, and you can smell death. Especially in the winter with the windows closed. Notice, too, any overpowering scents that might be used to mask those odors. Ask to talk to all of the other people who live in the house. Ask about their neighbors — how long have they known them. Remember, it's possible that Richard Eulie, our suspect, has only been living in the area for three years. He may be perceived as a relative newcomer. Any questions?"

God, she wished she were going out there, with them.

But even more than that, she wished Tracy had never disappeared.

And as long as she was making wishes, she wished Jenk were sitting there, looking back at her. Instead, he was with one of the teams that would be moving the sat dishes to new locations.

Lindsey didn't feel as frightened when he was beside her. The panic came when he was gone. What was she doing, telling him she'd think about going home with him for Christmas? Meeting his parents as if she were his girlfriend?

There were no questions — everyone was eager to get on their way.

Chains had been put on tires.

Weapons were checked and holstered. She herself had her usual setup — a pair of .22 caliber handguns, lightweight and easily concealable. Not extremely useful in long-range situations, but completely capable when up close and personal.

Not that she'd be needing a weapon.

Still, both Tom and Alyssa had checked with Lindsey and Tess, too, making sure they were armed.

As the motel cleared out, with the wind howling and the snow falling sideways, swirling around, the emptiness was decidedly creepy.

Lindsey went back to the maps, studying the twisting labyrinth of mountain roads.

If she were a serial killer, where would she be?

*   *   *

Visibility sucked.

And the tires kept slipping off the freaking road.

It wasn't due to the whiteout conditions caused by the wind and falling snow, although that didn't help.

It was the lack of guardrails or markers on these poorly maintained back roads that were screwing Jenk up the most. With a blanket of snow already on the ground, drifting high in places, he found himself unable to define just how wide the road was. He invariably ended up leaving the pavement with his right wheels.

The shoulder often sloped, sometimes rather steeply, but he was always able to wrestle the vehicle back.

Except for this time. *Shit.* "Hold on!"

He focused on keeping the car on all its wheels, managing only to slip and skid down into a ditch along the side of the road.

"Jesus, Jenkins." Gillman was less than pleased. "Will you let me drive now?"

"That was fucking awesome driving, asshole," Izzy came back at him. They were all already out of the car, working to get it back up to the road. He shouted over the howl of the wind. "He kept us from rolling over. You think pushing this is heavy? Try turning one of these fuckers over."

Getting the SUV back up the slippery hill wasn't going to happen with mere muscle. They needed traction. Jenk opened the rear door. There were shovels and bags of sand in the back.

"Danny's still freaked out," Lopez said, his voice muffled beneath his ski mask and hood, as he tore open one of the bags, "from that whole confrontation with Larry Decker."

"You were freaked, too," Gillman told Lopez. "Don't deny it. He's one scary mofo."

"Yeah, but I'm not the one who hit on Sophia," Lopez pointed out. "You're freaked out about *that*, too."

"I wouldn't have hit on her," Gillman said, "if I'd've known about . . . I mean, God, the shit she's been through. A woman like that should come with a warning label. I mean, she told me she had baggage, but, man."

"Will you fucking stop yapping and push?" Izzy said.

Jesus, it was cold. The windblown snow felt like needles of ice on Jenk's face. He climbed behind the wheel and put the vehicle in gear as his teammates dug in their boots and heaved. The engine whined and the tires spun—and finally caught.

And they were back on their way.

"My hair's entirely iced," Gillman complained as Lopez cranked the heater.

Izzy was unsympathetic. "Next time wear a hat, douche-bag." He turned to Lopez, who had the map. "How much farther?"

"Another three kilometers."

"Jenk," Gillman said, "you and Lindsey are pretty close, and she's friends with Sophia, right? Did she tell you about . . . ? You know."

Jenk did know. Gillman was talking about how Sophia had gotten those scars.

"No," he answered, looking at him in the rearview mirror. "But even if she had . . . Didn't you just promise Decker not to gossip?"

Larry Decker, who was not the type to make idle threats, had pointed to Gillman, Lopez, Izzy, Jenk, and Lieutenant MacInnough, back at the motel, while they were gearing up.

"The five of you," he'd said. "Over here. Now."

Once a former Navy SEAL chief, the man could put a boatload of authority into his voice when he wanted to. Even Mac, an officer, hopped to it at Deck's command.

"Stay away from Sophia Ghaffari," Deck had told them. The man was seriously pissed, but his voice was quiet. His delivery was far more effectively frightening than any angry shouting would have been. "Don't touch her. Don't talk to her. Don't even *look* at her. What she's been through is bad enough without you making it worse. And you see it as something to take advantage of. She's an easy target, right? *Wrong.* She's strong. And brave. More than you sons of bitches could ever hope to be. So when you gossip to your friends about her, about her scars? Be sure to mention that. And mention me, too. Because if anyone so much as looks at her sideways, I'll rip out their fucking throats."

Mac had been seriously confused. "What scars? Deck, I appreciate your concern for Sophia, but I've neither gossiped about her, nor seen any scars."

Decker looked at him hard, but it was very obvious that Mac wasn't bullshitting him. "Gillman and Lopez didn't tell you?" He was seriously taken aback.

The two SEALs in question were offended. "I didn't tell anyone," Gillman insisted.

"What kind of jerks do you think we are?" Lopez's mouth was tight with outrage.

Izzy, for once, just shook his head as Decker looked from him to Jenk.

"We respect Sophia," Jenk told him.

"Whatever they know about Sophia and her scars—God—none of these men shared it with me," Mac told Deck.

"You asked her to go to New York with you," Decker said as if that was proof of Mac's evildoing.

"Yeah," Mac said. "Dream big's always been my credo. If you want to know the truth, Chief, I asked her out because, yes, I had heard rumors that she was some sort of, I don't know, modern Mata Hari concubine over in some shithole Middle Eastern country and . . . See, I figured that everyone else had heard these rumors, too, and were completely intimidated by her—both by that and the fact that she's really beautiful. There's something I call *out of my league syndrome* that I use to my advantage. When women are too beautiful, no one ever asks them out. I thought this would be doubly the case with Sophia, because, you know. The rumors. I figured I had a real shot at dating her. *Dating* her."

"So she really is that Mata Hari operative everyone's been talking about?" Izzy asked. "Whoa."

"Aw fuck," Decker had breathed. "Gentlemen, I apologize. Please don't hold my brash actions against Sophia. I hope you'll continue to respect her and not spread these . . . rumors any further."

Rumors. Right.

"I'm not gossiping," Gillman said now. "Because we've all seen those scars. Gossiping would be me telling Silverman or Junior. Or calling Wild-Card Karmody in California. I would never do that. I'm . . . freaked is a good word for it. I mean, it's no secret either that I kissed her, at the hunting lodge. It never occurred to me that her silence wasn't an affirmative, that maybe I'd scared her, or . . . I don't know what. But I didn't even ask. I just frenched her. God, I feel awful. And the stupid part is that I still really like her. She's incredible. But now I don't know what to say to her. I'm all . . . yeah, freaked out."

"You should tell her," Izzy advised, as they drove through the storm, wipers ineffectively slapping, defroster blasting to keep the windshield from completely freezing. "Definitely tell her, Dan. Life's too short."

Jenk glanced at him in the mirror, wondering what it was that Izzy would tell Tracy if he had the chance.

Izzy caught his eye and shook his head. "Just shut up, Weeble."

"I didn't say anything," Jenk protested.

"Yeah, but I know you, and you were going to."

He was spared having to answer because his phone rang. He tossed it back to Zanella, because he needed both hands on the wheel, and Lopez was wrestling with the map.

"It's Lindsey," Izzy said, before he even opened the phone. "Please tell me that we found her alive and in one piece." There was a pause, then, "Oh, my Jesus God, pull over, pull over, Jenkins—pull *over!*"

Jenk didn't pull over. He didn't want to risk another trip into the ditch, but he hit the brakes and they skidded to a stop.

Zanella dropped the phone and bolted out of the car.

Gillman picked it up, grimly handing it to Jenk. "I think it was bad news."

As he put the phone to his ear, he could barely see Izzy, just standing there, a few feet from the side of the SUV. The falling snow was that heavy. "Linds."

"Is Zanella okay?" she asked.

"He needed to, um, make a pit stop." Jenk braced himself. "What's the news?"

"The DNA test came back. The body we recovered is that of Connie Smith, from Midland, Michigan."

Thank God. Poor Connie Smith, but thank *God.*

"Tracy's alive," Jenk told the others.

As Izzy got back into the car, no one commented on either his abrupt departure, or the fact that his face and eyes were red, as if he'd scrubbed himself with a handful of snow to hide whatever emotional reaction he'd had. Gillman just silently handed Iz some Burger King napkins that some-one had stuck into the pocket behind the front seat so he could blow his nose.

On the other end of the phone, Lindsey was being cautious. "We don't know that Tracy's alive," she reminded Jenk. "But we can say for sure that the body from the quarry wasn't hers."

"She's still alive," Jenk repeated his optimistic words. "Thanks for the update. FYI, we'll be going dark in just a few minutes. We're approaching the tower. It'll be shut down for the next thirty to forty minutes. We'll call in as soon as it's reset."

"Be safe, Mark" she said, and cut the connection. He tried not to be disappointed that she hadn't said, *As long as I'm giving you good news, I just thought I'd say yes to Christmas.* She had, after all, called him Mark in public. Small victories, he reminded himself.

"Can we please drive?" Izzy asked. "Because now we know that Tracy's with this motherfucker, and personally?" His voice actually shook. "I'm very fond of her eyes right where they are, securely in her head."

. . .

Tracy woke up in the dark, groggy and confused.

Wherever she was, it was cold and damp. Her neck hurt from sleeping on the floor, her head throbbed, and as she moved, a chain clanked, and she remembered.

The man with the gun, the dead man on the floor of the store, the woman in the bed with the gash on her arm.

A Tupperware bowl from the freezer that was filled with human eyes.

He'd dragged her into his kitchen where he'd showed her that nightmare, along with the awful eyeless thing that had once been a woman.

Dear God. Perhaps the darkness was due to the fact that Tracy herself no longer had eyes. But she felt her face, and it was still intact. Lids with eyes beneath them. Nose. Ears.

Clank. There was some sort of shackle around her ankle. She followed the chain to a bracket in what felt like a stone wall.

She had to be in some kind of subterranean room. A basement or cellar. She had no memory of coming down here, but she could remember him laughing at her screams as he stuck her with a needle.

God, how she'd screamed at the sight of that gruesome mutilated body, just sitting at his kitchen table, as if joining him for lunch.

Had he silenced Tracy because he was afraid someone would hear her?

If she screamed now, would he come down here and do to her what he'd done to that poor woman? Dear God, he'd scalped her, then stretched the skin in an embroidery hoop to dry. Whoever she was, she'd once had long, golden hair, which he'd washed until it shined.

The alternative was to wait in silence, at which point he'd probably kill her anyway.

"Help!" Tracy started to scream. "Someone help me!"

Dave tried to stomp the snow off his feet before getting back into the truck.

"Anything?" Deck asked.

He shook his head. "Just a pair of older ladies. They didn't want to invite me in at first because, well, their house smelled like pot. But I told them that was okay with me."

Deck looked at him.

"Medical marijuana," Dave explained. "One of them was bald from chemo—it was kind of obvious what was going on. They were friendly and willing to help, but they didn't recognize either Tracy or our Ralph Fiennes impersonator."

Deck nodded. "Single truck in the garage. The bulkhead to the basement was open, so I went in. It was spotless—I think they paint their basement floor."

After leaving the motel, they'd quickly established a pattern. Dave would go to the door, while Deck did a quick circuit of the outside of the house. He also checked any outbuildings or garages for a car with a nine in the license plate.

"Where to now?" Dave asked.

Deck turned on the interior light to check the map. "House number five is about four miles up the hill. It's the next house on the left. The road curves so take it slow."

As if there was any other way to travel in this weather. Dave put the truck in gear. He could barely see through the windshield. But they were definitely moving faster than they would've been able to on foot. Although frequently Decker had to get out and find the road for him, as he had to do right now.

It was then, when he was climbing back into the cab that Deck surprised the hell out of him.

"I really fucked up today," he said. "I don't know how I'm going to tell Sophia."

Dave glanced at him. "Tell her what?"

Deck pretended to look at the map, but Dave knew he was just avoiding eye contact. "I went all cowboy," he admitted. "On Gillman and MacInnough. And Zanella and Lopez and Jenkins. Jesus. I thought . . ." He exhaled his frustration. "I thought they'd found out about Sophia."

About how she'd used sex to stay alive in Bashir's palace.

"I thought their interest in her was inappropriate," Deck continued. "I was wrong. They didn't know. But they do now." At Dave's glance, he added, "Yeah. I managed to confirm the rumors. Brilliant, huh?"

Does everyone know?

Sophia was going to be upset, but Dave couldn't help but think that this would be, in the long run, a good thing.

"She has nothing to be ashamed of," he told Decker. "The truth is that she managed to survive a terrible situation. Keeping it a secret isn't going to change what happened. It'll never be just magically erased. Frankly, I think she'll be better off with everyone knowing. I think she should be talking about it. Maybe now she will."

Decker was just shaking his head.

"What, you disagree?"

"No," Deck said. "You're probably right. I just . . . *I'm* ashamed."

"Of Sophia?"

The look Deck shot him would've turned Dave into stone in another dimension. "Of myself."

Screw that!

"Get over it!" Dave said. "Do you have any clue at all just how much she cares about you? How many times do we have to have this conversation anyway?" He was gripping the steering wheel so hard his knuckles were white. "But this is it. The last time. Listen carefully, because after this, you are on your own. I'm not going to say this again. Ask her to dinner, and when she says yes—which she *will say* with an expression of total joy on her face—put your arms around her and kiss the hell out of her. Just do it! Don't think, don't analyze, don't argue, and for the love of God, don't, don't, *don't* feel ashamed. The past is over. Let it go. Start focusing on the future."

Decker didn't look convinced. "She told Mac it was too soon to start dating—"

"Yeah—to start dating *Mac.*" Dave completely lost it. He actually pounded on the steering wheel. "Do you have any idea, *any idea*, what I would give to be you, you stupid, stupid fool? I wouldn't have waited a second longer than I'd had to. By now she would be pregnant with my child, my ring around her finger. And she wouldn't have nightmares anymore, because I would be there at night, to talk to her, to hold her, to make sure she knew that she was safe forever. *God*, I am *so* in love with her, but you're the one she wants—you total fucking idiot. How can you just throw that away because you're ashamed of some mistake that you made a million years ago? A mistake that she's forgiven you for!"

Silence seemed to ring in the car, broken only by the sound of the tires and the windshield wiper laboring to clear away the falling snow.

"I didn't know," Decker finally said.

"Well, congratulations, now you do." Dave was so done. He used to think Deck would be good for Sophia, but now . . . It was over. He was no longer willing to help her find happiness by pushing Decker in her direction, by trying to talk him into spending time with her. He was finished with that. Finis. No more.

Yeah, and who was he kidding? He was done all right—until the next time Sophia looked longingly in Deck's direction. Shit. *Shit.*

"I'll do it," Decker said. "I'll ask her. To dinner. If that's really what she wants."

Dave took out his phone. "Great. Call her right now."

"We're in a dead zone."

"Not for the next few minutes," Dave told him. He dialed Sophia's number. Held the phone out to Decker. "Take it, it's ringing."

He took it, just as Sophia answered. Dave could hear her voice—his volume was up that loud. "Dave?"

"No, it's, uh, Deck."

"Is everything okay?" she asked. "Your timing is incredible!" She sounded excited.

"Uh, yeah," he said. "I was—" They must've both spoken at the same time, because he stopped. "I'm sorry—go ahead."

"I was just about to call you." Her voice crackled—the connection was tenuous at best, and Dave slowed down, afraid he was moving out of range. "We got a blip from Gillman's missing jacket on the computer, and you're the closest team."

Jenk was on the verge of going bullshit.

He'd handed over the driving to Gillman, so he could double-check the map, but there was no doubt about it.

Lindsey, at the motel, was the closest operative to the location of the blip that was being picked up by the computer. The blip that was Gillman's jacket that Tracy had taken from the cabin. The blip that was Tracy and/or a vicious and dangerous serial killer named Richard Eulie.

He dialed Lindsey's cell again.

She picked up—thank you, Jesus—and he didn't wait for her to say more than hello. "Please tell me you're waiting for backup."

"I'm meeting Dave and Decker there," she told him.

"And you'll wait for them, if you get there first, right?" This connection sucked. The wind wasn't helping.

"Oh, yeah," she said. "Believe me, I'm not crazy."

And yet she was alone in a vehicle, probably his POS rental car, without chains on the tires, rushing through a blizzard. Not crazy? No comment. In fact, Jenk clenched his teeth over any recriminations that might inadvertently pop out of his mouth. He wouldn't like it if she questioned his ability to handle a dangerous situation. She was an experienced, skilled operative—it had to go both ways.

Still, it was safe to say that, as far as their relationship went, this aspect of it was far less fun than having sex. In fact, it was going to take a lot of sex to make up for this.

Lindsey corrected herself. "I'm not too crazy."

"Yeah, that's what I'm afraid of," Jenk said.

"I thought Navy SEALs weren't afraid of anything," she teased.

"Seriously, Linds, wait for backup, okay?"

"I said that I would."

"We're on our way, too," Jenk reported. "We're probably thirty minutes behind Deck and Dave."

"That's good to know. Hey, I'm getting a beep. Hang on."

He hung. For longer than he'd hoped. He kept checking his phone to make sure he hadn't lost the connection. But then she was back.

"You're about to get a phone call," she told him, and sure enough, Lopez's phone rang.

"What's going on?"

"Sophia just got a call from the police," Lindsey informed him. "Someone saw Tracy on the night she disappeared with a man known as Todd Nortman. He's something of an eccentric—no one really knows him or trusts him. Apparently he gives food away, which makes everyone leery. He's too generous—small-town mentalities boggle my mind. Still, he fits our profile. He's lived—with a mother no one's ever seen—outside of town for two and a half years."

"You don't think he's our man," Jenk could hear her doubt.

"It just seems so obvious—the town freak's a killer? But everyone else likes him for this. The police chief sent a patrol car to his house—and, get this: Tracy's other mitten was spotted through the window of Nortman's car." She exhaled her exasperation. "It just seems so careless. But they're getting a search warrant, so we're diverting everyone in the immediate area—your team included—to his property. They want his house surrounded before they knock on his door."

"Nortman's property is not the same location as our computer blip," Jenk clarified as, sure enough, Gillman carefully turned their SUV around.

"Correct," Lindsey told him. "But it's within ten miles. I keep telling myself that the blip is just the jacket. Tracy may have taken it off hours ago. God, it's hard to see. You know what this is like? With the snow reflecting off my headlights? It's like making the jump into warp speed from the *Millennium Falcon*."

"Great," Jenk said. "Next you're going to say, *I've got a bad feeling about this*."

"Yeah, well, I do. I'm going to continue to investigate the blip. With Decker and Dave," she added, a smile in her voice.

"Good," he said.

"Do me a favor," Lindsey said. "When you get over to Nortman's, and you take a look at him . . . ? Give me a call and let me know if you think he fits Tracy's *hot guy* description, okay?"

"I don't know if I'm qualified," Jenk told her. "But I'll do my best."

Beth dreamed of the days when he'd first brought her down into his basement hell. She dreamed of Number Four, of the screaming that had gone on and on and on. Screaming, and crying. Unholy noises. Sounds that a wounded animal might make.

She dreamed of the horrific thing that he'd carried down the stairs, with its fingerless hands and empty eye sockets. It seemed impossible that it could still be alive, with its hair gone and part of its skull exposed, but it was. It moved. *She* moved.

And then she spoke, her words impossibly clear from behind that sutured-shut mouth: "Time for your pill."

Beth awoke with a start. It wasn't Number Four who'd spoken to her. It was *him*.

He carried a tray with a plastic bowl and spoon. One of the antibiotic pills sat beside a plastic cup of water. He'd somehow figured out which drug Tracy had given to Beth, even though she'd tried to hide it. Of course he had. He always knew everything.

"Chicken soup," he told her. He must've gotten it when he went out. She could picture him in a grocery store, pushing his cart down an aisle, waiting patiently for an elderly lady to select her favorite brand of oatmeal. Lord, he'd been in a grocery store, and no one had known that he was the devil.

The screams from her dream continued—they weren't Number Four's. They were Tracy's. Number Twenty-One's. She was still alive.

The wind was howling, making the house creak and shiver, but not loud enough to mask the sounds from the basement.

The chicken soup smelled unbelievably good. It would be the first hot food she'd had in . . . She couldn't remember how long.

"Thank you so much," she told him, because she had to do this right. She had to be polite, even though she wanted nothing more than to kill him with that plastic spoon. "Will you sit with me for a while?"

She couldn't let him bring Tracy back into the kitchen. God knows what he'd done to her already, although from the sound of her screams she still had her tongue.

It was hard to eat the soup with him watching her with those awful eyes, with Tracy crying now. But she did it. And she kept it down. Took the pill. "I'm feeling much better," she lied.

"You should rest," he said, standing up and taking the tray from her lap.

"Wait," she said. "Please."

He turned back to her.

"You've been so kind." She choked the words out, fighting the bile that was rising in her throat. "I'm asking for one more kindness. Let me fight Number Twenty-One. Let me finish her off."

He didn't say a thing. He just turned, taking the tray into the kitchen.

"Please," Beth called after him. "I'm begging you. I'll do it your way. With your knife, if you want me to."

It took him a few minutes, but he finally came back. He was wearing the plaid hunter's jacket he always wore when she fought, and her relief was mixed with sorrow.

He'd brought her a plastic cup, too. Handed it to her. "Drink."

It was ginger ale. She obeyed him. Gave him back the empty cup. He tucked it under his arm because he was holding both his deadly little gun and the keys that would unlock her chains.

He tossed her the keys.

Deck hadn't asked her.

Dave glanced at him as he drove through the storm. According to the map, the road ahead of them was straight for the next few miles, so he picked up speed even though visibility was next to nothing.

Deck being Deck, he knew what Dave was thinking. "I know," he said. "I'm a coward."

"It wasn't exactly the right time," Dave pointed out. And it wasn't, with the news about both the signal from Gillman's jacket and the search warrant for this Nortman guy's house. It was, as always, disappointing to be sent away from the action, but Lindsey was alone out here, and the danger wasn't just from a serial killer. These roads were treacherous.

"It'll never be the right time," Deck admitted. "Because I just don't know how to—"

"Hello, Sophia?" Dave interrupted him. "It's me, Deck, the idiot. I was hoping you and I could have dinner sometime soon. How does the first Friday after we get back to California sound?" He looked at Decker. "Do you need me to repeat that?"

Deck shook his head. Muscles jumping in his jaw, as if he were preparing to face a gang of murderous ninjas, he dialed his phone.

He was actually doing it, actually calling. Dave had this sudden urge to swerve off the road, to knock the phone from his hands, to rewind the past few days.

To let Decker and Sophia continue to drift apart.

Sophia would get over Deck eventually, wouldn't she? And when she did, Dave would be there.

Deck held the phone to his ear, clearing his throat as he waited for her to pick up.

But then his eyes narrowed and he leaned forward, looking through both the frosted windshield and the snow. "Dave!"

Oh, shit. An enormous tree was down in front of them, completely blocking the road, and all his brakes did was lock the tires—they were worse than useless.

"Hang on!"

They were skidding sideways now, Deck's side of the truck heading directly for . . .

The side window shattered right before metal crunched. Dave saw Deck's phone sail into the air.

But then he saw nothing as the air bag punched him right in the face.

Chapter
Twenty

Lindsey got there first.

The house, looming through the swirling snow, was pure Stephen King—one of those Victorian three-storied monsters that cost a fortune to maintain, let alone heat in the winter. There were quite a few of them in this area, built as summer homes, no doubt at the turn of the century when business at the old hunting lodge had been thriving.

Like most that Lindsey had driven past, this one, too, was in a shabby state of disrepair. Peeling paint, broken gutters, missing slates on the roof, sagging porch.

Big windows with rotting frames, like vacant, lifeless eyes. A center door like a mouth open in a silent scream.

Yeah, Lindsey couldn't have found a creepier-looking house if she'd gone to the local real estate office and asked to see something in classic Batesian psychopath.

There was an outbuilding—a barn from the looks of it—by the road. Lindsey had cut her headlights long before she'd pulled up alongside of it and now lurked there in the swirling snow and gloom.

The barn probably wasn't a garage, since there was a car parked out in front of the house—a little beat-up Nissan, half-buried in snow, with nary a nine in the plate number.

On the drive over, Lindsey had gotten some information from the police, via Sophia, about the home's owner—one Peter Thornton. He'd inherited the house from an elderly uncle, seven years ago. That didn't fit their profile for Richard Eulie, their suspected killer. But . . . apparently,

Peter's brother, Dick—Dick, Richard?—had moved in with him . . . wait for it . . . three years ago.

And that did fit.

Especially since, after the brother showed up, Peter conveniently retired to Florida, never to be seen again.

He was, perhaps in truth, stashed in the attic.

His mummified body would be a special feature when it came time to resell the house—for that ever-growing number of serial killers in the real estate market.

Lindsey dialed Dave's cell, but got bumped right to voice mail. This house was right on the edge of a dead zone. The fact that she couldn't reach them hopefully meant that Dave and Decker were nearby. Any second now, they'd appear. She squinted out the car's rear window at the road behind her.

Any second now . . .

But they didn't come. And they still didn't come. She finally called Sophia, and actually got through. "Any news from Nortman's?"

"Nothing yet."

"Have you heard from Decker or Dave?"

"They're not there yet?" Sophia asked, concern in her voice. "Deck just called in, a few minutes ago, but . . . It was weird—as if the connection was there, but no one was on the other end. I tried calling back, but I couldn't get through. I'm going to try again after I'm off with you."

Their own connection was dreadful. "The wind out here is pretty intense," Lindsey told her. "It's possible one of the towers came down."

"Tess says the wind alone can affect the signal," Sophia reported. "Even if the towers stand."

Wonderful. "The roads are awful, too," Lindsey said. "It took me three times longer than I thought it would to get here." She described the house to Sophia.

"I've dug up some more info on Dick Thornton," Sophia in turn told her. "Nobody in town knows him very well—he really keeps to himself. He shops in the grocery store, but never stops to talk. Apparently, he disappears, sometimes for weeks at a time—speculation is he travels for business. But, other than the extended trips, he seems to be retired—putters around his yard, working on his car . . . Some people think he made a fortune from some Internet business, others think he inherited money, but they all agree that he doesn't live as if he's rich. Stella told me Rob was hoping to get some work, fixing up the house, but Thornton hasn't done any renovations at all—other than to put in a security system, which, frankly, everyone thinks is weird. To quote Stella, *Who needs a security system out here? Most folks don't even lock their doors.*"

Unless the system wasn't to keep people from getting in, but rather from getting *out*. Creepier and creepier.

There didn't seem to be any lights on in the house, although it was so big, the kitchen could be in the back, lights blazing, oven on. Dick Thornton could be baking Christmas cookies, getting ready to hunker down for an evening of watching *Rudolph* and *The Grinch*.

"Will you do me a favor and try calling Dave and Deck again?" Lindsey asked. Or he could be getting ready to do embroidery on Tracy's face. "Maybe you'll get through on Dave's phone. I just want to get an estimate of when they'll be here. This place is *freaking* weird. My spidey senses are tingling."

"Do not approach that house," Sophia ordered. "I'll call you right back."

Izzy wasn't armed.

It wasn't that the senior chief didn't trust him. Well, okay, it *was* that the senior chief didn't trust him, considering that after this was said and done, with Tracy safely home, Izzy was going to take an extended trip to Punishmentland.

The senior had provided weapons for all the other SEALs in the SUV. And had given specific instructions to Gillman to keep them out of Izzy's disobedient hands.

Still, Izzy was a body, and he was here with his boyz, and about five of the local police officers of varying shapes, sizes, and probably skill levels, considering that the guy with the beer gut was also unarmed. Although there was one little redheaded waif who looked about fourteen, who got to carry. No doubt she'd earned her Girl Scout firearms badge.

With the stealth of a herd of goats, they moved into place outside of Todd Nortman's little house in the big woods.

And it was a little house. It was the New England equivalent of a shotgun shack. Two rooms, tops. Nortman's ancient car, parked in front, was almost larger.

The car had a nine in the plate, and Tracy's mitten on the floor of the front seat.

Jesus Lord of heaven and earth, please let them find her here, unharmed.

The local police were in charge of this takedown, a uniformed officer named Morris waiting until he got the signal from Lopez that he and Gillman were positioned outside the back door.

The delay—what the hell was taking them so long?—made Izzy want to scream in frustration.

Waddling through the deep snow, clearly challenged by the weight of his bulletproof vest, Morris finally knocked on Nortman's door.

It opened immediately, revealing a little, wizened turtle-looking man, with an underbite, a nonexistent chin, and a bald head that he attempted to hide with a comb-over.

"Officer Morris," Nortman said, genuinely pleased to see him. "What a surprise. Bless your heart for coming all the way out in this storm to check up on Mother and me! Won't you come inside?"

Jesus H. Christ on a pogo stick.

If this was their killer, Izzy was his own grandmother.

Tracy didn't hear the door open because she was crying.

She did, however, see the light streaming down the flight of rough cellar stairs.

She also got a look around, which would have made her cry even harder, except for the fact that she'd vowed never again to let him see just how frightened she was. If she was going to scream, it was going to be for help.

She was chained to a wall, just as she'd thought, in a basement, just as she'd thought.

What she hadn't imagined were the bloodstains on the rough concrete floor. The pile of—oh dear God—human fingers, some of them recently severed, most of them little more than bones.

How many women had he brought down here to kill? All those eyelids, all those eyes?

But it wasn't him coming down the stairs, it was Beth. She leaned heavily on the railing, taking one step at a time.

Hope bloomed, until Tracy saw that he was right behind her, the light gleaming off the barrel of his gun.

As Lindsey got out of the rental car, her cell phone rang.

It was Jenk, as if he'd telepathically known that—after waiting for Decker and Dave for what seemed like forever—she'd finally decided to investigate the contents of that barn.

She got back in the car, restarted the engine and the heater. "Hello?" Just that two-second exposure to the elements had chilled her to the bone.

"Where are you?" he asked.

"Sitting in the car, outside this creepy-ass house, still waiting for Deck and Dave," she was able to tell him honestly.

"I'm pretty sure Nortman's not our man," Jenk informed her. "He's cooperating completely—he's willing to help in any way he can—fingerprinting, DNA tests. We're taking him up on that, although it'll be a while before we get the results."

"What does he look like?" Lindsey asked.

"Well, unless Tracy has a secret thing for Don Knotts . . . Hang on," Jenk said. "I'm going to send you a picture. If I lose you, I'll call you right back."

And there it was, right on the screen of Lindsey's phone. A photo of Todd Nortman. Wide, bulgy eyes and a comb-over and . . . yeah. Even tanked on tequila, Tracy would never have described Todd Nortman as a hot guy.

"He says he picked up Tracy on the night of the exercise," Jenk told her, "on the road behind the cabin. She was in his car for well over an hour, helping him deliver food baskets to what he calls neighbors in need. Although, if you could see this guy's house, you'd wonder why he's not at the top of his own list. Anyway, he says he dropped Tracy at the pharmacy—it's also a bus station—because he had more deliveries to make, and going to the Motel-A-Rama would've taken him too far out of his way. His mother—she's real, she's about a hundred and fifty years old. Apparently she would've worried if he was gone that long. He said there was one other car in the parking lot at the store—a dark-colored Impala that he didn't recognize. And this is a guy who knows everyone in town."

"Have you relayed this information to Sophia?"

"Affirmative," Jenk said. "I'm already on my way to you, with Gillman, Lopez, and Zanella. She told me to tell you that Decker and Dave have fallen off the map. She needs you to backtrack, to try to find them. Got your map?"

"I do." Lindsey picked it up, squinting at it in the dim afternoon light. She was far enough from the house not to be seen from the windows, but that would change if she put on the overhead light. She marked the map as Jenk rattled off a series of roads—the route Dave and Deck had been taking to reach her.

"While you're waiting for us, head back that way. See if maybe they went off the road."

Lindsey couldn't not say it. "If we go inside this house—when you get here—and Tracy's there and we're too late . . ." God. "The idea of turning around, of leaving her in there . . ."

"You'll be back," Jenk said. "Think of it as getting in there sooner. If you can find Deck and Dave . . ."

And if she didn't? "Just hurry," she told him.

Tracy—Number Twenty-One—stood up, chin defiantly high, chains clanking.

He hadn't hurt her.

Relief made Beth stumble, and he caught her arm, barrel of his gun jammed into her spine.

Only, now what? She'd come down here, thinking she'd find Tracy already tortured, already half-dead. Her intention had been to dispense mercy. To end her suffering.

Instead Beth locked eyes with her, remembering the words she'd mouthed behind his back. *Two against one.*

Lord, she was weak and dizzy. It was hard to stand, let alone think. And yet she hated him touching her. She pulled her arm away, taking the rest of the stairs on her own, venturing out into the dimly lit basement.

She cradled her injured arm, using it as an excuse to bring her hands up against her chest, hidden from him. She held up two fingers. And then one. Please Jesus, let Tracy understand.

This was where he'd throw Tracy the keys to her shackles—except he didn't.

Instead, he threw a knife. A switchblade. It clattered on the concrete at Beth's feet, opening to reveal a long, deadly blade.

She turned to look at him, at the gun he still held on her. She could hear Tracy's fear in the sound of her breathing—rapid now.

"Finish her," he ordered.

"She's chained," Beth protested.

"You're weak," he said. "Just finish her." He paused. "Or leave her for me."

The sound of persistent ringing roused him. His cell phone.

Wow, it was cold—how long had he been out? The air bag had bent his glasses.

Dave deflated it and—Jesus.

The stump of a tree branch, its end pointed and jagged as if Mother Nature had fashioned a giant spear, had pierced the side window, pinning Decker to his seat.

Calling it a stump was probably misleading, since it was three feet long, with a diameter of at least twelve inches where it met the trunk of the fallen tree.

Dave reached both for his phone and for Decker's throat—to check for a pulse—and discovered that his right wrist was broken.

Holy Mother, it hurt.

The fact that Decker didn't move wasn't a good sign, since Dave had just shouted in his ear.

He cradled his wrist as he answered the phone—it was Sophia, of course—tucking it between his shoulder and right ear, as he reached across himself with his other hand, praying that he'd find Deck still alive.

"Dave! Where have you been?"

A pulse. Thank God. But it felt weak. How long had they been sitting here, with the wind and snow blowing through that broken window? Decker had snow on his right eyebrow and ear, his shoulder and . . .

The stump of the branch had smaller branches attached to it, and one of them had stabbed Decker in the side. Right through his jacket and his shirt. It had broken off, so he wasn't still attached to the tree, but . . .

And now Dave was thankful for that broken window and the cold that had surely stanched the flow of Deck's blood. As it was, he'd lost a lot, soaking his clothes and pooling on the floor at his feet.

"We've had an accident," Dave told Sophia, as he tried to get a better look at Deck's injuries. "A tree came down—it's blocking the road." He gave her their location—on Burlington Road, about a half mile from the intersection of Mt. Trent.

No, the branch pinning Deck in was only going to prove a logistical nightmare in getting him out of the truck—it hadn't hurt him. At least not in addition to the undetermined length of wood sticking into his gut. "The truck's totaled. Decker's badly hurt."

"Oh, my God," Sophia breathed as he described the injury. "I've called for help, but I don't know when they'll be able to get there."

"As long as we're asking for the impossible, we're going to need a medic," Dave said, as he looked at his map. "You might as well request that, too. As far as I can tell, the closest house is that of the Misses Rogers and Kittford." The pot ladies. Although their home was at least five miles back. Five miles, through a dead zone, where he'd have no contact, no chance to call for help. Which was moot, since there was no help to be had.

Apparently Sophia was looking at a map, too. "You're going to walk five miles through a blizzard, carrying an injured man?"

With a broken wrist, but she didn't need to know that.

"Who loves ya, baby?" Dave did his best Kojak, but of course she didn't recognize it. She was too young.

She said something back, but he couldn't make it out, not before their connection crackled and died. Which made the dead zone thing doubly moot.

Dave pocketed his phone—Decker's, too, grabbing it from the floor. "Okay, Deck," he said, taking several deep breaths, getting ready to take the unconscious man beneath his arms and pull him across the parking brake. There was no way he could do it without using his broken wrist. "I take comfort in knowing that this is going to hurt you as much as it hurts me."

"Finish her," the monster said, "or leave her for me."

Tracy could see indecision in Beth's eyes—the woman was actually considering it.

Two against one. Beth had been flashing hand signals to Tracy when she'd first come down here, two fingers and then one, but now she'd stopped. Now she looked at that knife as if she actually might use it. But then she looked back, hard, into Tracy's eyes.

"Look at her," Beth said. "She's terrified. Sure, she's standing there as if she's not, but I take one step toward her? She'll cower in the corner and cry."

Okay, there was a definite message there. Beth lifted her foot, took a deliberate step toward Tracy.

"Don't hurt me, don't hurt me," Tracy said, curling into herself. The tears were easy to produce, even while thinking, *please dear God, let Beth have some kind of a plan.* Two against one was well and good, but he had a gun. Of course, if they both attacked him, he could only shoot one of them at a time. Providing they were close enough to him . . .

"Let her have the keys," Beth told the monster.

"No," he said. "You have until ten, nine . . ."

Resignation replaced hope in Beth's feverish gaze. "I'm sorry," she whispered to Tracy. "I tried."

"Eight . . ."

"I'm so sorry. I'll make it quick, I promise." Beth advanced, holding that knife in a clearly practiced stance. "I can't let him take you."

"Seven . . ."

"Please don't," Tracy said, but Beth wasn't Beth anymore. She'd changed—into Number Five. Her eyes were feral, her face tight.

"I'll make it quick," she said again. "It'll be over, and you'll be free. Water will punch you, but you won't feel a thing."

Okay, now she sounded as well as looked crazy.

"Six . . ."

Tracy backed away from that blade, as far as her chains would allow her. "Don't do this," she said. Dear God, she didn't want to die. "Help! Someone *help me!*"

Lindsey couldn't do it.

She couldn't leave, not without checking the barn to see if another car was inside.

And sure enough, as she went through the side door, she could see it there, in the gloom. It was covered with a tarp. She lifted the heavy canvas and . . .

A dark blue Impala. New Hampshire plates. Complete with a nine.

She should have called Tom Paoletti right then and there. Except he would have ordered her back to her car, to wait for the freaking backup.

Instead, she made the decision to approach the house. Just to walk around the outside. Quietly. Stealthily. Maybe look in a window or two. Get as much information as she possibly could.

The wind was howling, and the snow was blowing. No one would see her or hear her. And even if they did, she'd do her so-called ninja thing and get herself to safety.

The shades were down in the front of the house.

Lindsey saw the security system that Sophia had told her about. Drat, she should have asked for more details. Although, with this wind, any motion detectors would have to be off, or the system would be tripped every ten seconds.

She rounded the back of the house. There was a little porch, and a back door that led into a drab kitchen, where a single light was on.

It was there, as she looked into the window, that she heard it.

Someone help me!

And then no words, just screams. Long, piercing, high-pitched screams.

She had her phone out and dialing. First Sophia. Then Tom Paoletti. Both times, she was bumped straight to voice mail.

She called Jenk. Same thing.

She left him a message: "Please don't be mad. And please, God, I hope you're close. I'm still here at the Thorntons'. There's an Impala in the barn, with a nine in the plate. I've heard screaming from the house— a female who sounds like Tracy begging for help. I can't wait for backup— I'm going in."

Lindsey pocketed her phone and looked more closely at the security system. No way was she getting into the house without Richard Eulie knowing about it.

Which meant that there was only one thing to do.

When the news came in about Dave and Decker's accident, Jenk asked Lopez, who was taking the call, to find out if Lindsey was with them.

"No," Lopez reported, "and Sophia says she hasn't heard from her in a while."

Those were not the words Jenk wanted to hear.

"We're approaching from a different direction," Lopez continued his phone conversation, "so we don't need to worry about the downed tree, but Danny's marking it on the map."

"Can't we go any faster?" Izzy fretted from the backseat.

"I'm going as fast as I can," Jenk told him. "Visibility's about eighteen inches. If I get up too much speed, same thing that happened to Dave and Deck could happen to us."

"I could fucking run faster than this," Izzy said. "Even in knee-deep snow."

Yeah, Jenk could, too. In fact . . . He jammed his hat onto his head, and zipped up his jacket. But stopping on these roads was a four-ring circus. Even if they didn't slide into a ditch, getting started again would be another whole event.

But at this speed, they didn't have to stop.

"Gillman, take the wheel," Jenk ordered. "Right now. Just slide over."

Gillman thrust the map he was holding back to Lopez, as Jenk opened the window. The wind was blowing too hard to open the door.

A boatload of snow swirled into the car, and the wind pushed the map up into Lopez's face. "Hey, I'm trying to talk on the phone! It's hard enough to hear . . ."

Jenk hoisted himself up so that he was sitting on the open window, with the SUV still in motion. Before he pulled his legs out, he turned on the brights, which, with the whiteout from the snow, brought visibility down to even less than eighteen inches. That, however, was going to change.

"Dude!" In the back, Izzy had rolled down his window, too. "You're the balls! I'll relieve you in ten."

Jenk nodded, and ran—easily—past the SUV. Without the glare from the windshield, his visibility increased—not by much, but by enough. Of course, it was a lot colder out here. Not that he felt it. He positioned him-

self about twenty feet in front of the vehicle, right where the headlights reflected off his jacket, and hauled ass.

Gillman, driving behind him, picked up speed.

Was there a good way to die?

Tracy had always thought that dying in her sleep would be the best
way to go. To just go to bed one night and never wake up. It would be
peaceful and painless.

Now, however, her two choices were both violent and painful—quick,
via Beth's knife, or slow, with the monster in his death-kitchen.

"Just close your eyes and it'll all be over soon," Beth said, over Tracy's
screams for help, as the monster droned on, "Six . . . Five . . ."

No. She couldn't. She wouldn't. If she was going to die, she would die
fighting.

Tracy stopped screaming and kicked at Beth with her best Tae Bo
roundhouse, knowing full well that she was probably going to get stabbed.
Tae Bo was about muscle toning, not self-defense. But she couldn't just
stand there and be slaughtered.

She missed the knife, instead hitting Beth's other arm—the injured one.

Beth cried out, fumbling with the knife. Tracy kicked her again—damn
this chain that jerked her back! But the knife fell to the floor with a clatter.

Her opponent was sick and injured—which was at least as big a handi-
cap as Tracy's chain—possibly more so. She tried to land a third kick, but this
time Beth was ready for her, grabbing her leg and knocking her off-balance.

Tracy landed on the concrete, on her back, all the air forced from her
lungs. Beth leaped on top of her, her hands around Tracy's throat.

Dear God, no! Now she really couldn't breathe.

But then, as she fought to throw Beth off of her, she could breathe.
Beth's grip had loosened, yet she still held on to her.

"Die!" Beth told her, shaking Tracy as if she were still squeezing the
life from her. "Die!"

And Tracy understood. She jerked and thrashed. And then went limp.
As Beth's hands left her throat, she forced herself not to move, not to gasp
for air. She could hear Beth breathing hard.

She heard the monster speak. Chidingly, churlishly. "You said you'd
use the knife."

"She overpowered me," Beth told him. "I'm not as well as I'd . . . oh . . ."

Tracy heard a sound that had to be Beth collapsing beside her, onto
the floor. She didn't dare open her eyes to look.

Would he approach? Thinking Tracy dead and Beth unconscious? Beth surely had that knife near her.

Unless she really had fainted.

Please let this work. Please God . . .

It was then that something hit Tracy, hard, in the back. It was all she could do not to move, to react, to flinch from the sudden pain.

It was water. From some sort of high-pressure hose.

Beth had warned her about this, back when Tracy thought she was talking crazy. *Water will punch you . . .*

He was testing her, testing them both.

She forced herself to remain limp, to let the water push her. And finally, after what seemed like minutes, but surely was mere seconds, he shut it off.

Tracy heard a *clunk* as he set down whatever it was—a tank?

She heard the steps creak as he descended the stairs, coming all the way into the basement. She heard his footsteps on the concrete.

And she braced herself, praying that Beth was bracing herself, too, ready to attack him—*two against one*—when he got close enough.

Ding-dong.

The man stopped.

What was that? Distant, from up the stairs . . . ?

It rang again. *Ding-dong.*

A doorbell?

He turned, and went back upstairs, picking up whatever he'd left on the steps. He shut the door behind him, locking them into darkness.

Lindsey stood on the sagging porch of Serial Killer Central, and rang the bell again.

She had her .22 in her hand, in her left jacket pocket, her finger on the trigger as the door opened, and there he was. Tracy's hot guy— although in truth he looked more like Sean Bean than Ralph Fiennes.

He had GQ stubble—and eyes that reminded her of a chicken's. Or maybe a snake's. Or both. She was convinced that birds and reptiles were more closely related than one would think, considering the seemingly vast difference between feathers and scales and okay, a little focus would be nice.

"I am *so* sorry," Lindsey said, doing her best impression of a small, help- less female, "my car went off the road about a mile back. I've been walking and walking and thank God I found your house. Please, may I come inside?"

CHAPTER
TWENTY-ONE

B eth's head pounded.

When he'd sprayed her, the water had pushed her back into the wall, and she'd hit her head. As if she wasn't dizzy enough from being ill.

She sat up in the darkness—he'd turned off the light—touching her head. Her hand came away wet. Warmer than the water. Sticky.

Bloody.

"Beth?"

She heard the clank of the chain as Tracy shifted.

"I'm still here," Beth said. Like she'd be anywhere else. She started to laugh, except it came out sounding like sobs.

"Thank you for not killing me," Tracy whispered.

Lot of good that had done. Lord, they had been so close. For the first time in forever, Beth had had real hope. *Two against one* . . . They could kill him and end this nightmare. But the truth was that she'd never be free, never again.

"It's occurred to me," Tracy said, "that he may not have bullets for his gun. Or maybe it's not real. He had it—the gun—in the pharmacy, but he killed the clerk by bashing in his head. Have you ever heard or seen him use it?"

"Shhh!"

The floorboards creaked directly overhead as he moved into the kitchen. Beth could hear the murmur of his voice—he was talking to someone. A reply—the second voice was higher-pitched. Female. The person who'd rung the doorbell was a woman, God help her.

Another wave of dizziness swept through her.

God help them all.

Marky-Mark's cell phone beeped from the slot in the dash, where he'd left it before he did his little Mario Andretti exit-the-car-from-the-window trick.

They were moving about three times faster than they had been, but fucking slow times three was still fucking slow. Still it was better than nothing.

Izzy leaned over the front seat, taking the phone and looking at it. Jenk had a message. From Lindsey—whom Sophia had lost contact with. "What's Jenkins's cell phone code?"

No one answered him.

"I know you know it, Lopez," Izzy insisted. "Cough it up, this could be important. It's from Lindsey."

"Yoda," Lopez told him. "You know—nine six three two."

Yoda. Right. Jenkins was a *Star Wars* nerd. Izzy keyed in the numbers, brought the phone to his ear. And listened to Lindsey tell Jenk that she wasn't waiting for backup. She'd heard screams that might be Tracy—Christ—and she was going inside.

Izzy opened his window and climbed out of the still-moving car.

Lindsey sat at the kitchen table while a kettle heated on the gas stove.

"This is a wonderful house," she lied. "Perfect for a large family."

Richard Eulie—and it had to be him. She was 95 percent certain. But Eulie hadn't offered to take her jacket, so she'd kept it on. Even if he had, she would have made some excuse about being too chilled to take it off, so she could keep her hand on her weapon. She kept its barrel aimed at the suspect as he moved about the kitchen, getting mugs and a canister of tea bags from a creaky-doored pantry.

Not that she'd actually drink anything he gave her, but when he'd offered, she had told him that a cup of something hot would be nice. It gave him something to do instead of sitting silently across from her at the table. He was extremely taciturn—he'd said maybe three sentences to her since he'd let her inside.

The kitchen was large but as shabby as the outside of the house. It had ancient linoleum—complete with a faded but totally un-PC picture of a smiling, turban-clad African American woman à la Aunt Jemima, right in the center of the room.

An old-style, stand-alone gas range with a griddle in the middle, was across from the door to the hallway. Its white ceramic sides were rounded, same as the ancient icebox over on the other side of the kitchen, but both were grimy and discolored. The sink, positioned in front of a window, had similar ceramic cabinets beneath it. Someone had attempted to build a counter in the corner between the sink and the stove, but their lack of skill left it crooked, like a badly constructed workbench. Its surface had at one time been covered with colorful Mexican tiles, many of which were missing. The rest were cracked and chipped.

Something definitely didn't smell right in here. Not as bad as if there were a body stuffed under the sink or in the pantry, but something was definitely funky.

And this table, at which she was sitting, had had its finish completely scoured off. It had been cleaned recently—she could feel the residue of the cleanser, gritty beneath her fingers.

The lights flickered but didn't go out. "Maybe we should light some candles," she said. "You know, before the power goes? It's probably better to find them now, rather than crashing around in the dark—"

"I don't have candles," he said.

Of course not. Serial killers thrived in the darkness. "Not even birthday cake candles?" she asked. "Everyone has birthday cake candles."

A can of Campbell's Chicken and Rice soup sat on the tiled counter, along with a handcrank opener. A two-liter bottle of ginger ale was next to a pill bottle—its label that of the pharmacy that had been robbed.

"I don't. Besides, the power's already out. The generator's on. It won't fail." He smiled. "Unless I want it to."

Okay. Lindsey wasn't close enough to check the name on that pill bottle, but she did gesture toward it. "Looks like someone in your house has been fighting a bug," she said, herself fighting the urge to just plug him. Right there. Pump him full of bullets until he was dead. Of course, if she turned out to be wrong about his identity, she'd never forgive herself. "I had *such* a sinus infection last month—it just would not go away. I had to have a double dose of the antibiotic. What a pain in the butt."

There was a door with a window next to the sink—it was that back door that she'd peered through when she'd heard those screams. All was silent now, but she'd definitely heard something. She hadn't imagined it.

What had he done to the woman who'd screamed?

A door, hanging half-open, knob gone, led to the dimness of the pantry. Another door, right next to it, was closed and locked with a series of dead bolts. Its hinges were shiny, as if they'd been replaced far more recently than the other renovations to the kitchen, which probably dated back to 1939.

"And of course the stomach flu's going around," Lindsey continued, "it's that time of year. You know I heard there's this new anti-nausea medication that really works and . . . Is it your wife who's sick?"

He made a sound that might've been yes, might've been no, as the kettle began to whistle. He turned off the gas, poured the water into the mugs. Tall and lean, he was one of those men who looked really good in faded jeans, especially from the rear. Yes, he had an attractive back-of-the-head, in a plaid hunting jacket and hiking boots kind of way. And his face would have been handsome, too, if not for those eyes.

No doubt about it, from the distance in particular, he might've been mistaken by Tracy as a very hot guy.

But up close . . . Brrrr.

"I'm so sorry," Lindsey told him. "And then for me to come barging in . . ."

It was then that she saw it. Hanging in the window, over the kitchen sink. Drying on what looked like an embroidery hoop.

He saw her see it—long golden hair. Human hair—Connie Smith's? Still attached to a scalp.

She considered bluffing—*what an interesting dream catcher*—but really, why bother? He'd seen her eyes widen.

"I'm armed, Mr. Eulie," she told him. "Keep your hands up, in sight, or I'll shoot you, right here, right now."

"I haven't been called that in a long time." He'd turned back to get the mugs, and now he froze, his better side to her, his hands on the counter. "Your hair's not long enough," he said. "It won't look as good. But you'll scream as I slip the knife between your scalp and your skull—"

"Don't talk," she ordered him, taking out her phone. "Don't move, don't talk."

"I'll miss this place," he said. "I liked it here."

"Shut. Up." She dialed Jenk's number. Nothing. Sophia. Tom. Dave. No one answered, damn it. How long was she going to have to sit here with him, like this?

He turned his head slightly to look at her reproachfully. "Be polite, and I'll kill you quick."

To hell with that. Lindsey pulled the trigger and shot him, right through the pocket of her jacket.

·   ·   ·

Jenk ran even faster.

"Mark," Izzy said, running alongside him. "Let me do this for a while. Go back to the car."

"How much farther?" he asked.

"I don't know exactly," Izzy told him. "Somewhere between three and five miles."

Lindsey should have waited. But *he* wouldn't have waited if he'd heard screaming.

"Go call her," Izzy persisted. "Maybe you'll get through. Maybe it's all over. Maybe she shot him when he answered the door."

And maybe she hadn't. Maybe he'd overpowered her. Maybe he was with her right now, cutting her.

"Call her," Izzy said. "Take five minutes, get warm, then get back out here. My ass is already freezing off."

Eulie didn't fall.

He dove for the doorway leading into the hall.

Lindsey fired again, but he was through it and gone.

There was no blood, no spatter, no spray. She'd hit him with that first shot—she'd seen his body jerk from the impact—so there should have been blood.

Unless he was wearing some kind of body armor beneath that jacket.

Weapon held at ready, in her right hand now, with her left steadying her grip, Lindsey stood with her back pressed against the kitchen wall, next to that door to the hall.

She looked—just a quick peek, leading with her handgun.

The hall to the right ended at the doorway to a small bathroom.

To the left, it led down for quite some ways. What looked to be a living room was off to the right of that, a series of closed doors to the left. It opened into the front foyer, where there was a curved staircase going up. Lindsey couldn't see it from the kitchen, but she knew it was there. She'd seen it when she'd first come in.

Eulie was nowhere in sight. She could only hope that he'd taken that first bullet and had crawled off somewhere to die.

And okay. All right. She would bet big money that Tracy was in the basement behind that door with the new hinges. How else could Lindsey have heard those screams so clearly while standing out in the backyard?

Once she found Tracy, they'd hunker down here in the kitchen, waiting for reinforcements to arrive.

Lindsey now quickly built a barricade, tipping the table onto its side. They could huddle here, between the table and the fridge. And Lindsey would shoot anyone who came through that kitchen door.

Although, God, what if there was a second route down to the basement? What if Lindsey was wrong, and that wasn't the basement at all, but instead another closet?

Before she could get to the door and unlock the bolts—as quietly as possible—the lights went out.

Great. She definitely hadn't killed Eulie. And now Eulie had killed the generator.

So much for her theory that he didn't have bullets for his gun. Tracy was shaking, but at least she wasn't dead yet. It felt very good to not be dead. "Do you think that he killed her?"

And who exactly was the woman who'd come to the door? Lindsey? Tess? Alyssa? Tracy knew that the Troubleshooters were looking for her. They had to be. Except it didn't make sense. Why send only one person—a woman—to the door? Why not bring an entire team crashing through the windows, like in the movies?

Unless the woman at the door was just an unlucky Mary Kay representative. Or a political petitioner, looking for a signature. Or . . .

"No." Beth's voice was grim in the darkness, even with its soft Southern twang. Grim, but slurred, almost as if she were drunk or on the verge of falling asleep. "He'd never shoot to kill. Never."

"Why isn't she screaming?" Tracy strained her ears, but she heard nothing. Not even the squeak of footsteps on the floor overhead.

"I don't know. Lord, I'm going to be sick. I'm going to . . . Connie Smith, Jennifer Denfield, Yvette Wallace, Paula Kettering . . ."

"Beth," Tracy said sharply, feeling for the other woman in the darkness, hands out, searching. "Don't lose it." And wasn't that just too crazy? She herself was on the verge of panic. It was crowding her throat, filling her with fear and dread—and *she* was the levelheaded one. "Stay with me. We need to make a plan."

"A plan."

She connected with Beth's leg. "Where's your hand?" There it was. Thin and cold, her grip not as strong as Tracy had hoped. Her chains clanked. Step one in any plan would involve getting out of these chains. "Do you know where he keeps his keys?"

"In the kitchen, on a hook by the door," Beth said, her voice getting even softer. Almost dreamy. "I've never seen it, but he told me. He always told me, because he knew I'd never get there, I'd never reach them. I was always chained—"

"You're not chained now," Tracy told her, giving her a shake. "Can you make it over to the stairs, and turn on the light? At least then we can see what our options are."

"If I turn on the light, he'll know. Connie Smith, Jennifer Denfield, Yvette Wallace—"

"Beth!"

"—Paula Kettering, Wendy Marino, Julia Telman . . . Lord, I think he . . . He must've . . . drugged me."

Beth pulled her hand free, and Tracy heard her scrambling away. She heard sounds of retching, as if Beth had jammed her finger down her throat.

"How did he drug you?" she asked. Dear God, she didn't want to be left alone here in the darkness.

"In the soup," Beth gasped. "Or the ginger ale. He usually drugs me . . . after the fight . . . so he can chain me back up . . . He must've . . . planned . . . Didn't unchain you . . . Knew it would be . . . fast . . ."

"Where's the knife?" Tracy asked, through the tears that she couldn't stop from streaming down her face. Beth was checking out, and she was going to be alone here in the dark. "At least let me have the knife."

And there it was. Cold and hard in her hand.

"Use it," Beth breathed. "Finish me."

"*What?*"

"When he finds out I didn't kill you . . . He'll take one of us upstairs," Beth told her, weeping now, too. "I don't want to die like that. Please . . . Please . . . Finish me."

Sophia couldn't stand it another second. Everyone was having trouble with the snow and ice. Everyone was moving as quickly as they could, but despite that, it was going to be hours before Dave and Decker got the help they needed.

"I'm leaving my post," she told Tess, who manned the computer.

"Sophia, you can't." Tess spoke the words, but her expression countered them.

Sophia knew that Tess was nearly as worried about Dave and Decker as she was. "I'll get Stella and Rob to help you. They know these roads much better than I do, anyway."

"Lindsey took the only car," Tess said.

"Rob's got a truck with a plow." His back was out, or he'd be out there using it himself. As it was, he could barely hobble from his bed to the restaurant and back.

"The plow that's attached to the truck that he doesn't even let Stella drive?" Tess asked. "You think he's going to let you borrow—"

"I'm not going to ask," Sophia said. "I don't need a key to get it started." She would hot-wire it. It was one of the skills she'd picked up, living on the streets of a third-world country.

Tess's eyebrows went up. But she wasn't convinced. "Have you ever used a plow before?"

"No, but when I applied to work for Troubleshooters Incorporated, I put on my résumé, *Up for Learning New Skills,*" Sophia said.

"I'm in charge here, and officially? I can't let you do this."

Sophia nodded. "Unofficially?"

Tess tossed over her motel room key. "I know you're allergic to wool, but tough, you'll just have to itch. Wear at least two of my sweaters. And at least two pairs of socks. Take plenty of supplies. Blankets. Wear one of the training jackets so I can track you. And take the first-aid kit from the kitchen. I am *so* going to get my butt kicked for this. Probably worst of all by Decker and Dave."

Provided Sophia found them alive.

Lindsey turned on the gas stove. All four burners. The flames lit the kitchen, creating shadows that leaped and jumped on the walls.

It was better than nothing.

She was ready for him, for when he came back. And he would come back, of that she had no doubt.

Was he really wearing body armor? If she got the opportunity to shoot him again, she'd aim for his head.

A far-more-burning question, though, was whether or not he was armed. For all she knew, he had a closet filled with AK-47s somewhere in this rambling house.

All she had were her handguns with their limited range—even more limited since she was now going for headshots. She was a decent enough marksman, but a human head was a very small target. Especially considering the adrenaline that was coursing through her system.

Lindsey had just unlocked the door to the basement, throwing the bolts as silently as possible, when her cell phone shook. It was Jenk, thank God.

"I'm in, it's him," she whispered, moving so that her back was to the wall, behind the barricade she'd made from the kitchen table. "What's your ETA? Please say *now* or *soon.*"

But he didn't. Instead, he said, "Shit. We're still at least three miles away. When we're moving, we're doing about an eight-minute mile, but the weather's getting worse. All the local backup has been shut down—everyone's been ordered to get to shelter."

"Shit," she agreed. "Because the next thing I was going to ask you for was an ambulance or a Medevac helicopter. I haven't found Tracy yet, but . . ." She had to take a deep breath, glancing at the gleaming ring of hair still hanging above the sink, remembering Eulie's words. *You'll scream as I slip the knife between your scalp and your skull . . .* "I have a nasty feeling we're going to need medical help when we do."

"I've got Lopez with me, and—damnit! There's ice on the roads, beneath the snow. We are just not making it up this hill. We've been in and out of the SUV, pushing it for twenty minutes now."

"Get to shelter," she told him, her heart sinking.

"Not a chance. We're—"

"Shhh," she said. What was that sound? Floorboards as someone crept closer? Or just the old house creaking in the wind? "Look, I came inside, pretending my car went off the road. He let me in, we talked, it became clear he was Eulie, so . . . God, Mark, I shot him. But I think he's wearing body armor, because it didn't drop him. No blood. He's somewhere in this house, the power's out, and I can't talk now—I've got to listen for him. Just . . . be safe."

She cut the connection, but her phone shook almost immediately as he text messaged her. *Hng on. On my way 2 U.*

Find shelter, she messaged back. *Dont die.*

On my way.

Cant help me if U R dead, she messaged.

Get out, he messaged back. *Wait fr us in ur car.*

Yeah? Like hell. *Cant leave Tracy,* she told him.

OK. I cant fnd shltr. Get it?

God, there was definitely a sound coming from the hallway. She dropped her phone and held her weapon with both hands.

And water exploded, directly into her face.

Lindsey covered her eyes with her left elbow, trying to move, but trapped between the table and the refrigerator, there was no place to go. He was spraying the wall across from her with some kind of high-pressure hose, and the water bounced off, drenching her, choking her, stinging and cold.

She turned, trying to spot him but, of course, he was standing out of range, way back in the hall. She fired her handgun anyway, trying to blast him right through the plaster wall.

Just as suddenly as it started, it stopped, and all she could hear was her heart hammering and water, dripping off the table, off her face, into the puddle she now sat in on the floor.

She was soaked to the skin.

The son of a bitch had limited her options. He'd made it impossible for her to grab Tracy and run. She wouldn't last ten minutes out in the freezing storm with wet clothes.

"I've got a team of Navy SEALs coming as backup," she called out to him. "They'll be here in minutes."

"Thanks for the tip," he called back from what sounded like the living room. "I'll work faster. Of course, when they come, I'll kill them, too."

And, with a shriek, the smoke alarm went off.

Beth was Tracy's only hope.

"No one's finished," she told Beth as somewhere in the house a smoke alarm started ringing. She couldn't think about what that meant—if the house truly was on fire and she was chained down here. "We're still fighting. We'll use this knife, but we'll use it on him. Now I need you to go up those stairs and turn on the light."

But Beth had given in to the drugs the monster had fed her. She'd given up.

The drugs he'd used must've been some sort of roofie-type deal, because Beth was still talking, still seemingly conscious, though very woozy. She was even able to move—she was just very compliant and relaxed.

"Please," Beth begged. "Finish me."

"I'll finish you," Tracy lied, "if that's really what you want. But wouldn't you rather be set free?"

Beth was back to muttering and chanting that list of names. Jennifer whatever and Cathy something.

"Go up those stairs," Tracy ordered her, "and turn on the light. Can you do that?"

Beth didn't answer. She just dragged herself away.

. . .

Jenk lost Lindsey.

It was as if her phone had gone completely dead.

"God damn it," he said. "Lopez, use your phone—try calling Lindsey."

He had his back to the rear of the SUV, as they all slipped and slid, trying to get enough traction to push the vehicle up the hill.

"I'm not getting through," Lopez reported.

"It's windy as shit," Izzy said. "Maybe a tower went down."

Or maybe Eulie had smashed Lindsey's phone, then smashed in her head, and . . .

The fucking SUV slid a good twenty-five feet back down the road, despite their efforts to prevent it from doing so.

Gillman swore. Loudly.

"Leave it," Jenk said. He opened the back to get his weapon, opened the front to get the map.

Lindsey needed him. Right now.

It was time to use the only form of transportation he could absolutely count on. It was time to run.

The piece of wood that had pierced Decker's side wasn't quite as long as Dave had feared.

He'd imagined a nine- or ten-inch spike, skewering all of Deck's internal organs.

Instead, it was about two inches long and skinny, like a giant splinter. Well, really, more like nature's own shiv. And yeah, Decker had bled, appropriately enough, like a stuck pig, but his unconscious state more likely came from a blow he'd received to his head.

He was still out, the bastard, which meant that Dave had to carry him. Through blowing snow that stung his face—like being hit with BBs made of ice. Through drifts that were sometimes as high as his hips.

He staggered and tweaked his broken wrist, almost dropping Deck as the pain made him shout. He cursed the storm, he cursed Deck, but most of all he cursed himself.

Back in the car, right before they'd crashed, he'd called Decker a coward. So what did that make him?

Who loves ya, baby?

No, really, he should have said to Sophia, when he'd had her on the phone. *Why don't you ever just stop and get your bearings? Take a deep breath and look around you—and see who really loves you.*

His world had shrunk down to pain and cold. But he would get through this—he'd been through worse. He'd carry Deck to safety, be the hero of the hour—not that anyone would notice him.

He'd watch, silently, while Sophia fell into Decker's arms.

"I should just drop you in a drift," he told Deck, who, of course, didn't respond.

The smoke alarms screamed—even before Eulie tossed what looked like draperies onto the lit gas stove.

At first Lindsey thought he was trying to cut the light, but then she realized he'd thrown newspaper onto it, too. It burst into flame.

He was trying to set the house on fire.

Gun held at ready—thank God she'd invested in a firearm that could withstand a good dousing—she moved to the hall doorway. He'd vanished again.

But her quick peek down the hall had revealed flickering light— flames—coming from the living room.

Yup. The house was on fire.

The good news was that if he tried to come down the hall again, he'd be silhouetted against the light from the flames.

The bad news was that the house was on fire. Lindsey's phone had been trashed by that high-pressure drenching. She was soaking wet, too.

And, oh yeah, outside? They were having the blizzard of the century.

Leaving the shelter of the house was not an option, but if she didn't put that fire out, soon, it would become a necessity.

Lindsey pulled the curtains and the paper from the stove, stomping out the flames.

She had to go into the living room—put out the fire he'd started there, too. Except that was what Eulie wanted her to do. He'd be waiting for her, ready to kill her, but not with a gun.

No, he'd told her how he wanted to kill her—with the blade of his knife.

Revulsion filled her, along with its companion, fear. And for the first time since she'd left her car and pressed her finger against that doorbell, Lindsey realized that she could very well die. Right here. At this man's hands.

Horribly.

Fear was not a new emotion—she'd been afraid, plenty of times before in her life. No one spent seven years on the LAPD without experiencing total, bowel-clearing fear.

And she'd had the added bonus of living in fear that her mother would die, starting back when she was a child.

Still, this particular fear was intense. She was all but alone in a dark house, in the height of a howling storm, with a true monster of a serial killer.

Lindsey had learned as a cop that it wasn't the fear but rather what she did with it that mattered. She had to set it aside. She had to think clearly, keep her wits about her. She had to find and then kill this beast, put out the fire he'd started, and locate Tracy. Then and only then would there be time to tremble and shake.

She took a deep breath, exhaled hard.

Another. And another.

She wished her phone still worked. Even just looking at Jenk's text messages would've helped. She wasn't afraid when he was around. Or maybe she was. Maybe, though, when she was with him she was just too busy living her life—enjoying her life—to notice just how frightened she was.

I cant fnd shltr. Get it?

Jenk couldn't find shelter the same way Lindsey couldn't leave Tracy. Not couldn't—*wouldn't*. She got it. She did. But it was too late to tell him so.

Okay, no. That was defeatist thinking. She would tell him. It wasn't too late. She had tentative plans with him. For this coming weekend, and for Christmas. Tentative could become definite—all she had to do was tell him yes.

And she would—as soon as she saw him again.

God, Lindsey was tired of living as if she didn't have a future. She wanted a life that was more than going to work and then hiding in her apartment. This was, of course, a hell of a time to realize that—while on the verge of having all of her choices taken from her in a very permanent way by a man who wanted to add her hair to his nasty-ass collection.

But maybe this was what she'd needed to get her life back on track. Serial killer therapy. Fifty minutes trapped in a house with Richard Eulie. If she survived with her scalp still attached, she'd emerge empowered with the knowledge of what truly was important in life.

Making Mark Jenkins laugh.

Smiling back at him.

Watching his eyes soften as he looked at her, when he thought she didn't notice.

His kisses, so sweet, turning to fire . . .

No way was she going to let Eulie hurt her. And double no way would she let him hurt Mark.

She was not going to lose him—not to some killer. She may have lived in fear of her mother dying, helpless to prevent things over which she had no control.

But this was completely different.

She knew what Eulie wanted—to look into her eyes and see her fear as she died. It was possible he would shoot her, but he wouldn't shoot to kill, only to wound.

Getting shot would hurt, but she'd been shot before.

She'd let him look into her eyes, all right.

Eulie wanted her in the living room? She'd go into that living room. She had to get this fire out, and then she had to find Tracy.

But first, she'd give this bastard more than he'd ever bargained for.

Number Five was halfway up the stairs—she was so dizzy, each step was a seemingly insurmountable challenge.

It was so dark, it would just be so easy to close her eyes.

"Keep going," Tracy called. Assuming that really was Tracy's voice and not some hallucination.

She was floating in that place where time and space warped and bent. There was a noise—a siren wailing. It got louder as she climbed. Danger. It was dangerous to come up these stairs. If he knew, if he found out . . .

Number Four was there with her, then, with her horrible face, with the whimpers of pain she made behind that mouth that was sewn shut.

"Oh Lord, oh Lord . . ."

"Beth?"

He'd shown her some of the others—what he'd done to them. But he'd done it after they were dead, after she'd killed them.

Five knew he'd shown them to her as a reminder. This was why she finished them. This was why she obeyed him, why she always did what he said.

"Beth, are you still there?"

Beth. Her name was Beth, not Number Five.

"I'm still here," she called back, her fingers finally closing on the light switch on the wall by the door.

But when she flipped it, nothing happened. No light. No change. No salvation.

Beth started to cry. She collapsed against the door—which creaked opened. And there she was. In his kitchen.

The stove was on, flames leaping and jumping.

This was where he'd done it—where he'd killed Number Four and cut up all the others.

And there was the key—right where he'd said it was, hanging on the wall, where he'd said she'd never reach it.

She grabbed it and stumbled back downstairs.

Dave's world had narrowed to one step and then one more step and then another step. Each time, he jarred his broken wrist. An inhale. An exhale. He breathed through the pain.

And sometimes he managed it by talking to Decker.

"The next time you give me that *you're not a Navy SEAL* scornful look, I want you to remember this. That I carried you. All this way. Without complaining. And a few months from now? When you and Sophia are making your wedding plans? I want you to remember who made you make that phone call. Because even though you may not have said the words, you dialed the phone. And she's going to mention that you called her, while she's sitting by your hospital bed, running her fingers through your hair, and you can say *Yeah, you know, funny, right before we hit that tree, I'd just pulled my head out of my ass and realized that I was, like, twelve months behind schedule to ask you out to dinner. That's one of the biggest problems about having my head up my ass. It's too dark to see my watch or a calendar. But what do you say? I know this great restaurant in Coronado. It's right on the water . . .*"

Dave stopped talking to Deck, not because Decker wasn't listening, but because a giant truck with a snowplow had appeared in the road in front of them.

It rumbled to a stop, and the driver climbed down from the cab—and morphed into Sophia.

Great. Dave kept walking. He wasn't certain that a symptom of hypothermia was hallucinating, but hallucinating in general was never a good sign.

"Dave!" Sophia followed him. "Come on—let's get Decker into the truck. Lopez—he's a medic—he's heading toward the Thornton place— you know, where Gillman's jacket made the computer blip?"

She was real.

Sophia was real, and she tried to help him with Decker—by grabbing Dave's broken wrist.

Son of a bitch. He went down into the snow, and she realized that he'd left out certain details when they'd spoken on the phone, after the accident.

She was tight-lipped as they got Decker into the truck, as she helped Dave in, too. Then she climbed behind the wheel, put the truck in gear.

"Any other injuries?" she asked, as the plow ground forward, as Dave tried to crawl inside the dashboard heater. "You know, besides your obviously broken nose?"

His nose was broken? He looked into the mirror on the flip side of the sun visor. Yep. Broken.

"No," he said, shivering so hard he could barely speak. "I'm okay."

She was terribly upset—the sight of Decker unconscious was pretty rattling—but she was driving this monster like a total pro.

"Deck's going to be okay, too," he reassured her. "He's going to be just fine."

Sophia just shook her head, glared at the snow, and drove.

Izzy added running through deep snow in a blizzard to his list of crappy ways to spend a December afternoon.

Christmas shopping at a mall where the parking garage was being renovated and was therefore inaccessible would have been more fun. Yeah, death threats from other drivers trying to cram into the remaining parking lot, fender benders as cars played chicken to gain a suddenly available slot, twenty solid minutes of gridlock while people double-parked, shouts of *Fuck you, asshole!* Way to spread the glad tidings and holiday cheer.

Yeah, that definitely sucked. But this was ten times worse.

Jenkins was determined to set a new world record for the most consecutive seven-minute miles through blizzard conditions. Izzy was winded and lagging, and *he* wanted to get to the Thornton house very badly.

And Jenkie was the one who was leading the way. He was breaking through the crust on the snow, making it that much easier for the rest of them to follow.

Lopez was muttering in Spanish.

Gillman had actually zipped up his jacket and put on a hat.

Yeah, it was freaking *frio*, all right.

Jenk turned and shouted something back at them.

"What the fuck did he say?" Izzy asked.

"I think he said halfway there," Gillman repeated.

"We're way more than halfway," Izzy said. Weren't they? Please God.

"I think he said he smelled smoke," Lopez said. Although how he could have heard Jenk with his hood up was a mystery.

But then Izzy smelled it, too. It was definitely smoke. Damn, that couldn't be good. A fire, in this weather?

Ahead of them, Jenk was running even faster—pointing at something just ahead.

Izzy manufactured a second wind, and as he rounded the corner, he saw what Jenk had spotted.

Less than a quarter mile down the hill, there it sat. The biggest fucking haunted house in the world, with smoke pouring out of a first-floor window.

Lindsey froze in the hallway, certain she'd heard a noise from the kitchen—a noise that wasn't the freaking annoying smoke alarm.

Push it away. She pushed it away—the endless high-pitched squealing—and concentrated on moving soundlessly down the hall.

The living room was large and cluttered with furniture. Shadows jumped around the room from the burning draperies, and smoke curled, not just around the high ceiling, but lower, too, making it hard to breathe.

And hard to see, too. Not just for her, but for him.

A window was open across the room. Was she supposed to believe Eulie had left—maybe made his escape? What did she look like? The queen of wishful thinking?

Still, she went toward it, because he so obviously wanted her to.

It was then that she heard him. Behind her. She spun to face him—as he hit her again with that powerful stream of water.

It was different this time. She was being hit directly, instead of getting the splashback, and it pushed her off her feet.

Shit! She got off a shot—a wild one—as she hit the floor. The water smashed at her, and she couldn't keep her head from smacking the sturdy leg of a heavy oak chair, and she actually saw stars.

Her weapon left her right hand, and he used the water to push it farther from her. She crawled toward it on her belly and elbows, but it skittered away.

He hit her again in the head—it was like taking a punch from a professional boxer—and she heard herself cry out, heard Eulie laugh.

She struggled to reach her handgun, and once again he smacked her with the water—*whap!*—right in the head.

He didn't do it if she didn't move. Lindsey looked at the weapon. It was too far away. She'd never reach it in time.

Eulie, however, was coming closer.

And closer.

He held the pressure hose and its heavy tank at the ready, in case she tried once again to go for her gun.

But Lindsey didn't need to. She had her backup, her even smaller .22, already in her left hand.

He finally came into range, and she blasted him, right in the face, and he fell, the water tank clattering beside him on the floor.

She twisted onto her stomach, sealing the deal with two more bullets, sent directly into his head.

"Hey!"

She spun to face the hallway, weapon up and ready—to find herself staring through the swirling smoke, into the barrel of a submachine gun, held by the abominable snowman.

"Lindsey!" The snowman knew her name. He had ice on his hat, on his jacket, in his hair, on his eyebrows. And three other snowmen were right behind him.

"Ryan Seacrest," Lindsey said as she lowered her weapon. "I knew you'd come."

Jenk laughed—it was either that or cry. It was just like Lindsey—soaking wet, shivering, and looking as if she'd been dragged through hell—to make not just a joke, but one that referred to the phone conversation she'd had with him and Izzy the night they'd babysat for Charlie Paoletti. The night Oz had gotten free.

The night he'd fallen in love with Lindsey but was too stupid to know it.

It was also clear, just as she'd pointed out that night, that she really hadn't needed a team of Navy SEALs to save her.

She done just fine by herself.

"Let's get this fire out," Jenk ordered Izzy, Gillman, and Lopez, who leaped into action, pulling down the flaming drapes, opening windows.

Weapon still at ready, Jenk went over to the body. Eulie was definitely dead.

Lindsey was back on her feet. She'd picked up some kind of tank and hose and was using it to spray the flames. "Is he wearing body armor?" she asked.

"He is," Jenk reported, taking his jacket off, shaking the snow from it. "Gillman."

"Where's Tracy?" Izzy asked.

"I haven't found her yet," Lindsey said, as Gillman took the tank from her. "She might be in the basement." Jenk wrapped his jacket around her and she looked at him. "Mark, I haven't heard her since I came inside."

"Where's the basement?" Izzy demanded.

"I think there's a door in the kitchen," Lindsey told him, starting to show him the way.

But Jenk held onto her. "Let him go."

"It's down that hall," she said. "And Iz?" He was already gone, so she raised her voice. "Brace yourself."

Izzy took a deep breath and his flashlight from his pack, and went into the darkness of the kitchen.

Only to be lunged at by a crazy woman with a knife.

"Ow! Shit!" The blade was incredibly sharp. He'd cut his hand just blocking the blow. "What the fuck . . . ?"

"Izzy?"

He turned on his flashlight. "Trace?"

She was alive. She was bruised and dirty and scraped up pretty badly, but sweet, sweet Jesus, she was alive.

"We need to get out of here," she whispered urgently. "I need some help with Beth. There's this awful man, and he's—"

"Dead," Izzy told her, so damn glad to see her in one piece that he nearly burst into tears like a great big baby. "His name was Dick Eulie. Did you hear those gunshots? That was Lindsey, just saying no. Don't ever piss her off." He realized what she said. "Who's Beth?"

Tracy pointed and there, curled up on the floor, was a woman who looked like she'd been raised by wolves. "She was his prisoner, for I don't know how long. She's injured—she's very ill—she needs a hospital. Plus, he drugged her, and—"

"Okay," Izzy said. Tracy was soaking wet, just as Lindsey had been. "All right. Let's take care of you first. Let's get you out to the other room and—"

"I'm not leaving her," Tracy dug in her heels. "Not in here. There are horrible things in the freezer. Down in the basement, too. This Dick guy, he . . . collected body parts. From his victims. He showed me. He was going . . . I was . . . I was supposed to be Number Twenty-one."

She was trying to lift Beth, and Izzy realized that Tracy had probably carried the other woman all the way up the basement stairs. "I got her," he said. Wolf-girl was fragile—much too skinny. And, damn, but she smelled. Tracy, however, didn't seem to care. She stayed close.

"Was that really Lindsey who came to the door?" Tracy asked. "She just rang the bell and walked in."

No shit. Lindsey had huge balls. "She was supposed to wait for us, but . . . we were delayed by the weather," he told her.

She looked at him, and her remarkable blue eyes widened. "Is it snowing?" she asked.

"Yeah," Izzy said past the lump in his throat. Thank God they'd found her in time. "A little."

All three of the women were soaking wet. But none of them wanted to borrow any articles of clothing—not even a blanket—from Richard Eulie's house.

The fire was out. Gillman had gotten the generator up and running. The heat was working, and the snow was still coming down like a bitch, but Lindsey was the only one of the women willing to stay in the house to warm up.

And Jenk suspected that was only because *he* was there.

The other two women—Tracy and Beth—were out in the rental car Lindsey had driven from the motel, heater blasting. Lopez was with them, cleaning up their various scrapes. Although Beth definitely needed a hospital stay—and a serious delousing.

"You okay?" he asked Lindsey.

He'd wrapped his and Lopez's jackets around her, sat her down next to an electric heater, but she was still shivering.

"He's really dead, right?" she asked him, not for the first time. She knew it, too. "I'm sorry, I'm just . . . I can't imagine what Beth and Tracy have been through. The short time I spent with the man was plenty long enough."

"He's very dead." Jenk put his arms around her, and she rested her head on his shoulder. "You want to see the body again?"

She shook her head.

"Sophia's here with the plow," he told her. "Dave and Decker need medical attention, then we're going to head back to the motel. Gillman'll drive the car, right behind the plow. We're also going to pick up the SUV."

"What about the body?" she asked, sitting up to look at him. "We're not just going to leave it here—with all the evidence . . . ?"

She sounded so outraged at the idea, that he had to smile. Once a cop, always a cop. "You know that FBI agent who flew up from DC?" he asked. "He's actually on his way, with a forensics team. They'll be here before we leave. I think we can trust them with the crime scene."

Lindsey leaned forward and kissed him. Her mouth was so soft and sweet. Jenk could taste the tea Lopez had made for her. He was just starting to get into it, when she pulled back. "Yes," she said.

"Yes?" he repeated, not certain what she meant.

"To the weekend," she explained. "I'd like—very much—to see you this weekend." Her voice shook. "And for Christmas. Yes to Christmas, if the invitation is still open."

As if it wouldn't be. As if he wasn't about to starting weeping from happiness.

"Of course it is," he managed to say. He cupped his hand against the softness of her face, lost in the darkness of her beautiful eyes. "Although I have to be honest. When I first invited you? I lied when I said I wasn't in love with you. And I know that might scare you but—"

"When I was here, alone with Eulie, and I thought . . . it could go either way," she whispered. "I didn't just not want to die." Tears brimmed and one escaped, sliding down her cheek. "I wanted to live."

Jenk kissed her, because he got her message. Loud and clear. She didn't need to say the words. But then, because she was Lindsey, because she always surprised him, always made him laugh, she did say it.

"I love you, too, Mark." She laughed, then, wiping her eyes with her hands. "I promised myself that if I came out of this with my scalp still attached to my head, I'd tell you. I would've texted it to you, but my phone got wet."

Jenk couldn't speak. He didn't know what to say, couldn't find any words to describe the sheer happiness he was feeling. Instead, he just sat and breathed, with his arm around Lindsey, holding her close.

"So what do you want to do this weekend?" she asked, and he kissed her again.

CHAPTER
TWENTY-TWO

W hen Tracy's doorbell rang, she was certain it was Lyle, coming back for one last attempt to talk her into returning to New
York.

"I said I'd think about it," she told him as she opened the door.

Except it wasn't Lyle standing there. It was Izzy. What was *he* doing
here?

She hadn't seen him at all in the past week and a half. Not since she'd
cut him with that knife in Richard Eulie's kitchen.

He was wearing jeans and a T-shirt. Sneakers on his feet. Sunglasses
that hid his eyes. He took them off.

"I saw—was it Lyle? Leaving," he said. He was carrying a present,
wrapped in festive paper and a bow. "Don't tell me you're seriously thinking about getting back with him?"

Izzy wasn't the only one who was outraged that Lyle didn't come to
New Hampshire when Tracy had first gone missing. In fact, it was three
whole days after the rescue before he'd appeared—apparently he'd had an
important court case and couldn't leave New York.

Sophia was thoroughly disgusted with Lyle, too. She'd called Tracy,
every day for the past week, trying to talk her into staying on as Troubleshooters' receptionist. She'd gotten Dave and Lindsey and even Tom to
call, too.

"I don't know," Tracy said, stepping back to let Izzy in. "I'm not sleeping too well. I'm not sure I can handle living alone."

"This place is big enough for a roommate," he said, looking around
the living room.

"I don't know," Tracy said again. "There's only one bedroom."

"Jenk told me you went to see Beth at the hospital before you left New Hampshire." He was obviously nervous. He kept flipping that package over and over in his big hands. He walked all the way to the window— looked out. "Nice view."

"Of the street?" she asked.

He glanced at her. "I've lived in places that look out on a brick wall, four feet away. This is a nice view. How *is* Beth?"

"I don't know." Tracy was starting to feel like a broken record. But the truth was, since New Hampshire, she didn't know much of anything. "Her mother and brother were there. Her brother, Bobby, just came back from Iraq. She cut her hair—really short. I think it was impossible to get the knots out. She seemed . . . Shell-shocked."

"It's going to take time," Izzy said.

"Yeah, I guess," Tracy said.

"I have to go," he said. He held out the package. "This is for you. I also wanted to apologize to you again—"

"Forget it," Tracy said as she tore the paper. Beneath it was a box from a store called Leather World. Great. This was either going to be embarrassing or awkward.

She opened the lid of the box.

A belt was inside, made of rich brown leather. Nothing fancy. Except it had two notches cut into it.

And okay, she was wrong. This was both embarrassing *and* awkward. Her cheeks heated.

"Only two?" she said, her voice tight. "You were number three. Or is this your way of saying that night never happened?"

Izzy actually looked surprised and then aghast. "No," he said. "Wait. You think this is . . . No, no, no. Whoa, whoa. This isn't about sex. This isn't . . . These notches are for the lives you saved. Yours and Beth's."

The lives she'd saved.

Tracy felt her eyes fill with tears. The lives *she'd* saved.

"Really?" she asked.

Izzy nodded. "You know, it just occurred to me, that in some countries, when you save someone's life, you become responsible for them. You saved your own life, Trace. Don't you think you owe it to yourself to do something worthwhile with it? Not just throw it away on some asshole like Lyle?"

She looked at him, really looked at him. He was serious. "Thank you," she said. "This is a very nice present."

"You're welcome." He gazed at her steadily. "I really hope you'll think about what I said."

"Tom and his wife, Kelly, are having a New Year's Eve party," she told him—the words just coming out of her mouth, unstoppable. "Will I see you there?" She actually hoped he'd be there. How crazy was that?

But Izzy shook his head. "I have to, um, go away. It's going to be a while before I'm back."

"Oh," Tracy said. "I didn't know."

"Yeah," he said. "It's one of those assignments that no one wants, but someone has to do it, especially when they do something stupid or illegal and get into trouble." He made a face. "But I'll, you know, call you when I'm back in town. If you're still interested. Because I'm, you know, interested. But it's going to be a while. About six months."

"Wow," she said.

"Yeah," he said. "I know. That's much too long." He glanced at his watch. "I really have to go."

"Thank you," Tracy said, walking him to the door. "For the belt and for . . ."

For one long moment, she was sure he was going to kiss her good-bye. But he didn't. He just nodded and then was gone.

Tracy went to the window and saw him exit her building. He took a left and went down the street. She watched until he turned the corner, disappearing from view.

And then she picked up her phone and dialed. She connected with Lyle's voice mail almost immediately. "Hi," she said, as she looked at the rich leather of the belt that Izzy had given her, as she ran her finger across those two little notches, as she smiled. "It's me. I've made up my mind. I'm staying in California. I love my job, and . . . I really don't want to marry you. Good luck and . . . good-bye."

Tracy hung up the phone, and went to change into jeans—so she could try on her new belt.

Decker was moving painfully as he came into the Troubleshooters' office. But at least the son of a bitch was moving.

Dave, on the other hand, was finding out just how many things he couldn't do with a broken wrist.

"I'll get you some coffee," Sophia said, as Dave maneuvered himself behind his desk.

"Yeah," he called after her. "And will you also type for me and tie my shoes and button my shirts and cut my food. This is like being a child again. I can't stand it—it's driving me mad!"

"Hey, Dave," Dan Gillman said. "Is Sophia around?"

Okay, now the morning truly was a nightmare. Dan Gillman was actually standing in Dave's office. In dress whites.

"She's not in here," Dave said. He put his hand in front of his eyes. "You're blinding me."

"Yeah," Dan said. "Ha-ha. I haven't heard that one before. Isn't this her office over here?"

"Yes, she's right to the left of me." Dave managed to get to his feet without screaming. His leg muscles still hadn't recovered from that workout during the storm. "Is there something I can help you with?"

"Nope," Dan said. "I'll wait in her office."

Decker was across the hall, and Dave went into his office, where he had a clear shot of Gillman through the open door. "What's this about?" Dave asked quietly.

Deck shook his head.

"Did you," Dave asked, "you know . . . ?" Finally invite Sophia to dinner?

Again, Deck shook his head.

Dave shut his mouth over the blistering names he was about to call Decker, because Sophia had come back.

"I'm putting your coffee on your desk," she called to Dave.

"Thanks," he said.

"Oh, hi," she greeted Gillman. "What a . . . surprise."

"A nice one, I hope," he said.

"Of course," she obviously lied.

"Look, I'm just going to be honest, okay?" the SEAL said. "I haven't been able to stop thinking about you. I really enjoyed the time we spent together, and yeah, I got a little freaked out—because I hate the thought of anyone hurting you. You're beautiful, you're amazing, and I know you have reservations, but I really hope you'll put them aside and give yourself a chance to get to know me. I'd like to take you out for dinner, or lunch, or coffee or a drink or a movie or . . ." He laughed. "I know I sound insane, but bottom line, I really want to see you again."

Sophia said something, but her voice was too low for Dave to hear her.

Dan, however, stood up. His voice carried quite nicely. "Friday's great. Friday's perfect. Seven o'clock? Well, great, I'm . . . thrilled. I'm looking forward to it. I'm . . . going now, so you can get to work and I'll . . . see you. On Friday."

Dan Gillman came out of Sophia's office walking like a man who was on top of the world.

Dave didn't even bother to look at Decker. He just went into his office and closed his door.

Jenk was waiting on the steps of Lindsey's apartment when she came home from work, a pizza box and a pile of DVDs beside him.

"Hey," she greeted him.

"Hey," he replied. "I had the entire day off. I have something I wanted to show you, and I was in the neighborhood, so . . ."

Lindsey kissed him. "You want to do me," she translated, "and think I'll put out for a pizza."

"I always want to do you," he said, catching her and pulling her onto his lap. He kissed her again.

"Honey, I'm home," she said, leaning her forehead against his, looking into his eyes. "God, I could get used to this."

"Good." He was grinning at her. "Aren't you going to ask me what I did on my day off?"

Lindsey stood up. Unlocked her apartment door. "What did you do on your day off?"

"I made you some DVDs," he told her as he followed her inside. "See, I know this guy, who knows this other guy who works at a nursing home, where there's this World War II vet. He was a survivor of a POW camp in the Philippines."

She looked up at that.

"Yeah," he continued, bringing the pizza into the kitchen. "He was one of the men your grandfather saved. He knew your grandmother, too—she was one of the guerillas who staged the rescue. It was her knowledge of the camp that made it all possible. Did you know that?"

Speechless, Lindsey shook her head.

"Her name was Keiko, right? I know you never knew her, and I just thought, you know, this guy—his name's Bruce Wendell—he's in his nineties. He may not be around much longer. So I went to the home and videotaped an interview. I thought your father might like seeing it, too. According to Bruce, Keiko—your grandmother—was really something special."

Her heart was in her throat. "I can't believe you did that—on your day off."

"It was fun," Jenk told her as he opened the pizza box, got plates down from her cabinet. "He was a nice guy. It was interesting talking to him. I think this pie's going to need reheating."

Lindsey watched as he took a couple of bottles of beer from the fridge. "Thank you. I just . . . I don't know what to say."

"You just said it." He kissed her. He opened the bottle and handed it to her. "And you're welcome. So what do you want to watch first? The Bruce Wendell interviews, or *The Empire Strikes Back?*"

Star Wars, of course. "Which one is that, again?"

"The best one," Jenk told her. "The one where Luke finds out that Darth Vader was his father. Which means that Darth was Princess Leia's father, too. And I don't know if you know this, but in the *Star Wars* books, Leia and Han Solo get married. Han doesn't have any problem with Leia being the mother of his children, and Darth's, like, a bigger mass murderer than Hitler even. I mean, he wiped out entire planets and—"

"I get it," Lindsey said, laughing, as she put a slice of pizza on her plate and set the microwave for a quick zap. "And by the way? You can stop working so hard. You're definitely getting some tonight—you had me at *Luke, I am your father.*"

Jenk laughed. But then got serious. "I didn't make that videotape because I wanted—"

"I know," she cut him off as the microwave dinged. "I finished my Christmas shopping this afternoon. I'm now officially ready to have a stress-free holiday."

"That's really great," Jenk said. "Because I'm suddenly completely stressed about it."

She looked up from testing the temperature of her pizza with her finger. He wasn't kidding.

"I'm completely terrified that when you meet my mother she's going to say . . . I don't know what she's going to say," he admitted. "I've been having nightmares that she'll greet you at the door with a pile of bridal magazines and menus from catering halls. See, I've never brought anyone home with me before."

"She's going to think we're really serious," Lindsey realized. She bit her lower lip. "That could be uncomfortable."

He didn't realize she was teasing him. "I don't know how to—"

"Yeah, it could be *really* uncomfortable," Lindsey interrupted him. "If, you know, it weren't true."

Jenk gazed at her. "So are you saying that you won't mind if my mother goes a little overboard?"

"I'm saying don't stress."

He wasn't done. "Or are you saying that you'll marry me? Because you know I want to marry you."

Lindsey stuck her fingers in her ears. "Don't frighten me, don't frighten me, don't frighten me," she said. "La, la, la, la, la."

Laughing, Jenk took her fingers from her ears. "Aren't you the unflappable woman who went one-on-one with the most horrible serial killer of the decade?"

"That wasn't half as terrifying as planning for the unforeseeable future." Lindsey was only half-kidding. "Tell me that we'll take it slowly, really, really slowly."

"We'll take it slowly," he promised.

Looking into his dancing eyes, Lindsey nodded. With this man beside her, she could do anything. "But not so slowly that you shouldn't, you know, kiss me. Right now."

Jenk laughed and kissed her.

And then Lindsey gave herself the best Christmas present ever.

"I've been thinking," she told him, working to keep her voice from wobbling—she was that nervous. "That when you leave the Navy, we should maybe travel for a year or so. Work overseas. And then, you know, think about getting married and . . ." She cleared her throat. "Maybe even have kids."

The love she saw in Mark Jenkins's eyes took her breath away.

"Sounds like a plan," he whispered. And this time when he kissed her, he didn't stop.

PARTNERS—AND LOVERS—
SAM STARRETT AND
ALYSSA LOCKE TEAM UP AGAIN
IN AN EXCLUSIVE SHORT STORY!

SAM TAKES
AN ASSIGNMENT
IN ITALY

"Why," Sam bitched into his cell phone on Tuesday night, "did Tom have to send *me* out here?"

His wife, Alyssa, didn't answer, because she wasn't on the other end. She was out handling a real case—an *important* case—so he was just leaving voice mail.

A known sex offender had gone missing. The man's sister had hired Troubleshooters Incorporated to find him before he hurt anyone else. Alyssa had taken the assignment and was in Richmond, Virginia, tracking him down.

Meanwhile Sam sat here, halfway around the world, the newest poster child for Murphy's Law. *Whatever can go wrong,* will *go wrong.*

And oh, how it had.

And you there, trying to glass-half-full this disaster? It's obviously not painful enough for you, so let Mr. Murphy supersize it, 'kay?

No doubt about it, Murphy had been riding Sam's ass from the moment he'd kissed Alyssa good-bye far too many weeks ago. This so-called easy assignment setting up security at a corporate honcho's big fat Italian wedding had turned into a nightmare. Four days had turned into a week, and then that week had turned into an unbelievable three.

Yeah sure, the little coastal town was beautiful—all blue sky and ocean, gorgeous beaches, bright sunshine. Yeah sure, Sam was making a fortune for Tom Paoletti's security company, Troubleshooters Incorporated—and yeah, all right, he'd earned himself one hell of a bonus for his trouble, too—but come *on.*

The inefficiency of the honcho's staff was mind-numbing. Sam could have made bricks by hand and constructed a wall around the wedding chapel himself in the time it took them just to make the decision to set up a temporary chain-link fence and then hide it with a decorative one.

First the ceremony was going to be held indoors. Then out. Then in. Then on the beach. Each time the location shifted, Sam reworked the details that would keep the VIPs safe and the paparazzi at bay. He hadn't written this many reports since college.

And then—God please help him—there were the bridesmaids from hell. Four spoiled daughters of both the bride and the groom—this was a third or fourth marriage for the client, Sam had lost count—they all had far too much time on their hands. Ashley, Heather, Sabrina, and Chloe.

Ashley and Chloe were the worst. They followed Sam constantly, refusing to let him be. He'd flashed his wedding ring and mentioned his wife when they were first introduced. When they hadn't seemed to get the hint, he'd flat-out told them that he loved Alyssa more than life itself. He'd even showed them a photo of her, but they just did not let up.

Which led to tonight's phone call and Sam's desperate plea for Alyssa to hurry up and find the man she was looking for, get her butt on a plane, and join him.

"It's like trying to work in the middle of a *Girls Gone Wild* video," he complained, and of course, again, she said nothing.

"I miss you, Lys," he whispered, which was, in fact, his biggest problem. He could handle an entire army of Ashleys and Chloes. He could rewrite a report for the hundredth time if he had to. He could attend dozens more meetings that redefined *boring*.

What he couldn't do was survive too many more mornings waking up thousands of miles away from the woman that he loved. And it wasn't just that he missed her in his bed. He missed her smile, her voice, her very presence in his life.

"Please come and save me," he begged and cut the connection.

Wednesday brought more perfect weather—and another teeth-gritting delay in the impending nuptials. Chloe informed him over breakfast that the wedding had now been moved to Sunday—just a day later than Saturday, but still.

She also told him that her father would be out of touch until Thursday morning—which left Sam with just enough time to *not* be able to squeeze in a round-trip to Richmond.

Of course, if he'd been told about this yesterday morning, he could have made it there and back.

Sam worked off his frustration—or tried to anyway—with a ten-mile run. It was nearly noon before he returned to the resort.

He was drenched with perspiration, his hair literally dripping with sweat. He would have stuck to the shade and gone straight up to his room without talking to anyone, except there was some sort of commotion by the pool.

The hellsmaids—three of them anyway, Chloe was AWOL—were giving their full, shrill attention to a man dressed in a snugly-fitting blue T-shirt and linen pants. He was height-challenged, with dark hair and . . .

"Hey, sweetie," he said as he spotted Sam dripping on the stone walkway beneath the arches, turning to greet him with a wide smile. "Rumor has it you need some TLC."

Alyssa apparently couldn't make it here to Italy, but she'd called their good friend and her former partner in the FBI, Jules Cassidy, as a stand-in.

He came right over and gave Sam a hug, despite the high sweat and slime factor. In fact, Jules gave him a big hug. A much, much, *much* too long of a hug.

For once, Heather, Ashley, and Sabrina were wide-eyed and silent, staring at them, definitely wondering . . .

So Sam cleared his throat. "It's good to see you," he told Jules. Which was no lie. But when he cleared his throat again and gruffly added, "Sweetie," it definitely boosted any potential misperceptions.

Jules laughed his ass off, of course. "Alyssa is going to love hearing about this," he whispered as he hugged Sam again.

Yeah, she would. Provided they would ever be in the same country at the same time again.

"I was in Dubai," Jules said, as Sam pulled two bottles of cold water from his suite's kitchen fridge. He tossed one to Jules. "Thanks. It's not *quite* the same neighborhood, but close enough. Closer than Richmond. I had some time off coming, so . . . Here I am."

"Checking up on me." Sam toasted him then took a long swig from his bottle.

"Absolutely not," Jules said. Up close, the FBI agent looked tired. His usually bright smile even seemed a touch forced. He sank into one of the leather armchairs in the suite's sitting area. "Your wife trusts you completely. Although, that *Girls Gone Wild* comment? It was probably not her most favorite thing she's ever heard you say."

"I was trying to get a rise out of her. And no offense," Sam said, half-sitting on the desk where his laptop was out and open, "but I was kind of hoping she'd be the one to show."

"She sounded pretty pissed off when I spoke to her," Jules reported. "This guy she's looking for? He knows she's looking. He's been messing with her. Playing games."

"Thanks. I love hearing that." Sam's blood pressure was up so high, his ears were ringing. "Motherfucker's a sex offender."

"And if Alyssa were ten years old, she'd be in danger," Jules reassured him. "She finally called in for backup, by the way. Lindsey and . . . damn, I'm blanking on his name . . . former CIA . . . ?"

"Dave Malkoff," Sam supplied the name of the Troubleshooters' operative.

"That's him." Jules glanced at his watch. "They're probably in Richmond with Alyssa right now, cuffing the guy."

"Good." Which meant Alyssa could be *here* by tomorrow night.

"Yeah, you're way too happy at that news," Jules said. "You haven't checked your e-mail, have you?"

Sam shifted his laptop so he could see the screen, jumped on line and . . . Sure enough, there was an e-mail from Alyssa. Subject: *I'm needed in San Diego.* "No. No, no, no . . ."

He clicked on it, skimmed it. The good news was that she, Lindsey, and Dave had indeed caught the game-playing sex offender. The bad news was that their boss, Tom Paoletti, had another assignment waiting for Alyssa. Which meant it would be . . . *What?*

"She's going OCONUS," Sam told Jules, using the military term for outside of the United States. "Unless I can somehow get home by Friday morning, it's going to be another two weeks—at least—before I see her." She'd added a P.S. that Sam didn't understand. *"Tell Jules that Dave's a maybe?* What does that mean?"

Jules took another swig from his water bottle. "Don't get too excited, because I haven't cleared it yet with Tom. Or Max. I have to wait a few more hours before I call either of them. But if they give me the thumbs-up, I'll be able to hang here, hold down the fort for you, until a replacement arrives. Alyssa told me she was going to ask Dave Malkoff."

Sam shook his head. "As an FBI agent, you can't—"

"I won't," Jules said. "You just told me the wedding's not until Sunday, and the client's gone until Thursday. Dave—or someone else—will definitely be here before then. I'm just going to hang here, pass along the message that you had to leave, that your replacement is on his way. I'm not getting paid, I'm just doing you a favor."

It was one hell of a big-ass favor. "You don't get much vacation time," Sam pointed out. "Wouldn't you rather, I don't know, go on a cruise?"

"With who?" Jules gazed at him. "Ben?" He rolled his eyes as he shook his head. "Just take a shower, let's go get lunch. If you really want to hear it, I'll tell you the whole terrible Ben story. But I definitely need nourishment first."

"He did what?" Sam said.

"Brought his beard," Jules repeated. He sat back to let the waiter take his plate. They sat in a little outdoor restaurant, overlooking the harbor below. The food had been unbelievable, the owner himself coming out of the kitchen to make sure everything was to their liking. "Beard is slang for a woman who pretends to be a closeted gay man's wife or girlfriend. Ben's beard is named Amanda. She's his roommate. His own parents actually think she's his fiancée."

Sam struggled to comprehend. "So, this guy lives with a woman, except he's gay and . . . she's okay with that?"

"She's not really his fiancée. They have separate bedrooms," Jules told him. "She's a grad student—they're friends from high school. Plus, he lets her live in his condo for free."

Sam had to make sure he understood. "So Amanda helps Ben fool everyone into thinking he's straight."

Jules nodded. *"Don't ask, don't tell*—I think you've probably heard of the policy? It sounds so innocuous, but it forces servicemen and -women into the closet. They have to hide who they are, pretend to be something they're not. It's okay to be gay in the military, as long as no one knows." He was disgusted. "Ben takes Amanda to all kinds of functions—including this date he had, with me."

"It was really a date?" Sam asked, as the waiter poured them each a cup of coffee. Alyssa had told him that when it came to dating, Jules was remarkably gun-shy—and yeah, okay that was probably an unfortunate expression to use.

But Alyssa's going theory was that Jules was still hung up on some actor he'd met out in Los Angeles—Robin something. The SOB had hurt Jules badly—their relationship had been a total train wreck. Still, Lys had been urging her old friend to get back into circulation. This Marine captain, Ben, had been calling him for a while—apparently Jules had finally taken that first date step.

"Ben calls and goes, *Hey, how are you? I just got back from overseas. I was wondering if you wanted to get together, maybe have dinner at my place?*" Jules reported. "I wasn't ready for that. So I suggested we meet at a restaurant. It wasn't even downtown. It was suburban and discreet, and . . . he brought Amanda anyway. So we all sit down to dinner and it's way weird. I mean, she was nice, but, what the hell . . . ? She finally gets up to, you know, hit the ladies' room, and Ben goes, *I'm career military. This is how I've made it work.* He knew I was freaked out. He said, *You should've come over. It's easier, more comfortable,* and I said, *Not for me.* I said, *I'm not climbing into your closet with you,* and . . . that was that. I haven't seen him since." He paused. "The stupid thing is, I really like him. The *really* stupid thing? I'd be genuinely upset if he resigned his commission. The Marines need more officers like Ben."

"I'm sorry it didn't work out," Sam said.

"Thanks."

They sat in silence for a moment.

"Thing is, I'm thinking about doing it." Jules finally spoke. "Calling him and . . . Maybe if it's just sex, it won't bother me. As much. You know, keeping it on the down low."

Sam took a sip of his coffee, choosing his words carefully. "I guess whether or not you decide to do that should really depend on what you want. If it's sex . . ."

"Who doesn't want sex?" Jules pointed out.

"If it's *just* sex," Sam said, "there's a waiter over there who's been checking you out." Part of him could not believe he was having this conversation. "Personally, I don't think it's a good idea, some stranger . . ."

At least Jules wouldn't get him pregnant. Years ago, Sam had had sex with a stranger—a bar bunny—and he now had a daughter, Haley, and an ex-wife, Mary Lou. Talk about careless mistakes. Although Haley was definitely the best mistake he'd ever made. She was a real peach of a kid. It had all worked out in the end, but for years it was bad. He'd messed up his life, along with Mary Lou's, Haley's, and even Alyssa's.

"Ben's not a stranger," Jules pointed out, taking out his wallet and paying the bill.

"What happens when you fall in love with . . . him?" Sam asked. It was another question that he couldn't believe he was asking. Still, the words needed to be said. "You know, I should pay that."

Jules shook his head to both the question and the offer. "That won't happen." He said it with such finality and stood up as punctuation. "Let's get back. I want to make those phone calls."

"How much do I owe you?" Sam persisted, opening his own wallet.

Jules waved him off. "It's on me."

"You come out here to do me a favor, *and* you pay for lunch . . . ?"

"You have no idea how much I appreciate your friendship," Jules said.

Sam held out several bills. "Yeah, actually I do," he said. "It's probably as much as I appreciate yours."

Jules couldn't just take the money and be done with it. He had to go and hug Sam. "Thanks."

Of course, now the gay waiter was checking Sam out, too. He even followed them out into the square as they headed up the road.

Which turned out to be provident, since they hadn't gone far before a group of men, ranging in ages from teens to much older, blocked their path. They were scowling and grim, and their postures were clearly meant to menace.

Jules stepped in front of Sam, his body language relaxed, a smile on his face. "Good afternoon, gentlemen," he said in close to perfect Italian. "Is there a problem?"

Sam counted them quickly. There were nine, but only three—red shirt, goatee, and tattoo—looked capable of holding their own in a brawl.

Tattoo let out a stream of Italian that was far too rapid-fire for Sam to understand. He definitely caught the words *Rome* and *the Pope* along with what sounded like negative language. He wasn't quite sure what the man was saying, but there was no mistaking his intention when he roughly shoved Jules.

And just like that, the talking was over. Well, almost over. "I got tattoo and red shirt," Jules announced, as he effortlessly took down the man who'd shoved him.

That left goatee for Sam. But ouch, the man had a fishing knife. Sam quickly adiosed it, breaking more than a few fingers in the process.

That was all it took. Goatee ran home, crying for his mommy, eating the dust of the rest of the gang. They'd all long since am-scrayed, except for the delusional man in the red shirt, who actually still believed he could get a piece of Jules.

The FBI agent was subcompact and tended to have a far better fashion sense than Alyssa, but he knew how to bring it in hand-to-hand combat. He fought with an efficiency of movement that Sam admired. It was beautiful, actually. Jules fought with his brain, unlike Red Shirt, who'd let loose his inner Neanderthal, swinging blindly, flailing mindlessly—making himself good and winded in the process.

Jules, on the other hand, was breathing about as hard as he'd been during lunch.

Red Shirt came at him one too many times, and Jules dodged him yet again, this time tripping him on his way past, using an expertly placed elbow to help the man greet the ground that much harder. He didn't get back up.

The gay waiter, meanwhile, had run to get the entire serving staff of the restaurant, including the owner.

As Sam watched, Jules turned to face this new threat, ready to take them all out if necessary. But—again, since his brain was fully functioning—he immediately recognized them for what they were. The cavalry come to save them. Not that they'd needed it.

The owner of the restaurant spoke fluent English. "This is not the first time such an outrage has happened here. Such anti-American sentiment is not helpful to our town. Tourism is down as it is."

Anti-*American*? Not anti-gay?

The man ushered them into his kitchen, ordering his staff to bring the first-aid kit, and ice for Jules's raw knuckles. Sam looked at Jules, but he was playing right along, talking about the anti-American protests in Greece and even Dubai, as he helped Sam over to a table and pushed him into a chair.

It was then Sam realized he was bleeding. He'd gotten cut by that knife.

It wasn't too much more than a scratch, but the restaurant owner—who was also the chef—wasn't about to let them leave without cleaning them up. And feeding them a sampling of all his desserts, which was fine by Sam.

The man even drove them back to the resort in his little Mini. It was only then, after they said their good-byes, as they headed down the pathway past the pool, that Sam asked, "Anti-American?"

But Jules's phone rang. It was his boss's administrative assistant, Laronda. It was okay with Max if Jules wanted to take a few more days off. Which meant . . .

"Let's get you a flight home," Jules said.

But Sam shook his head. "Anti-American, my ass. I've been here for weeks. That was not about us being American. That was about you being gay. I'm not leaving you here alone."

Jules rolled his eyes. "That's ridiculous."

Sam held out his bandaged hand. "No, it's not."

"Yes, it is."

This was going nowhere fast, but Sam couldn't let it go. "Jules—"

"Don't you get it?" Jules asked, leading the way up the stairs to Sam's hotel suite. "This is my life. I could be jumped—not just here, but in any town in virtually any country in the world. Particularly in the United States, by the way. Are you going to follow me home to DC, Sam? Lots of hate crimes happen there, you know."

"Then maybe *you* should have a beard." Sam knew as soon as the words left his mouth that it was the wrong thing to say. But then he unlocked the door to his suite, and the situation went from bad to worse.

Chloe, dressed in only a pair of leopard-print thong panties and some very high heels, was dancing to music on the radio while fixing herself a drink at his wet bar.

A drink? *Another* drink. Clearly, she'd had quite a few already. "There you are," she said, as she caught sight of Sam. "I've been waiting for you."

Once again, Jules stepped in front of Sam. "You must be Chloe. I *love* your shoes."

She grabbed for her robe—apparently just as Jules had hoped she would. In fact, he even helped her into it. "Pack," he ordered Sam over his shoulder, as he led Chloe out onto the balcony.

"You remind me of Scarlett Johansson," Sam heard him saying to the girl. "You must get that all the time—you *don't*? Really? You look a *lot* like her . . ."

Sam was almost completely packed, but he wasn't going anywhere without Jules. He stood in the bathroom. It didn't make sense to pack up his toilet kit, only to unpack it again tonight when he went to bed. His clothes were no problem. He could easily live out of his suitcase. He'd look slightly more rumpled than usual, but . . .

"I got you on the four o'clock flight to London." Jules stood in the door.

Sam looked at him in the mirror. "I'm not leaving you behind."

Jules nodded. "I appreciate your loyalty, but Chloe had a little confession that, well, she asked me to share with you."

Sam waited.

"The bride and groom have apparently eloped," Jules told him. "The wedding party is indefinitely postponed. Your services are no longer needed—as of last night, as a matter of fact."

"What?"

"Apparently Chloe neglected to tell her sisters about this, too. She wanted to stay a few extra days, and . . . She's young and misdirected. Apparently she's got quite the crush on you, cowboy."

Sam used one arm to sweep what Jules would call his "products" off the sink counter and into his bag. "The four o'clock to London will only get me home in time if nothing goes wrong," he said tightly. No delays, no canceled flights, no screwups between connecting flights. "And I'm still not leaving unless you've got a flight out of here, too."

"Yeah, about that," Jules said. "Confession part two. Apparently she hired those men to, well, as she put it, make me go away."

Sam looked at him. "Young, misdirected—and vicious."

"She is a little socially disengaged," Jules said. "But she's leaving, too. With her sisters. I thought I'd hang for a few days. Maybe get to know Paolo a little better."

"Paolo?" Sam asked.

"He owns that restaurant," Jules admitted. "While you were washing out that cut on your hand, we got to talking and . . . He, um, offered to give me cooking lessons."

Sam laughed. "That's a new way of saying it." The restaurant owner was an older man with gray at his temples—good-looking in a kind of Italian Tom Hanks way. Sam hadn't even realized the man was gay. He sobered fast. "Are you sure you want to . . . ?"

"Sweetie, the only thing I'm *absolutely* sure about is that I don't want a beard," Jules said.

"I shouldn't have said that," Sam told his friend. "I didn't mean it. But I worry about you."

"I know. I forgive you. I just . . . I want a relationship with someone like Paolo who's not afraid to be himself," Jules said. "God, I really want someone I'm in such a hurry to go home to that I'll pack in that horrific way that you just did." He laughed, but then stopped. "You know, before? When you asked me what I want? I want what you have with Alyssa, Sam. I want what Max has with Gina, what Jack has with Scott. I won't have that with Ben. *Or* with Robin, who's in fucking London right now promoting his latest movie, so I'm *not* going to London with you, thanks but no thanks."

Maybe Alyssa was right. It sure seemed that all roads led back to this Robin guy.

"I remember," Sam said, "being in love with Alyssa, but she didn't want anything to do with me. I was so desperate not to think about her, and . . . Nobody could compete. Messing around with other women . . . that didn't help. It only made me miss her more. Plus someone usually ended up hurt, which sucked."

"I hear what you're saying." Jules nodded. "And I appreciate your candor. But you need to go, or you're going to miss that plane."

Sam grabbed his bags. Opened the door. "Thanks again for everything."

"I'll give you a call in a coupla days," Jules said. "Kiss the shit out of Alyssa for me, okay?"

Sam laughed. "Absolutely."

Alyssa wasn't waiting for him at LAX. She was in San Diego, at the Troubleshooters Incorporated office, organizing the gear her team—Sam included—would need for this next assignment. It was cold where they were going, and they'd need to stay hidden, which meant camping without the benefit of fire.

Freeze-your-balls-off-style camping was definitely not Sam's favorite thing to do, but this time, he absolutely couldn't wait. A pup tent, a two-person thermal sleeping bag, and his incredible wife . . .

Yeah, he'd find a way to keep plenty warm.

Traffic was heavy, not just on the Five, but off it as well. He finally arrived, and, yes. There she was, in the parking lot. His wife. Working to fit three truckloads of supplies into two tiny packing crates. And getting the job done with room to spare.

Sam just stood there for a moment, watching her, just letting his heart swell. Her dark hair was long enough to pull back into a ponytail, but tendrils escaped, curling around her face. She was, without a doubt, the most beautiful woman in the entire world, even without any makeup, dressed down in forest cammie-print BDUs and lumberjack boots for two weeks of stomping around in the woods.

She was using her former naval officer voice—no-nonsense with a hint of dominatrix. But then she turned and saw him, and smiled. When she spoke again, her voice was honey. "Sam. You made it."

"Thanks to Jules," he said. She seemed happy to just stand there and look at him, too. He was grinning at her like an idiot.

"He called me," she said. "Told me all about the thong incident. Poor Chloe."

"Poor *Chloe*?" Sam protested. "What about poor me?"

"Poor Sam, having such a *trying* few weeks, in the most beautiful part of Italy, with naked women throwing themselves at you . . ." She was trying to sound sarcastic, but her amusement bubbled through. She mocked him even more. "It must've been terrible, like . . . like . . . working in a *Girls Gone Wild* video!"

That was it for the just-let-me-look-at-you part of their long-awaited reunion. Sam dropped his bag and went for her. She met him more than halfway. He knew she'd missed him badly, too, because she didn't even bother to look around to see who might be watching them—they were, after all, at work. But she didn't care.

She just kissed him, and as he kissed the shit out of her, he thought of Jules, of how lonely he was. *You asked me what I want? I want what you have with Alyssa . . .*

It didn't matter to Sam where they slept tonight—in their own bed, or in a five-star hotel, or even in a tent. As long as Alyssa was beside him, Sam was home.

ABOUT THE AUTHOR

Since her explosion onto the publishing scene more than ten years ago, SUZANNE BROCKMANN has written more than forty books, and is now widely recognized as a leading voice in romantic suspense. Her work has earned her repeated appearances on *USA Today* and *New York Times* bestseller lists, as well as numerous awards, including Romance Writers of America's #1 Favorite Book of the Year—three years running in 2000, 2001, and 2002—two RITA Awards, and many *Romantic Times* Reviewers' Choice Awards. Suzanne Brockmann lives west of Boston with her husband, Dell author Ed Gaffney. Visit her website at www.suzannebrockmann.com.

ABOUT THE TYPE

This book was set in Electra, a typeface designed for Linotype by W. A. Dwiggins, the renowned type designer (1880–1956). Electra is a fluid typeface, avoiding the contrasts of thick and thin strokes that are prevalent in most modern typefaces.